W9-CQX-379

continued . . .

Praise for
Sisters of Cain

"A most entertaining and satisfying story. Should appeal to Civil War enthusiasts, mystery buffs, and historical fiction fans alike."
—*Library Journal*

"Monfredo's historical accuracy provides a solid foundation for the exploits of both sisters . . . [Her] skillful characterizations of historical figures (Lincoln, General McClellan, Dix, etc.) blend easily with her fictional creations . . . An intriguing novel."
—*Publishers Weekly*

"An exciting historical mystery that includes sensational characters with mainstream appeal."
—*Midwest Book Review*

"A most intriguing read. The story rings with historic authenticity and the espionage adventures will have you glued to the pages."
—*Romantic Times*

Praise for
Must the Maiden Die

"Written beautifully, richly satisfying both to the head and to the heart."
—*Anne Perry*

"The imaginative research and lucid writing create a fine balance."
—*Chicago Tribune*

"Monfredo spins a clever, suspenseful tale that involves gun-smuggling and sexual abuse. She's at her best pulling plot twists out of actual events. Her research is evident on every page."
—*Publishers Weekly*

CHILDREN OF CAIN

Book III of the Cain Trilogy

Miriam Grace Monfredo

BERKLEY PRIME CRIME, NEW YORK

CHILDREN OF CAIN

A Berkley Prime Crime Book / published by arrangement with
the author

PRINTING HISTORY
Berkley Prime Crime hardcover edition / September 2002
Berkley Prime Crime mass-market edition / August 2003

For the children of my children,
Christopher, Alyssa, Zachary, and Davis

ACKNOWLEDGMENTS

I wish to thank again those previously acknowledged in *Sisters of Cain* and *Brothers of Cain*. Each contributed in various ways to all three books of the Cain trilogy. I would like, however, to express my continuing gratitude to Berkley editor Natalee Rosenstein, as well as to Eivind Boe, David Minor, Rachel Monfredo Gee, and, as ever, Frank Monfredo.

AUTHOR'S NOTE

Children of Cain, like the preceding *Sisters of Cain* and *Brothers of Cain,* is based on the historic 1862 Virginia Peninsula Campaign. The Federal plans to capture the Confederate capital of Richmond became the single largest campaign of the American Civil War, and the campaign's long-term consequences on the course of that war, as well as on the young American nation, were significant. Owing to the optimistic mood of those in the North, few there questioned whether the gates of Richmond could be breached and the secession rebellion crushed. The absence of organized intelligence gathering would prove to be a crucial factor in the campaign's outcome.

The major characters in *Children of Cain* are fictitious, but historic figures frequently appear. Some information on those who are lesser known is given in the Historical Notes section at the end of the novel. Although *Children of Cain* is a work of fiction, recognized historical facts have not knowingly been altered.

Visit Miriam Grace Monfredo's website at
www.miriamgracemonfredo.com

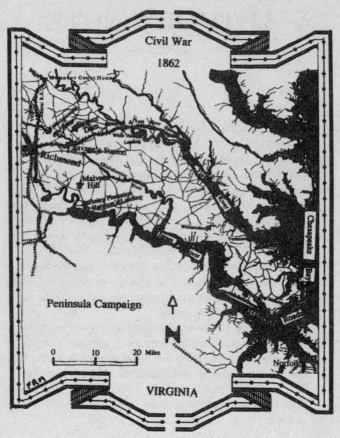

1862 Virginia Peninsula Campaign

Hence, fratricide! Henceforth that word is Cain
Through all the coming myriads of mankind,
Who shall abhor thee though thou wert their sire.

—BYRON, *Cain*

PRELUDE

------ ∞ ------

*The question . . . was whether Richmond should
be surrendered to the young Napoleon, with his
invincible host, or defended even to its altars
and its firesides.*
—Sallie Brock Putnam, Richmond, June 1862

JUNE 23, 1862
General Lee's Headquarters

*T*he afternoon had turned sultry with a metallic smell
to the air that threatened rain. While heat simmered Richmond's cobblestone streets, crowded with refugees fleeing
the threatened countryside, at the High Meadows farmhouse beyond the city the first summoned officer rode up
its dirt lane.

General Thomas "Stonewall" Jackson and his horse
sweated heavily under thick gritty coats of dust. Jackson's
eyes were threaded with red, the lids swollen half-shut over
slivers of blue, and he slumped forward in the saddle, nodding rhythmically to the animal's plodding gait. It was
the fourth horse Jackson had ridden in the past fourteen
hours, during which he had traveled nearly fifty miles to
the south of his command.

Dismounting near the front porch, he was told by an
aide, "You're expected, sir, but General Lee cannot see you
just yet. He asks that you wait."

Jackson yanked his battered forage cap down over his forehead and went to prop himself against a post-and-rail fence. Some time passed before his brother-in-law, General D. H. Hill, rode up the lane, clearly surprised to see Jackson there. The last Hill had heard, Stonewall was shooting Yankees in the Shenandoah Valley. Then again, Lee's order bringing them here had emphasized the meeting's secret nature. And no one approved of secrecy more than Jackson.

The next quarter hour brought two more dusty, sweating generals: gaunt, impetuous A. P. Hill and massive, deliberate James Longstreet.

The erect figure of General Robert E. Lee stepped onto the porch to cordially call his generals inside. Leading the four to a back room of the farmhouse, he gestured to chairs placed around an ancient, oak table. Once the council of war began in this room, only those bringing refreshments gained entry. The silent slave women came and went, as unobserved as the battered legs bearing the generals' table.

"We have had ample time to observe the enemy's advance," Lee began. "Today he stands so near the city it is said our church bells can be heard in his camps. To save Richmond—and there can be no question that it *must* be saved—we are obliged to act swiftly."

He stopped to look at each man there. Grave, determined expressions met his eyes, signaling their common resolve.

"The enemy's commander and I," Lee went on, "both served in the Corps of Engineers during the Mexican War. He is disciplined and cautious, and he has trained his army well. His numbers are twice those of ours, but he takes position to position under cover of his heavy guns, so we cannot get at him without storming his works. To engage him, we must force him from his present position."

Upon this reading of his adversary, Lee was prepared to launch a daring strategy to save the Confederate capital.

Fifty-six thousand troops, massed under the four chosen generals, would strike the railroad supplying the huge Federal army's base twenty-three miles northeast of Richmond. To execute the operation, Lee's generals and their troops must first cross the rain-swollen Chickahominy River.

"Once its bridges are passed," he continued, "we will sweep down the river. I am confident that a sudden blow will force the enemy to retreat from the gates of our city and move north to defend his vital supply lines."

It was the tactic of a wily gray wolf. A wolf that lures a mountain lion away from his mate and den of pups; while at the same time leading his pack to strike with fangs bared where the lion least expects it.

The seated officers had listened in tense silence to their commander's bold plan, but now Jackson grunted as he lunged across the table for a blue and white pitcher of lemonade. With the sound of liquid splashing into a glass, the others shifted themselves on their straight-backed chairs.

"There will be risk," Lee responded to the question hanging there unspoken. "When we cross north of the Chickahominy, we can spare only twenty-nine thousand troops to be positioned here, south of the river, to defend Richmond. Seven thousand more will remain in reserve, but this number cannot hold the city. Not if the enemy attacks while our main force is on the river's far side."

Such an attack might not appear imminent, given the enemy's cautious, unhurried pace, but it was widely rumored that Abraham Lincoln had become impatient with his general's sluggish advance. And Confederate intelligence had learned from a spy in the enemy military that an assault on Richmond might be expected before long. This spy was currently placed in a position to know.

Lee, intent on seizing the offensive, set his aggressive, if perilous, plan in motion.

Hours were spent on the operation's intricate logistics, and it was dusk before Lee adjourned his council. As the generals left the farmhouse to resume their commands, Longstreet said to Lee, "When can we expect more British rifles and ammunition? They're sorely needed."

"Arrangements on our behalf have been made," Lee answered. "I am assured that more will arrive shortly."

Jackson looked close to exhaustion when he mounted his horse for what would be a long return ride. After rejoining his eighteen thousand troops, he must immediately turn around and march them south to link with Lee's main army. An army that in the meantime would have crossed the river.

Lee stressed again the need for stealth. "To be efficacious, the movement *must* be secret."

As the remaining officers watched Jackson ride north in a drenching rain, D. H. Hill expressed what Longstreet had earlier mentioned. "General Lee, we must have those weapons, sir."

Lee, his mind on the complex maneuvers ahead, responded with merely a nod. The others did not press him further, but all were aware that the need for European-made weapons, smuggled into Southern ports by blockade-running ships, would become even more urgent if the conflict were to last throughout the summer.

JUST forty-eight hours after Stonewall Jackson left High Meadows and rode into that wet June night, the Northern and Southern armies would begin to race on a fateful course. The prize to be saved or lost was no less than the capital of the Confederacy.

And if Richmond were to fall, while Federal armies appeared invincible in the West, that prize could well become the war itself.

Part One

—⚡—

Ye elms that wave on Malvern Hill
  In prime of morn and May
Recall ye how McClellan's men
    Here stood at bay?
While deep within yon forest dim
  Our rigid comrades lay—
Some with cartridges in their mouth,
Others with fixed arms lifted South—
    Invoking so
The cypress glades? Ah wilds of woe!

—HERMAN MELVILLE,
    "Malvern Hill"

1

It is variously estimated that the Rebel army at Richmond and vicinity numbers from 150,000 to 200,000 men.

—Allan Pinkerton, June 1862

Chickahominy River, Virginia

Dawn was only a glow of bronze to the east when Federal Treasury agent Bronwen Llyr reined in her Morgan horse. Stretching forward in the saddle, she cupped one ear and listened to the ominous rumble from somewhere in the misty countryside ahead, before raising a hand to warn her brother.

"Seth, hold!" the young woman called over her shoulder, afraid he might not have caught the signal. His aging mare's pace kept him some distance behind the Morgan.

She was still unable to see the source of the noise. Although it had been increasing in volume, what alarmed her now were the suddenly recognizable sounds that told of large numbers of men, horses, and wheeled transports. When she lifted her hand to again signal Seth, he was just pulling the mare alongside.

Bronwen looked beyond him to where the horizon was now flaming to gold, and only then did she believe the long night was finally over. Several hours before midnight she had engineered her brother's flight from Richmond's Libby Prison, escaping his scheduled execution by a single day. Now they were bound for the Union lines. They had been traveling the fairly steep grade of a bluff rising above the Chickahominy River, and by this time must be some four miles north of Richmond.

"Sounds like troop movement ahead," Seth speculated. "Too many wagons clattering to be a prisoner manhunt."

"I never did think enough civilians could be rounded up for a manhunt. They're all hunkered down behind doors, expecting their city to be stormed at any minute."

"But could Union troops be this near Richmond without the Rebs giving them a fight?"

"I doubt it," she said, reaching behind the saddle for her small field telescope, or spy glass, as she preferred to call it; spying was, after all, what it did. "Sun's coming up, so let's leave the horses here and take a look."

On foot they warily climbed the remainder of the way through scrub growth that slowly yielded to tall grass. The noise ahead should have given ample forewarning, but even so, when they crept to the edge of the bluff, Bronwen was not prepared for what revealed itself below. She and Seth instinctively threw themselves facedown and scrabbled backward in the grass.

"Good God," Seth whispered at her side, "it's Rebels! Thousands of them! What are they doing down there?"

She took a glance around before worming forward on her belly for another look. Below the bluff, endless ranks of gray-uniformed troops were massing along the river-bank with their shouldered muskets bristling like trees in a vast forest. Sleek cavalry horses, the scabbards of their riders' sabers glinting in the new sun, paced well away from countless heavy draft horses drawing the field car-riages of bleak black cannon. Rolling caissons and limbers held huge ammunition chests while swirling over it all were regimental flags, their colors a shifting blur of blood red and blue.

When Bronwen managed to tear her gaze from the scene below, she realized that thousands more troops, as far as the eye could see, were advancing in long smoky columns over a road that must be the turnpike approach to Mechanicsville Bridge.

Why were they here? *Here,* when they should be dug in before Richmond, ready to defend their capital against McClellan's threatened assault?

Her memory spooled out the past days, over the bits of information she'd heard without paying close attention while she focused on her brother's peril. Not finding an answer, she raised the spyglass to scan farther upriver. And sucked in her breath when she saw still more thousands of troops gathering at the approach to Meadow Bridge. It, too, spanned the Chickahominy.

She lowered the glass and handed it to Seth, frantically searching her mind for an explanation. When one came to her, it seemed so risky, so foolhardy of Confederate command that she nearly discarded it. Until she recalled the gleeful accounts in Richmond newspapers of General Jeb Stuart's flamboyant raid when his cavalry circled the Union army. The papers treated it as a romp designed to humiliate General McClellan, but Bronwen had believed at the time that Stuart's was almost certainly an intelligence mission, his cavalry dispatched by Confederate command to learn the enemy's position and strength.

The troops massed below might be the first phase of an operation based on Stuart's reconnaissance. But to leave Richmond unprotected? It must be a strategy born of desperation, or else a confident gamble that McClellan, despite weeks of preparation, was still not ready to attack.

Seth gave her a nudge. "What are you thinking?"

"That after those troops cross the river, they'll advance northeast toward White House Landing. You were captured, Seth, before White House became McClellan's main supply base. The army's dependent on it, and its railroad and river access to Chesapeake Bay."

He nodded. "Tens of thousands of troops in enemy territory can't survive without a supply line. Where's McClellan now?"

"His current headquarters are supposed to be somewhere near Savage's Station on the railroad. And that station's on *this* side of the Chickahominy. If we can reach Union lines—"

But Seth was already on his feet, running toward their tethered horses. Bronwen, after taking one last scan with her glass, sprinted after him.

Minutes later they descended to flat, low-lying farmland. When they urged the horses eastward on a course parallel to the flooded Chickahominy, Bronwen felt both relieved and worried by the eerie silence on every side. Relieved because there were no gray troops here, worried because the Confederates were so plainly launching an offensive.

And McClellan, lacking reliable intelligence capability, might not know it until disaster struck.

A vast sprawl of tents and striped flags led to the Union lines, where the first pickets directed them to the farm owned by a Dr. Trent. Trent's large house and outbuildings north of the railroad tracks, the pickets said, served as General McClellan's headquarters.

When the farmhouse came into view, Seth asked of a passing soldier, "Are there New York regiments camped nearby?"

"Plenty of 'em. 'Bout a mile or so down the tracks."

Seth turned in the saddle to give his sister a long look. Her eyes smarting, Bronwen returned his gaze with a nod that she understood it was the only thing he could give her. The concealing bibbed overalls, loose shirt, and straw hat she wore portrayed a farmhand, a male farmhand, who was simply delivering a lost soldier to his army.

Dismounting to watch her brother ride off, she brushed at her eyes and told herself no good came from fearing an unknown tomorrow. For now, today, Seth was alive and well. And he was as safe as any of them could be in a hostile land.

A short distance away, a handful of soldiers straddled the rail fence enclosing more than a dozen sound-looking horses. Bronwen glanced over the men, trying to spot a sympathetic face. Seeing a likely candidate, she tugged the straw hat down until its brim skimmed her eyebrows. No point in announcing to the entire camp that here was possibly the only female within miles.

With her voice pitched as deep as she could make it, she told the soldier, "Take good care of this horse," when giving him the Morgan's reins. "He's a fine animal, even if he was more or less borrowed from a Confederate officer."

The soldier grinned in response. "That bein' the case, we'll take damn good care of him!"

The sun stood high overhead as Bronwen walked quickly to the frame farmhouse, where two young privates posted at its steps sweated in their wool flannel uniforms. Before approaching them, she paused to swipe at her face with a dirt-smudged hand. After flicking weeds and dust from her boots and overalls, she again hauled down the hat brim and pulled from her pocket a gold coin bearing the United States Treasury seal.

"I need to see General McClellan," she told one of the soldiers. Keeping her face averted, she handed him the calling card.

The coin brought first a look of surprise, then a frown, as the soldier eyed her patched, dusty overalls. She had expected skepticism, but the coin should prevent her from being dismissed outright.

"Who wants to see him?"

"Agent Llyr," she responded promptly, knowing it would create even more doubt if she appeared less than confident. "Is the general in camp—and if not, where can I find him? I have information to report, and I don't want one of his aides."

The private gave her another dubious glance, while bouncing the coin in his palm as if weighing its authenticity and maybe assessing its worth. Then he shrugged. "Okay, wait here."

He turned to climb the steps.

While she waited, Bronwen looked over her shoulder to where row upon row of army tents, battery wagons, and field artillery carriages littered the green Virginia pasture land. McClellan would have made his headquarters here for its ready access to the railroad running supplies from White House Landing. At a short distance to the north flowed the Chickahominy. When Bronwen and Seth had ridden in, the countryside seemed tranquil, but it would not remain tranquil for long. Not when two huge armies were about to collide.

General McClellan had persuaded the Federal War Department that only his massive campaign could end the secession war in a matter of weeks.

"I shall soon leave here on the wing for Richmond—which you may be certain I will take," McClellan was said to have told a friend.

In the past three months, he had first conducted a protracted siege before Yorktown, broken when Confederate troops packed up and stole away into the night. This "brilliant success," as reported by McClellan, had been followed by a modest Union victory at Williamsburg, where Seth had been captured. A subsequent engagement at Seven Pines had produced a staggering number of casualties on either side, but the two days of combat had ended in stalemate. Among the heavy toll of wounded had been the Confederate army's commander Joseph Johnston.

Command had then passed to Robert E. Lee.

Since then, McClellan's engineers had been building bridges, elaborate and expensive bridges, across the unpredictable Chickahominy. These projects—which some critics complained rivaled those of ancient Rome during the whole of Caesar's campaigns—had brought the Army of the Potomac's advance to a standstill. Union troops battled not Rebels but malaria, dysentery, and typhoid. Confederate troops, with time to spare, entrenched to the east of Richmond.

And McClellan must believe Lee's army was entrenched there still, Bronwen concluded as she noted the unhurried pace of the Union encampment.

Lack of intelligence information had plagued the North since the war's beginning. McClellan seemed content to rely solely on Pinkerton's private detective agency, despite the fact that the agency had next to no experience in espionage. But Allan Pinkerton, with typical conceit, had lately taken to calling himself The Secret Service.

Bronwen plucked at the collar of her yoked shirt. It was so humid it might as well have been raining, and the sun's heat had become breathtaking. Her skin itched from the coarse-woven cotton, and sweat plastered her hair to her skull. It was no consolation that the remaining young private appeared to feel just as wretched.

She was beginning to think her request to see McClellan must not have carried enough urgency. If he wasn't here, why didn't someone say so?

At the sound of a door creaking open, Bronwen started

forward, but stopped short upon seeing the man who was lumbering down the steps. With a nasty jolt, she recognized the stubby, cigar-smoking Allan Pinkerton.

It had been little more than a year ago when Pinkerton, unaware that President-elect Lincoln was within earshot, had loosed an angry tirade. "You, Llyr, have committed your last act of insubordination. You'll never set foot inside my agency again, because you're fired!"

As it had happened, Bronwen's insubordinate act might well have saved Lincoln from assassination in Baltimore, where a secessionist conspiracy had been put in motion. But Pinkerton had detested her even before causing himself that very public embarrassment.

Her immediate superior at Treasury had repeatedly warned, no, *ordered* her to avoid Pinkerton. At the moment, Bronwen could not see how to comply short of bolting for the river, and the information she held was too crucial for her to turn tail and run.

As the detective approached, she stood her ground, determined not to be cowed by his intimidating glare. A reddish brush mustache and wiry hair made Pinkerton most resemble a pugnacious, short-legged terrier, and she noticed that, unlike most Union soldiers, he had put on weight, probably from dining at McClellan's table. It was rumored to offer lavish fare brought here from Washington by way of the York River and its railroad.

Several paces beyond her, he came to a standstill, yanked the cigar from his mouth, and jabbed it at her like a smoldering thumb.

"Llyr, I want you out of this camp. Now!"

"I'll leave as soon as I've reported to General McClellan."

"You'll leave *now!*" The cigar swung in tight circles, scattering live ashes that flitted over the dirt like fireflies.

Before asking to see McClellan, she should have made certain Pinkerton was not in camp, but given the events of her ride here with Seth, it had not even crossed her mind. It could be a costly mistake, but it was her mistake and not one for which Union soldiers should have to suffer.

She gave him a level look and forced a conciliatory tone. "I wouldn't have risked confronting you over something minor."

"You either leave voluntarily, or I'll have you removed."

"I need to see General McClellan—"

"Now!"

"—because I have some vital information. And it's too important to let our . . . our differences prevent McClellan from hearing it. Believe me, I wouldn't be here otherwise."

"I'll decide what's important," he said, continuing to glower. At least he had stopped jabbing the cigar at her. He stuck it back in his mouth and muttered around it, "What's this information?"

"I should report it directly to McClellan."

Pinkerton's face flushed an angrier shade of red, and he turned toward the steps as if to summon the two soldiers.

"All right!" Bronwen conceded. Just a few months ago she would have flung him an insult and stalked off. She had since learned that her natural tendencies carried the risk of costing others too high a price for her conscience to bear. Pinkerton was also capable of having her forcibly detained, although he must guess she was in Virginia because Lincoln had sent her. But Lincoln was not here to say so.

Pinkerton would jealously guard his position as McClellan's sole conduit for intelligence information, but surely even he would not deliberately conceal something important just because it came from her.

"Can I be assured McClellan will hear this immediately?" she asked, taking a stab at learning the general's whereabouts.

"You have exactly one minute to tell me what you know, or I'll have you arrested for trespass!"

Bronwen shot a glance at the house guards who were both listening to this exchange with obvious interest. It could be the most action they had seen in weeks. "Pinkerton, can we move away from our audience?"

"*Half* a minute!"

She saw no alternative. "Earlier this morning, I was on a bluff south of the Chickahominy. Confederate troops were massing at two bridges there, readying to cross over to the north—and when I say massing, I mean there were thousands of them."

Pinkerton's small eyes flared. "How many?"

"There could well have been forty thousand or more. Probably more."

Pinkerton scowled, shaking his head, and then fell uncharacteristically silent.

Because she didn't want to sound too absolutely sure of her figure, she hedged, "Of course that estimate was made more or less on the run." She had not arrived at it alone, but Seth did not need Pinkerton hauling him in for interrogation.

Since the detective was still silent, she added, "I admit it seems reckless of General Lee to move all those troops away from Richmond. But they were there, at the Mechanicsville and Meadow Bridges."

Pinkerton glanced around, and then clamped her shoulder, marching her toward a grove of peach trees some distance from the eavesdroppers.

"You've been in Richmond?" He said it gruffly, as if it pained him to ask.

"I just came from there."

"What did you hear about Stonewall Jackson?"

She didn't immediately respond. If she told him what she had learned of Jackson's position, would he demand to know *how* she had learned? It had been during an assignment for Lincoln and Treasury, and she did not want to remind Pinkerton of their past.

But he was now staring off into space as if he didn't expect an answer. His expression was baffling; in fact, he looked almost stricken. It took her aback, because she had never seen this man lacking bluster.

He abruptly jerked his head at her, saying, "A deserter was brought into camp yesterday. He swore Jackson is near here and ready to strike."

How could Pinkerton risk believing anything said by a deserter, who could deliberately be planted to give false information?

"That doesn't sound possible," she told him, deciding their past was outranked by the dangerous present. "Jackson's troops are marching south from the Shenandoah Valley along the Virginia Central Railroad tracks. They couldn't be within striking distance yet."

"You're wrong," he stated flatly, not even asking how she had come by something so explicit.

"Pinkerton, why worry about Jackson when you should be much more alarmed by all those Confederates I saw at the river? Lee's army is obviously preparing to march north!"

"You are worse than useless if you believe that!" he growled, although his ruddy complexion had become distinctly paler. "Lee marching north—that's rubbish! He would never leave Richmond vulnerable, not when most of our troops are *south* of the river. What you saw only confirms that Jackson and Beauregard are arriving. And that Lee now has under his command upwards to two hundred thousand troops. More than twice our number."

She knew she was gaping at him, but couldn't help herself. "That can't be right. When I was in Richmond I heard nothing about Beauregard. Nothing! And Jackson *cannot* be this far south yet. From what I saw at the Chickahominy, I'd wager almost anything that Lee didn't have that many troops. And won't have even when Jackson arrives."

"I'm not interested in your wagers, and there's no time for this. I want you out of—"

"How can you ignore what I'm telling you? Especially when by doing it you're wasting even more time!"

He was already starting back toward the farmhouse, so in desperation she caught hold of his coat sleeve. "Please *listen* to me, Pinkerton! I heard from someone in Richmond, someone in a position to know, that Lee was about to launch something . . . 'audacious' was the word used."

"Your source for that?"

"I'd rather not say."

He wrenched his sleeve from her grasp.

With her frustration mushrooming, Bronwen said, "If it's the only way you'll take this seriously, my source was a British intelligence agent. A Colonel de Warde."

"And you *listened?* To someone who has a vested interest in seeing the South win this war? You're damn undisciplined, Llyr, but I didn't think you were stupid!"

He plodded on toward the house with Bronwen determinedly matching his strides. "What that agent strongly implied, Pinkerton, was that Lee was about to take the offensive."

"Nonsense!"

"It is *not* nonsense! You just want to discount what I'm saying because you have no agents of your own in Richmond. Which means you're as good as blind and putting God knows how much in jeopardy. You can't rely on deserters and prisoners of war for information. It's too dangerous!"

Seeing him motion to the two soldiers, she refrained from saying more about his methods. And while his pigheaded refusal to consider what she said was infuriating, far too much was at stake for her to give up.

When the soldiers approached, she dug in her heels. "I *insist* upon seeing McClellan!"

"Get this woman out of here," Pinkerton said to the soldiers. When they looked around, apparently confused by his reference to a woman, he pointed the cigar at her. "This hysterical female is disrupting military operations. Put her in the stockade!"

"No!" Bronwen protested. "No, you can't do that."

"I can and will—"

He broke off, and all of them spun toward a sudden staccato of musket fire from the southeast. A sustained rumble of heavy artillery immediately followed it.

Pinkerton turned back to Bronwen. "Notice where that gunfire is coming from? It's *south* of the river. So much for your vital intelligence information!"

"I know what I saw. And it stands to reason that Lee would have left some troops to guard the capital."

"Put her in the stockade," he repeated to the soldiers, "and do it *now*! If she tries to escape, you can shoot her!"

2

*Curiously enough there was almost always
something for McClellan to do more important
than to fight his own battles.*

—Francis Palfrey, 20th Massachusetts, 1862

Union Headquarters

By biting her tongue, Bronwen managed to keep quiet.
Cursing Pinkerton couldn't make matters any better than
they were, and it might make them worse, so she seethed
in silence.

Meanwhile he glowered at the soldiers. "I gave you men
an order!"

One of the two finally mumbled, "If you say so, Mr.
Pinkerton."

"I say so! Now do it!" Pinkerton turned on his heel and
made for the farmhouse, pausing only when another round
of artillery sounded.

Bronwen fought back the urge to snatch the stiletto
from her boot and nail the jackass to the nearest tree. Right
between his nasty little eyes.

She absolutely could not allow herself to be confined. If
Pinkerton wouldn't listen, her Treasury superior likely
would, though from the sound of that artillery it might

already be too late. She needed to find the telegraph here and send a wire to Washington.

The two soldiers were still just standing there, looking confused, and throwing anxious glances toward the gunfire. Given what she had seen at the Chickahominy, it could be a Confederate tactic to focus attention south of the river while Lee's main force moved north.

Where was the telegraph?

She took off her hat and raked her fingers through a damp tangle of hair. It would take something other than beauty to free herself. "Soldiers," she began, "I know both you men are here to fight Rebels and not helpless women. Surely you won't take orders from a civilian."

She gave them a submissive smile to prove she was not the disruptive madwoman Pinkerton had claimed. "I have to leave for Washington immediately," she said, adding the truth for good measure, "to file a report with my Treasury superior. So I don't have time to spend in a stockade, grand a place as it may be."

Hope swelled when one of them smiled back at her. But the other, drawing himself up to a lofty height, announced, "Mr. Pinkerton is a civilian all right, but he's also an adviser to General McClellan. Afraid we have to obey him, miss."

He motioned for her to follow him just as another round of artillery boomed. When both soldiers whipped toward the sound, Bronwen inched sideways in an attempt to put herself beyond reach. But the taller of the two caught the move and took hold of her upper arm. "Come along now, miss. I don't like it much, but we've got no choice."

As he tugged her toward a fenced enclosure that stood some distance from the first trees of a thick wood, she shot a glance at the second soldier. He looked younger than the other, and his expression showed dislike for this detail. What was the saying? Divide and conquer?

Targeting the younger one, she said, "Private, do you suppose I might at least first see my brother? He's with a New York regiment."

"Your *brother*? He's here?"

"Yes, and he'll be wondering where I am."

"Richter," this one said, "don't you think maybe we could let her—"

"No, we can't! And quit smilin' at her, Sully. Makes no difference if her brother's here. Orders are to put her in the stockade."

"Civilian orders," Sully grumbled.

"Coming from him, they're good as from Mac himself."

Bronwen recalled it being said that McClellan's men idolized him. At least the younger ones did, those who had initially been scared, bumbling greenhorns and were now proud to call themselves Union soldiers. Even her fellow Treasury agent Kerry O'Hara, who had nothing else good to say about McClellan, admitted, "Young Napoleon has done one hell of a job training his army. Question is, does he have the guts to use it?"

Growing desperate, she glanced around, willing just one chance for escape to show itself. Her Treasury training had taught her how to use the telegraph, if only she could find one.

As they neared the fencing, all three of them jerked to a halt, startled by a boom of cannon that sounded to Bronwen like Zeus-hurled thunderbolts. The hold on her arm loosened only slightly, but it was all she needed. Wrenching herself from Richter's grasp, she gave him a forceful shove, and he staggered sideways into young Sully. Before either of them could recover their balance, she dashed forward, past the fencing and on into the first trees.

Straightaway a knot of roots tripped her. She stumbled, thrusting out her hands to break her fall. As two sets of boots pounded up behind her, Bronwen regained her foot-

ing and twisted away from an outstretched hand. She heard
a muffled thump and several grunts, hoped one of them
had careened into the other, and sprinted in the direction
of the river.

She likely had more experience fleeing pursuers than
these privates had at pursuit, and with luck they couldn't
swim. Ignoring their angry shouts, she kept running,
forced to veer around tree trunks as the woods grew denser.
Despite Pinkerton's threat, she doubted the soldiers would
actually shoot.

She was wrong. A bullet winged over her head and
thudded into a tree trunk. She couldn't know whether it
had been a warning shot or one fired in earnest. Either way
they must be falling behind if they were resorting to weapons. But as she zigzagged around a stand of large maples,
thinking she just might make the river, she heard a stomp-
ing noise coming from somewhere ahead. Suddenly, low-
hanging branches parted directly in her path. When she
tried to slow and dodge whatever was there, momentum
carried her straight into the grip of fingers like iron bands.

"Well, now, what have we here in the forest primeval?"
came a deafening bellow.

Struggling to free herself, Bronwen saw the hairy face
of what at first appeared to be a large brown bear. Her
struggles only made the iron hold on her shoulders tighten.
She made herself go limp, waiting for the grip to loosen
enough for her to reach her stiletto.

The soldiers, having caught up, stood there panting,
while she took another look at her newest captor. He was
hatless, and his rolled-up flannel shirtsleeves told her nothing, but his blue kersey trousers carried the wide stripe of
a sergeant. The only features visible through the bushy hair
and beard were brown eyes, a prominent nose, and a cav-
ernous mouth.

"She was trying to . . . escape . . . and she's our prisoner," Richter said between breaths.

"She? Did you say *she?*" came the thunderous response. "Am I to understand you're chasing some wood nymph? If so, I can tell you, boys, that it's bad practice. *'Nymph, in thy orisons / Be all my sins remember'd.'* Thus spake the bard."

Bronwen was sure her jaw must have dropped as far as the soldiers', but she couldn't waste an opportunity no matter what shape it took.

"I believe, Sergeant," she said, guessing wildly, "that it must be Shakespeare you're quoting?"

"A nymph who's literate? I am confounded! *'Sweet Echo, sweetest nymph, that liv'st unseen within thy airy shell.'* " The bear's voice had dropped to a whisper. "Needless to say that's Milton, not Shakespeare."

Abruptly switching volume, he roared at the soldiers, "Just what in hell were you boys thinking, abandoning your posts? Both ought to be court-martialed!"

More cannon fire to the southeast diverted the sergeant momentarily. Bronwen now spotted six or seven other soldiers scattered in the general vicinity, walking slowly with their heads bent as if searching the ground for something.

"Find it?" the sergeant yelled at them.

"Nope," came the reply. "Nothin' yet."

"Well, open your damn eyes and keep looking!"

The sergeant returned his attention to Sully and Richter. "Do you so-called soldiers suppose that instead of chasing nymphs, you should be investigating that noisy ruckus down the Williamsburg road?"

"We were ordered to take this woman to the stockade," murmured Richter, looking none too eager to investigate the "ruckus," but more than eager to leave.

"*Who* ordered you?"

"Mr. Pinkerton."

"Pinkerton? A disagreeable fellow. *'Squat like a toad, close to the ear of Eve.'* Also Milton."

When Bronwen forgot herself and instinctively smiled in agreement, the grip on her shoulders slackened. She cautiously edged away from what was either a savior or a raving lunatic, or maybe both. Her frustration was soaring at the valuable time being consumed.

"Sergeant," she said, determined to end this, "do you know where the telegraph is?"

He didn't appear to have heard, since he was once again instructing her former captors.

"Soldiers do *not* take orders from civilians!" he stated at full bellow. "*I,* however, am ordering you to get the hell back to where you can shoot some Rebels. *They* are the enemy, my boys, or have you forgotten it in your pursuit of this defenseless maid? Now, move out!"

The soldiers backed up, poised for flight.

"Wait," Bronwen said to them, "my gold coin. Did Pinkerton keep it?"

"Ah, no . . . I . . . I forgot I had it," stammered Sully. Red-faced, he stuck his hand into a pocket and fished out the Treasury coin.

As he handed it to her, the sergeant growled, "Do we now need to add thievery to your sins?"

"I don't believe we do, sir," Bronwen said quickly, willing to say anything that would let her move on. "I gave it to him voluntarily."

When the sergeant swung wide-eyed to her, the two privates turned and made off through the trees. The other soldiers, who still had their eyes more or less fixed on the ground, glanced up but then resumed their mysterious hunt.

"Thank you, Sergeant, for your gallant rescue," Bronwen said, though if it weren't for him, she wouldn't have been so delayed. Since her impatience was reaching epic proportions, she was ready to bolt again, although questioned whether she could evade the half-dozen soldiers whose search had brought them nearer, within a few score yards.

"You're welcome, I'm sure," the sergeant answered in a moderate voice. "But why the gold coin? Aren't a Rebel sympathizer, are you, scheming to make those boys neglect their duties?"

"I gave it to the soldier as identification, but it's the only one I had." She thrust out her hand with the coin on her palm lying face up. "Notice the seal on it, sir? I'm an agent with the U.S. Treasury."

"Egad, no!"

"Yes."

"You're not a nymph, then?" Dark eyes twinkled through the bush of hair.

"I'm sorry, no, I'm not, sir."

"I'm disappointed to hear that. But why would the U.S. Treasury send a maid 'mongst the dogs of war?"

"I'm a fast runner," she sidestepped, trying to curb the impatience in her voice. "I need to report to General McClellan, Sergeant, but Pinkerton refused my request to see the general. When I insisted, he ordered me to the stockade. So I need to send a telegram to Washington . . . unless you would know where McClellan is."

"No, but from the sounds of that hullabaloo on the Williamsburg road, I know where he is *not*!"

"Pardon?"

"Our general is taking a novel approach to command. One that keeps him as far as possible from a battlefield."

Bronwen, having heard the same thing from Kerry O'Hara, swallowed a groan.

"Here!" came a sudden yell from one of the soldiers. "Found it, Sergeant, but you ain't gonna like it."

Turning, the sergeant walked rapidly toward the soldier, his step surprisingly nimble for such a big man, and bent over the spot that was being pointed out. When he straightened he held up two lengths of what was obviously telegraph wire.

This time Bronwen couldn't restrain the groan. "How long has the line been down?" she asked.

"An hour or two, maybe more."

"Is there another line?"

"There was."

"You mean the *second* one's down, too?"

"Take a closer look, Miss Treasury Agent, and see what you think."

He handed her the wire lengths and she saw immediately what he meant. "This line's been cut! Slashed clean through. And the other one?"

"The same. It seems our lines fell afoul of a Rebel sympathizer, or, worse, a traitorous rat 'mongst our own ranks. If so, he is long gone, because I cannot detect the smell of either Rebels or rats."

"So headquarters is without telegraph capability?"

"It is until we lay another line."

"I can't wait that long!" She stood staring down at the severed line. Either of the sergeant's proposed saboteurs could be linked to the Confederate offensive; interrupting telegraph transmission to keep McClellan's headquarters isolated would gain Lee more time. For her purposes it didn't matter who had cut the line, only that she was prevented from sending word to Washington from here. She couldn't risk running into Pinkerton again.

"Sergeant, how far are the York River Railroad tracks? I can't go back into camp, and I need to jump a train to White House Landing. There must be a working telegraph there."

"You intend to *jump* a train? Surely not."

"I've done it before, and please, Sergeant, time is critical here."

He looked dubious, but glanced at the sun and then pointed to his right. "The track will be east of here, and it's not a long hike." He said to the soldiers who had gathered, "You boys head back and let the telegraph operator know what we found."

Bronwen had begun edging away, thanking the sergeant again, when he shook his head and motioned for her to move along. "I'll go a distance with you, just to make certain there are no rats lurking. And while we're about it, you can tell me what's so damnably urgent."

After they had started in the direction of the tracks, Bronwen decided there was no harm in relating what she had seen at the Chickahominy. He would learn soon enough anyway, and no one else here had cared to listen.

To her surprise, when she finished describing the scene below the river bluff, the sergeant nodded. "That makes some sense of it then."

"Of what?" she asked, kicking aside a tangle of vines in her path and ducking under a tree limb.

"Earlier this morning, a gold-braided array of naval officers came on a train from White House Landing. They all trooped into the farmhouse, where McClellan was having his leisurely breakfast. Plainly those officers had been summoned."

"Meaning?"

"Meaning the general might have been issuing orders to move the navy gunboats from White House. Our commander might not be much on advancing, but he's likely very good at retreating."

"Retreat!" McClellan, like Pinkerton, must believe that a force of a 200,000 Confederates stood against him. "But where could he retreat to?"

The sergeant gave a dramatic shrug. "I cannot say. Could be to the Chesapeake. That's the route he brought us here to fight *'mongst the livery of hell.'* Shakespeare must have served in the army."

It sounded as if McClellan recognized that circling Confederate cavalry for the reconnaissance mission it had been. Which meant he also recognized that his supply base could be endangered. But did he know how soon, and from what direction?

"Your railroad tracks will be straight ahead," the sergeant told her. "The trains run frequently, thus you won't have long to wait. I'd best head back to camp, and see the new lines get laid."

"Sergeant, thank you again." She extended her hand, and he took it in what she thought of as his paw.

"I bid you Godspeed, Miss . . . what is your name?"

"Bronwen Llyr."

"A Welsh maid, I should have known, and from the ancient Celtic line of Llyr! Just think, lass, one of your forefathers might have been King Arthur. Now, if only *he* were in command of the Union army."

"If only," she agreed, thinking that at least Arthur had been spared reliance on Allan Pinkerton.

"Miss Llyr, should you chance upon Mr. Lincoln in Washington, please inform him that he had my vote. And that immediately upon his request for able-bodied men, I left the stage of my beloved theater."

The curtain lifted, not that Bronwen was by this time at all surprised. "I'll tell Mr. Lincoln that." As she started for the tracks, she called over her shoulder, "And what's *your* name, Sergeant?"

"Berringer. Claudius Berringer, but others call me simply"—

"Bear!" she finished with certainty. Hearing the whistle of an approaching train, she turned to send him a wave before making for the tracks.

" *'Once more into the breach,'* Bronwen Llyr!" he bellowed

after her. " '*And when the blast of war blows in our ears, then imitate the action of a tiger.*' "

SHE had been at White House Landing before, having stopped to see her sister when Kathryn worked as a nurse with the U.S. Sanitary Commission hospital ships. While the train steamed to a stop, Bronwen saw a heightened level of activity that tended to support the sergeant's speculation. The Pamunkey River's natural harbor was overflowing with navy gunboats and artillery barges that appeared to be taking on cargo. Officers shouted orders at sweating, harried-looking soldiers, while mules hauled battery wagons to the wharves. But it seemed beyond reason to believe that McClellan would consider abandoning this supply base.

After she cautiously climbed from the freight car, she asked the nearest soldier the location of the telegraph. Upon reaching a tent with huge spools of wire outside it, she found frantic activity there too.

She went to one of the operators seated at a long table, and drawing the coin from her pocket, quietly identified herself as a Treasury agent. "I need to send a wire to my superior in Washington."

"Can't," the soldier said without even glancing up from his clicking machine.

"It's important. Very important!"

"Can't *do* it! The lines are busy."

"Well, then, as soon as possible?" she persisted.

"For cripes sake, can't you see we're swamped?"

"Are you receiving from field headquarters?" she asked, although given the severed lines it seemed improbable that communication would have been restored yet.

He didn't respond, and Bronwen stood waiting. When

there was a lull in the clicking, she started to ask again to send a wire, but was interrupted.

"No, damn it!" the operator snapped. "The frigging line's down again!" He threw himself back in his chair, slapping his palms on the table.

Her Treasury superior Rhys Bevan knew she would have to pass through White House at some point, and he might also believe her sister was still there. Because she had been out of touch with Rhys for some days, she asked the operator, "Have any messages come in recently for Agent Llyr?"

When he ignored her, she repeated the question in a less civil tone, adding pointedly, "They would have been from the War Department."

With that he finally looked up at her. "What did you say your name was?"

"Llyr. *L-l-y-r.*"

After rifling through stacks of the yellow foolscap used when transcribing the telegraph's Morse code, the operator thrust at her two messages. She recognized the Treasury unit's cipher and, grabbing a pencil, found an unoccupied spot farther down the table. The messages were identical, and only took a minute to decode. When finished, she bent over to prop her elbows on the table and stare at what she had written.

LLYR: ASSUMING BROTHER RETRIEVED RETURN WASHINGTON IMMEDIATELY. REPEAT IMMEDIATELY. BEVAN

One was dated yesterday, the other today. Rhys Bevan knew she would never have left Richmond, at least not left alive, without freeing Seth.

As she was tearing the paper into bits she heard

"Llyr!" and straightened to see the telegraph operator waving another yellow sheet.

When he handed it to her, she saw its message was not in code. "Is this for me?"

"Says *Llyr*, doesn't it? Came in today."

She nodded, thanked him, and walked away with the paper. By then she had seen it was addressed to Kathryn Llyr, and had been sent from Savage's Station.

KATHRYN: YOU ARE NEEDED HERE. COME AT ONCE.
PLEASE. GT

So Dr. Gregg Travis was familiar with the word *please* after all, Bronwen noted with disgust, even if his use of it did appear to be an afterthought.

Pocketing her scraps until she found a campfire to dispose of them in, she stood debating what to do with Travis's wire. Much as she wanted to spare her sister more grief, she couldn't destroy something that wasn't hers. Kathryn should read the message, and rip it to shreds herself, which was what Travis deserved.

Bronwen stuffed it into her pocket, and after checking that the telegraph was still not operating, she left the tent.

Her eyes searched the crowded wharves for a supply ship that could take her at least as far as Fort Monroe on the Chesapeake. The only vessels she could spot were the gunboats and barges, but how could she get aboard one of them? That she was with Treasury would not impress a navy commander. Unless . . .

She could not take in the entire riverfront from where she stood and glanced about for a higher vantage point. Her need being urgent, she settled for the first thing at hand, and climbed onto the back of a harnessed mule standing nearby.

"Hey, you damn fool!" yelled the mule's driver. "What

d'you think you're doin', you crazy farmer? Get the hell off government property!"

"Forgive me, sir. I'm just borrowing it a minute," she told him, but his continued cursing indicated he was an unforgiving man.

Balanced on the mule's back, and ignoring the driver's oaths, she rapidly scanned the river and wharves. Given the amount of commotion nearby, no one seemed to pay much attention to where she was planted or to the driver's outrage, although one soldier glanced her way with a startled expression. Bronwen finally spotted the black gunboat and broad-shouldered naval officer she had hoped to find.

"My apologies," she said to the driver when she had jumped down, quickly moving away before he could stop swearing and start asking questions.

She covered the distance to the gunboat's wharf with her gaze locked on Lieutenant Commander Alain Farrar, afraid his ship would steam off downriver before she reached it.

Three months ago in Baltimore, Farrar had come to her rescue during what had been considered by Treasury as a routine surveillance assignment. It had become anything but routine. When three armed men had pursued her, she sought refuge in one of Baltimore's waterfront taverns, having been previously told that Treasury had an unidentified deep cover contact there. The tavern keeper's wife, later revealed to be the contact, had alerted Farrar and other navy men at the tavern, who captured the thugs and imprisoned them aboard Farrar's ship. Subsequently Farrar's ensign had allowed them to escape. This ensign had later been killed while attempting to sabotage the Union ironclad *Monitor*.

Bronwen had seen Farrar only once since then, a few weeks ago here at White House Landing.

When she reached the wharf, Farrar was watching sailors

who were loading onto the gunboat numerous barrels labeled FLOUR. Bread might be a staple of a ship's galley, but its main ingredient did not seem to warrant the attention it was receiving.

"Is that really flour in those barrels?" she said, coming up behind Farrar.

When he didn't turn, she added in jest, "Or is it something more interesting? Like bourbon?"

When Farrar swung around, a frown creased his square, smooth-shaven face. "What the devil—" He broke off, and stared at her with a half-annoyed, half-perplexed expression.

Then Bronwen remembered her concealing hat and whipped it off. Farrar's frown wavered before it vanished in a wide compelling smile, something in his ice-blue eyes reminding her of sunlight reflecting from a frozen pond.

"Miss Braveheart! Is it you?"

"It is."

"What a splendid surprise to see you again. But why are you here?"

"To catch a ride on your ship, if you please."

"Doesn't Treasury provide transport for its employees?" he said, still smiling.

"Are you bound for Fort Monroe?"

He put up a hand for her to wait, and turned to the men who had finished loading the flour barrels. "That's it for now. Dismissed." He turned back to her, saying, "Come along the wharf with me."

"Do you always supervise the cargo?" she asked as they walked at a brisk pace toward the shoreline. "Even when it's flour?"

"Especially when it's flour! The bread I cast upon the waters should at least be dry to start with. Last time, we had mold and maggots the second day out. Now, why do you need passage to Fort Monroe?"

"I have to return to Washington and thought I'd stand a chance of finding a steamer heading north there at the fort."

"Is Treasury recalling you from the field? I hope so, because it's no place for a beautiful young woman. Although you never seem to go out of your way to avoid perilous assignments, Braveheart."

"I also need the fort's telegraph."

"There are several lines here."

"They're down."

An ensign was coming toward them, and Farrar returned his salute, and then said to him, "Round up the staff officers ashore on the double."

"I'm not bound for Fort Monroe," he told Bronwen after the ensign dashed off, and they had started back toward the ship. "But I can put you ashore there when I pass through Hampton Roads."

She glanced at the ships that were steaming away downriver. "Where *are* you bound?" she asked, thinking back to Berringer's earlier comment about naval officers arriving at McClellan's headquarters. "Surely all these ships can't be abandoning this base for the Chesapeake?"

"You're supposed to be the one with information, Braveheart," he said with a sideways glance.

"I've been in Richmond and out of touch for a few days."

"You've just come from Richmond? Why is Treasury risking the life of a valuable agent by sending you there? Virginians are thirsting for Yankee blood."

He hadn't answered her original question, and she was sure it had been intentional, so she simply shook her head in reply to his. But if he were passing through Hampton Roads, he might be bound for the Norfolk naval base.

"Lieutenant, why all the activity here? Does McClellan plan to use gunboats in combination with his infantry?"

she asked, recalling in stark detail the thousands of Confederate troops she had earlier seen.

Although Farrar gave her only a brief smile, Bronwen saw it as one of irony rather than simple evasion. Either way it was a disturbing response to her question.

3

In peace, children inter their parents. War violates the order of nature and causes parents to inter their children.

—Herodotus, 425 B.C.

Seneca Falls, New York

Glynis Tryon stood at a fence bordering the cemetery, but even from there she could hear the soft heartrending cries of a young widow's grief. Over them came the voice of Reverend Eames speaking the ancient words of burial.

"I am the resurrection and the life, saith the Lord; he that believeth in me, though he were dead, yet shall he live."

Glynis had slipped away from the others following the pine casket and its bearers up the slope behind the church, and had gone to where she could look across the village of Seneca Falls and its river. On the opposite slope rose her own fieldstone library. Beyond the roads of the town lay the green and gold patchwork that was fields of young corn and maturing winter wheat.

"To everything there is a season . . . a time to be born and a time to die."

From where Glynis stood, she could hear water washing against the concrete canal walls that channeled the river through the village. She could hear, too, the rattle of wagons on an adjacent farm and the shouts of youngsters at a nearby swimming hole. The usually welcome sounds of summer now seemed an intrusion.

"We are the children of God, and if children, then heirs."

And they were here today at this gravesite, Glynis thought, because they were also the heirs of Cain.

She had not been raised here in this village in the Finger Lakes region of western New York, but over the years it had become her home, its people now her people. Today they were burying one of their own. Young John Carey had not been the first Seneca Falls soldier to fall in the war, but if the North's current campaign in Virginia proved successful, he might be among the last.

There was good reason to believe a swift end to the war was nearly within grasp. Since early spring the newspapers in every Northern town and city had trumpeted accounts of Federal victories in the West. Control of the great rivers within the South's heartland was again, or soon would be, in Union hands.

"Thou turnest men to destruction; and sayest, Return, ye children of men."

The morning was warm even for June, and as Reverend Eames read from the *Book of Common Prayer*, he ran a finger inside the rim of his white linen collar. Gathered around the raw earth of the gravesite were mostly local farm families. The fabric of long black skirts whispered in a hot wind, and dark wool coats and trousers, worn only on special occasions, smelled of camphor balls and cedar chests. Standing somewhat apart from the others was an aged man, hunched over a crooked staff, his face bearing the pain of one whose life had been hard even before this last, cruelest blow. He was old John Carey, the dead soldier's father.

"And the places that knew them shall know them no more."

The whimper of a small child, sleepily rubbing his eyes,

broke through the stillness following this passage, and Amanda Carey bent down to lift the toddler in her arms. This child, Johnny, had been named for his father and grandfather. Two other children, as thin and pale as the toddler, stood beside the woman, hiding their faces in the folds of her cotton skirt. The skirt had doubtless once been black, but now showed the rust-colored hue of many launderings.

"I will lift up mine eyes unto the hills; from whence cometh my help? My help cometh even from the Lord, who hath made heaven and earth."

The Carey family had barely scratched out a living. How would those remaining survive? Their small farm and the rough house that sat on it carried a mortgage at the Red Mills Bank. When young John had joined a Seneca County regiment bound for the South, he told his wife and father that he would be gone for ninety days. His army pay, he had said, could hire workers to help harvest the acreages of wheat planted the previous autumn. Now, with only a young mother and a lame old man to reap it, most of the wheat would rot in the fields. Neighbors had their own crops to harvest, and scores of families were headed by women whose husbands had answered Lincoln's call to arms.

How many would find themselves in poverty if the war was not over soon? How many like old John Carey would end their days grieving?

"My soul fleeth unto the Lord before the morning watch."

Reverend Eames closed the book and motioned to the pallbearers, who then grasped the ropes that cradled the casket. As they lowered it into the ground, the three children began to cry, Johnny clinging to his mother with arms clasped around her neck. Weeping, Amanda Carey buried her face in the child's hair. Her free hand blindly sought the other two children to draw them closer, while in the church steeple below, a bell began its mournful toll. *"Earth to earth, ashes to ashes, dust to dust."*

"THANK you for coming, Miss Tryon," murmured Amanda Carey at the steps of the church. The three children pressed against her, anxiously searching their mother's face. Did they understand what had just been done, or would they forever be waiting for their father to come home?

"Please let me know if I can help in some way, Mrs. Carey," Glynis responded, dropping coins discreetly into the collection basket so as not to embarrass the young widow. They were the usual well-meaning things one said and did, but they meant very little. What could anyone do?

Her thoughts on the war and its victims, Glynis walked down the slope and crossed the river bridge to Fall Street, the wide dirt road that ran east and west through the village. Three members of her family, two nieces and a nephew, were involved in the struggle to save the young nation. Glynis lived with nagging concern for them, and for Seneca Falls constable Cullen Stuart, who had left to join a Seneca County regiment in Virginia. She felt his absence with what was still acute grief.

Several weeks had passed since Glynis had last heard word of any of them, except for her nephew Seth.

A week ago, the content of a telegram relayed by letter to Glynis had raised her concern to full-blown fear. The War Department had notified her sister and brother-in-law in Rochester that their son was missing. It was possible, her sister Gwen had written, that Seth had been captured. Glynis, reading between the lines, knew Gwen could not even begin to consider the obvious alternative.

Now, as she neared the library, someone calling her

name made her turn to see the village telegraph operator. Her heart began to thud with dread, since he was waving a sheet of yellow paper.

"Telegram, Miss Tryon!" said Mr. Grimes as he hurried up to her.

His bland expression told her nothing, but this was a practiced act on his part. Everyone knew it was an act, because while Mr. Grimes prided himself on being a disinterested messenger, he was, in truth, the most meddlesome busybody in western New York. He often learned the calamities visited on townsfolk long before the ones most affected did, and many of those who received hand-delivered telegrams suspected him of being the glad bearer of bad tidings.

"Thank you, Mr. Grimes," said Glynis, extending her hand for the telegram and willing it not to tremble.

"Sent from Washington," he announced, gripping the paper so tightly that Glynis wondered if she would need to pry his fingers open to claim it.

He added, in unnaturally hushed tone as if everyone on Fall Street hadn't already been alerted, "It's from that fellow you know at the Treasury Department. So I expect you'll be needing to send a——"

Her dread by now grown unbearable, Glynis cut him off by snatching the telegram.

4

—⁂—

The rebel force is stated at 200,000, including Jackson and Beauregard. I shall have to contend against vastly superior odds ... the responsibility cannot be thrown on my shoulders.
—General George B. McClellan, June 1862

Washington City

It was early evening, but the summer solstice meant daylight was not even fading when Bronwen reached the far boundary of Lafayette Park. She stopped and lowered her carpetbag to the sparse grass before starting down the next street. A scan of the quiet, well-kept neighborhood told her vagrants could be at risk here, and she better not linger because she must look like one. Three hack drivers had passed her by after only a glance.

She had just learned at the Treasury Building that her superior Rhys Bevan had left his office an hour earlier. The guard on duty there had handed her a slip of paper bearing only a street address. She had recognized Rhys's handwriting and the address as being a short distance from her former boardinghouse.

Picking up her carpetbag with a groan, she trudged from the park. Halfway down the street, she glanced at the slip of paper, and then up at the brass numerals on the front door of the nearest neat, brick house. After passing through its low gate, she was walking toward the entrance when the door swung open.

Coming through it to stand three steps above her was Rhys Bevan. He was obviously dressed for an evening out, the well-tailored black evening suit, sparkling white shirt, and polished boots giving his clean-shaven good looks even more elegance than usual. She felt a stab of resentment until reminding herself of his role in the war effort. Proximity to so many mud-streaked, sweating men in uniforms or farm clothes had nearly made her forget the ones who worked behind the scenes.

Rhys was regarding her with an unreadable expression. Because he could rarely be taken by surprise, and hardly ever showed it if he had been, he must be concealing the distaste anyone would have at finding a bedraggled tramp on his doorstep. When Bronwen glanced down at her filthy boots and frayed overalls, a sudden embarrassment, unwarranted but there just the same, made her reach for her usual shield of flippancy.

She thrust out a dirty palm to him. "Alms for the poor, sir?"

Instead of the smiling response she had aimed for, his expression remained the same. He came down the steps and grasped her shoulder, propelling her ahead of him up the steps and through the doorway into a cool, dimly lit entry hall.

"Mrs. Petersen?" he called up the stairs. At the same time he plucked off Bronwen's straw hat, then held her at arm's length, inspecting her as he might someone who had survived, but might still be carrying, the plague.

"So, Agent Llyr, you're all in one piece," he finally commented. "And your brother? He's back behind Union lines?"

When she nodded, he said, "Earlier today I wired your

aunt in Seneca Falls that he was free of Libby Prison."

"How did you know?" she asked, and then guessed he must have received word from Agent O'Hara.

"We'll get to that later."

"Chief, I have some information you need to hear."

"It will have to wait. I'm just on my way to a supper engagement."

She opened her mouth to retort but caught herself when she heard a skirt rustling on the stairs. Coming down them was an angular woman who looked to be somewhat past middle age. Although her features were not overly severe, dark hair skinned back into a bun seemed to emphasize narrowed, disapproving eyes.

Rhys turned to the woman, who was apparently his housekeeper, because he said, "Please draw a bath for Miss Llyr."

"No, not yet," Bronwen protested. "We need to talk first."

Rhys glanced at the hall clock. "It will have to be when I return, since—"

"It will have to be *now*!" she broke in, bringing an exclamation from the woman and even a look of surprise from Rhys.

She knew she was offending both of them, but couldn't stop herself. The frustration and fear of the past weeks, which she'd been forced to bury out of sight if not out of mind, came bursting to the surface.

"Rhys, I haven't spent long hot hours scrambling to get here for a *bath*! Yes, I'm dirty, but the assignment *you* gave me didn't leave much time for soap and water. I was too busy being scared! Believe me, I wouldn't keep you from your frigging supper if it weren't important. And if you dislike my language, then don't make me spend so much time with the military!"

The clock ticked loudly into the silence that followed,

and at a gesture from Rhys, the tight-lipped Mrs. Petersen turned on her heel and left. Bronwen sagged back against the wall, flexing the fingers she had unconsciously clenched into fists, and started to sputter an apology. Rhys dismissed it with a wave of his hand. While he didn't appear angry about her outburst, his expression again held something she couldn't name. It almost seemed to reflect sadness. He said nothing, just reached for her arm and drew her into an adjoining room. A room that housed more books than she'd ever seen in one place other than her aunt's western New York library.

"Please, sit down," Rhys told her, indicating an arched-back sofa, and pulling out a chair from the kneehole of a mahogany desk.

She took one glance at the richly upholstered sofa, which was probably an antique, and then down at her overalls. "I think I'd better stand."

"Bronwen, sit!"

She perched herself at the edge of the sofa.

Not once did he interrupt while she told him what, by a twist of fate, she had witnessed at the Chickahominy River. She finished with a much-abbreviated version of her confrontation with Allan Pinkerton.

"I should have somehow avoided him," she admitted. "And seeing him did no good anyway, because he wouldn't even consider what I said. But Seth saw those troops, too, and he agreed with my numbers."

"We've learned of an engagement on the Williamsburg road," Rhys said. "It reportedly came about when McClellan attempted to advance his siege guns to within range of Richmond and instead ran into a Confederate force. So that indicates there are at least some of Lee's troops south of the Chickahominy."

"But wouldn't he have left a few brigades at the earthworks before Richmond—he's had his men digging them for the past month—to make it appear the city was fully defended? While his main force crossed to the north?"

"If true," Rhys said, "it would be a daring tactic. But that's what you thought Colonel de Warde had implied?"

At the time the British agent said it, he'd had good reason to be more forthcoming than usual, so she tended to believe it. She believed little else de Warde ever said.

"He strongly implied," she answered, "that Lee was about to launch some operation, and the word de Warde used to describe it was 'audacious.' I agree it seems a startling maneuver for Lee to pull most of his army away from Richmond, but I know what I saw."

"What did you hear in Richmond about General Beauregard?" asked Rhys. "Anything to suggest he was on his way from Mississippi?"

"Nothing at all, and I think there would have been rumblings of it if Beauregard were expected anytime soon. Why?"

"McClellan's last wire to the War Department stated that Beauregard has already arrived."

"Pinkerton insisted the same thing. But he's relying on a story given by a so-called Rebel deserter, who was probably planted to unnerve Union command with exaggerated troop figures."

"If so, it may have succeeded. McClellan sounds convinced that the number of enemy troops now stands at two hundred thousand."

"Pinkerton used the same figure. I just don't believe it's that great."

"It seems inflated, I agree. Our estimate here indicates the number as being somewhere between sixty thousand and one hundred thousand."

"O'Hara told me he did see Jackson's troops heading south toward Richmond. Since you knew about Seth's escape, I assume you've heard from O'Hara?"

"He sent a wire from West Virginia, saying the British tobacco is safely on its way north by rail to Canada. For which he gave you full credit."

Surprised by O'Hara's generosity, she murmured, "I don't deserve all of it. He engineered the train. But, Chief, when I got to White House Landing, there was, to put it mildly, heightened activity there. The telegraph operators had messages coming in apace until the line went down. And the gunboats were leaving. By the way, do you remember Lieutenant Commander Farrar?"

Rhys nodded. "Our War Department contact when he was stationed at Baltimore."

"I found him at White House, and begged a ride to Fort Monroe on his ship. Other than mentioning Hampton Roads, he wouldn't say where his orders were sending him."

"I haven't heard of any navy reassignments, but when I stop at the War Department to file your report, I'll look into it. The president may even be there. McClellan stated he would not be sending wires regularly, but despite it Lincoln's been haunting the telegraph room."

"How is he?"

"As he would phrase it, 'Doing tolerably.' He'll want to see you at some point."

She had known she would have to eventually face the president with some bad news involving her assignment in Richmond, but pushed the thought aside for the time being.

"Rhys, I'm positive about the troops I saw."

"And I'll report it. But while I've not known you to exaggerate your information—"

When she tried to interrupt, in a repeat of the same frustration she'd experienced earlier, he held up a hand to stop her and went on, "Estimating troop numbers is tricky business. It's possible there were fewer Rebels at the river bridges than you could calculate on the run. But I agree that many there at all is troubling."

He got to his feet, saying, "I really must go now. We'll talk more tonight. Meanwhile I'll have Mrs. Petersen fetch you something to eat."

"First I need to find a room. If you recall, I no longer have a boardinghouse." Her sister Kathryn had barely escaped with her life when that house had been torched by a deranged Confederate agent.

"Incidentally," Bronwen said, "you might want to know that Mrs. Bleuette—a.k.a. Agent Bluebell—fell victim to what I'd call a deserved and long overdue assassination. But it wasn't by my hand. I'm fairly sure Confederate intelligence arranged it. She'd become too unpredictable to control and too dangerous to be useful."

"I can't say I'm sorry to hear it. The woman was indeed dangerous, and even here in Washington there are still entirely too many secessionist sympathizers running around loose for peace of mind. Some of this city's more fanatical ones may have assassination designs as well."

Bronwen jerked forward on the sofa. "Have there been new threats against the president?"

"They've never really stopped since he took office. It takes more agents than we have available to run down every last one of them. And, as you know, Lincoln does not want us to enact extra precautions that would make him inaccessible to the public."

"Even if he's in danger?"

"We can only hope the threats aren't credible. But about a room—you won't find one in this overcrowded city, and certainly not at this hour. You'll stay here," Rhys said briskly as he started for the hall, but then turned to ask, "Do you have any money left?"

Without waiting for a reply, he withdrew several gold coins from his waistcoat pocket.

"I don't need that much," she protested.

"You might. The hack drivers here, along with everybody else in Washington, have raised their fares, and after you've bathed I want you to come to Willard's. I'm due there now."

"*Willard's?* I can't go there! I have exactly one dress in that carpetbag and it's torn and wrinkled."

"Mrs. Petersen can mend and press it."

"She can't mend scratches and ratty hair—" She broke off at his bemused expression. Ordinarily it wouldn't much matter to her how she looked provided she was at least clean, but she didn't fancy drawing attention at the stylish Willard's because she resembled a Gorgon.

"Bronwen, what are you fussing about, when you're one of the most . . . most resourceful women in Washington."

She had caught his hesitation and its possible implication, but was too drained for even Rhys to hold his usual appeal.

"Is this a command performance?" she persisted. "Because if it isn't, I'd rather sleep. I caught some on the ship but that's all I've had for a good while."

"I know you're tired, and I'd rather not request that you do this. However, it's not my request." He gave her a faint smile when adding, "You were recalled because one of your admirers has been asking for you. He'll be at Willard's tonight."

"Who will?"

As he made for the door, the smile was his only reply.

5

Nine-tenths of all vessels now engaged in the business [of blockade-running] were built and fitted out in England by Englishmen and with English capital, and are now owned by Englishmen.

—Thomas Haines Dudley, U.S. consul,
Liverpool, England, 1862

Washington City

When the hack driver pulled his horse to a halt on Fourteenth Street, Bronwen craned her neck to look up at the imposing structure that was Willard's hotel. It rose four tall stories above its sprawling ground floor. Adding to its height were the numerous United States flags flying from poles affixed to its roof top. Not only was Willard's considered to be *the* meeting place in Washington, but some also swore that a good deal of the government's business was conducted in its barroom.

"You'll be wanting the ladies' entrance, miss," the driver told her, pointing to a recessed door some distance beyond the barroom's double ones.

After Bronwen climbed from the carriage, she paused before the entry to shake dust from the hem of her rehabilitated green dress. She already missed the carefree comfort of overalls. Wisps of hair still damp from the bath brushed her face, and she made a half-hearted attempt to push them back under the large, flat velvet bow that hid the hastily contrived, untidy knot at the nape of her neck.

Her hair had been shortened weeks ago at Rhys Bevan's express order. It had been dyed a dark auburn, also at his order: "It is dangerous, not to say stupid, for an undercover agent in the field to own highly distinctive red hair!"

Time and the rains of Virginia had begun to somewhat restore the hair's natural length and color, and although Rhys had earlier said nothing about it, by this time Bronwen had been forced to agree with him. Danger had become too familiar for her to scorn disguise.

Once through the ladies' entrance of the hotel, she stopped in confusion. Half of Washington must have crammed itself into Willard's tonight. The bluish haze of cigar smoke made any attempt at visual reckoning a wasted effort, but the mouth-watering smell of roast beef and fowl led her to a mammoth dining room, where candlelight from the scores of chandeliers flickered over stylishly dressed diners. A dozen or more white-coated waiters were maneuvering around the closely placed tables while they balanced food platters the size of tombstones.

A minute after Bronwen gave an assumed name to the maître d', Rhys Bevan appeared. He took her arm and led her past the main dining room, and then down a corridor to the open door of a smaller, more intimate room. "Forgo the colorful military language, if you please," he told her.

As they entered the room, the only other person there rose to his feet immediately, and with surprise Bronwen recognized Gustavus Fox. President Lincoln had thought highly enough of this man to create the office of assistant navy secretary expressly for him.

"Miss Llyr, a pleasure to see you again."

"And you, Mr. Secretary."

Bronwen thought, as she had on their first meeting, that Fox wore his name well. His bright eyes missed little, and a receding hairline was more than compensated for by a brushy brown mustache and short beard. When he drew out a chair for her, his movements were quick and energetic. Fox had been one of the first supporters of the newly designed ironclad ships, and Bronwen had met him when assigned to investigate the threatened sabotage of the *Monitor*. He had stipulated that the navy's role in foiling the sabotage plot must be a covert one. As far as she knew, it had remained so to this day.

At the time, her nagging suspicion that all the conspirators in the *Monitor* plot had not been exposed brought almost no interest from either Fox or Rhys. And it seemed unlikely to be the reason she had been summoned here tonight. So why had she been?

"On the way here I stopped at the War Department," Rhys told her after they seated themselves. "There's been another engagement near Richmond. At least one Confederate division launched a surprise attack against McClellan's right flank—meaning about a third of the Union troops, namely, those who had remained north of the Chickahominy. Two-thirds of them are now south of the river."

Bronwen winced, recognizing again that she had been right about General Lee's intentions. Keeping her disappointment at having been ignored to herself, she only asked, "Where do things stand now?"

"The Confederates were driven back," answered Fox. "General McClellan wired War Secretary Stanton that, and I quote the general: 'victory was complete and against great odds.' McClellan's message concluded, and this is also a quote: 'I almost begin to think we are invincible.' "

Fox and Rhys exchanged a glance, the meaning of which Bronwen could only guess.

"There's been no extended contact with Union command since then," Rhys said, as he poured a glass of claret for her. "I expect we'll soon hear something more, but right now it would appear that your report was accurate."

Curse Pinkerton and his pigheaded self-importance!

She of course did not voice this, and only when she sensed both men's gaze on her did she realize she had been twisting the tablecloth between her fingers. Releasing it, she reached for the wine glass just as a waiter appeared.

"Did Mrs. Petersen feed you?" asked Rhys.

"Scones," Bronwen replied briefly, knowing neither man would be interested in her opinion of scones as food.

When Rhys asked for a menu, Gustavus Fox said with a smile, "I think, Miss Llyr, that under the circumstances the U.S. Navy can afford something more substantial, and certainly more appropriate, than British quick bread. Perhaps one of Willard's excellent steaks?"

"Yes, thank you," she answered quickly enough, but her feelings were mixed. The navy secretary had sounded as though he might be offering the condemned a last meal. She glanced at Rhys, hoping he would confirm that this was an absurd impression, but he was too busy giving the waiter their orders to notice.

"I'm assuming," Fox said to her in an abrupt change of topic, "that you know the purpose of the Atlantic blockade?"

The question was so unexpected that she repeated blankly, "Blockade?" The thought occurred that she might be ordered aboard a frigate, possibly even before the steaks arrived.

A temporary reprieve came from a waiter bearing bowls of clam chowder. After several spoonfuls, Fox said, as if he hadn't asked the question, "The blockade's meant to keep foreign-made goods from entering Southern ports, and to prevent the South's products from leaving."

He efficiently applied a napkin to his mustache before continuing, "There are over three thousand miles of coastline to patrol, and as yet our navy doesn't have anywhere near enough warships to make the blockade effective."

Bronwen nodded, but wondered what coastlines and lack of warships had to do with her. She could swim, yes, but her sailing skills, scant as they were, could hardly recommend her for oceanic patrol duty.

"We're stationing what ships we have at the most obvious points of entry," Fox went on, "but the blockade-running steamers are fast, and at night they're nearly invisible. Their captains are skillful, paid princely sums to take risks, which they do."

The soup bowls were whisked away to be replaced by small plates of salmon garnished with sliced cucumber. Bronwen, to show that she was paying attention and therefore deserved this fare, though truly she did not have any burning desire to know, asked Fox, "How much is actually making it through the blockade?"

"We estimate that upwards of sixty percent of Confederate weapons and ammunition will soon be arriving on blockade-runners. They're primarily British-made, and the vast majority of ships running the blockade fly the British flag."

Rhys added, "British goods are delivered on large, deep-draft, oceangoing freighters to neutral ports like Nassau and Bermuda. The cargo is off-loaded there, and then reloaded onto shallow-draft steamers for the run through the blockade to Southern ports."

As he was speaking the steaks arrived, marble-veined and still sizzling, surrounded by mushrooms and brown-crusted potatoes. By this time Bronwen's appetite was not quite what it had been. The discussion appeared to be heading into perilous waters, so to speak. And both men's pointed references to Britain made her fear she would again be expected to bargain with Colonel de Warde. Those in the Federal government who knew she had helped rescue his endangered tobacco stored in Richmond might conclude de Warde owed them a favor.

But no one, not even Rhys, could know the Englishman owed her for more than his tobacco. She intended to keep it that way, if it meant she could avoid ever again crossing de Warde's crooked path.

After too few minutes had been focused on the food, Fox put down his knife and fork to say, "There's been a recent turn of events, Miss Llyr, that has us particularly concerned."

Here it comes. Toying with her silverware, she regretfully eyed the remainder of her steak.

"First some background," the secretary said. "Once the blockade-runners have slipped through our deepwater blockading net, they're nearly scot-free."

"Because their shallow-draft ships can run closer to shore?"

"Correct. And when I said 'blockading net,' I used the phrase loosely—picture our ships as a few tiny gnats on an immense block of Swiss cheese. We're building steam-propelled warships and converting merchant sailors to steam, but in the meantime we're capturing only a small number of the runners. For every one caught, seven slip through."

He paused, and from the corner of her eye, Bronwen saw the waiter approaching empty-handed, which probably meant her uneaten portion of steak would leave when he did. She grasped the edge of her plate, hoping her fingers couldn't be observed.

"I don't believe the lady is quite finished," the sharp-eyed Fox told the waiter. "Just bring our coffee and whatever fruit is fresh."

Rhys looked merely amused when Fox added, "Do you regularly starve your operatives, Bevan? Please eat, Miss Llyr, since I take it you haven't recently had a square meal.

Does that mean Richmond is beginning to feel a pinch?"

"Yes, sir, not only is there scarcity, but the prices of meat and other perishables are soaring."

Nodding, he said, "Earlier I mentioned a new concern. It involves Richmond."

These days, what did not involve Richmond? But what could an inland city have to do with the Atlantic blockade?

"We have learned," said Fox, "that in the past weeks two large shipments of guns and ammunition arrived there aboard blockade-runners."

"Arrived in *Richmond?*" Bronwen echoed in surprise.

"We know they came up the James River, obviously by way of the Chesapeake and past Norfolk through Hampton Roads."

His remark increased her confusion. A month ago, when Confederate troops had withdrawn from Norfolk to rush back to their endangered capital, Union forces regained control of the strategic naval base. Both she and Fox had been there in Norfolk that day. The same day *Monitor* and its crew were to have been blown up by means of a lighted fuse leading to its powder magazine. She still cringed whenever she thought of the intended explosion.

"But how," she asked, "could blockade-runners slip past the Union ships there?"

"That, Miss Llyr, is precisely the question. And because of your recent success in Richmond, it's a question I think you might help to answer. Wherever the leak, it must be plugged!"

That was one way, she supposed uneasily, to portray a damaging lapse of attention by those at Norfolk. But if it were as simple or innocent as that, Fox would not be asking for Treasury assistance.

• • • •

IT was another hour before she and Rhys Bevan left Willard's in a closed carriage. Bronwen shifted position several times on its leather seat, being in the uncomfortable state where her body felt leaden with fatigue while her mind raced in several directions.

She said to Rhys, "Secretary Fox never did name the source of that information about the guns and Richmond."

"We don't know the source. The loyalist Union network there passed us the information, but the source of it insisted on remaining anonymous. And there could be any number of explanations for that."

"But do we know it's reliable?"

"There's no reason yet to suspect it's not. The same source identified the blockade-runner's captain, who in both instances was a Thomas Lockwood. Fox learned that before the war Lockwood captained U.S. mail steamers. He was known for bringing his ships through violent weather, equipment failure, and anything else he ran into."

Not a man to let a few Federal frigates worry him, Bronwen thought, and one who would make a dangerous opponent. Luckily, she did not have to find him, but only his method of sneaking past Norfolk.

"Fox's staff tracked down some men who served with Lockwood on the mail steamers," Rhys added. "They described him as 'daring' and 'quick-witted,' not coincidentally, Agent Llyr, the words Fox uses to describe you. Which is why he wants you assigned to this."

Bronwen sagged against the back of the carriage seat. She felt anything but quick-witted. And since under the circumstances her bad news could not be put off any longer, she said, "Chief, there are a few things I should tell you."

"Tomorrow is soon enough."

"I have to leave Washington tomorrow."

"Not without sufficient rest you don't. And other than seeing the president tomorrow——"

"When?" she interrupted. "What time do I see him?"

"I scheduled it for late morning. Why?"

"Because I need to leave."

"Given what I took to be a lack of enthusiasm at Willard's, your eagerness to start this assignment is surprising. But you should rest, and the Norfolk situation can wait one more day."

"I can't go directly to Norfolk. That's why I have to leave here tomorrow."

Rhys changed his position to peer at her more closely by the glow of the carriage lamp. "Leave for *where*?"

Bronwen was now tempted to evade, but knew she couldn't succeed, not with Rhys. "For Richmond."

"No, you are not going there! You heard me tell Fox I wouldn't allow that, not so soon after your brother's escape. It's too risky."

"Richmond has tens of thousands of people swarming in and out of it because of McClellan's advance. The city's a turnstile. Looking for me there would be like searching for a moving needle in a haystack, if anyone were to even bother."

"Confederate intelligence will bother——you can depend on it. The answer is *no*."

"It wasn't a question."

The carriage had shuddered to a halt. Rhys leaned across her to unlatch and push open its door, telling her brusquely, "We'll continue this inside."

Climbing from the carriage, Bronwen was exasperated by having to even mention Richmond, but she hadn't expected to be recalled to Washington so soon. Then again, if she could gain Rhys's support, he might find a way for Treasury to assist in what needed to be done.

A glance at his expression told her that prospect did not appear promising.

Once in the house, Rhys said to his housekeeper, "Please bring a glass of warmed milk for Miss Llyr."

Clasping Bronwen's shoulder, he prodded her none too gently into his study. While he poured himself a brandy from one of several decanters on a pier table, she said, "I'd rather brandy than milk."

When she started toward the table, he gripped her arm and sat her down on the sofa. "You will explain your suicidal urge regarding Richmond, Agent Llyr, without the benefit of spirits! Now talk. And don't hedge, dodge, or mislead me."

Given his uncharacteristic display of bad temper, she had considered doing just that.

"I may already have misled you," she began, groping for a way to present this in its most compelling light.

"I'll decide that."

"The truth of it is that I didn't complete my last assignment. I tried to tell you when I first arrived here, but—if you recall—you hurried me into giving you only the most urgent details."

"Get on with it."

"When I said you may have been misled, I meant the city of Richmond is not *precisely* where I have to go."

"My patience, Bronwen, is not inexhaustible! And stalling will not—"

He broke off as a knock on the door announced the milk. "Thank you," Rhys said to Mrs. Petersen, taking from her a small tray. "That will be all for tonight."

When the housekeeper went out, she looked even more disapproving than she had earlier. Bronwen found this faintly amusing. If the woman were entertaining some risqué ideas about her employer and his guest, maybe one of them should inform her that milk was not commonly used as an instrument of seduction.

Rhys closed the door and, handing Bronwen the glass, said, "I was mentioning my lack of patience?"

"I don't need to go all the way into Richmond. Just east of it to Chimborazo."

"The hospital? You mean Marsh wasn't removed from there?"

When Treasury agent Tristan Marshall had been wounded on a previous assignment, Bronwen and O'Hara had disguised him as a Confederate soldier before taking him to the nearest hospital. Chimborazo had been opened earlier that year and was reputed to be the largest military hospital in the world. Having seen it, Bronwen had no reason to doubt its reputation.

"Marsh is still there," she answered. "I was told his vision hasn't cleared yet and he's unsteady on his feet. I believed it, since my sister was the one who told me."

"Your sister Kathryn? How would she know?"

"Because she's at Chimborazo, too."

Rhys sat forward with a mutter of surprise, and then, as if suddenly recalling something, said, "So that's what his letter was about."

"Whose letter?"

"Dr. Travis wrote asking if I knew where your sister was. But let's not complicate this anymore right now."

"It's already more complicated, because Kathryn and Marsh aren't the only ones trapped there. So is the orphan boy Natty. You do remember Natty?"

"How could anyone forget him? So you're saying there are three Northerners imprisoned there at Chimborazo—"

"Actually, there are four."

At Rhys's incredulous look, she quickly added, "But they aren't all imprisoned . . . not exactly. Bear in mind that Marsh truly is a patient, although no one knows his real identity. Kathryn is serving as the nurse she is, except that . . ."

She stopped herself, having nearly said that her sister was nursing sick and wounded Confederate soldiers. It could be viewed as "giving aid and comfort to the enemy," which was a treasonous offense. Kathryn didn't see it that way, and Rhys probably wouldn't either, but others well might.

His expression told her he had already grasped this, even before he said, "I do not want to know the details of your sister's *forced servitude* in a Confederate installation. Understood?"

She nodded, and deliberately mumbled, "You don't need the other name, do you?"

"I didn't hear you."

"The fourth isn't someone connected to Treasury."

"That's a relief," he replied, skipping over this as she had hoped he would. "At least you've explained yourself. Which is not to say I agree with your Richmond request, not by a long stretch. In fact, my answer is still *no*."

"But Rhys—"

"My objection is the same one it was when you proposed going there to free your brother. If you're caught, and interrogated, other members of the Treasury unit could be put in jeopardy."

Bronwen chewed her lower lip. Would it be more persuasive if she revealed the identity of that fourth person? But it couldn't matter tonight, not when he was being so inflexible. She needed to think through how to handle this, and right now fatigue combined with the milk was making her groggy.

When she tried to stand, her legs nearly buckled under her. "I have to get some sleep."

Rhys, who had been staring at the ceiling, said, "I do agree to that."

As they left the study and started up the stairs, she tried once more, if only as a forewarning. "I told those four people I'd come back. And even if I hadn't promised, I can't abandon them. My own sister?"

He said nothing.

AFTER unpinning the knot of hair, she slipped into a clean cotton shift that had been hung next to the commode, and crawled into the feather bed.

The sheets and pillowcases smelled of lavender, reminding her of the house she had been raised in, and she fought back a surge of homesickness. She couldn't recall when she had last written to any of her family, not even to Aunt Glynis. She also could not recall when she had last slept in a real bed. Her legs of their own volition moved restlessly between the sheets, as if she were still on the run . . . it seemed as if she had been running forever . . .

Her eyes opened at a light rap, and the door swung into the room. As he came toward the bed, Rhys was holding a dimly lit oil lamp and a pear-shaped glass.

"Here's some brandy," he said, placing the lamp and glass on the bedside table. "Or were you already asleep?"

"Not quite. I can't seem to stop running."

She glanced up to see if he understood.

And he nodded as he sat down at the foot of the bed. "Which is exactly why, Bronwen, I can't allow you to go anywhere near Richmond. It's too risky, and in the past few weeks you've been exposed to more than enough risk. That's my decision and you have to accept it."

"I've explained why I can't!" she protested, struggling upright against the pillows.

"I did not come in here to begin that again."

When she leaned forward to shift the pillows behind her, she smelled pipe tobacco and brandy on his breath, and came wide awake. "So why *are* you here?"

"Don't look at me that way," he said, a smile playing around his mouth. "I told you once before, you're too young for me."

"I'm older every minute."

"In any case, I'm your superior—" his smile broadened "—at least in terms of employment I am."

"You're not my employer, Treasury is. And I resign."

His laugh was soft. "I came in to see if you were comfortable. You must be, since you sound more like yourself. Earlier I almost missed your irreverence. Repeat, *almost*."

"Speaking of irreverence, where is O'Hara?"

"I thought you disliked and distrusted O'Hara."

"He became somewhat more trustworthy in Richmond. But about Rich—"

"I've said all I intend to say about that."

Did he really believe she was unaware of the danger?

"Rhys, everyone who joined the Treasury intelligence unit knew it could involve risk. You yourself warned us of that at length, so you certainly knew it too. Why are you making such an issue of it now?"

When he didn't respond, she said without thinking, "Besides, recalling my recent missions, since when have you been concerned with my safety?"

She had meant it flippantly, but when his smile withdrew, she saw he hadn't heard it that way.

"Rhys, I shouldn't have said that. I'm sorry if it sounded as if . . . as if you don't care about the hazards when you hand out assignments. I know that can't be true."

"You don't know the half of it, Bronwen."

He stood up and took the lamp from the table, saying, "Get some sleep."

"First I'd like to know if you're in a forgiving mood."

"And since when," he said, "have you been concerned with my state of mind?"

He turned toward the door, but not before she had caught the smallest hint of a smile.

6

*Now therefore I, Abraham Lincoln . . . have fur-
ther deemed it advisable to set on foot a blockade of the ports of the States aforesaid.*
                                    —April 19, 1861

"Weigh anchor!" ordered Lockwood, his decision voiced
with crisp authority.

For hours his lean gray ship, blown off course by a storm,
had been wallowing in dense fog. Like a hunted wolf forced
onto unknown ground, the *Portia* was becoming more endangered than dangerous and, despite the risk, her captain
meant to get under way. Excessive caution was rarely prof-
itable, and Thomas Lockwood was not by nature a cautious
man.

In response to the order, his pilot Artemus muttered,
"Can't see nothin' worth a damn in this fish stew."

Lockwood, fingering his neat black beard as he studied
the coastal charts, let the remark pass, too self-possessed to
take issue with what another might hear as criticism.
Moreover, he had made the decision after a glance at the

pilot's dour face told him their position was unlikely to improve. The tide was turning, the wind was dying, and the fog was not lifting. Each held its own hazards for a blockade-runner. The passage of time held yet another for a ship loaded with three thousand cavalry sabers, twenty-five thousand British-made rifles, and close to a million ball cartridges. In addition to the medical supplies concealing the weapons, all were urgently needed by Confederate troops.

Lockwood's sleek side-wheeler *Portia* had been launched at a Liverpool shipyard, and this was her third run from the British warehouses at Nassau. An English agent had sought out Lockwood there, saying, "I have heard you are by far the most successful runner, Captain."

A mere nod had been Lockwood's initial response.

"I have sound reason to believe," Colonel Dorian de Warde had gone on, "that the new Confederate commander Robert E. Lee is preparing to mount an offensive against the Union force now threatening Richmond."

De Warde had accompanied this prediction with a knowing smile. No more inducement was necessary. Lockwood instantly recognized there was a fortune to be made in the timely delivery of weapons.

"What are you offering, de Warde," he had demanded, "and what will it cost me?"

Now, after setting his fifteen-man crew to hoisting the *Portia*'s anchor in fog that bound them as surely as iron shackles, Lockwood warned once again against noise. They created little of it. Sound skimmed effortlessly over water, and all were aware their cargo and possibly their freedom depended on stealth. So did the sizable bounty paid each for a successful trip.

Lockwood, standing at the helm, turned his head slowly from side to side while he listened intently. His hearing was acute, saving previous cargoes more than once, and he had earlier caught a sound that made him suspicious. At the time he had ordered the steamer's profile reduced; her fore and aft masts for auxiliary sails, along with her two smokestacks, had been telescoped to a deck only four feet above the waterline. He had heard nothing since.

After again scanning his charts, he turned to the pilot. "Any sense yet where we are?"

"Long way north of where we're s'posed to be," Artemus muttered through his thick beard, its copper hue as vivid as a Bahamas sunrise.

Nassau was where Lockwood had hired him, having been told the pilot knew the treacherous shoals of the Southern coast like the back of his hand. It was their second run together, this time bound for an inlet of the Cape Fear River that led to the railroad hub at Wilmington, North Carolina. But now they could be almost anywhere. They might even have been blown into the shipping lanes of the Union's Atlantic Blockading Squadron, or, just as perilous, close upon sand bars and coastal reefs. Lockwood's charts were useless without bearings.

For two and a half days out of Nassau, wind had filled the *Portia*'s sails, conserving the coal supply needed for her return trip. As she reached the rippling edge of the Gulf Stream, Lockwood had been ordering steam to thrust her through the northerly-flowing current when shouts from the stern made him pause.

"Sails, ho! Sails to the south!"

Raising his telescope, Lockwood had sighted two frigates. At the same time a carpet of thick black clouds began unrolling from the same direction, and shortly after that the *Portia* was struck by gale-force winds. For most of the night she had been driven relentlessly northward. The storm, when finally spent, had left in its wake the fog.

Artemus now appeared ready to expand on his dark view of their bearings, but Lockwood held up a hand for silence.

He had just heard a repeat of what had earlier sounded like the squeal of rats at the far end of a warehouse. With scant hope that it might be only seagulls, and fair certainty that it was another ship's rigging, he lifted his glass to peer into the murky gray mist. And received a jolt when, like a great white shark, a three-masted, fully rigged frigate hove into view. Seconds before fog swallowed the vessel whole, Lockwood sighted its Federal flag.

Where there was one patrolling warship, there could be others.

Lockwood called down the tube to the engine room, "Fire the boiler!" and told the pilot, "Take more soundings fast!"

The deep-draft sailing ships of the blockading squadron were able to chase side-wheeling steamers landward only so far or risk running aground, but their cannon were capable of a longer reach. Their prey was deliberately never armed with heavy guns, because a charge of piracy carried more severe consequences than that of blockade-running.

In response to Lockwood's order, Artemis said, "If it were me, Capt'n, I'd lay by." The pilot glanced in the direction of the frigate, adding, "Some swear these low-slung steamers can't been spotted more than three or four hundred yards away."

"I'm in no mood to test that, Pilot. These weapons need to be delivered to Wilmington by noon this day."

"Where they bound after Wilmington?"

"Richmond, by noon tomorrow."

"Won't make it."

"Longer and the city could fall or be under siege. I doubt the U.S. will be eager to pay for Rebel contraband!"

"Can't do it! Not with fog and Union blockaders standin' between us and Cape Fear—an' I reckon we're a far sight north of it."

Lockwood fingered his beard. "If so, those warships will

wait for *Portia* to turn south. They won't expect her to head north."

Artemus scowled. "Not by chance thinkin' of Norfolk again?"

"We did it twice before. Straight up the James River to Richmond."

"You got repute for takin' risks, Capt'n, but I say the odds of us slippin' in there again are poor."

"Find us shallow water!" replied Lockwood. He swung his glass toward shore, where a sudden brightness was coming from a tunnel of light just opened in the fog bank. At its far end was the brown of land. He started to point, but Artemus already had his own glass raised.

The tunnel broadened, and after a long search, the pilot lowered his glass. "Ain't good news, Capt'n. We got blown a damn sight nor'east, past Hatteras and—"

He broke off as a young crewmember came dashing forward.

"Capt'n, two warships spotted due south! They're both flyin' Union flags, sir, and the fog's liftin' fast."

Artemus said without enthusiasm, "Could be we got no choice, Capt'n, but to steer north."

"Short of running straight into Federal warships," Lockwood said briskly, "we have no choice at all." He told the crewman, "Raise a U.S. flag."

He had considered the alternative course when the fog first came, but his pilot did not need to know that. Lockwood trusted no man's counsel more than his own.

He immediately called for more steam. The big paddlewheels turned faster, and to muffle their hammering, he ordered canvas thrown over their housings. There was still a remote chance the *Portia* had not been sighted.

Minutes later that hope died when two calcium flares shone white against the clearing sky. A booming roar fol-

lowed, and a rain of shells sent water spouting short of
Portia's stern.

"That Federal captain's not playing by the rules," Lockwood said with a sardonic smile. "Supposed to send a shot
across the bow! But those flares are doubtless signaling the
second ship, and maybe others, with our position. How
the hell did he find us?"

"Reckon he saw us b'fore the storm hit," Artemus answered, his face impassive. "Maybe even got blown north
hisself."

"Let's play his game and even the odds some," Lockwood
said, still smiling, and his blood up by now. As another
shell sprayed water over the deck, he ordered two of *Portia*'s
own flares fired.

They might confuse the second ship's captain and keep
him busy trying to figure out who were the hunters and
who was the hunted. When *Portia*'s flares bloomed white
overhead, Lockwood called another order down the tube.
The answering steam whistled like a chorus of tin fifes,
and the churning paddle wheels whipped the water to
froth. The *Portia*'s bow lifted as she leapt forward.

Lockwood steered the ship in a zigzagging course, her
speed nearly eleven knots, evading shells as he made for
shallow water. The first frigate, dependent on fair wind
and deep water, began to fall back. The second ship had
already dropped below the horizon.

BY the dim light of a cloud-covered moon, the *Portia* edged
warily into the broad channel of water between Norfolk
and Fort Monroe known as Hampton Roads. She hugged
the ragged southern shore as closely as Lockwood dared;
more than one blockade-runner had been captured by running aground. Her steam was being blown off underwater,

her lights had been extinguished, and tarpaulins hid the glow from engine and fire room hatches. Except for the muted engine throb and paddlewheel thumps, the lead-gray *Portia* was one shadow gliding among many. But protected only by stealth and her captain's boldness, she was courting disaster by remaining there.

In lowered voice, Lockwood ordered a lantern to be flashed toward land with the coded message: *One, if by land, and two, if by sea.*

While he watched the shore for a response, Lockwood experienced a rare tension. Had the Englishman's continued assurance of safe passage been just empty words in return for a share of the expected profit? De Warde had little at risk. Lockwood risked not only capture, but without taking on more coal at Richmond, he would not have fuel enough for the return trip.

He glanced uneasily at the eastern horizon and noted the pilot doing likewise. Daybreak might still be hours away, but they needed to be through Hampton Roads long before it came. Time was running out. Lockwood could not wait much longer . . . but . . . there it was! An answering signal in the winks of a tiny blue shore light.

Cloaked in blackness the *Portia* slipped around anchored ships to steal into the river's mouth. The pilot suddenly gripped Lockwood's shoulder, pointing to starboard. A dark shape was steaming directly toward their bow. It slowed a short distance away, and appeared to be maneuvering for a closer inspection. In a calculated bluff, Lockwood ordered the *Portia*'s speed decreased.

After a heart-stopping interval the other steamer abruptly veered away, blending into the dark water to vanish. Leaving Lockwood to ponder if it had been friend or foe, or neither.

"You're a darin' man, Capt'n," said Artemus. "A mighty lucky one again, too."

"That's what I'm paid to be, Pilot. Now let's get these weapons to Richmond. We can dock and deliver by high noon—and demand a bonus for both in the bargain!"

7

If I save this Army now I tell you plainly that I owe no thanks to you or any other person in Washington—you have done your best to sacrifice this Army.

—General George B. McClellan, June 1862

Washington City

She came suddenly awake, gasping for air under a suffocating weight pressed over her face. When she struggled beneath it, trying to dislodge it, two pale misshapen lumps flew upward; her arms torn off by mortar shells. But there was no pain and no cannon thunder. For a long terrifying moment, Bronwen had no idea where she was or what she had been fighting. Then the room came into focus, while a few feathers drifted from the two pillows now lying on the floor beside the bed.

Still panting, she sat up, waiting for her breath and pulse to slow. The irony of it was not lost on her. Here she was, safe and dry for the first time in recent memory, with her heart pounding from the phantoms of nightmare.

Several sharp knocks sounded on the bedroom door. Before she could respond, Mrs. Petersen flung it open to announce, "Mr. Bevan said you're to meet him at noon. You must rise!"

Untangling herself from the sheets, Bronwen swung her bare feet to a hook rug beside the bed. "Is that coffee I smell, Mrs. Petersen?"

In answer the woman turned to disappear through the doorway, reappearing with a large tray.

"Mr. Bevan said you were to sleep as long as needed, but it is now eleven o'clock." Mrs. Petersen placed the tray on the bedside table and poured coffee into a bone-china cup.

Bronwen took one look at a plate of crusty French toast awash in butter and syrup, surrounded by crisp brown sausages, and was instantly ravenous. Beside the plate was a white bowl mounded with cherries and blueberries, the colors abruptly bringing to mind both the Federal and Confederate flags. It was an unwelcome reminder of what lay ahead.

"Thank you, Mrs. Petersen."

The woman did not go so far as to smile, but her pursed lips parted. "You had best eat quickly," she urged. "And you're woefully thin, so have all of it."

Bronwen, having decided after the first swallow of excellent coffee that she could not afford to be offended, simply nodded.

When the housekeeper went to open the closed draperies, Bronwen caught a glimpse of something pale green that almost looked like mist floating in the open door of a wardrobe closet. As the draperies parted to let in a burst of sunlight, she identified the mist as a graceful, cotton lawn frock. That it did not include even a stitch of trimming meant someone knew her aversion to frills. She doubted it had been Mrs. Petersen.

"The frock was delivered earlier," the housekeeper told her. "Together with a message from Mr. Bevan saying you were not to meet him at the Treasury Building. You're to go directly to the War Department telegraph room."

It rang an ominous note, but Bronwen told herself the nightmare had left her overly apprehensive. That, and having so lately witnessed the potential for disaster on the Virginia peninsula.

THE minute she stepped inside the building, she knew something earthshaking had happened. Considering the anxious faces of clerks, who were clutching papers and scurrying up and down the War Department corridors, whatever it was, it had not been good.

After presenting her Treasury pass to a guard, and being told to proceed, she hurried toward the telegraph room. By the time she neared its door, she had overheard enough to know the news must be worse than not good.

Huddled just outside the room were War Secretary Edwin Stanton, Navy Secretary Gideon Welles, and Treasury Secretary Salmon Chase. Stanton was alternately tugging at the strands of his sparse, grizzled beard and gesturing in agitation. Welles looked reasonably composed, as he usually did, but Chase's receding hairline exposed a forehead slick with perspiration.

Bronwen jumped when a hand clamped her shoulder, and then Rhys Bevan was steering her back down the corridor.

"What's happened?" she asked.

"There's a vacant office at the end of the hall," was the reply.

When they entered the small room, Bronwen tried again. "Has there been a battle?"

"Yesterday, and there was more than one," Rhys answered, going to the single window and closing it. "The largest engagement was north of the Chickahominy, so your speculation about Lee's intent was sound."

"I gather the news is bad?"

"Confederates attacked McClellan's corps remaining north of the river. And yes, it's possible Lee was attempting to clear the way to the railroad and White House Landing. The Union troops had been holding a defensive line near a place called Boatswain Swamp, but subsequent reports said that late in the day the line broke, forcing our troops to the Chickahominy. During the night, they managed to retreat south across the river. The first approximation of casualties is staggering."

Bronwen's stomach lurched, her first thought being of her brother. Her next thought was of Pinkerton, and only Rhys's tight face kept her silent.

"There was a second engagement yesterday, but it took place *south* of the river. The reason for the furor here right now," he said, "are reports that Confederates have launched another attack there today. We don't have many details yet."

"How close is the fighting to Richmond?" she asked, her mind having jumped to those at Chimborazo Hospital.

"It can't be much more than four or five miles. Mc-Clellan's initial report said that Lee's force includes troops of Jackson and Beauregard. And that these Confederate offensives signal the beginning of an all-out assault."

Rhys paused, before adding, "We have since received reliable word that Beauregard is *not* there. But McClellan still swears he is outnumbered at least two to one. And for this he blames Lincoln and Secretary Stanton."

"He *what*?"

Rhys closed the office door before saying, "This is not to be repeated. Last night, or early this morning, McClellan sent a wire to Stanton. Telegraph operator David Bates transcribed it, but he didn't deliver it to Stanton. Instead Bates gave it to his superior, Colonel Sanford. Just before you arrived, Sanford confided to me that the original message so shocked him that he struck its closing sentence.

And had the message rewritten before it went to Stanton."

Bronwen stared at him in astonishment. "Did Sanford tell you what McClellan said?"

"That by not sending him more troops when he demanded them, Stanton and the president have made every effort to sacrifice the army."

She couldn't have heard him correctly, but his expression said otherwise. "Is McClellan out of his head?"

"I don't know what he is," Rhys answered, "but it's clear his notorious contempt for Lincoln knows no bounds. His accusation is nothing less than treasonous, and of course Sanford recognized it. I'm telling you now only because Lincoln is here in the telegraph room—and has been most of the night and this morning—and he may still intend to see you. In the meantime Sanford might have owned up to his lapse in judgment. He had no business trying to shield the president from his own commander, no matter how well meaning it was. But don't you compound the matter by bringing up your row with Pinkerton."

"So you passed on what I saw at the Chickahominy?"

"Only to Stanton. Lincoln wasn't available at the time. But Stanton dislikes McClellan so intensely that I'm assuming he took the first chance to inform the president. Lincoln's already aware that the number of Confederate troops McClellan insists are arrayed against him must be an inflated one. Our own rough calculations now suggest the numbers on both sides may be close to equal, but that McClellan definitely has the edge."

Not bothering to mask her disgust, she said, "And here I thought Confederate command must be insane to leave Richmond exposed. Clearly Lee knows something of McClellan!"

"Which you should not be voicing too freely."

"My *brother* is out there in the field!"

Rhys didn't immediately respond, but then he glanced

toward the door before saying quietly, "It's not been made public yet, but McClellan has ordered a full-scale withdrawal."

"Withdrawal? Meaning he won't try to recross the river to defend White House Landing?"

"That's what it means. McClellan's calling it a *change of base*, but no matter what he calls it, the reality is that he's retreating. And some here have begun to question whether our army can be saved."

Bronwen dropped into the nearest chair. For months McClellan's turtle-paced advance had been threatening Richmond, and now, almost overnight, the Union army itself was threatened. Except that it wasn't just some abstract army out there, it was men like her brother who were endangered.

And soldiers would not be the only ones, she remembered with a jolt. "Chief, you said the first casualty estimates were high. Those would have been only for the Union, right?"

"Yes," he answered, "but the fighting has reportedly been fierce, so we can take the other side's casualties for granted. Why?"

"Because Chimborazo Hospital must be where many of the Confederate wounded are being taken. Once Southerners start seeing their maimed and dying soldiers, it won't be anyplace for Kathryn and the others."

"I very much regret that, Bronwen, but there's no possibility of removing them from there. Not until the smoke clears."

"I think there might be a way."

"I don't!"

Obviously the direct approach would take her nowhere. Bronwen made herself stop and change course before she asked, "Where does McClellan plan to withdraw? The Chesapeake? Fort Monroe?"

"Navy Secretary Welles said that two days ago McClellan began ordering gunboats to the James River. Presumably to cover his retreat."

So that was where Lieutenant Commander Farrar had been bound. McClellan, she recalled, had originally wanted a naval force on the James. The Confederate *Merrimack* prowling at the river's mouth had prevented it, but since then the Rebels, after abandoning Norfolk, had destroyed their ironclad.

"Where on the James is McClellan withdrawing?" she asked. "It has to be somewhere below the point where the river narrows."

Rhys eyed her warily. "Why are you asking?"

"I need a map," she dodged, getting to her feet and scanning the room.

"Bronwen, I don't want you moving one inch from Washington. I can send other agents to Virginia when the worst is over, but right now neither you nor anyone else should wade into the meleé surrounding Richmond!"

She had already decided not to argue when the door opened a crack. A young man whom Bronwen recognized as one of Lincoln's junior secretaries stuck his head around it.

"Mr. Bevan, the president wishes to see you and Miss Llyr in his office. He left for there a short time ago."

THEY followed the secretary down the short, well-trodden dirt path from the War Department building to the Executive Mansion. Once inside, they met secretaries Welles and Fox just coming from Lincoln's office. Welles went on, but Fox stopped and motioned Bronwen into an anteroom.

"Miss Llyr, regarding that matter we discussed last evening?"

When she nodded, he went on, "Given the unfolding military situation in Virginia, the matter could prove to be more difficult than I had first thought."

"That goes without saying," Rhys inserted. "I'm reluctant to proceed with it at this time."

"The information we need has acquired more urgency," Fox said. "Europe may view a Union withdrawal from the Richmond campaign as a sign the North is weakening. And that the South, with some assistance, could win this war. In which case, the British might make even more-determined efforts to thwart the Federal blockade."

Rhys looked ready to further urge postponement of the mission, but Bronwen, guessing it was the president who had insisted Fox spell this out for her, said quickly, "I understand the risk, Mr. Secretary."

She did not of course. No risk could be fully understood until it was met head-on, and by then it was too late to plead ignorance. Fox knew this, too, but she recognized that he wanted to hear her say it. In return, she wanted something from him, but for the moment it would have to wait.

"Very good, Miss Llyr," he said. "Should you need to find me, I expect to be either in my office or in the telegraph room."

As Fox walked away, presidential secretary John Hay appeared in the doorway and motioned them inside the office.

When they entered, the president was standing at the window, his shoulders hunched forward and his large hands clasped behind his back. When he turned to them, his pallor startled Bronwen. The deep-set gray eyes under reddened lids gave the impression he had not slept for several days.

"Sir, I'll finish preparing those papers for your signature," Hay said and went out, closing the door behind him.

Lincoln gestured to a chair and lowered himself into his own behind the desk. Bronwen took the offered seat, and Rhys, as had become customary during these sessions, stationed himself near the door.

"I presume Mr. Bevan has outlined the current circumstances in Virginia," Lincoln said to her, whatever fatigue he suffered not evident in his voice. "Did you see Secretary Fox when you came in?"

"Yes, sir, I did."

"He gave you fair warning?"

Bronwen concealed her surprise at his directness, since ordinarily the president couched his questions and requests in veiled terms. But their past meetings had not taken place during a crisis. Still, he hadn't spoken in specific terms, so neither should she.

"Yes, sir, Secretary Fox explained the added importance of what's needed."

"We are obliged to you for agreeing to look into it, Miss Llyr. While I'm troubled by asking you to ride straight into this storm again, we've just received something in the way of a gift horse. It's gone far to persuade Secretary Fox and myself that you should be the one to pursue the matter."

He picked up a cream-colored envelope, drew from it a sheet of high-quality paper, and handed it to her across the desk.

She took what was obviously a letter, but before reading its content, she looked at the signature. And very nearly dropped the paper.

When she glanced at Rhys, he shook his head to indicate he had no knowledge of it, his expression alone enough to tell Bronwen he was as puzzled as she.

To His Eminence President Lincoln:

I have been instructed by your worthy emissary Miss Llyr to convey my appreciation. Thus, sir, I indeed offer my gratitude. Your generosity has expedited a satisfactory conclusion to what had become a vexing affair.

I should be remiss if I did not also state that the aforementioned emissary must be commended for executing her role with uncommon resource and valor.

> *I remain your humble servant,*
> *Colonel Dorian de Warde*
> *Office of War and the Colonies of Great Britain*

Bronwen lowered the paper and, having managed not to break into laughter, looked up to find an almost wistful expression on Lincoln's face.

"Hand that to Mr. Bevan to read," he said. "And by all means enjoy it, Miss Llyr. I just wish there weren't so little else to congratulate ourselves for these days."

After Rhys finished reading, he replaced the letter on the desk, saying dryly to Bronwen, "Consider yourself commended."

"I'm astonished by this," she admitted, "but knowing de Warde, I'm suspicious, too. While I did tell him that he should thank you, Mr. President, I said it mostly to remind him who was responsible for his tobacco's safe passage. I never dreamed he'd actually do it. So I'm skeptical, because de Warde may have some ulterior motive. He almost always does."

While she was speaking, Lincoln had been looking rather curiously at her, and now he said, "I expect we'll find out what he wants soon enough. But you appear to have seasoned some since we first met, Miss Llyr, and while the colonel's being so agreeable, you might want to have a friendly chat with him. I expect it won't do much good— but likely won't do much harm either—if you were to mention that the British Office of the Colonies shouldn't set its heart on reclaiming the brightest jewel lost from its Crown."

She said, "Yes, sir," readily enough, but the prospect of fencing with de Warde again made her unconsciously sink back into the chair. When she realized it, she straightened quickly. If the president, now getting to his feet, saw her reaction, he chose to ignore it.

When she also rose, Rhys was motioning to her, as though she couldn't see it was time to leave. Knowing it had to be now or never, she drew in her breath and said rapidly, "Mr. President, I have something unfortunate to report."

From the corner of her eye she saw Rhys stiffen. If he suspected that she would request permission to remove her sister from Chimborazo, he would be wrong, but not very far wrong.

Lincoln remained behind his desk, and she rushed on, "I know it's not a good time for this, sir, but—"

"No, it is not a good time," Rhys interrupted and reached for her arm just as a rap sounded on the office door. She stepped away from him, and he caught only a handful of green lawn sleeve.

John Hay came into the room and advanced to the desk with several documents. "Mr. President, if you would sign these, sir, before you go?"

At this point, Rhys had gripped Bronwen's arm and was fixing her with a glacial stare, but Lincoln gave her a slight nod as he took the papers.

"It's not every day I get a thank-you note from the British," the president said, "so you've earned yourself a listen, Miss Llyr. Just let me sign these, and you can have your say while we walk to the War Department."

He bent over the desk to extract a pen from its inkwell, and began putting his signature to the documents. Without looking up, he added, "I trust your news can't be any worse than what I've already heard today?"

"No, sir." How could anything be worse than word that McClellan was retreating?

Rhys's fingers were locked so tightly around her arm she could feel her hand growing numb, but her rebellion was of his own making. If he hadn't refused her permission to rescue Kathryn and the others, she wouldn't need to be circumventing him. She hated doing it, but saw it as the only tactic left.

Lincoln had been handing each signed document to the secretary, and after the last signature, he rounded the desk. "You know where to find me, Mr. Hay."

As he moved toward the door, he said over his shoulder, "Come along, Miss Llyr, if you're able to slip your leash."

When Rhys released her and they left the office, she tried to ignore his cold stare. Once more on the path, she fell into step beside the president as he said, "Well, now, what's the bad news?"

She glanced around and seeing no one other than Rhys directly behind her, she said quietly, "It's about your friend James Quiller, sir. He's being held in the Confederate hospital outside Richmond."

She sensed rather than saw Rhys come to a sudden halt. The president also stopped walking, and asked, "Was Jimmy taken sick?"

"No, sir. Confederate intelligence seized him at the Richmond train station and substituted an impostor. Since I'd never met him, I didn't know a switch had been made until later when I was introduced to the genuine James Quiller. He's in good health, Mr. Lincoln, but is obviously being held against his will."

Lincoln glanced around. "I think this talk is best continued inside."

As they entered the War Department building, Rhys muttered, "Why didn't you tell me?"

"You didn't ask to be told. Will it do any good if I apologize?"

"None whatsoever."

The president had stopped before one of the first doors, and stood looking down the hall toward the telegraph room. The earlier commotion there had quieted. As if satisfied he could spare another minute, he rapped on the door before opening and peering around it like a burglar about to break and enter. "Seems empty," he announced.

It was a large office, well appointed, and with a thick carpet underfoot. Hanging on two walls were immense maps of the eastern states, and Bronwen briefly wondered if it might once have been McClellan's office. Lincoln folded himself into a chair, and said, as if there had been no interval, "Why did they put Jimmy in a hospital?"

"Confederate intelligence is aware he's an acquaintance of yours, sir. I have to assume that's the reason he is being treated relatively well. Again, his health is good, but they have him confined as if . . . as if he were insane."

"You mean with restraints?" asked Rhys.

"I'm afraid so. Mr. Lincoln, there's a good deal more to this story, but for now I'll just say that I wasn't able to remove Mr. Quiller from there. I'm sorry, sir, but first I had to free my brother. At the time, his scheduled execution was only hours away."

She stopped, waiting uneasily for his reaction.

"Under the circumstances, Miss Llyr, I expect I would have done the same."

She had thought that would be his response, but let out a relieved breath. "When I left Chimborazo, I believed Mr. Quiller would be safe for a few more days, since my sister Kathryn is also there. As is an injured Treasury agent."

"And now?" asked Lincoln.

"They all need to be removed immediately. With Confederate wounded pouring into that hospital, it's bound to be a dangerous place for any Northerner."

"What do you need from me, Miss Llyr?"

She glanced guiltily at the stone-faced Rhys before answering, "Permission, sir."

Lincoln had evidently seen the glance. "Mr. Bevan, is there reason not to grant it?"

"I had already refused Agent Llyr leave to go to Richmond," Rhys replied. "While at the time I wasn't aware of Mr. Quiller's situation, I should have known that a mere refusal wouldn't stop her. As witnessed by this last-resort appeal to you."

When Lincoln said nothing, Bronwen feared she had gone too far. She had risked almost all on this strategy, but if Lincoln denied her appeal . . .

"Frankly, Mr. President," Rhys continued, his voice betraying not even a hint of anger, "if Agent Llyr were a member of the military, she would by now have been court-martialed several times over. However, since she is not a soldier in the strictest sense, that remedy is unavailable."

With perspiration trickling down her back, Bronwen watched Lincoln. He seemed to be waiting for Rhys to add something.

When Rhys did, it was to say, "Short of us chaining her in Old Capitol Prison, I think she will proceed with or without permission. Her inventiveness in evading rules can be exasperating, but I strive to remember that it's the same inventiveness which makes her a valuable agent."

He ignored the look of gratitude she sent him as Lincoln got to his feet. "Permission granted."

"Thank you, sir. When the first matter is resolved, I'll go directly to Norfolk."

For the Chimborazo rescue, she needed cooperation from the assistant navy secretary. Fox had been her sole remaining ace to play.

Lincoln paused with his hand on the door. "Please keep in mind, Miss Llyr, that I cannot afford to lose inventive soldiers in any sense. Proceed with your missions accordingly. I trust it is needless to say that I wish you Godspeed."

When he opened the door, it was to renewed clamor down the hall.

"YOU'LL never forgive me, will you?"

"I very much doubt it. It may take an act of Congress to restore you to my good graces. Now listen to me, Agent Llyr, and listen well! If you're captured in Richmond, I will disavow any connection you may say you have with Treasury. Understood?"

"I need to find Fox's office. And isn't O'Hara due back here? I want—"

"Can I have heard correctly?" Rhys interrupted. "You want *O'Hara*? O'Hara who is, and I quote you, 'a fountain of lies,' and 'a walking powder keg'? Whom you accused of consorting in his youth with what are now Confederate officers?"

"In his *youth*? A Virginian at West Point military academy?"

"A *western* Virginian!"

"In any case, I don't want O'Hara. I only need to borrow him."

8

---~~~---

*The month of July 1862 can never be forgotten
in Richmond. We lived in one immense hospital,
and breathed the vapors of the charnel house.*
——Sallie Brock Putnam, 1862

Chimborazo

A stiff warm breeze from the Chesapeake filled the
sloop's sail, taking Bronwen and O'Hara toward Richmond
faster than she could have dared to hope. With the prow
of the boat cutting cleanly through dark water, she glanced
past O'Hara to the near riverbank. Under a waxing moon,
trees seemed to loom like sentries guarding Virginia
against its invaders. There was altogether too much light
for Bronwen's peace of mind, but a few other ships dotted
the winding upper James this night, and there was no
reason for any particular one to stand out. So she kept
telling herself.

Secretary Fox had ordered a navy gunboat to tow the
sloop as far upriver from Fort Monroe as prudent without
drawing fire from a Confederate fort some eight miles below Richmond. This fort on Drewry's Bluff, which
McClellan had declined to capture when an earlier opportunity arose, now blocked the navy's approach to the Con-

federate capital. But below this point, shallow-draft gunboats and the new ironclad *Galena* were steaming from the Chesapeake to cover the perilous withdrawal of Union troops.

"Which gives the Norfolk mission added urgency," Fox had told Bronwen before she and O'Hara left Washington. "The blockade-runner Lockwood has managed to slip past when it was relatively quiet. But shortly, what with troop and hospital ships steaming in and out of the Bay, it will be even less difficult to steal unnoticed into the James."

And Bronwen, now gazing downriver at the sloop's wake, recognized uneasily that not only a blockade-runner but also a saboteur's ship bearing explosives would not be any more conspicuous than this sloop was.

O'Hara suddenly asked her, too loudly, "Anything look familiar yet, Red? As, for example, a hospital? And why the hell did the Rebs name it *Chimborazo*? Does Jefferson Davis expect compensation in the form of Spanish troops?"

"Please keep your voice down," she whispered.

"Yes, sir! Aye, aye, sir!" came his low, mocking response. The wind barely ruffled the short-clipped blond beard as his jaw lifted in silent laughter.

O'Hara's compact, well-proportioned frame did not straightaway suggest the considerable strength he owned, and Bronwen had been surprised by it more than once. It also surprised her, although she wouldn't acknowledge it aloud, when she discovered tonight that O'Hara was a good sailing hand. Just as over time she had discovered that he was good at any number of things. Some of them he might have learned at the U.S. Military Academy before he had been dismissed for carousing.

Her keen distrust of him had lessened, but it had not disappeared entirely. It had started when, on reconnaissance in northern Virginia, they had met by chance Confederate cavalry general Jeb Stuart. The officer had greeted O'Hara with hearty familiarity. O'Hara had later tried to brush off this familiarity by saying that he and Stuart had attended the academy at the same time and had gambled together on occasion. Bronwen still had her doubts that this was the full extent of it.

"O'Hara, remember when several weeks ago you told me about a blockade-runner that had been seized in the Chesapeake? The day Confederate troops abandoned Norfolk?"

"It came up when you mentioned your great chum Colonel de Warde. His name, as I recall, was on the runner's cargo manifest. But that ship carried bales of cotton, Red, not weapons."

"Even so, you said that before the captain of it could be questioned, he tried to escape and was killed."

"What about it?" he asked, raking fingers through his thick, fair hair.

"Because I asked you to find out the name of that captain."

"Forgot about it—time to satisfy your infamous curiosity has been scarce." This was clearly a not-so-subtle reference to her mistrust of him, because his eyes flashed, their lucent turquoise nearly visible even in the darkness.

The gray Confederate navy jacket O'Hara would shortly put on had come from a prisoner of war. Two more such jackets were stashed in the sloop's bow. Bronwen wore her loose shirt and farmer's overalls, one of its pockets holding a double-derringer. And inside one of her soft, lightweight leather boots, which she had bought in Washington, was her thin, sheathed stiletto.

O'Hara now asked, "Where'd you learn to sail a boat?"

"On the Chesapeake with Marsh. He taught me what I know—which isn't much, so let me concentrate."

"Just what else did Marshall teach you whilst frolicking

on the Bay? And is that why we're risking my life and limb to retrieve him?"

"O'Hara, *please* lower your voice!"

"Who's to hear in the middle of a river? You afraid maybe the Rebs have armed the fish? Better not suggest that to our fearless commanding general, or he'll grab an observation balloon and airlift himself out of this mess he's made. Next time I tell you McClellan's a blustering coward, I trust you'll pay attention!"

"The wind's changing, O'Hara, and we need to tack again. Ready about!"

"Aye, aye, sir!"

They ducked under the swinging boom, and as the sloop veered, Bronwen saw up ahead a thick string of flickering lights. They must be from the hospital sprawled over a hill above the James.

"O'Hara—"

"I see them! Hard to miss up there, and I'd say we've got a climb ahead of us, my girl. I still can't figure how you expect to fit four more people in this tub."

"The boy Natty is slight, but if it's too crowded, you can swim back to Fort Monroe."

"You're a hard woman to love, Red."

WHEN Kathryn cautiously entered the long, low shed that housed one of Chimborazo's kitchens, she found only a few workers kneading dough at its far end. Since this shed was the farthest one from the road and the wards, other hospital workers had laughingly said its seclusion made it an ideal place for trysts. Relieved to find none currently taking place, Kathryn stood for a minute to get her bearings. The sudden quiet after the noisy tumult of the wards was disorienting, as was the slowly receding numbness she forced upon herself when dealing with wounded men.

More than anything else, she needed to breathe some air free of chloroform.

Meager light cast by two hanging lanterns made the dried blood on her hands and arms look like a coating of rust. After washing it off in a water bucket, and then tossing the water outside, she broke off a piece of bread from one of the loaves stacked on a table. Glancing around she spotted a stool by the door and sank onto it.

"You look worn out, miss," a ward-master had told her during a momentary lull in the rising flood of casualties. "You've been at this longer than I have, so before you fall over, go and find yourself some food and fresh air."

He was a kind-hearted man, and didn't steal from the whiskey supply issued for the wounded as some did. There was nothing to be done about the stealing; the word of a female nurse against that of any man's was discounted.

Although she had left reluctantly, she knew the ward-master was right. If she didn't clear her head and eat something, she would become a casualty herself. Confederate wounded had been streaming in steadily, and medical personnel were desperately needed. So far none had questioned Kathryn's Northern accent or her loyalty.

Tents had been raised beside the road, so most wounded were receiving water and food soon after they arrived, with protection from the scorching sun while they waited for medical attention. She had heard that the citizens of Richmond were giving shelter to many. In stark contrast, Union wounded after the battle at Seven Pines had lain in the open for hours, even days, before receiving care, because there were not enough ambulance wagons to remove them from the battlefield. Remembering how terrible the conditions had been then, what must those soldiers be suffering now?

At first she had not made a distinction; wounded men were wounded men, no matter the color of their uniforms. She still believed that, but after a few days at Chimborazo she recognized that Southern soldiers were at least among their own people in their own homeland. Her Northern countrymen were in a hostile land. But she couldn't return to White House Landing. When she had wanted to see her brother in a Richmond prison, surgeon Gregg Travis had forbidden it.

"You cannot simply walk away from your obligations here," he had said angrily.

Kathryn wiped her eyes with a corner of her apron and resolved, once again, not to think of him.

Where had Natty been all evening? More than likely pinching scraps for the handsome young dog that seemed to have adopted him. Much, she recalled, as Natty had adopted her. He claimed the dog had belonged to a wounded Confederate officer who subsequently died here at Chimborazo, but he might have shaded the truth. It wouldn't have been the first time.

A round of shouting from outside, accompanied by the distant clatter of wagons on the road fronting the hospital, meant more wounded were coming in. Kathryn made herself swallow the last of the bread, and was getting to her feet when the kitchen door burst open.

"Lady!" came Natty's high-pitched voice as his straw-colored mop of hair appeared around the doorjamb. "Lady, c'mere fast!" he hissed.

"What is it, Natty?"

"Jest c'mere, will ya! And be quick 'bout it!"

A lantern swung from the eave and as Kathryn stepped through the doorway, she could see the black-and-white, longhaired dog at Natty's side. Behind the dog stood a shadowed figure.

This figure stepped forward, whispering, "Kathryn, it's me."

"Bronwen!"

Her sister put down a canvas knapsack before pulling Kathryn into shadows to ask tersely, "Where's Marsh?"

"In the ambulatory ward."

"He's able to walk?"

"Yes, and he's regained his vision in one eye, but the other's not completely cleared yet. What are you planning?"

"To get you out of here. Mr. Quiller's already gone. I remembered the way to that isolated room where he was being held, and once O'Hara had filed through the chain confining the 'patient,' Quiller had no trouble crawling out through a window. With luck he and O'Hara should already be halfway to the boat."

"Boat?"

"A sloop moored at one of the wharves below. Right now there are only a few supply ships down there, and with all the commotion up here, I doubt anybody but Natty saw us steal past a few guards."

"Will all of us fit into a small boat?"

"We'll have to. Couldn't risk the attention a larger one might attract—"

Bronwen stopped at a low growl from the dog.

"What'sa matter, Dog?" Natty whispered, bending over it. As if reading its mind, he reared up whispering, "Somebody's comin'. Maybe more'n one body."

"Quick, into the kitchen!" Kathryn told her sister. "There's another door, halfway down the left wall. It opens to the east, facing the ambulatory ward, so go straight ahead after you get back outside. We'll meet you there."

"No, there might be some delay, so head straight to the

wharves. And keep your eyes peeled for trouble while you're doing it!" Bronwen cautioned, grabbing her knapsack before she bolted into the kitchen.

Now several voices could be heard, talking softly as their owners approached the building. The dog had continued to growl.

"Natty," warned Kathryn, "please be quiet. But if you must answer someone, be careful what you say."

He gave her a look of annoyance. " 'Course I will! I wanna git outta this stinkin' pest house, 'cause everybody's dyin' here!"

"Hush!" A moment later she said with emphasis, in case Bronwen was still within earshot, "Good evening to you, Mrs. Lynne. And to you, *sir*."

The attractive hospital matron had stopped abruptly at the kitchen entrance, the naval officer behind her stopping just as abruptly. As he began to back up, keeping his face averted, the dog stepped forward to sniff at his trouser leg. It jumped aside with a sharp bark, having narrowly missed being kicked.

"Hey!" Natty yelped at the rapidly retreating officer. "What'd ya do thet fer? Dog's jest bein' friendly."

"Take that animal away from the kitchen this minute!" said the matron. "Boy, I have told you repeatedly to get rid of the dog. Since you have ignored me, I must order that it be destroyed."

"The bloody 'ell ya will!" Natty shouted. "You leave Dog alone, you mean ol' bat!"

"Natty!" gasped Kathryn, seizing his arm. "Apologize at once to the matron."

Natty, glaring at the woman, shook his head.

"Miss Tryon," began Mrs. Lynne, and Kathryn in her anxiety nearly looked around before remembering that *she* was Miss Tryon. When she had arrived here, she hadn't dared use her real name, since the Richmond newspapers had most likely carried the story of her brother's trial.

"Miss Tryon!" the matron said again. "Because you are so sorely needed I have tolerated the often deplorable conduct of your charge. But I cannot and will not continue to do so."

"Ya gonna order *me* dis-troyed, too?" snapped Natty, his tone anything but contrite.

Kathryn gripped his arm so hard he yelped, fearing that at any second the matron would call the kitchen workers for assistance. Thus possibly alerting the hospital to the escape of the "insane" prisoner Quiller and threatening all their freedom, to say nothing of the lives of three U.S. Treasury agents.

Desperate straits, as Bronwen would say, called for desperate measures. Sending Natty a silent plea for cooperation, but squeezing his arm even harder, Kathryn said, "Forgive me, Mrs. Lynne, but wasn't that a naval officer I just saw with you? He seems to have left rather hastily. I heard that you might have a . . . ah . . . a friend."

The woman's face darkened as she drew in her breath. Turning on her solid square heels, she swiftly walked away, but not before Kathryn had caught the look of embarrassed fury on her face.

"Stop grinning," Kathryn told Natty, ashamed she had resorted to such a shabby tactic.

"Leggo! Yer am-pu-tatin' my arm," he said accusingly. "An' she *is* an old bat! She an' thet there Reb officer—jest like I told ya b'fore—they been doin' some mighty pee-cu-yer stuff when he comes round. Ya should see 'em when they figger nobody's lookin'. Makes ya wanna toss yer supper! If ya kin b'lieve it, he puts—"

"I've heard enough!" Kathryn released his arm when the dog began to whine.

"Okay, but I shure did git the light off a' yer sister now,

dint I? Long 'nough fer her to find Marsh. An' I helped git Mr. Killer out, too."

"Mr. *Quiller*. While Bronwen would doubtless applaud your intentions, you nearly put us in very serious trouble."

"Who cares 'bout trouble if'n we're leavin'?"

"We've lost so much time, we had better go quickly to the wharves. And please go *quietly*, Natty. But what about the dog?"

"Dog's goin'! Ain't leavin' him here! No, ma'am!"

"Then we'll need to muzzle him."

"He won't make no noise if'n I tell him not to."

Kathryn tended to believe this, but she stepped back into the kitchen, snatching a towel to muzzle the dog should his and Natty's eerie way of communicating break down. With a twinge of guilt, she also took a fresh loaf of bread.

"All right, let's go," she told Natty. "And remember, this could be dangerous for my sister."

"Thet's nothin' new fer her—everythin' she does is danger-us!"

As they warily made for the path leading down to the river, the dog followed closely, and silently, on their heels.

9

---∿∿---

Mother had a charming chamber, with new matting and pretty curtains, all prepared for Genl. McClellan, and for a long time we called [it] Genl. McClellan's room.
—Elizabeth Van Lew, Richmond, 1862

James River

"Are you managing all right?" Bronwen said quietly to Marsh, who was just behind her on the path.

A pugnacious thrust of the young man's chin, which now bore an abundant beard, accompanied his sullen "Stop asking me that! I told you I'm *fine*!"

He was not fine, but hell would freeze over before he admitted it. His gait was cautious, even halting, which Bronwen assumed was due to the clouded vision in his one eye, and whereas he had formerly been lean, he was now what could only be called gaunt. She knew better than to offer sympathy. Weeks in a Confederate hospital had not improved his moody temperament, either.

As she had anticipated, all of Chimborazo's wards were jammed with wounded soldiers, together with anxious Richmond relatives searching for survivors, and the turmoil had allowed her to spirit Marsh outside. There had been no time to tell him what to expect. Once they reached the path to the river, Bronwen paused only long enough to yank the gray Confederate jacket from her knapsack.

Throwing it over his shoulders she said, "Just follow me," not giving him a chance for questions.

Her chief concern now was whether, after his long confinement, Marsh had strength enough to make the wharves. But she would not leave him here, even if it meant dragging him down the hill feet-first.

And there was more than enough else to worry her.

Were Kathryn and Natty safely aboard the sloop, and had Quiller's escape been discovered? If it had, the clamor of ambulance wagons with incoming wounded would have drowned any noise of pursuers.

Clouds had begun gliding across the moon. The cover they gave was welcome, but the path became nearly invisible as it wove through waist-high scrub growth, forcing her to keep her eyes on the ground ahead. She was just turning to see how Marsh was faring when he gripped her shoulder. After pointing down at the river, he went into a crouch. Bronwen, when she craned her neck and saw what he meant, instantly sank beside him.

Still at some distance, the wharves below seemed awash in lantern light and men in dusky uniforms. And where was the sloop? She couldn't see it where she and O'Hara had docked.

"Is this your idea of sneaking away under cover of darkness?" muttered Marsh. "Looks like high noon down there. And those are Rebels below, in case you were wondering. Even *I* can see that."

She cast another anxious glance over the scene. Where were Kathryn and the boy? *Don't let them be at those wharves!*

While fumbling in the knapsack for her spyglass, she suddenly heard voices coming toward them.

"Marsh, stay down and follow me."

On her hands and knees, Bronwen crawled forward,

struggling to clear a way through the tangled growth. Behind her, Marsh's labored breathing gave evidence of his weakened condition. When her outstretched hands finally found what seemed to be an opening in the brush, she heard the voices again, sounding as if only yards away. She flattened herself on her belly, and hoped Marsh was doing the same.

"Lot of lights at the river," said a male voice that Bronwen could have sworn was only a few feet from her. "Some kind of trouble down there?"

"Could be lookin' for them escapin' Yankees!" said another, making Bronwen's pulse race.

"Maybe so. Heard they're fixin' to hightail it back North. And before they do, Gen'l Lee's gonna make 'em mighty sorry they tried to whup us!"

Bronwen heard a soft intake of breath, and prayed Marsh didn't intend to waste what little strength he had by defending Northern honor. He couldn't know that the man they just heard had it very nearly right.

A distant shout resulted in a shuffling noise from the path as if heavy articles were being shifted. Then the tread of footsteps trailed away to be replaced by silence.

Just as Bronwen's pulse was beginning to slow, something clamped her outstretched forearm. Startled, she instinctively jerked it back. The hold was immediately released, but her arm felt wet. Had it been some soldier's bloody hand?

Not daring to move, she peered into the darkness. When something nudged her shoulder, she struck out blindly, and connected with what felt like silken hair.

"What's the matter?" Marsh whispered behind her.

"I think," she muttered, "or at least I hope, that it's Natty's dog."

Marsh mumbled an oath while Bronwen warily felt her way forward into the tall grass of what must be a field or pasture. When the clouds thinned, moonlight showed the dog in a half-crouch just beyond. He sprang forward to clamp her hand in his soft mouth, released it, and sprang away.

"I'm guessing he wants to be followed," she told Marsh.

"Are you crazy?"

"I've watched these dogs herding sheep back home, and one of them alone can round up an entire flock. They're smarter than some people I know, and a whole lot more trustworthy. So no, I'm not crazy. Not yet."

She listened for sounds indicating Quiller's absence had been discovered, prompting a search, and heard nothing but the same chaotic noise from the road and hospital. Signaling to Marsh, and keeping her body low to the ground, she started after the dog. It was moving in an easy loping stride on a course parallel to the river.

"This is the wrong direction," breathed Marsh.

Bronwen's response was to gesture toward the wharves, where lanterns were still lit, if fewer than before. And now, directly ahead, rose the outline of trees. She resisted the urge to stop and use her spyglass to see what was happening below, but feared it might involve O'Hara and Quiller. She didn't tell Marsh that. He knew nothing of what they all were risking.

The dog had disappeared into the first trees of a wooded area. With Marsh now at some distance behind her, Bronwen took a few guarded steps into the woods, then stopped short at a blur of movement just ahead.

She ducked, and her fingers had closed around the derringer in her pocket when she heard a high-pitched, "Shure took ya long 'nough to git here!"

Moonlight filtering through branches showed her the boy and dog standing beside Kathryn.

"Are you all right, Bronwen?" her sister whispered.

"I'm okay. Are you?"

"Yes, but I've been worried about—"

She broke off as Marsh came panting up. Bronwen noted with alarm that he was not only out of breath but was nearly staggering.

Kathryn, stepping forward and taking his arm, drew him down beside her on the leaf-strewn floor of the woods, saying, "I'm exhausted, Marsh. Just sit with me a minute or two, while I'm catching my breath."

Without a murmur of protest, Marsh sank back against the trunk of a tree. Bronwen didn't need Natty's knowing sideways glance to recognize her sister's flawless managing of an unmanageable patient. He would have snapped anyone else's head off.

While she groped in the knapsack for her spyglass, she asked Kathryn, "What happened at the wharves? Do you know?"

"We were at the top of the path when lanterns below began to flare, and I heard raised voices. I thought one of them was Kerry O'Hara's. He was talking so loudly—in fact, he was shouting—that I guessed he was trying to warn us off."

"And?" prodded Bronwen, thinking that O'Hara always talked too loudly, but maybe this time with good reason.

"There was so much commotion I couldn't see clearly, but obviously something had gone wrong. I grabbed Natty and we ran for these woods."

"It was me thet told Dog to go git ya," he inserted.

Bronwen didn't inquire how he went about conveying an abstract concept to a dog. "If O'Hara was there at the wharves," she said to Kathryn, "then Mr. Quiller must have been too."

"I didn't see him, but Natty did."

"You *saw* Quiller at that distance?" Bronwen said to him skeptically. "How could you?"

"I snuck down the hill," answered Natty matter-of-factly.

"I couldn't stop him," Kathryn explained.

"Well, what did you see?" Bronwen asked.

"Lotta supply boats, and Rebs standin' 'round thet big-mouth Oh-haira. He was wearin' a Reb coat, but ya couldn't mis-take *his* blabbin'! An' Mr. Kil—Mr. What-sisname from the loony ward was there too."

"Mr. *Quiller*?"

"Yeah, him, but he weren't talkin' none. Oh-haira, he said he hadda git under way, 'cause thet Mr. Whatsisname was a . . . a under-the-covers gent. An' he got top-secret orders from a War Apartment."

"Secret orders?" Marsh repeated.

"Yeah, to scout out them there damn Yankees who's a-comin up the river! An' Oh-haira, he's wavin' this piece a' paper in everybody's face."

"One of O'Hara's talents is forgery," Bronwen said, her tension somewhat eased as she dropped beside her sister. "Confederate War Department documents are child's play to him—I won't go into his checkered past just now. Natty, what happened then?"

"Nothin' much. Everybody jest keeps lookin' at the pa-per whilst Oh-haira climbs into a sailboat. He pulls Mr. Whatsisname into it, too. Then he yells, 'S'long, mates! Gotta spy on them Yankees.' An' he pushes off with a oar and starts rowin' into the river. Thet's it!"

Marsh broke into Bronwen's relief with "So O'Hara just *left* us here?" his tone suggesting that she was single-handedly responsible for the desertion.

"What did you expect him to do, Marsh? Announce that, oh, by the way, I can't leave yet because I have to wait for two other U.S. Treasury agents? O'Hara and I took the potential for trouble into account before we started out—and he rightly left with Quiller, who was the one most endangered. It was always an option that he pick us up later."

"Where?" both Marsh and Natty chorused.

"Where he can do it unobserved."

"In other words, you don't know *where*," said Marsh accusingly.

Bronwen retorted, "I've had about enough of your bad temp—" and stopped herself. He was well aware he couldn't pull his weight, and that would make anyone bad-tempered, especially someone as proud as Marsh.

Kathryn had been unrolling a towel from which she now lifted a loaf of bread. Breaking off two pieces, she handed the larger one to Natty, and gave the rest of the loaf to Marsh, saying, "We should eat something while we have the chance."

Bronwen sent her sister a grateful nod. It was an indisputable truth, and one every smart woman learned early, that all men's dispositions were vastly improved by food.

After breaking off a chunk of bread, Marsh offered Bronwen the remaining loaf with a forced half-smile that probably indicated apology. She was about to refuse the bread, leaving more for him, and then decided she should keep up her own strength. Kathryn had been right: Who knew when they could eat again?

She took the remaining piece, noting that Natty was feeding part of his bread to Dog, and gave Marsh a sideways glance. He seemed better, although he was still perspiring heavily.

He had needed the rest, but she was growing edgier by the second. The area was crawling with Confederates, and here were the four of them breaking bread! After listening for hostile voices again, she scrambled to her feet.

"We've been lucky so far," she quietly announced, "but

sooner or later Quiller's escape will be discovered. We need to move out. Now!"

BRONWEN, holding up her hand to signal the others, calculated they had covered perhaps another three miles since she last called a stop. At first their course had followed the James, but heavy undergrowth along its bank had finally forced them to veer away from it. While the North Star had guided them for a time, the sky had long since filled with clouds. Now a misty rain was falling.

Between the darkness and the rain, the spyglass was useless. At this point Bronwen was not certain exactly where they were, and she needed to reconnoiter before they stumbled into the Confederate fort at Drewry's Bluff. That they hadn't already collided with enemy troops was presumably due to the dog's constant watchful circling as they trudged through the wooded terrain. Guarding his simpleminded sheep, she concluded.

"Dog won't let none a' them Rebs sneak up on us," Natty had insisted. She half-shared his confidence. What choice did she have?

During the first stop, while Marsh and Natty slumped wearily against tree trunks, she had taken her sister aside. "I was surprised, Kathryn, that you agreed to leave Chimborazo so readily. Relieved, but surprised. Why did you?"

"Our Union soldiers. I know how inadequate the military medical service has been. And remember, when I first arrived at Chimborazo, there were no battles taking place."

When Bronwen had said nothing, her sister added, "And there's another reason. Southerners say their slaves are treated well, are perfectly happy with their lot, and until now I'd never seen slavery firsthand, so I guess I wanted to believe it. But while it may be true of some slaves, I've seen hundreds of them fleeing for the Union lines. People don't run from something familiar to something unknown unless they're desperate."

"I agree."

"I know, you've said the same yourself. I guess now I'll try to find a Union field hospital near the battlefront. I can't go back to White House Landing, not with Gregg Travis there."

"Travis is not at White House."

"He's not?"

"And you couldn't go back there anyway, Kathryn, because McClellan is withdrawing to somewhere on the James."

"*Withdrawing?*"

"As in 'retreating.' "

"Dear Lord, does that mean our troops are in danger? Seth, too?"

"Great danger, and yes, Seth, too. The army is fighting its way south right now, so I assume Travis is no longer at Savage's Station where he was a few days ago."

"How . . . how do you know that?"

Her sister's voice held too much emotion for Bronwen to evade the question. "He wrote Rhys Bevan in Washington asking where you were. And I picked up a telegram intended for you."

She fished the damp paper out of a pocket and handed it to Kathryn.

"Bronwen, it's too dark to read it."

"It's a short message from Travis—obviously sent before McClellan ordered White House abandoned—saying he wants you to return. That you're needed. It ends, believe it or not, with the word *please*."

She sensed her sister's agitation, but kept herself from offering an opinion of the overbearing Travis. Kathryn would have to come to terms with him and his request on her own. "I'm sorry, Kathryn, but there's no more time. We have to keep moving."

The rain had started shortly thereafter. Now, as they stopped once again, Marsh collapsed on the wet ground in exhaustion. Bronwen knew that she, far more than O'Hara, should have foreseen that Marsh would hold them back, keeping their pace too slow to rendezvous as planned. And there was no alternative.

Darkness meant there was little hope of finding landmarks, with or without the spyglass, to pinpoint their location. She no longer had a reliable sense of the time either, and was certain only that the river lay somewhere to her right. Whatever else might be there, such as Confederate troops, was too frightening to consider. Every time the wind shifted it seemed to carry the muffled sound of artillery fire, though it might be only her overtaxed imagination.

Withdrawing from her knapsack a rolled rubber poncho, she gave it to Kathryn. "Rain's getting heavier, so take this for cover. Soldiers even make tents of these things. It's big enough for you three, and even for Natty's furry friend, too. I need to scout what's ahead."

When both Kathryn and Marsh started to protest, she cut them off. "If trouble approaches, the dog will warn you. Just remember, Marsh, you're a lost Rebel soldier trying to find your regiment. Here, take my derringer, although I can't think anyone would harm you, or your sister and younger brother here."

It sounded hollow, even to her. But their further objections fell on deaf ears as Bronwen struck out in what she trusted was the direction of the river.

It was only a few minutes later, as the woods began to thin, that she caught a rustle of leaves. Edging behind the nearest tree, she slipped out the stiletto. And then heard a low bark.

"Dog!" she whispered in exasperation. "Go back!"

"He ain't gonna go nowheres," came a voice behind her. "Some scout ya are! Dint even hear us!"

"You nearly got yourself knifed, my man!"

She began to walk again, the dog trotting just ahead of her. "Okay, Natty, you've had your fun, now go on back to the others." She was surprised that he had left Lady, but not that he ignored her order.

"I thought we was s'posed to meet thet there Oh-haira," he said, having fallen into step beside her. "So where's he at?"

"By now he might have sailed halfway to the Chesapeake. Then again, he might not."

"D'ya trust him?"

"Right now, I have to trust him. How about you?"

"Mebbe. He's kinda smart, even if'n he's pee-cu-yer."

"He's peculiar all right."

"Think we's gonna git captured by Rebs?"

"Not if I can help it. I don't suppose you could ask Dog to find us the river?"

"Don'cha know where it's at?"

Bronwen, ignoring this little jab, again ordered him to go back while knowing he would not. A few seconds later the dog went streaking off ahead of them.

"Where's he going?"

"To the river, a' course."

THE James was where Bronwen had calculated it would be. She and Natty followed the dog onto a relatively open bluff, and stood staring at what lay downriver.

The pale gray in the eastern sky gave enough light to see the squat profiles of warships riding at anchor.

"Is thet our boats down there?" Natty asked.

"Spyglass says they're U.S. Navy."

After searching again with the glass, she debated with herself, and then said to Natty with some reluctance, "Would you and Dog be able to find your way back to the others?"

"What fer?"

"To lead them here."

"Why? It's a long ways to them boats. 'Sides, I cain't swim."

"Just do what I asked."

"But what're *you* gonna do?" he asked, looking at her with narrowed hazel eyes. "I s'pect it'll be danger-us, huh?"

"I'll meet you right here at this spot, as quick as you can make it, okay? Now go!"

He muttered something under his breath. The dog bounded back into the woods, and after Natty stopped once to cast an odd glance at her over his shoulder, he followed. Bronwen had already begun hurriedly rooting in her knapsack. She needed to act before the sky became much brighter.

As her fingers closed around several cylinders, and then a box of matches and lengths of cotton yarn, she could only hope that her fragile trust in O'Hara was justified.

10

This is the first time we ever had reason to believe that the highest and first duty of a general, on the day of battle, was separating himself from his army, to reconnoiter a place for retreat.

—Brig. General John Barnard, USA, 1862

James River

While Bronwen waited for the others, pacing back and forth on the bluff, her impatience was mixed with apprehension. She had fired off two rocket flares to signal O'Hara, but with the gathering dawn she didn't dare risk firing another, not when Confederate troops might be in the vicinity. If O'Hara had deserted her, she hoped it meant he was transporting James Quiller downriver to Fort Monroe. If, on the other hand, he had betrayed her. . . . She could not bring herself to consider that yet.

In the meantime, where were the others? By now Natty should have been returned here with them, unless Marsh had collapsed, or they had run into even more serious trouble. She was sorely tempted to look for them, but hours could be wasted wandering around in the woods passing one another unknowingly. And O'Hara might return. She should strain for patience and wait.

First light was bringing with it an eerie quiet that belied

the presence of warships downriver. Even the earlier snatches of artillery grumbling had ceased. Glancing around her, Bronwen experienced a skin-prickling sense of foreboding. It felt as if the entire world was stopping to draw one last sane breath before plunging into madness.

Attempting to shake off her dread, she was again scanning the river when a low whistle made her spin to her left. From behind some bushes, a grim-faced man in Confederate jacket came sprinting toward her.

"O'Hara, thank God!"

"We need to move fast! Where are the others?"

"What took you so long?"

"No time for that. I *said*, where're the others?"

"Supposed to be here by this time."

"We have to go *now*, Red, or not at all!"

"Where's Quill—"

She broke off as the dog came loping from the trees, followed by Natty, and then the others. Kathryn appeared to be supporting the ashen Marsh, who was all but gasping for breath.

O'Hara sent Bronwen a dark look, muttering, "Hell! All we need right now is an invalid."

"We don't have a choice. Where's the sloop?"

"Downriver." He turned to Marsh, saying briskly, "Can you last another mile or so?"

"Yes, damn it!" Marsh retorted, jerking away from Kathryn.

O'Hara shrugged, swung his arm for them to follow, and struck out in the direction from which he had come. The pace he set over the uneven ground was one Bronwen worried that Marsh could not match for long.

Since the mid-summer sun had risen in a clear sky, it was already hot, and little time elapsed before Marsh began dropping back. When Kathryn slowed her own steps,

Bronwen said to her quietly, "You and Natty should go on ahead with O'Hara. I'll stay with—"

"No!" interrupted Marsh. "All of you just get to the boat. I'll be right behind."

"Please go on, Kathryn," Bronwen urged, adding lamely to persuade her sister, "you're responsible for the boy."

Kathryn was not persuaded, and they moved forward at what felt like a crawl. Bronwen was becoming infected with O'Hara's urgency, having heard what sounded like several long rolls of thunder.

As Natty threw her a questioning glance, O'Hara turned and came dashing back to them. "Hear that? It's not thunder, it's Reb cannons! And Marshall, if you can't keep up—"

"Move on!" Marsh broke in, his voice cracking in what had to be frustration. "Make for the sloop! I'll either get there or I won't."

O'Hara gave Bronwen a look that said "you heard him," but she shook her head. "Take Natty and my sister," she told him.

When Kathryn and, surprisingly, Natty too began to object, O'Hara brushed past them to stand directly in front of Marsh. "There's still a ways to go, chum, and we need to do it fast, so I'll carry you."

"Like hell you will."

"Don't be an ass, Marshall! You're putting all of us at risk, you selfish bastard."

Bronwen heard this as a deliberate goad, but before she could stop Marsh from reacting, he had raised his fists and was lurching forward. O'Hara, moving so fast that all Bronwen saw was a blur, struck him a chopping blow to the base of his skull. As Marsh fell sideways, O'Hara caught and heaved him over his shoulder like a sack of grain.

"Okay, let's move," was all he said.

No one else uttered a word as they went forward. The dog, trotting around them in tight circles, seemed to regard this as all in a day's work, but Bronwen found herself resenting his smooth, tireless gait.

Despite his burden, O'Hara did not appear to be tiring either. He had a wiry strength and, Bronwen had learned before now, the stamina to match.

After they had hiked down a slight, rock-strewn incline, scattered with stringy pines, the river's edge was finally before them. "How much farther is the sloop?" Bronwen asked O'Hara.

"Not far," he grunted, shifting his load. Marsh, his arms dangling limply, appeared to be only half-conscious.

The sloop was so well hidden on a short finger of water surrounded by scrub growth that they almost fell into it. Bronwen did not see anyone else there.

"O'Hara, where's Quiller?"

"Aboard a navy gunboat."

"*Gunboat?* How did . . . is he safe?"

"Fairly, which is more than can be said of us," he answered, after dropping Marsh into the sloop. "No more questions for now, Red."

O'Hara motioned for the others to climb aboard, but when the dog jumped into the bow, he said to Bronwen, "Tell the boy, no dog."

"Whaddaya mean?" Natty said, scowling fiercely.

"Just what I said. No dog. There's barely space for us, and this is no Sunday afternoon cruise we're taking."

"Dog's goin' or I ain't!"

"Natty . . ." began Kathryn, and then simply shook her head.

Natty's eyes were tearing, something Bronwen had never seen from him even in the direst circumstances. She said to O'Hara, "The dog won't take up much room if he stays in the bow."

"No, dammit! We might have to sneak past Rebs, and dogs bark!"

"He ain't gonna bark, Oh-haira! I swear he ain't. But he's gotta come. He's the only thing I ever had thet was mine."

Bronwen, looking at a boy who had somehow survived alone on the streets, who didn't know his last name, or even his age, told O'Hara, "We can use a muzzle if necessary. The dog comes!"

THE current would have taken the sloop downriver even without its sail, and Bronwen watched over her shoulder as O'Hara's harbor swiftly receded. There were no gunboats this far upriver. From her vantage point, there were few other boats at all, which wasn't surprising, given the almost constant growl of artillery from somewhere to the north.

Marsh at last appeared to be coming around. Kathryn, kneeling on the floorboards amidships, hovered beside him, frequently reaching over the side to wet the towel and apply it to his forehead and bruised neck. In the bow, the dog had his front paws up on the rail, his ears pricked forward, and his twitching nose pointed straight ahead. Natty crouched beside him with an arm flung over the animal's well-muscled haunches.

While they were getting under way, O'Hara had said, "Believe me, Red, if we're captured, I'm handing you over to the Rebs on a mutiny charge. You defied my orders, and for what? A mouthy kid, an invalid, and a dog! Do I look like a captain of the good ship *Samaritan*?"

When she had ignored him, he added, "And I *am* the captain now, because I know what's up ahead and you don't. No argument!"

She hadn't intended to argue, because O'Hara was as good a sailor as she. Neither of them were anywhere near as experienced as Marsh, but he had still been groggy.

Since she had never known O'Hara to hold a grudge—other than against McClellan—she now ducked under the boom and asked him, "Okay, what all's happened?"

"Where would you like me to start? With the disastrous happenings, or the only slightly less disastrous happenings?"

Thinking of her brother, she said, "What have you heard, if anything, about Union troops?"

"They're struggling to reach the river here, having to battle every step forward during the day, and march south by night."

"How do you know?"

"There was a minor hitch last night at the Spanish *hospicio*—"

"I heard about it," she interrupted, adding dryly, "Natty was spying."

"Then you know those wharves were swarming with supply ships and Reb navy, and I needed to remove Quiller fast. And later, when you weren't where our alternate Plan B called for you to be, I went to Plan C. Which meant taking Quiller downriver, putting him ashore temporarily, and then coming back for you. He and I were moving at a good clip some south of here"—he gestured toward the wooded riverbank—"when we met up with a U.S. Navy gunboat."

"This far upriver?"

"Captain was scouting possible enemy positions, after escorting the warship *Galena* on a jaunt from McClellan's headquarters at Haxall's Landing. Even though Quiller and I quick ran up the Stars and Stripes, we were ordered aboard the gunboat. Those navy boys weren't taking any chances on a Rebel attack by sloop! Anyway, we climbed aboard."

"And you left Quiller there?"

"Damn right I did! When the captain learned it was

Lincoln's chum I was transporting, he insisted. Said he could put Quiller on the next ship bound for Fort Monroe. So you bet I left him! One less to worry about."

"I would have done the same, O'Hara."

"Don't tell me we agree on something!"

"And I haven't thanked you for coming back for us."

"I'll exact my reward later. But Quiller's the only thing you can be relieved about, Red. Aboard the gunboat, I caught the latest reports. None of them good."

Bronwen was trying to prepare herself for the worst when the wind abruptly shifted. O'Hara shouted, "Loop of the river coming. Ready about!" as the sloop heeled precariously.

Marsh mumbled an oath about seamanship that sounded mutinous.

After they were again on course, Bronwen said over her shoulder to Kathryn, "How's he doing?"

"I'm *fine*!" came the irritated response.

"Such a sweet-tempered chap," O'Hara muttered. "I notice, Red, you didn't bother asking how *I* am. And why worry about Marshall when there's a dashingly handsome, good-natured fellow like me aboard."

Natty glanced back at O'Hara with skepticism. His head rested against the dog's sloping shoulder with the wind roughing both the fair and dark hair.

"What more did you hear about our troops?" Bronwen pressed.

"Reports are that in the past twenty-four hours there've been massive engagements south of the Chickahominy. And I mean *massive*. Before that—Sunday, I think—there was heavy fighting along the railroad near Savage's Station."

Bronwen heard her sister's sharp intake of breath.

O'Hara waited, but when Kathryn said nothing, he went on, "All we can hope for now is that our army makes it here to the James. Columns of wagon trains with provisions and ammunition have been pushing south during the night, but you know how treacherous the terrain is."

"And the troops?"

"Frankly, Red, it'll be a marvel if the Union army survives Lee's assault. McClellan, one hopes, might not survive this—and I don't mean physically, since he'll never put himself in harm's way. But Young Napoleon should face an accounting by his commander in chief. Or, better still, a firing squad."

Telling herself that O'Hara's remarks about McClellan were likely an exaggeration, she hoped the same was true for reports about the army. "How far south are the troops now?"

"Head of the supply column is supposed to be at or near Haxall's Landing. And yesterday the artillery's big guns were being positioned along the bluff of Malvern Hill to protect the troops' retreat."

"Where's that?"

"Just north of the landing and smack in the path of our army. North-south roads are scarce and swamps and bogs are aplenty, so to reach the river our army has to pass Malvern Hill. With Rebs advancing behind them, and their backs to the river, it's the last line of defense. If Lee attacks with his full force—and he's looking too aggressive not to—there'll be one hell of a fight. It may have already started, from the sound of it."

Bronwen, trying to push aside fear for Seth, couldn't bring herself to ask if any casualty figures had been reported.

But Kathryn suddenly said, "Confederate wounded were flooding into Chimborazo, so Union casualties must be great, too. What's being done for them?"

"Not much, I'm afraid," O'Hara said. "Savage's Station was vacated, and that's where the large Union field hospital is . . . was."

After a stunned silence, Kathryn persisted, "But if our army's being pursued, what about the *wounded*?"

O'Hara shot an uncomfortable look at Bronwen, before telling Kathryn, "When troops need to retreat fast, there's not much to be done for the ones who can't keep up."

"You don't mean injured men might have been abandoned? Left to die or be captured?" Kathryn's voice was trembling when she repeated, "You can't mean *that*."

"We're losing the wind," O'Hara said. "Need to tack again. Ready about!"

As the boom swung overhead, Bronwen caught a glimpse of her sister's distressed face, but Kathryn said nothing more.

A long rumble of cannon fire made all their heads swivel toward land. As it died away, Bronwen, determined to believe the army would escape, said, "O'Hara, where on the James is the nearest area large enough for an encampment? Of thousands of troops?"

"A good question," he responded, clearly relieved to deal with something other than Kathryn's horrifying ones. "But fear not, Red, because our McClellan, not content to leave reconnoitering to mere minions—such as the engineers who designed and built all his damned bridges—is himself personally selecting the site."

"I don't understand."

"Who *could*? It seems that while Young Napoleon's troops were fighting for their lives in stinking swamps and woods, he was taking his ease on the James River."

"O'Hara, I know you hate McClellan—"

"—but that sounds too far-fetched even for him? I was assured of its truth by the gunboat captain. Who also seemed to find it 'curious,' given all the unpleasantness just north of here, that Mac boarded the *Galena* yesterday afternoon, and after steaming upstream to order a few shells tossed at some Rebel column, stayed to dine at its captain's table. I was informed that he and his companions greatly enjoyed the white linen tablecloths, good food, and fine wine. Which little excursion, of course, put him conveniently beyond reach of telegraphic communication. To say nothing of his army."

Bronwen stared at him dumbstruck. He, in turn, was staring bitterly at the water. She glanced back at Kathryn and was met by her sister's shocked look of disbelief.

"That . . . that just can't be true," Kathryn said to O'Hara.

"It's true."

"I can believe it," Marsh said, unexpectedly raising himself on one elbow. He looked as weakened as he had earlier, but was typically exerting heroic effort to disguise it. "From what I've heard, McClellan has managed to be someplace else at every damn battle fought down here. Man talks a good game, but he's spineless when it comes time to play it."

"I would imagine in war everyone has fear," Kathryn ventured softly.

O'Hara, his voice cold, said, " '*Everyone*' is not a commanding general!"

As Bronwen thought over the past months, she had to agree with O'Hara's point. Which only made the present more terrifying, because if fear had overpowered McClellan's ability to command, it was unlikely he had the moral courage to acknowledge it.

A sharp booming roar from somewhere ahead made her glance at O'Hara, and she found him studying her. "So you've finally seen the light," he concluded, his voice holding no satisfaction.

"That cannon fire sounds too close," she told him. "I think we should make for shore before we sail right into a battle."

The river bend was straightening and the James was

broadening, but the sloop was in mid-stream. Something caught her eye, and she seized O'Hara's shoulder. "Look there ahead—off the port bow!"

As she grabbed her spyglass to scan the first visible warships, a thunderous barrage issued from one of them.

"Gawd a'mighty!" Natty gasped, clutching the dog's hindquarters as it tried to scrabble over the bow.

"O'Hara!" Bronwen shouted over another blast from what she had identified as the ironclad *Galena*. "Take us into shore!"

"Guns couldn't be aimed at *us*," he argued.

Natty, struggling to keep the terrified dog from jumping overboard, yelled, "How do them boats know who 'us' *is*?"

When the firing suddenly ceased, leaving a haze of unfurling smoke, O'Hara muttered, "Can't get into shore with no wind."

An instant later the guns roared again, spitting fire across the water. Natty tackled the dog as it leapt forward, and they went crashing to the floorboards as sudden gusts of wind sent the sloop skimming toward the ships.

Marsh, who had risen to a crouch and was letting out a line, shouted, "Ready about! Everybody down and hold on!"

As the boom flew over their heads, the sloop careened perilously, canting so far that its starboard rail was under water. Bronwen, sure the boat could not right itself before capsizing, clung to the opposite rail as the others were doing.

"Dog!" shrieked Natty when the animal tried to scramble over them. Bronwen reached up to grab the dog's tail while abruptly recalling that Natty could not swim. Suddenly the boat rocked violently, and then it righted, flinging them all to the floorboards. When Bronwen caught her breath and looked up, they were moving, if ever so slowly, toward land.

O'Hara said nothing about Marsh's seizure of command.

In the next instant several shells sprayed the water to starboard. While everyone instinctively ducked, Bronwen assumed the shelling had been accidental. It had to have come from one of the navy ships, which couldn't intentionally be wasting ammunition on a small sloop!

But more shells splashing into the water made Marsh yell, "Who the hell's shooting at us?"

"Can't see where they're coming from," O'Hara yelled back.

"Run up the flag!"

They had deliberately not flown one for fear of attracting unfriendly interest. Bronwen crawled toward O'Hara to help him hoist the flag, hand over hand, and while doing it, saw with shocked recognition his gray sleeve.

"O'Hara, your Rebel *jacket*—it's probably why we're being fired on! Take it off! Marsh, you too!"

She and Kathryn pulled away the jackets after the two men wriggled out of them, but Bronwen feared it might be too late. If some officer had ordered gunners to shell a sloop bearing Confederates, how likely was it that the same officer would desist now?

A volley of gunfire from land to the north made Bronwen jerk toward it. When it continued without letup, she looked at O'Hara.

He nodded, shouting, "Could be from Malvern Hill."

If that were true, the now ominous silence from the ironclad and gunboats made her assume they were waiting for signals to resume firing. But signals from where?

The sloop was rocking gently as it made slight headway, and Bronwen eyed the remaining distance to shore. If necessary she could probably swim it. O'Hara could too. Kathryn, maybe, but not Marsh in his condition . . . and then there was Natty.

After a few minutes of watching their slow progress, she

said impatiently, "Marsh, let's break out the oars. They won't help much, but we can't just sit here—"

A sudden thunder of guns drowned her words, and fire shot from the ships. The sloop seemed to be vibrating as O'Hara thrust an oar at her. "No room to sit together, so you go closer to the stern where there's another oarlock."

No sooner had they begun pulling toward land than a shower of shells threw up spray alongside the sloop.

"Somebody's shootin' at *us* 'gain!" Natty yelped, clutching the dog tightly against him.

Bronwen heard another rain of shells come whining through the air to strike the water just short of the sloop. Almost instantly she heard the deadly whine again and looked up, catching only a glimpse of the one descending directly above the stern.

A crashing thud with a burst of light sent wood and rigging spewing in every direction. The sloop shuddered, its bow heaving out of the water, and immediately began to founder. What was left of the stern began to slide slowly beneath the surface.

Bronwen, her head barely clearing the water that swept over her, looked in vain for the others while grabbing at anything that might float. It was then she realized that her left arm wouldn't move and seem pinned to her side. Something on the wreckage had caught her, trapping her in a swirl of water and debris. Twisting her body in a desperate attempt to free herself, she kicked hard to keep from being drawn to the river bottom with the sinking boat. But whatever had snared her held fast, and she couldn't overcome the relentless downward pull.

She heard a high-pitched, garbled scream just before she was dragged under.

11

—∞—

*People had shaken themselves down, as it were,
to the grim reality of a fight that must be fought.
'Let the war bleed, and let the mighty fall' was
the spirit of their cry.*
—Constance Cary Harrison, Richmond, 1862

West of Haxall's Landing

Bronwen struggled to hold her breath while working to
tug the stiletto from her soft boot. *Keep your wits,* she told
herself, trying to curb the panic that would make her gasp
for air. *It can't be worse than breaking through ice on the Erie
Canal.*

She knew by now it was the tough cotton fabric of her
sleeve, snagged on something in the wreckage, that was
trapping her, and her fingers fumbled frantically with the
knife's sheath. Blood throbbed behind her eyes, the need
to breathe becoming intolerable. Then her right hand
found and closed on the stiletto grip. In one desperate
stroke, she whipped its razor-sharp blade upward through
the sleeve. As the pieces parted, she broke free, and with
lungs bursting, fought her way to the surface.

Taking great gulps of air, she scanned the water for the
others. Her waterlogged overalls were threatening to sink

her again even faster than the boots, and she had to scissor-kick hard to keep her head above water.

"Kathryn?" she called. "Kathryn, are you all right?"

Straining to hear her sister's voice, and listening for the whine of more shells, she heard instead, "Red! Over here! Catch the line!"

A length of rope snaked overhead and splashed inches away. After she had grabbed it, she saw O'Hara at its other end, treading water next to what appeared to be the overturned bow section of the sloop.

"Where're the others?" she shouted, casting frantic glances over the water as O'Hara hauled her toward him. "The boy can't swim!"

"He's here, Bronwen!" It was, thank heavens, Kathryn's voice. "We're all here!"

Bronwen was so relieved, it barely registered that the shelling had stopped. When she reached the overturned half of the sloop, she saw Kathryn and Marsh holding onto its side opposite O'Hara, and then she spotted Natty. His face ghastly white, he was gripping the paddling dog with one hand and Kathryn's shoulder with the other.

"Just keep holding the dog, Natty, and breathe deeply," Kathryn was saying to him, as if imminent drowning was nothing unusual. "The dog won't let you sink, and it's only for a minute longer. Just hold on."

She repeated this until O'Hara, after prying the dog's jaws open to release the waistband of Natty's trousers, hoisted the boy onto the floating hull. The dog, with a boost from Bronwen, scrabbled up to lie panting beside him.

"Damned if that dog didn't save the kid's life," O'Hara told her.

When she looked up at Natty, he simply nodded, seeming, for the first time in memory, to have lost his voice.

"Marsh," she asked, "are you okay?"

"I'm *fine*!"

"Kathryn?"

Her sister also nodded, and gave Bronwen a wan smile, saying, "At least it's warmer than the day you broke through the canal ice."

"I remembered that day, too."

Bronwen snatched one of the floating ropes still attached to the remaining hull, and glanced around her, instinctively reaching for the spyglass before recalling it must be at the bottom of the James. They were not only drifting slowly downstream but also into the path of the currently silent gunboats. Since rumbles of the inland artillery had become more concentrated, the quiet here on the river would almost certainly not last long. Where were the orders to fire being transmitted to the ships? If Federal signal officers were stationed along the shore, deliverance might be at hand.

"When did the ships stop shelling?" she asked O'Hara.

"About the time they sank us."

"You can't think the two are related."

"Probably not."

"Those wharves I see a little farther downriver—are they at Haxall's Landing?"

"They are."

"We need to avoid McClellan's headquarters, because Pinkerton might be there. Another boat's our only answer, O'Hara, so one of us has to swim to shore for help."

"Want to draw straws?"

Bronwen pulled off her boots underwater and, after handing them up to Natty along with the stiletto, was beginning to wriggle out of her overalls when Marsh protested, "O'Hara, you can't let *her* swim alone to shore!"

O'Hara's expression warned of a sarcastic reply, such as an offer to let Marsh swim it himself, but surprisingly he said only, "Red's a strong swimmer, as you must know. It's smarter for me to stay here . . ."

His voice trailed off. Under the circumstances, that he hadn't said "Stay here with a mouthy kid, an invalid, and a dog!" brought Bronwen close to forgiving him just about anything.

Until, as he watched her squirm out of the overalls, he moved along the hull to whisper, "Since I've waited weeks for this, Red, naturally I'm overjoyed, but do you think this is really the time?"

"You might have the decency to look the other way."

"Not a chance! This is more fun than a box seat at Barnum's sideshow."

She finally dragged off the overalls, but the thought of splashing ashore to meet who knew what in only a ripped shirt and mid-thigh-length cotton drawers made her pause.

"Better tie them trouser legs round yer neck," Natty commented with his first words. "An' yer bootlaces, too."

"Spoken like a true man of the world," said O'Hara, "who's seen many a wench in similar straits."

"Mr. O'Hara, please," Kathryn murmured, whatever else she intended to say lost in renewed fire from the gunboats.

For now the arcing shells seemed to be aimed solely toward land.

WHEN Bronwen waded ashore, she was already beginning to perspire in the breath-taking heat. As she had guessed, acting Federal signal officers were stationed along the waterline, manning red, white, and black flags affixed to jointed hickory staffs. Just galloping up a long rise was a horse whose rider was probably their courier. The reverberations of artillery fire to the north were intensified here, and almost continuous, but the flags were not in motion and the gunboats were again silent.

"Saw your sloop take a shell," a weary-looking, young officer said as he approached her. He seemed to be the only one of the dozen men there not openly gaping at a partially clothed female. This officer even looked down at his boots in obvious embarrassment while she pulled on her dripping overalls. Her own boots would have to wait.

Bronwen, eyeing his field glasses, replied, "If you saw that shelling, then you must know there are survivors out there. They need rescuing."

"And you must know we've got our hands full, miss," he said. "There's heavy engagement just north of here, and rescuing Rebs is not a priority."

"They're not Rebels."

He shook his head and said almost regretfully, "We saw Confederate jackets."

Bronwen pushed wet strands of hair from her eyes to peer at his insignia, while jamming a hand into a deep pocket to fish out a coin. "Lieutenant, those jackets were used by Federal Treasury agents as disguise behind enemy lines. I can understand your skepticism, so here's some identification."

She thrust the gold coin at him. He turned it over several times, but shook his head again.

If he and his fellow officers had seen the sloop struck by Union gunboats, and then watched her swim to shore, the role of a dithering, helpless female in distress would not play here. And since this lieutenant looked tired but not stupid, the truth, no matter how implausible, would have to serve.

"Please look at that coin again, Lieutenant. Hard as it might be to believe, I'm also a Treasury agent. Two others are in the river."

"I'm afraid you're right—it's hard to believe."

"Where's your commanding officer?"

"Directly behind you!" growled an emphatically angry voice. "What in hell goes on here? Lieutenant, I assume this is not your designated position?"

"No, sir, Major Cook," the lieutenant said, and handed the coin to a slim, sharp-featured officer, whose weather-beaten skin and granite gray eyes magnified his don't-trifle-with-me expression. The lieutenant murmured something to him, but all Bronwen could hear of it was "Treasury" and "rescue."

Before dismissing him, the major said, "Lieutenant, if that courier doesn't return within a quarter hour, send another with the same message. Emphasize again that we must, repeat, *must* maintain continuous contact with command."

Not even glancing at the coin, he pivoted toward Bronwen. "Young woman, if you do not leave this area right now, I will have you placed under arrest."

"I don't want to be *in* this area, Major Cook," she told him, after taking his measure and deciding tears or hysteria would not move him one inch. With an anxious glance at the river, she said, "Sir, my fellow agents are in need of immediate help. If you won't oblige, would you tell me where to find the telegraph?"

His eyebrows shot up. "What for? Do you plan to wire an appeal to Jefferson Davis?"

Bronwen caught the wry twist of his mouth. Which meant there was hope, since this man also did not look stupid, and the furrows around his eyes indicated that he smiled often. Or used to.

"Sir, those people out there are not Rebels, as I can verify by wiring Washington."

"There is no telegraph line here. Even if there were, by the time Washington responds, your comrades will be at the bottom of the James, and you know it."

Desperate to keep him from dismissing her, she admitted, "Yes, sir, I do, so may I please, *please* have leave to explain what happened? I swear to you it will be the truth."

His narrowed eyes went to her bare feet and moved to her face, which he studied briefly before snapping, "Be quick about it."

"We've just escaped from Richmond's Chimborazo Hospital. My orders from Treasury were to retrieve a fellow agent as well as a civilian gentleman, both of whom were being held there. I believe the latter is presently aboard one of our gunboats, if you care to confirm it."

"And risk having myself thought a lunatic? Just what is your name, young woman, and are you a fiction writer of any note?"

"Bronwen Llyr, sir, and it's not fiction! My superior at Treasury will vouch for my identity and my mission. But sir, those gunboats fired on an unarmed civilian vessel, so there are two other people—"

"Miss Llyr," he interrupted, "our troops are in the midst of a hazardous operation. And if we weren't now waiting on further orders, I would not be indulging you!"

"I'm aware of the Union withdrawal—"

"Change of base!" he corrected, but looked so plainly disgusted with the euphemism that she once more grasped at hope.

"Major, my brother and his New York regiment are with the Union troops, so I wouldn't ask for anything that might jeopardize them or the operation. But please, sir, if you can't help us, then let me borrow one of your longboats over there. Please."

When his eyes again scanned her face, she pressed, "I beg you, sir, for your assistance. In addition to the Federal agents—one of them wounded in service to his country—the other two persons clinging to that wreckage are civilians. They are a female nurse and a frail, terrified little child. Who can't swim!"

Her "terrified little child" gambit brought a slight change in his expression. Bouncing the coin in his hand, he suddenly asked, "What's the Treasury secretary's first name?"

Startled, she managed to sputter, "Salmon."

"Middle initial?"

"Ah . . . it's *P. P* for Portland. Salmon Portland Chase."

"And his son's name?"

By glancing toward the river, she managed to check her impatience with his grilling, and answered, "The secretary doesn't have a son. He has two daughters, and the older one's name is Kate. I don't know the younger one's."

She returned his probing gaze levelly, and as if she had nothing to hide. And other than stretching the truth in describing Natty, for once she didn't.

"Very well," he said, "I won't chance non-combatants being harmed. But if you're lying, young woman, I'll see you imprisoned until your hair turns gray!"

"Yes, sir, and thank you. I am very grateful."

"Lieutenant!" he ordered, "take a longboat and three *armed* men, and retrieve those survivors. At the double-quick!"

As Bronwen started forward to join them, he seized her shoulder. "Not so fast! I intend to see for myself the 'female nurse' and 'frail child' whose case you have pleaded. You stay put, young woman, unless and until I say otherwise."

Since Bronwen didn't dare waste more time by arguing, she readily agreed. Now all she could do was hope that Allan Pinkerton didn't appear.

SHE used some extra field glasses, given her by a Captain Rutherford, to watch the retrieval maneuver. The ground on which she was pacing had begun to vibrate from intensified cannon fire to the north, and the noise of shells and musketry was becoming constant. Major Cook appeared increasingly impatient while he waited for his courier's return, and he too started to pace.

As the longboat approached, the major sent yet another courier galloping up the rising slope.

When the dog jumped from the boat and came splashing ashore, the major gave Bronwen a dark look. Although its meaning was clear, he strode to where she stood to say cuttingly, "I sent four of my men for a *dog*?"

"I confess, Major," she replied with a straight face, "that the dog was once a Rebel. But after seeing the error of his ways, he saved the boy from drowning."

"And is that boy," he said, pointing to Natty, "the 'child' you described?"

"Yes, sir."

"Young woman, he looks neither frail nor terrified."

"Well, no, sir, not now he's on dry land."

The major clearly found this disingenuous, and might have said more, but galloping hooves heralded a courier racing toward them. By this time, O'Hara and Natty, followed by Kathryn and Marsh, were coming ashore. They all looked pale but hardy enough, although her sister was again supporting Marsh.

"Major Cook, sir!" the panting courier said with a less-than-crisp salute. "General Porter is still in command of the field. He requests that gunboat fire be suspended. The shells are falling short of the enemy's position, sir, and are striking his men—"

He broke off, waiting while Major Cook gave an order to the signal officers.

As the flags were put in motion, he said to the still-winded courier, "Go on!"

"General Porter requests that you take a position mid-way up the hill, sir."

The courier paused to point at the rise of land that looked to Bronwen more like a plateau than a hill, its crest wreathed with battle smoke.

"Beyond some trees," the courier said, "is an area in front of Malvern House, which is General Porter's command headquarters. The general requests the gunboat fire be directed from there, and with the use of compass to ensure improved accuracy."

O'Hara had come forward, having left the others dripping at the river's edge, and asked Bronwen in a low voice, "Did he say *Porter* was in command?"

"That's what I heard," she said after stepping away from the officers. "Is everyone else okay?"

O'Hara just nodded, obviously more concerned with the courier's message. "Porter is one of McClellan's pets," he said, "but capable enough just the same. And he damn well better be, from the sounds of it. But where the hell is—"

"While I was waiting," she interrupted, knowing what he was about to ask, "one of the signal officers told me McClellan left his headquarters this morning. He's supposedly aboard the *Galena*, gone to inspect the site for the army's change of base. It's to be at Harrison's Landing, downriver at Berkeley Plantation, because the navy can't guarantee control of the river any farther upstream. Army advance units and the head of the supply columns reached the landing yesterday."

O'Hara's expression told her what he thought of McClellan's most recent desertion, but before he could comment, Major Cook began rapidly issuing orders.

When Bronwen reached Kathryn and the others, the first thing her sister asked was: "Can we learn the location of the field hospitals? And there must be at least one surgical unit behind the battle lines."

Before Bronwen could reply that she had no idea, the young lieutenant appeared beside them. "Major Cook has ordered this site to be evacuated immediately. He advises that he cannot be responsible for your safety, so suggests you take cover in those trees—the ones standing about halfway up the hill."

"Where are the Union lines?" said O'Hara before Bronwen could ask the same obvious question.

She had already concluded they had no alternative but to follow the signal officers. If it had been only her and O'Hara, and Kathryn, whose staying power equaled her own, she would have considered striking out for Harrison's Landing. But it was miles from here, and unknown terrain could make the trek as dangerous as chanced-upon Confederate units. Natty might bear up with some help, but Marsh's condition made it too risky a proposition.

"Right now we Federals are holding that hill," the lieutenant was telling O'Hara. "On its far side, our lines are more or less U-shaped, pointing roughly northeast, with the open end facing south toward the river here. The lines are fortified by heavy artillery at the summit, and even though the enemy's made several assaults, it hasn't succeeded in penetrating them."

"Not yet," murmured O'Hara.

Bronwen had raised the field glasses to scan the slope and asked the lieutenant, "I can see up there, to the northwest, a red-brick building. Is that Malvern House, and if so, how far is it?"

"That's General Porter's headquarters, and it's close to a mile distant."

Kathryn started to ask him if it housed a field hospital, but was interrupted by Major Cook's "Move out!"

Bronwen, thanking the lieutenant as he backed away, turned uneasily to O'Hara.

He must have read her mind. "Given the wobbly state of your entourage here, Red, what choice is there? I strongly encourage finding a front row seat for that shootin' match up there, and wait it out."

"O'Hara, I can't ask you to stay."

"Right, you can't."

"There's no reason you shouldn't start out for Harrison's Landing."

"Right again."

Turning away so he wouldn't see her disappointment, she was motioning to Kathryn and the others when suddenly shots crackled from the trees to her left. She instinctively ducked as O'Hara yelled, "Enemy fire! Everybody down!"

Throwing herself to the ground, she saw Natty, Marsh, and the dog diving behind the longboat, and O'Hara shoving Kathryn toward it. There were sharp reports to her right as Captain Rutherford and the remaining signal officers returned the fire. Bronwen waited for them to reload before darting to the boat.

For some unknown reason, the firing from the trees had ceased, as abruptly as it began, but the very air vibrated with the more resounding artillery fire to the north.

"You have a revolver, Red?"

"No, just the water-soaked derringer, and Marsh has that." Looking around, she asked, "Is everyone all right?"

Kathryn's soft "Yes" was countered by Natty's healthy-sounding "I ain't awright, 'cause I wanna git outta here 'fore we git kilt!"

"I'll second that," muttered Marsh, as O'Hara and Bronwen peered warily around the boat.

One of the last three signal officers was rotating

his arm to indicate the way was clear while yelling, "Better move out!"

Captain Rutherford had dropped to one knee beside the third man, who was lying motionless. When Bronwen reached him, she saw that the man on the ground was the young lieutenant.

As Kathryn hurried up, the shaken-looking Rutherford rose and shook his head at her. "He took a bullet in the forehead—he's gone, miss. We'll come back for him later."

Rutherford was the one who had earlier told Bronwen about Harrison's Landing, and now said to her, "Agent Llyr, you might want to take his revolver. And you better follow us."

A fierce cannonade from above was again making the ground tremble as the two officers started up the rise. Natty, craning his neck to see the dead man, was steered away by Kathryn with the dog close at their heels. Bronwen stood biting her lip and gazing down at the young soldier who only minutes before had been very much alive.

O'Hara removed the lieutenant's revolver and handed it to her. "Take it, Red. And I say we get moving before those snipers come back."

"*We* . . . you aren't leaving?"

"What, and miss the biggest damn battle McClellan never commanded?"

12

'Tis blood, my blood—
My brother's and my own and shed by me.
— Byron, Cain

JULY 1, 1862
Malvern Hill

With unknown dangers threatening on every side if they remained at the river, Bronwen and O'Hara told the others they had no choice but to follow the signal officers. As they began a reluctant climb toward Malvern House, the stifling heat was growing more intense and the artillery fire more deafening. Acrid smoke and cinders made their eyes water, and adding to their nervousness, with every cannon boom the ground underfoot shuddered. The closer they moved to the unseen field of combat, the plainer it became that a battle of unimaginable ferocity was being waged.

"I can't see a damn thing in this smoke," O'Hara complained. "Can you?"

Bronwen, peering vainly into the thickening haze, shook her head. "I think for now we should just keep going," she told him. "If Malvern House is in Union hands, we're bound to meet up with stretchermen—or with troops. Let's just pray they're ours."

The plateau's crest still lay some distance beyond, but shimmering heat gave it the illusion of moving ever farther away, and since the swirling smoke had obscured any trace of the house, each step forward was taken in blind hope.

Frequently, riderless horses would gallop past, trailing their reins and kicking up flurries of red dust. Marsh, who seemed to be holding up remarkably well, walked beside Kathryn and Natty, and at first the dog loped around those three, but before long he began anxiously circling all five of them. Although he flinched at every cannonade, when Bronwen and Natty tried to corral him, he refused to abandon his herding duties. At last, stretchermen began emerging from the smoke, the groans of the wounded on their litters a heartrending sign that a field hospital must be nearby.

Bronwen raised her hand. "Let's stop!" she shouted to the others over renewed thunderclaps of artillery.

After wiping sweaty palms on her overalls, she raised the field glasses but expected to see little, Captain Rutherford and the other officer having completely vanished. In the meantime, the sky had turned an angry red from a descending sun barely visible through the haze. It must by now be late afternoon or early evening.

When a pause in the cannon fire and slight breeze brought a thinning of smoke, her sister seized Bronwen's arm, pointing toward a large, gabled house of brick that had just become visible. A half-dozen tents pitched in front of it were nearly hidden by what must have been hundreds of wounded soldiers. Other men in bloodied aprons and rolled-up shirtsleeves, and hunched over long tables set under the shade of elms, were evidently performing surgery.

"O'Hara," she yelled in his ear, "have you seen those signal officers?"

He pointed toward Malvern House. "Isn't that them dancing a jig up there?"

The field glasses showed her twirling flags manned by the signal officers in precarious, shifting stances on the roof.

"Yes, it's them," she agreed. "I was afraid they'd run into advancing Rebels. But I haven't seen any evidence of Union troops retreating, have you?"

"Only McClellan."

"Bronwen," said her sister, "what can you see at the house?"

"That it's being used as a hospital."

"Then I need to be there." Kathryn began walking toward it, followed by Marsh and Natty. The dog trotted after them, but kept looking over his shoulder as if wanting to gather in the stragglers.

Bronwen stood debating with herself, having previously seen a field hospital in operation. And that one had not been behind a battlefield. She could not for the life of her understand Kathryn's composure—or what passed for composure—in the face of mangled bodies and gruesome surgical procedures.

Apparently neither could O'Hara, who told her, "I can forgo a hospital visit. I'm for taking a look at what Young Napoleon's missing."

"O'Hara, why this fixation with McClellan?"

"I though you'd never ask! But as usual, Red, your timing's rotten." He started forward, saying, "Are you coming?"

"I haven't the stomach for it or the field hospital either. I'll stay here and keep an eye on the others."

O'Hara trudged off, but the dog dashed after him as if

chasing a wayward sheep. "Hold onto that dog!" Bronwen shouted to Natty.

Marsh turned and yelled, "C'mon this way! We shouldn't be separating!"

Before she could say he was probably right, a barrage of cannon fire brought billowing smoke and Natty's shrieks of "Dog! Dog, stop!" as the boy ran past her.

She sprinted uphill after him. "Natty, you little fool! Come back here!"

With every boom of artillery the ground trembled and smoke rolled to envelop her, until Bronwen couldn't sense if Natty was anywhere near or not. And despite the cannon, she could now hear a swelling, tumultuous din made by men and horses. She crept forward, methodically scanning from side to side, but could not see the boy. Then unexpectedly, she found herself on level ground. Guarded steps took her into a relatively smokeless area at the crest of a gently sloping wheat field, where she stared straight into hell.

An inferno of bellowing men, stripped to the waist, were darting between ranks of roaring cannon spitting long orange flames. Cannoneers and weapons were blanketed with ash, and as withering heat rode over Bronwen, her eyes and nostrils burned from the scorching metal. At each earthshaking barrage, horses and mules wheeled in terror, lunging into the path of stretchermen who trudged in single file up the slope. In a patch of ground behind the cannon were a handful of youngsters, black-skinned and white, all of them huddled against the side of an ammunition wagon. Their terrified expressions, along with the tattered straw hats, denim trousers, and frayed cotton shirts they wore, made them likely to be Virginia farm boys, perhaps drawn here first by curiosity and now trapped in a howling tempest.

Bronwen, her eyes tearing from cinders, raised the

glasses to look farther down the slope. It appeared to be crawling, as wounded men clawed their way through a once golden field, where in places the harvested wheat still stood upright in tied shocks. She shakily moved the glasses to where ragged lines of gray were plunging from a woods to advance on solid ranks of blue positioned on a low ridge above them. When they met crackling musketry and hail-storms of shot, white Rebel faces became the dots on dominoes toppling backward before the sweeping Union fire.

Bursting from behind more trees, another brigade of Rebel infantry charged with bloodcurdling yells, battle flags swirling and fixed bayonets glinting red in the light of a fiery plummeting sun. As they advanced on the massed artillery, whole ranks of them were mown down, men and flags torn apart and strewn like husks of grain over the trampled field. And still they kept coming.

Bronwen stood stunned, wanting to look away and unable to do it, or to convince herself that Seth could not be down there. How long would Confederate command order troops to charge the entrenched Union artillery holding this higher ground? But when she found the will to move her glasses to the right, bloodied gray-jacketed corpses sprawled beyond the sharpshooters crouching behind shocks of wheat indicated that at some point the hold had nearly been broken.

She jumped at an explosion behind her, and spun toward it to see chunks of the ammunition wagon flaming to earth with what looked like straw-hatted rag dolls. Before she could fully grasp what she was seeing, men rushing forward with water buckets made her leap out of their way. She banged into another wagon, and was just regaining her balance when she was swept up and carried along by troops running in the direction of a frame house and two cabins that must be slave quarters. Straining to stay on her feet, she wormed herself sideways to the edge of the troops and staggered free short of the house just as a driving rain of shells and bullets hurtled overhead. Flinging herself to the ground, and desperately looking for cover, she saw something that made her blood chill.

Darting across the rutted slope adjacent to the cannon was Natty.

She scrambled to her feet and ran forward to tackle him, both of them rolling to within a few feet of some upended farm wagons near the cabins. Bronwen caught his legs and dragged him, struggling, behind the first squat structure.

"Are you crazy?" she yelled. "What are you doing here?"

"Dog! He runned away! I gotta find him!"

"No! We'll be lucky to get out of here alive!"

"There he is! Dog!" he screamed, wrenching free. "Dog, come 'ere!"

Before she could stop him he was tearing toward a unit of crouched soldiers, their weapons aimed at advancing Rebels. The dog, skidding to a halt well before he reached the Union troops, whirled around several times before dashing toward Natty. When the rifles fired, the dog launched himself forward a few feet before flattening to lie still. Bronwen thought surely he must have been hit, but an instant later, he began creeping forward. Natty had stopped, but now bolted again toward the dog.

As Bronwen went after him, another round of artillery blasted. She dropped in place, smoke smothering her, and began inching forward on her hands and knees, glancing back and forth to maintain her bearings and keep inside the trajectory of shrieking shells. And then she saw the boy. He was lying facedown over the dog, and from what she could pick out through the haze, neither of them was moving.

After another swarm of shells soared overhead, followed by a fierce volley of fire from the troops below her, the hellish noise seemed to abruptly diminish as she crept with heart thudding toward the motionless boy. But coming from out of nowhere, something struck her hard between the shoulder blades and shoved her into the churned earth. When she jerked her head up, it was to see Marsh stumbling toward Natty.

She heard a whistling sound, and a single shell exploded dead ahead. The light momentarily blinded her, but not before she had seen Marsh leap forward to throw himself over the boy. As she continued crawling toward them, she imagined someone was shouting her name, but she kept closing on the small heap of bodies now silhouetted in an eerie purple light. She was only a few yards from Marsh when another lone shell burst. The explosion knocked her flat, and burning pain shot through her left shoulder. It instantly receded, but when she tried climbing to her feet, her legs buckled under her. Just ahead lay Marsh's outstretched arm, so she squirmed forward on her belly and grasped his hand.

"Marsh? Natty? Are you okay? *Please say something!*"

With a surge of hope she saw Marsh moving, and then realized it was because Natty and the dog were wriggling out from underneath him. The boy was drenched with blood. The dog was not.

"Natty, you're hurt!"

"Nah, I ain't." He sat up unsteadily, glancing at the dog panting beside him. "Guess Dog's okay, too. But—"

He broke off when a third solitary shell went winging overhead, and dove head first into Bronwen with the dog burrowing into his shoulder. When the shell burst, it was a good distance away. She gave Marsh's hand another tug as she became aware that the cannon fire had ceased, and saw that the peculiar violet glow surrounding her was the light of a fading sunset.

An unfamiliar hush now seemed to hang suspended

from the darkening sky, while in the field below keened the terrible anguished cries of the wounded and dying. She could not bear to think that her brother might be among them. When a spasm of violent shudders seized her, she pressed her face into the stubbles of what had been vibrant golden wheat.

As she lay there, the echo of a long-ago voice from an all-but-forgotten pulpit whispered over her, and then passed on across the field with the soft rushing murmur of summer wind. *For Abel was a keeper of sheep, but Cain was a tiller of the ground . . . and the Lord said unto Cain, Where is Abel thy brother?*

Am I my brother's keeper?

The shudders were gradually subsiding, leaving in their stead a chill that flowed like ice water through her body.

From directly above her came another voice. "Red! For God's sake, Red, are you all right?"

It took a long time to register whose voice it was, although O'Hara had now dropped to one knee beside her.

"I'm all right, but I think Marsh was wounded by a shell," she finally managed to answer between chattering teeth. She shook his hand again. "Marsh, can you hear me?"

O'Hara draped a jacket around her shoulders, making her wince, and then he asked Natty something.

"Dog an' me're okay."

"Red, the firing's stopped, and they're saying the fight's about over, but we need to get out of here. You're shivering and your shoulder's bleeding . . . think you can stand up?"

"First see where Marsh is hurt."

O'Hara bent over him while she forced herself onto her knees, still holding Marsh's hand. There was so much blood dripping from her ripped left sleeve she couldn't see her upper arm. She also couldn't feel anything, until she tried to raise the arm and pain made her lightheaded. So don't move the arm, she told herself, wondering if dizziness was a sign she was about to faint. No, she couldn't do that.

She looked at O'Hara, who was upright again but saying nothing, just standing there and staring down at her. Natty and the dog were behind him, and the wide-eyed boy was silent, too. For both O'Hara and Natty, of all people, to be struck dumb at the same time was extraordinary enough to be disturbing. Maybe her injury was worse than it felt. Her sister would know. Where *was* Kathryn? She should be here to help Marsh. And someone should bring a blanket for him, because it was so cold.

"Marsh?" She pulled again on his limp hand. "Marsh, will you please answer me?"

O'Hara reached down and locked his arm around her waist as if to lift her. His breath felt warm on her cheek, the only thing she could feel, when he said, "Let go of his hand."

"O'Hara, you can't be listening, because I told you Marsh must be hurt."

"Bronwen!" he said sharply, and crouched in front of her. "Bronwen, look at me."

She tried to, but her eyes were watering too much to see him.

He grasped her chin and tilted her face toward him, then passed a hand several times in front of her eyes, saying, "You've lost a lot of blood and could be going into shock. I need to carry you to the field hospital. Put your arms around my neck and help me lift you. We have to leave *now*."

"We can't leave! When Marsh comes around there'll be no one here."

His arm circled her waist again, and tightened its grip.

"Bronwen, he won't come around. Marsh is dead."

Part Two

I am rather inclined to think that this is the land God gave to Cain.

— JACQUES CARTIER

When once the offensive has been assumed, it must be sustained to the last extremity. However skillful the maneuvers, a retreat will always weaken the morale of an army.

— NAPOLEON BONAPARTE

13

***

*The news from Richmond is so fearfully
bloody. . . . It is astonishing to see the* Boston
Journal *jubilant over a "victory" which leaves
twenty thousand of our men on the field, dead
or wounded.*

—Hannah Ropes, Washington, July 1862

Malvern House

Lanterns hooked over tree branches cast a sickly yellow
glow over the swirling pandemonium of wounded flooding
from the battlefield. Kathryn, working at one of the dressing stations in the path of the flood, resolved time and
again to remain numb and concentrate solely on the suffering man directly before her. It was the only way, she
had learned, to avoid being overwhelmed, and thus useless,
in the face of such immense need. Even so, she could not
keep herself from glancing anxiously over the endless,
blood-soaked torrent. Hundreds of men were being
brought shrieking on litters, and even more were somehow
managing to stagger in on their own or with the support
of fellow soldiers. Union casualties, it was now estimated,
would number in the thousands.

Recent arrivals confirmed that at dusk the battle had
finally ended. These men's voices held an almost palpable
sense of satisfaction and self-respect, since theirs had been

a hard-fought, decisive victory. Kathryn had heard count-less hoarse shouts of "On to Richmond!"

But where were her sister and the others?

At first she had been eager to tell Bronwen some hopeful news. A wounded officer had said their brother's New York regiment, held in reserve today, had by early afternoon started the march south to Harrison's Landing. But now concern overrode the comfort Kathryn took from that news, because nearly an hour had passed since the last can-non thundered into Malvern Hill's gathering darkness. *Where were the others?*

And then, her heart all but stopping, she saw them com-ing, somewhat removed from the soldiers streaming from the hill. Natty's head drooped, and his shirt and trousers seemed to be drenched in blood as he stumbled alongside O'Hara. O'Hara, who was staggering under the weight of Marsh carried over one of his shoulders, had his free arm clamped around Bronwen's waist and was dragging her forward. She looked deathly pale, and blood dripped from her left arm with every forced step. To Kathryn's fright-ened gaze, only the circling dog appeared to be whole.

She snatched up a blanket and a fistful of cotton band-aging, rushing to them as O'Hara released her sister and lowered Marsh to the ground. When Bronwen sank shiv-ering to her knees, Kathryn knelt beside her, still collected enough to note the clammy skin and to gently wrap the blanket around the hunched shoulders.

"Bronwen? Bronwen, can you hear me?" said Kathryn, her softly voiced question laced with dread. At the same time, she began tying a tourniquet just below her sister's left shoulder, having found the source of the bleeding.

She received no response.

"I think she's in shock," O'Hara said. "Took shrapnel in her arm, and she's lost a lot of blood."

Kathryn had seen that Natty was apparently not seriously hurt in spite of the blood, but a look down at the motionless body at her feet made her eyes fill even before she asked, "And Marsh?"

O'Hara shook his head.

"Dear Lord, no!" Kathryn whispered, but there was no time to grieve when her sister so obviously needed help.

They should move, since what had now become a broad river of walking wounded meant soldiers had to stumble around them. Kathryn could not completely control her tears, but she forced enough discipline on herself to tell O'Hara, "Please carry Bronwen around to the rear of the house. It's less crowded than the front. And Natty, are you all right?"

"Yeah, I am, but kin you fix her?" he said, pointing at Bronwen.

"I pray so."

O'Hara swept up the frighteningly mute Bronwen, and they rounded the house to where it was less congested; some of the regimental surgeons had relocated there, and stewards had roped off the area around the operating tables. Those of the waiting soldiers who could still stand were being herded into long queues. Stretchermen deposited the others on piles of straw.

Kathryn gave the tables a wide berth. The fumes of chloroform could somewhat mask the smells of blood and vomit and urine, but they could not disguise the rising mounds of amputated limbs. She led O'Hara to a patch of trampled grass well beyond the farthest table, which was clearly a door of the house ripped from its hinges, and where the only light came from sperm candles and small campfires.

"Natty, there are blankets folded under that nearest operating table. Would you please fetch one?"

When he came back with it, he looked so shaken that he was nearly as white as Bronwen. After he and Kathryn spread the blanket on the ground, O'Hara eased her sister onto the center of it and pulled the remaining part around her. She was still shivering as Kathryn quickly untied the tourniquet and pressed wads of cotton lint to the bleeding arm.

"Hold this cotton in place," she said to O'Hara, "while I try to find some forceps and—"

She broke off at the sight of a lanky, curly-haired man with blood-streaked linen apron loping toward them from one of the tables.

"Thought I saw you, Miss Llyr," he said, pushing his wire-rimmed spectacles back in place. "And is this your sister?"

"Yes, Dr. Rosen. I was about to try removing the shrapnel in her arm myself because . . . well, there are so many wounded soldiers . . ." Her voice trailed off.

"From what I've heard, she's a soldier too, isn't she?" he said matter-of-factly, bending down and waving O'Hara back. "I need more light."

Natty dashed off, returning almost immediately with a lantern. Since he had survived on the streets of Washington due to his skill as a pickpocket, Kathryn did not ask how he acquired it. Neither did anyone else.

The surgeon withdrew a forceps from the pocket of his apron, along with a white-tipped probe that would show gray marks when it contacted metal. Kathryn, not wanting to appear ungrateful or meddling, had to push herself to murmur, "Dr. Rosen, may I please put those instruments in the fire first?"

He gave her a wry smile. "So Gregg has indoctrinated you, too? Yes, go ahead—his ideas about infection may prove sound. In the meantime, you others find me some clean water. It's being hauled in barrels from the river to the front of the house. Find some whiskey, too."

Micah Rosen had gone to medical school with Gregg

Travis, and it was Gregg who had sent for him, a civilian surgeon, to bolster the inadequate supply of army medical doctors. Kathryn had first met Rosen while nursing in a makeshift Washington infirmary under Gregg's supervision. When she had arrived here at Malvern House earlier, the male nurses and surgeons either ignored her or demanded that she leave. It had been Dr. Rosen who vouched for her experience and urged that she be allowed to assist. Once the number of incoming wounded began skyrocketing, there had been no further objections.

Whiskey arrived, and Bronwen swallowed some in compliant silence. After Kathryn cleaned her arm and swabbed it with carbolic acid, as Gregg insisted on before all his surgeries, Dr. Rosen swiftly probed for and extracted the shrapnel. Thankfully, three of the four jagged pieces were not deeply embedded. Bronwen's jaw was rigid, and she made little sound other than the groans escaping between her clenched teeth, but sweat broke out on her forehead and tears coursed down her face. Natty, after persistently asking to hold the lantern, seemed to be transfixed by the procedure. Kathryn managed to pour much of a tin cup of beef broth into her sister, and O'Hara drank what remained. His expression said he would have preferred the whiskey.

When at one point he squatted beside Bronwen and asked, "Are you okay, Red?" she stared at him as if he were a stranger.

"She hasn't said anything yet," Kathryn told Rosen. "But she isn't in shock, is she?"

"Not dangerously so. She does seem withdrawn, which isn't particularly unusual. Didn't you say she just came off the battlefield—and after losing a friend?"

"Yes, we all lost a friend," Kathryn said, the tears welling again, and she glanced at O'Hara. His face held no emotion, and she wondered if it was as forced a façade as the one she was attempting with such meager success.

"Is Red gonna be okay?" a sober-faced Natty asked Dr. Rosen. Kathryn suddenly realized he had never called Bronwen anything other than "You," or "she" and "her." O'Hara used "Red" to annoy her, at least he had originally, and he was now studying Natty with an unreadable look.

"She's lost a good amount of blood," Dr. Rosen told him, "and there's the threat of infection. But unless the shrapnel has shattered bone—and right now I can't find any evidence of that—we'll hope for the best. She seems healthy otherwise."

"Yeah, 'cept fer now, she's tuff as a alley cat."

After Rosen used a few sutures to close the lacerated edges of the worst gash, Kathryn again swabbed the affected area with carbolic. While she bandaged the arm with wads of lint held in place by cotton strips, the surgeon got to his feet saying, "You know what to look for. Give her liquids and keep her warm, but at the first sign of infection . . . well, let's hope there isn't any."

Kathryn knew he meant if bone had been shattered and infection occurred, amputation of the arm would probably be necessary. In which case she feared Bronwen would prefer to die.

"Thank you, Dr. Rosen. I'm very grateful."

He stood surveying the efforts being made by regimental stewards to impose some sort of order, and said, "They're moving several of the dressing stations back here, so work at one of those to keep an eye on your sister. And you can assist me if needed."

He dipped his hands into a bucket of water, and while wiping them on a square of cotton Kathryn handed him, said to her, "When this nightmare is over, perhaps you'll tell me why you left White House Landing so abruptly."

When she said nothing, Rosen added quietly, "Gregg's been trying to find you, Kathryn. He's gone on ahead to set up surgical units at Harrison's Landing, but given the resounding victory here tonight, a retreat now seems less likely."

Kathryn nodded, thanking him again. He walked briskly back to the surgery table, as if he had just come from a ten-minute respite.

WHILE wrapping a length of bandaging around a sergeant's shredded calf, Kathryn glanced once again at her sister. Bronwen now sat on the blanket close to a nearby campfire, her back against the base of an elm and knees drawn under her chin, staring upward at dispersing streamers of battle smoke. Although she had stopped shivering, she had not uttered a single word since reaching Malvern House.

Kathryn finished the bandaging, certain a bullet was embedded in the sergeant's leg and should be removed without delay, but equally certain he would have a long wait before a surgeon could see him. There were too many wounded and too few doctors. Even more disturbing were the reports of untold legions of men still lying in torment on Malvern Hill. An ambulance driver said the devastated wheat field was dotted with winking lanterns, as both Union and Confederate workers attempted to retrieve their thousands of wounded. Often these workers, who had earlier been enemies with orders to kill, now passed within several yards of one another in an effort to save. They passed in silence and without confrontation.

"I'm obliged, miss," the sergeant said to her, and hobbled to the end of a line of others waiting quietly, patiently, for one of the surgeons. Most of them, even ones in severe pain, were showing signs of the lassitude Kathryn had observed once before in troops following a brutal battle. It seemed different from straightforward exhaustion, and as if these men, fierce warriors just hours ago, were now so drained they could not even summon the will to fear death.

As another soldier shuffled toward her, holding a rag to his forehead, Kathryn gestured to O'Hara, who was coming from the rear door of Malvern House. "Could you please check Bronwen's arm for signs of infection?"

"What do I look for?"

"Purple-red streaks or swelling from the edges of the bandaging."

He was just picking up Natty's lantern, which Kathryn had been using, when a sudden gust of cheering came from those nearest the house. She saw a handsome, black-mustached officer in spotless uniform, and mounted magnificently on a chestnut horse, rounding the staff tents as if reviewing troops. When the officer removed his hat with a sweeping flourish, the volume of cheers rose.

At her shoulder, O'Hara made an unintelligible remark.

"Who is that?" she asked him, although she had a pretty good idea.

"It's Young Napoleon himself," O'Hara muttered. "Just arrived from his safely removed bunker to inspect the battle lines—now the battle's over."

His biting tone made Kathryn cringe as she turned back to the soldier.

In the course of the next few hours, army and navy officers came and went through the doors of the temporary command headquarters. They included, Kathryn learned from those she tended, the artillery commander, Colonel Hunt, whose guns had so effectively held Malvern Hill. The day's victory had prevented the Confederate army, after nearly a week of aggressive and unforeseen assaults, from reaching and destroying the miles of vulnerable Union troops and supply wagon trains stealthily retreating southeast to the James. The Army of the Potomac had been saved, but at very great cost. And McClellan had been driven from his position at the gates of Richmond.

At one point, when raised voices began coming through the open windows, someone slammed the windows shut with a series of sharp bangs, and rumors of Rebel snipers sent waves of alarm rippling through the field hospital. Adding to the misery of the wounded was a light rain.

After O'Hara reported no change in Bronwen's arm, he had gone to station himself below a window near Malvern House's rear entrance door. Bronwen rested her head on her knees, while Natty and the dog curled up beside her on the blanket and slept. Uncomplaining wounded continued to wait for exhausted surgeons. Hundreds died as they waited, and from somewhere at the fringes of candle and firelight came the thuds of earth being thrown by gravediggers. There were so many dead that Marsh had been buried in a common grave.

Kathryn was checking Bronwen's arm herself when a sudden flurry of activity at the house brought O'Hara sprinting back from his window post, just before several officers came striding through the rear doorway.

An unmistakably enraged voice could be heard saying, "This can only be prompted by cowardice or treason!"

"We should *advance*, not withdraw," another snapped. "Stealing away in the night after such a victory is galling!"

Kathryn, kneeling beside Bronwen, said to O'Hara, "Do you know what they mean?"

"Yes, good eavesdropping agent that I am, I do know." He glanced down at Bronwen before saying, "McClellan has ordered a full retreat."

"A retreat?" Kathryn repeated blankly, as Bronwen stirred on the blanket. "When?"

"Now."

"*Now?* No, that can't be!" Kathryn objected, quickly getting to her feet. "What will happen to these injured men? And the ones still on the battlefield? There aren't anywhere near enough ambulance wagons to transport them."

"Now," said O'Hara again.

For some reason he had bent down and was groping under a corner of the blanket. While Kathryn desperately tried to grasp this inexplicable order, which could amount to a death sentence for the severely wounded here, O'Hara yanked out a leather cartridge pouch. Pulling his revolver out of its holster, he began to load the gun.

"Why are you doing that?" she whispered.

"To amuse myself." His lowered voice was edged with malice and, looking at Bronwen sideways, he added, "Thought maybe I'd bag myself a general."

Startled, Kathryn protested, "How in heaven's name can you joke at a time like this?" and looked around to see who might have overheard.

"Why assume I'm joking?" O'Hara's voice was still lowered but even more malicious. "Our exalted commander plans to abandon these soldiers to die or be captured, so I think he should at least keep them company."

Few of the nearby soldiers were regarding O'Hara with anything but faint curiosity, and Kathryn just hoped they hadn't heard what he said. They must not have, because no one moved to block his way when he raised the revolver and turned toward the house.

She thought his incongruous tomfoolery should be stopped, but didn't know what, if anything, she could do. Starting toward him, she caught from the corner of her eye a sudden blur of movement. In what seemed less than a split-second, Bronwen was standing behind O'Hara, the stiletto gripped in her right hand, its glinting blade held against the side of his neck. A single twist of her wrist, and the blade would slice straight through a carotid artery.

"Put it down, O'Hara."

Her voice sounded hoarse, and though not loud it must have carried to the first soldiers in line. Several of them started hesitantly toward her and O'Hara, but their faces reflected more confusion than anything else.

"Put it down!" repeated Bronwen, her voice stronger.

O'Hara's mouth twitched slightly before it stretched into his usual incandescent grin, and he lowered the gun. When Bronwen moved the stiletto aside, he slowly turned his head, his gaze going beyond her to the soldiers.

"At ease, men!" he chuckled, his eyes alight with what might have been mischief. "And welcome home, Red! Figured something was needed to jolt you back into life. This is no time to be lying down on the job."

Bronwen's only response was to motion with the stiletto toward the revolver. The soldiers, who had stopped a few yards away, still appeared bewildered.

O'Hara made an elaborate show of returning the gun to its holster. "Just indulging a whimsy, Red—no need to look so damn grim," he laughed, gesturing toward the soldiers. "And call off the palace guards."

Wordlessly, Bronwen dropped her hand to her side and backed into the stunned Kathryn, sagging against her as if the effort had taken whatever strength she had left. She seemed drained, like the soldiers, and now ignored O'Hara. It was almost as though she were sleepwalking. Or had been.

And Kathryn, slipping an arm around Bronwen's shoulders, was forced to wonder if her sister's actions had been fully conscious ones. Could they instead have been instinctive? If so, her distrust of O'Hara must have deep roots. She would know far better than Kathryn, who had met O'Hara only once before, what he was capable of doing and what he *would* do. Had her reaction been only because of his very public loathing of McClellan, or had it been something less obvious? Much of O'Hara's charm lay not only in his boyish good looks but also in his refusal to take anything too seriously, both of which made it easy to forget he was an intelligence agent. Was his allegiance to Treasury, and thus to the Federal government, what Bronwen distrusted?

The soldiers, looking relieved and a little sheepish, limped back into line. A few had even smiled at O'Hara's infectious laughter. But only moments later an outburst of frenzied activity at the house, with officers shouting commands and wheeling their horses toward the river road, sent the field hospital spiraling into chaos.

The order had come to move out.

14

—⚬—

[It was] ... a regular stampede, each man going off on his own hook, guns in the road at full gallop, teams on one side in the fields, infantry on the other in the woods.
—Captain Richard Auchmuty, USA, July 1862

River Road

The midnight showers had become by now more fog than rain, and dawn's first light filtered through a weeping gray mist that shrouded the road. Although the word "road," Kathryn thought bleakly, did not begin to describe the rutted swath of clumped red mud they were struggling to walk. The bottom of her skirt was crusted with dirt, but she was too tired to keep lifting its hem. Barely visible to her right stood the ugly raw stumps of what had been woodland, the pines nearest the road having been felled for bonfires to light the path of retreat.

"Watch those sparks!" Micah Rosen warned as fresh-cut wood once again sent them arcing over the road.

Wearily Kathryn nodded and moved aside, batting at the few sparks that landed on her skirt, while the smell of burning southern pine brought a wrenching image of home and a northern Christmas. Trampled fields lay to her left, whatever crops had been growing there now ground to dust by countless wheels, hooves of horses and mules, and many thousands of thumping feet.

When she stumbled avoiding a rain puddle, it rattled the few remaining bottles of chloroform and opium pills she carried stowed with bandages in a canvas bag. She felt a hand lightly touch her wrist, together with a quiet, "How are you faring?"

"All right, Dr. Rosen." She paused to adjust the strap of the bag hanging from her shoulder.

"Since we are swimming upstream in what appears to be the River Styx, Kathryn, I think we can dispense with formality."

At another time she would have smiled. Now she only murmured, "I would think so, Micah," and cast a sideways glance at his ordinary but thoroughly likable face. Without his spectacles, which he said were too fogged to be useful, he faintly resembled Abraham Lincoln, if the president had owned light brown hair and eyes of the same unremarkable color. He carried large canvas bags slung over both shoulders.

"Hey, doc!" yelled a soldier ahead of them in one of the last ambulance wagons. "Can you give us a hand here, doc?" The wagon was bumping noisily to a halt.

Dr. Rosen and Kathryn hurried forward at the edge of the road, dimly illuminated by the dying bonfires and candles sputtering their last. He climbed into the canvas-covered wagon while Kathryn waited below. The previous call for help, from the ambulance in front of this one, had required the surgeon to stop the blood flow from a soldier's arteries by tying ligatures, while he knelt in the wagon lit only by candles. A short time ago, he had performed another roadside amputation, and Kathryn now worried because she had so little chloroform left.

"Miss," another soldier called down to her, "there's a

couple men here who're in real bad pain. You got anything that could help?"

Nodding, she handed him up some opium pills wrapped in a small strip of cotton. "Do you need any more bandages?" she asked.

"No, but thank you kindly, miss. Most here've either stopped bleedin' 'cause they's dead, or wish they'd die and get it done with."

Dr. Rosen was bending over one of the soldiers lying on straw strewn over the wagon's rough-planked floor. A minute later he straightened, shaking his head.

After he climbed down and the wagon jolted forward, Kathryn didn't ask the outcome. They had been through the same sad event too many times since abandoning the field hospital.

"We can't leave these men," Kathryn had protested over and over as the chaotic evacuation swirled around Malvern House. "And there are still soldiers lying out there on the battlefield. In the rain!"

"Miss, we've got our orders," the attendants had kept telling her. "Rebs could strike again at first light, so we have to leave!"

Others had shouted over the din to the injured soldiers, "Any of you men who can walk, c'mon! Get moving!"

Rain drizzled over officers and enlisted men alike in the roiling bedlam, while Kathryn resolutely continued to clean and bandage. The deafening clamor rose and fell as more and more regiments departed, followed by wounded who could barely manage to hobble after them.

Dr. Rosen had argued against the evacuation for nearly two hours, saying he wanted to remain there regardless of what the "damned order says." But he finally told Kathryn, "I'm afraid there's no choice, Miss Llyr. I've been directed to leave because I'm a civilian, and threatened with immediate arrest if I don't. But my arrest isn't going to help the men who *can* be transported and badly need medical treatment."

"It's heartless beyond measure, and I don't care if they do arrest me," she replied.

"I think maybe you'd better care," said O'Hara. "If you're forcibly removed—and you will be—your sister's going to be left in the lurch. If the Rebs arrive—and they will—I doubt you want her to be captured. In case you need reminding, she's probably on every Wanted list in Richmond."

Kathryn hadn't thought of that, and her resolve faded when she realized that O'Hara could be right.

"Those last ambulance wagons are leaving now," he went on. "It's eight or nine miles to Harrison's Landing, and the wounded will need help when they get there."

"One of the army surgeons, John Swinburne, told me," said Micah, "that he and a few other medical officers have been granted permission to stay. And if the medical service at Harrison's Landing authorizes it, the unloaded ambulances can return to retrieve the rest of those here who . . ."

His voice had trailed off, but he clearly meant "those who are still alive."

Kathryn would never forget the faces of the worst-wounded when they learned they were being abandoned. Their heartbreaking cries and pleas and curses still echoed in her mind. She had stumbled away, half-blinded by tears of remorse and fury, and prayed she could be forgiven for wishing that O'Hara *had* intended to shoot McClellan.

Now, as she and Micah Rosen resumed walking, she glanced back at a small open cart of medical supplies, one of the last in the long, disordered train from Malvern House. By the dawning gray light she saw to her chagrin that Bronwen was walking alongside it. The dog was trotting at her heels, but Kathryn hoped Natty was still asleep in the cart. There was no sign of O'Hara, who had disappeared shortly after they descended the slope to River Road.

She stopped and waited for the mule and cart to catch up. "You shouldn't be taxing yourself, Bronwen. You promised to ride."

"I did ride. And I'm fine——" She broke off with a flinch of her shoulders, the words undoubtedly recalling Marsh's repeated phrase.

"I'm all right," she mumbled, staring at her feet.

"But you're not."

"I need to walk."

"You lost a great deal of blood and you're still frighteningly pale. And your arm needs to heal."

"The arm's okay. I know you mean well, Kathryn, but please, just let me be."

As they went forward, Micah Rosen looked questioningly over his shoulder, but Kathryn waved him on. It would be futile to argue further with Bronwen. She had never needed to be concerned about her health, but now she acted as if her well-being didn't matter in the least. And profound grief, Kathryn had learned, could often do that.

"Bronwen," she began, desperately wanting to ease her sister's misery, "I spent time with Marsh at Chimborazo, and I miss him, too. But it helps me to remember that he died saving another's life, and——"

"I don't want to talk about it," Bronwen interrupted. "Not now, and not ever. Please, Kathryn, please just leave me alone."

Kathryn could have disregarded bitterness or anger, which was what she had expected to hear, but the plaintive sorrow in her sister's voice silenced her. It sounded so completely unlike Bronwen that it was disorienting, in the way it would be if an eagle began cooing like a dove.

The rain had commenced again in earnest. What had formerly been showers became a steady downpour. The dirt underfoot had liquefied to the consistency of sludge, and the mule brayed in complaint with every unwilling step. Its driver jumped down and took hold of its harness to tug it forward, while its hindquarters lowered in resistance.

For some minutes there had been more agitated shouting than usual from up the road. Now its volume was sharply escalating, and Kathryn thought she also heard bursts of artillery. The ambulance wagon ahead slowed and then halted, bringing a hand signal from Micah.

"What's happened?" Kathryn asked when he walked back to them.

There had been constant warnings of possible Confederate attacks at dawn, which must have intimidated General McClellan more than it did his officers, because he was said to have again boarded the ironclad *Galena*.

"No one knows where that firing is coming from, but rain's making the road a sea of mud," Micah said with a worried expression. "The artillery wagons are sinking hub-deep in it, and all the vehicles up ahead are stopped, or else they've been abandoned. An ambulance driver said some of them are even being burned. Needless to say the road's completely clogged and nothing is moving."

"We ain't there *yet*?" came a grumbled complaint as Natty jumped from the cart. "So how fer is thet there Harry-son's Land?"

"Probably another mile," Micah told him.

"One and a half," corrected Bronwen unexpectedly.

"The men in those two ambulances ahead are in rough shape, and most of them need surgery," Micah said. "I doubt some can survive much longer without it."

The cart driver joined them, and the driver of the ambulance approached, too, asking, "What d'we do, doc?

Could be hours, maybe even a day or two, 'fore the road's cleared. Don't like them sounds of artillery none, neither. We're sittin' ducks here."

Micah was shaking his head helplessly as calls for medical assistance came from the two ambulances.

At another eruption of artillery fire, Kathryn and the others looked anxiously toward the woods, half-expecting to see a Rebel brigade hurtling from the pines. Her mind was so clouded by lack of sleep that she couldn't think straight. She heard Bronwen suddenly ask the ambulance driver, "How many mules do you have up there?"

"One's all they lemme have."

She frowned in concentration, and then pointed to the supply cart's obstinate mule. "If we unhitch this one and harness it with the other, it may be less likely to balk."

"You some kinda expert on mules?" the cart driver said dubiously.

"I'm an expert on stubbornness." Bronwen turned to Micah, saying, "The most-needed medical supplies can be unloaded from the cart and distributed between both ambulances ahead. Since the road's not passable, and you say those wounded men have no time to spare, we'll have to cross the fields. I know the way to Harrison's Landing."

"There ain't no more room in them ambulances," the driver objected.

"Aren't some of those men dead?"

"Yeah," he said. "Doc here can tell you that."

Bronwen looked at Micah Rosen. "How many?"

"Four, so far."

"Bronwen," Kathryn began, relieved to see her sister come to life, but troubled by what she was implying, "if you mean to abandon those men's remains—"

"They can be buried later. We can't just wait here to be fired on or captured, and shouldn't the ones still living be given a chance to survive?"

"But it seems so . . ." Kathryn stopped, groping for words, but at another rumble of artillery the two drivers started at a run for the ambulances.

"She's tuff as a alley cat," Natty said, casting a glance at Bronwen, and his voice held a foreign note of respect.

THE artillery fire became louder and more distinct before it abruptly ceased. It was almost noon and pouring rain when the wagons jounced across a last trampled field of what had been ripened wheat, the few stalks of it still standing as high as the mules' backs. All but the most incapacitated wounded were struggling forward on foot. The ground, saturated with water, was more swamp than field, and with every step Kathryn wondered if she would be the first to drop from fatigue. But at last they had apparently reached the field's crest, because Bronwen was pointing southeast to a vast, sodden plain sloping to the river.

"There's the James, and Harrison's Landing. Not exactly what I'd describe as the Promised Land."

"No," Kathryn agreed reluctantly, "it looks more like land where the Lord exiled Cain."

Directly below them was yet another Virginia field churned by thousands of troops, but unlike Malvern Hill, this one had become a sea of liquid soil. Everything visible was awash in mud, both men and horses forced to wallow through it, and even the oil blankets that soldiers were rigging as tents were caked with it. The scene looked, Kathryn thought, like the ancient world east of Eden must have looked when the waters of the Flood began to recede.

Beyond, on the broad gray breast of the James, rose the masts and smokestacks of what must be scores of Union supply and war ships.

Kathryn glanced with concern at her sister. Bronwen

looked chalk-white and was undoubtedly in pain, although she kept denying it. She held her left arm at an unnatural angle and gripped the side of the wagon with her right hand as if afraid her legs would give way.

"I ain't takin' no wagon down in that muck," Kathryn heard the driver tell Micah Rosen. "Mules'll sink up to their ears in it. What now, doc?"

"I'm hungry," announced Natty for perhaps the tenth time. The only food any of them had eaten for hours was ripe cherries from a tree somehow overlooked by the passing troops.

"Berkeley's plantation house is probably being used as a field hospital," Bronwen said. "It's straight ahead on this high ground."

She started to point with her left hand, but after raising her arm, she slumped limply against the wagon, grasping the elbow of the injured arm with her other hand. Her face was so pale that the few freckles on her nose resembled nutmeg speckling the cream of yuletide eggnog. Kathryn had time to wonder only briefly why the image of Christmas kept coming to her in July, and when the world around her so plainly belonged to Cain and not to a prince of peace.

Knowing Bronwen would reject any offer of help, Kathryn had to clench her teeth to contain her distress when Micah said to her sister, "Miss Llyr, you should be in a wagon."

"There's no room," was Bronwen's reply over her shoulder as she started forward. "Let's just get to the house with these wounded."

After a glance at the ambulances, Micah didn't argue, but followed her.

Kathryn noted that Bronwen, like herself, was continually scanning the drawn faces of soldiers they passed in hope of seeing their brother. Not only did the bedraggled troops seem exhausted, but they also held a sullen dispirited look, as if it was they, and not the Confederates, who had been defeated at Malvern Hill. Some of their officers were still muttering angrily about the disgrace of a victorious army leaving its wounded behind on the battlefield.

Another hike over a wheat field of an adjacent plantation brought the ambulances within hailing distance of Berkeley's stately, three-story brick mansion. It and several smaller structures were surrounded by stumps of what had likely been fruit trees, chopped down by the soldiers to use as tent poles.

"I'm gonna go git somethin' to eat," declared Natty. "Where there's sol-jurs, there's gotta be food." After muttering to the dog, they went off toward one of the smaller buildings. Kathryn was too tired to object.

"I'll go ahead and find assistance to unload the wounded," Micah said, and started toward the mansion.

Bronwen, after taking one lurching step after him, crumpled to the ground. Kathryn was beside her in a minute and even before lifting one of Bronwen's eyelids, she feared this was no harmless fainting spell.

15

Lo, in that house of misery
A lady with a lamp I see
Pass through the glimmering gloom
And flit from room to room.
              —Henry Wadsworth Longfellow

Berkeley Plantation House

Kathryn hurried over the threshold and into the mansion's immense entry hall just ahead of a sympathetic soldier who had offered to carry her sister. Bronwen had come to her senses momentarily, but then seemed to fall back into a semi-conscious state. That she didn't resist being slung over the soldier's shoulder was to Kathryn a telling sign of her sister's weakened spirit.

"Please wait," she said to the soldier as she surveyed the tragic aftermath of the battlefield.

Nearly every square inch of the floor held muddied, bleeding, and dying men. Some of them sprawled across thick-napped green-and-gold Brussels carpets, and others slumped over richly upholstered chairs and sofas that had been shoved back along the wainscoted walls. The green-flocked wallpaper was already stained with countless, large rust-colored splatters. A quantity of gold velvet draperies, ripped from windows for use as blankets, cast a soft if bizarre glow over the suffering, much as if sunlight were gilding the garden of Gethsemane. The army medical attendants, stepping gingerly around the wounded, were trying to determine which ones most urgently needed surgery.

"Miss Llyr, there's no place to set your sister down," said the soldier. "Where should I take her?"

"I don't know where until I locate Dr. Rosen," she answered, wondering how she would ever find him in this floodtide of misery. Her legs were beginning to tremble, and fatigue washed over her as she scanned the spacious entry, which was more ornate than many a Northern town's concert hall. It was not lost on her that Berkeley Plantation's mansion portrayed an opulent way of life that most white Southerners were willing to die to preserve, including the majority of them who owned neither mansions nor slaves.

At last she spotted Micah just inside an archway that led to a high-ceilinged drawing room. He was speaking to a tall, black-haired man in uniform who stood with his back to her, and in relief Kathryn started toward them. But then something in the uniformed man's stance made her hesitate, and when he pivoted toward the hall in a forceful manner, it jarred her into recognition even before his strong features did. Despite a nearly irresistible urge to bolt, her sister's plight kept her there.

She should have been prepared, because she recalled Micah telling her that Gregg Travis was bound for Harrison's Landing; so much had happened in the interim she must have thrust it to the back of her mind. His gaze was now sweeping relentlessly over the hall, and caught off guard as she'd been, her cheeks burned with an uncontrollable flush. When he found her, she averted her eyes.

Micah, after wading toward her through the ocean of wounded, told her, "Gregg said to take your sister into the study at the end of this hallway. He's using it for his field office."

Before she could think of an alternative, the soldier carrying Bronwen had started down the hall. Kathryn followed him until he paused before the last door, which was standing open.

"Is this the one, miss?" he asked her.

She looked into the room and nodded reluctantly, having seen a Queen Anne's pier table overflowing with paper folders and haphazardly stacked medical journals, and a mahogany desk holding a familiar, battered black surgeon's case.

After the soldier lowered Bronwen onto a sofa set between two heavily draperied windows, Kathryn voiced her gratitude.

"Glad to do it, miss. Guess you wouldn't remember, but you patched me up at Seven Pines. Made sure I got fed, too, and I thank you for it."

As he left, Kathryn hurried to the sofa, skirting the clumps of mud left on a thick maroon-and-cream rug that looked to be an Aubusson.

Bronwen startled her by mumbling, "Where are we?"

Kneeling beside her, Kathryn answered, "We're inside Berkeley's plantation house. How long have you been conscious?"

"Long enough to know I'm not dead."

"Let me examine your arm."

"Kathryn, please don't fret. I'm fi—" Her voice broke off, the echo of Marsh's "I'm *fine!*" hanging ghost-like in the air.

"You are not *fine*," Kathryn said, hoping that by saying it aloud the haunting echo would be exorcised. "You fainted dead away and you're white as a sheet. And I wish you'd stop acting so heroic! For one thing, I've seen too many men do it to convince themselves they're fearless, when they're really scared to death."

"An interesting observation," came a crisp, commanding voice from the doorway.

Kathryn quickly got to her feet as Gregg Travis rounded the table, coming to stand within a yard of her. When the smell of lye soap, ether, and pipe tobacco reached her, it evoked a painful memory of their last words at White House Landing's field hospital. Although several weeks had passed since then, it seemed like only yesterday. At the time she had just learned of the looming peril in Richmond for Seth, imprisoned under a death sentence, and for Bronwen, who had vowed to free him. The ultimatum Gregg had angrily given her then had not lost its sting: "Your obligations are here, Kathryn, and if you chose to disobey my orders and leave for Richmond, then do *not* come back!"

She had not seen him again until now. But if he held the same memory—and Kathryn couldn't imagine he failed to remember that day—his manner gave no evidence of it. He began in typically abrupt fashion by saying, "I've had reports on the bloodbath at Malvern Hill."

After she did not respond, his intense dark eyes searched her face, and his tone was not as crisp when he said, "You look tired, but are you otherwise well?"

"I am," she answered guardedly, "but Bronwen was injured by shrapnel." She looked at her sister, who seemed to be asleep.

Gregg glanced at Bronwen, nodding as if he already knew this. "Micah's told me some of what happened. He also said you worked through the night, and then walked the entire way here. Obviously you need rest."

He gestured toward a cot in the corner that Kathryn barely took in, so troubled was she by his lack of reference to that day at White House Landing. Did he think his words would be erased if left unmentioned?

Taking off his uniform jacket and slinging it over the desk chair, he said, "I had that cot brought in for myself. I arrived here earlier, during some enemy fire, and haven't used it. I haven't even begun surgery yet."

"I don't know if Dr. Rosen also told you," she said, determined to keep her distress concealed, "that the order to evacuate the field hospital came very suddenly. We were forced to leave behind more than a thousand wounded, some of them still on the battlefield."

"I'm aware of that."

"My understanding was that after the ambulance wagons were unloaded here, those men could be retrieved."

When he didn't immediately reply, she added, "I want to return with those wagons."

"You are sorely needed in the surgical unit here," he said in what was clearly an evasion and unlike him.

"I want to return," she repeated.

"We'll talk after you've had some sleep."

"I don't want sleep at the expense of—"

"You cannot go back, Kathryn!" he interrupted, his tone shifting from conciliatory to an unyielding one she had heard before. "We are in very real danger of renewed enemy attack. Now, I've said all I'm at liberty to say about evacuating those still at Malvern Hill."

Even though she knew it would be futile to persist, her conscience would have made her try had it not been for Bronwen's condition.

"My surgery," he went on, "will be located in the large dining room off the hall. It holds a priceless Chippendale table and chairs that will likely serve us better than they did their owners. After you've slept, come there."

Kathryn glanced again at Bronwen and saw with alarm that if possible, she was paler, her breathing seemed harsher, and her eyelids were fluttering as if too heavy to lift. She brushed past Gregg to kneel beside the sofa.

"Bronwen? Bronwen, if you can hear me, open your eyes." Receiving no response, Kathryn grasped her sister's wrist. When she found the pulse, its beat seemed steady enough, but when Bronwen's eyes opened their pupils were huge and black, only a narrow ring of green still visible.

By now Gregg was also bending over her, gripping her other wrist. "Move aside," he said to Kathryn, the brisk efficiency in his voice making her own pulse somewhat slow its racing pace.

"She collapsed right after we arrived here," Kathryn told him, "but she had insisted on walking two-thirds of the distance."

"Which, I assume, did not surprise you," he said dryly. "Her pulse is stable, but let's have a look at that arm. I need more light, so pull back those draperies."

As he unwrapped the bandaging, Kathryn watched with apprehension as the cotton strips fell away. While three of the four wounds had closed cleanly with only a trace of pink in the surrounding flesh, the fourth made her rock forward with a moan. The flesh between and around the stitches was purple and swollen. There was also an inflamed-looking welt at one edge that had not been present before.

"Get my instrument case on the table," Gregg told her. "The carbolic's there, too—did you apply it to the wounds, before and after Micah removed the shrapnel?"

"Yes. Yes, of course I did," she answered. She laid the case on the sofa and, without even thinking, handed him a forceps and scalpel. "You taught me that."

"I wasn't questioning your intention," he said, taking the instruments after rolling up his sleeves. "Only if you had carbolic there at the field hospital."

"We did, and I used it generously. But what *is* that?" she asked, pointing to the raised area.

"I think it's a piece of shrapnel trying to work itself out. Did Micah think he found it all?"

He drew the shining blade of the scalpel and a small-tipped forceps through the piece of cotton she had soaked with carbolic.

"There wasn't much light available there," Kathryn murmured. "Only some candles and small campfires, so he certainly could have missed a piece of it."

"Were conditions as bad as at Seven Pines?"

"Worse. Once again there were nowhere near enough tents or supplies. And one steward said there was ambulance transportation for only three hundred wounded in a corps of thirty thousand men."

Gregg cursed under his breath as he bent over Bronwen. When he removed the stitches and lanced the wound, Kathryn exhaled in relief when she saw blood but no sign of pus.

"So far so good," he said. "Swab carbolic on that now before I go any further. I'm convinced it prevents or holds off infection—even if we aren't sure why—but only if it's used *before* infection sets in."

While he probed for the shrapnel, Kathryn wished her sister would wince, or even cry out to indicate she had not fallen into a stupor.

"She looks so unresponsive, and her skin feels clammy," Kathryn said, pushing back damp hair from Bronwen's forehead.

"It's shock and exhaustion. Micah said she was found on the battlefield. Is that true?"

"Yes. And another Treasury agent, a longtime friend of hers, was killed by a shell right in front of her." Kathryn didn't have the strength to go into detail, and added only, "For hours afterward she didn't speak at all."

"But she's spoken since then? And sounded coherent?"

"On the way here she almost seemed to be herself, temporarily at least. When River Road was jammed with miles of stampeding troops and artillery wagons mired in mud, and even the ambulances couldn't get through, Bronwen led two of them across the fields."

"Aren't you being overly harsh in describing the troops?"

"I didn't mean to fault them. They were thoroughly exhausted men, ordered to retreat after they'd just won a long, brutally fought battle, and made to abandon their wounded. When heavy rain started pouring down, along with the sound of artillery fire ahead, I think it was the crowning blow. What began as a hurried, more or less ragged march became a headlong flight, and they likely couldn't stop themselves. But Bronwen got both wagons here safely—and they were filled with wounded," Kathryn added with emphasis.

Gregg disapproved of her sister, and one of the charges he leveled against her in the past had been that she was "undisciplined."

He now said nothing in reply. Although his jaw tightened as it did when he restrained emotion, it was probably because the failures of the army medical service continued to madden him. As he bent over Bronwen in concentration, Kathryn watched his deft square hands move as surely as they always did, with skill she admired without reservation.

"Here it is," he muttered, lifting the forceps that held a bloodied shard of metal. "Let's hope there's no other, and you should keep applying the carbolic. I know you're anxious, but if there's no additional infection, her chances of coming through this are good. Her willpower is certainly strong enough."

"I pray it still is," Kathryn murmured. When he gave her a questioning frown, she said only, "Something about her seems . . . missing. But did you find any other sign of injury? Micah said bone might have been shattered."

"I saw no evidence of it. I'll check her again later, but I'm needed now in surgery."

"Of course, and thank you," Kathryn said, getting to her feet when he did. "I'm grateful that you took the time."

He nodded and started toward the door, then turned and raised his hand, almost as if he meant to touch her face as he had in the past. But she stepped back, the memory of their last parting too painful and her feelings for him too confused to respond otherwise, and his hand dropped.

"Get some rest," he said, his tone crisp again. "I'll have some food sent in. And if you can manage it, make your sister take liquids."

Then he picked up the medical case and strode out of the room.

When Kathryn felt a smart of tears, she tried without success to blame them on exhaustion. After impatiently brushing her eyes, she took the discarded uniform jacket from the chair and covered Bronwen with it.

16

_____

[I] see the speech of Adam to Eve in a new light. Women will not stay at home—will go out to see and be seen, even if it be by the Devil himself.

—Mary Chesnut, 1862

Berkeley Plantation at Harrison's Landing

When darkness had gathered outside the dining room windows, candles were lit in the graceful crystal chandeliers and the silver candelabra and wall sconces. Other than this, Kathryn had no sense of time or its passage, not until Gregg Travis ordered her from the surgery.

"You've been working steadily for hours, and you're swaying on your feet," he said as yet another soldier was strapped to the Chippendale table. By now it was scarred and gouged by saw and scalpel, and stained with blood that pooled before dripping onto the polished oak floor. The table had held men from every Northern state save one.

"I know I am, Dr. Travis, and I'm sorry."

"Don't apologize—just take a respite. And when did you last eat?"

"I can't remember."

"Well, do it now. Most of those smaller, brick outbuildings are being set up as hospitals, but one of them holds the mansion's kitchen."

Natty had previously reported this, stating his intention to camp on the kitchen porch with the dog " 'til we kin git outta this here 'ell hole. It ain't no fit place to be, not fer men nor beasts neither. An' thet there Gen'l Mac-lemon outta be 'shamed makin' sol-jurs sleep in mud!"

He had gotten no argument from Kathryn.

Five hours of interrupted sleep was all she had managed earlier, waking frequently to check on her sister. Except for one heartening incident, when Bronwen had roused enough to take some beef broth, her condition seemed unchanged. Thankfully, the wounds so far all looked free of infection.

Before she left the surgery, Gregg said, "Stop at the two hospital tents that have been raised for men coming in who are sick but uninjured. If they're diseased, we don't want them here in the house with the surgical patients, but they should be examined soon nonetheless. Try to estimate numbers, since we may need to send more doctors out there."

When Kathryn gave him a nod, he added, "As soon as I've finished with this patient, I'll look in on your sister, so when you come back, go directly to my office."

As she made her way from the mansion, her lantern sent flickering shadows across the mounting number of soldiers outside its doors, forced to wait anxious, pain-filled hours for admittance to surgeons. Caring for them was like dipping the ocean out with a teaspoon. The wounded and sick were still coming in, not only from Malvern Hill, but also from the bloody engagements of the six days preceding it. Those had been fought on the Peninsula's low-lying swamplands, and to no one's surprise, apart from the army medical service, malaria and typhoid were now running rampant through the troops. The medical supply of quinine, the only known malarial treatment, ebbed and flowed with the timetable of Northern ships bringing it rather than with need.

Kathryn had grown increasingly worried about her brother, since the casualty numbers being estimated for the seven days of fighting were overwhelming. And she had heard soldiers tell of more than three thousand wounded who had been cruelly abandoned at Savage's Station, where she knew Seth's regiment had fought. Every New York soldier she treated was asked if he had come across Second Lieutenant Seth Llyr. As yet no one had word of him.

A stone walk ran to the building that housed the kitchen, and where she now found soldiers and a handful of the plantation's slaves working the brick ovens. Berkeley's Virginia owner had fled weeks ago, Kathryn had been told, instructing his slaves to take care of his property. Understandably, most of the slaves had seen this as an opportunity to likewise flee.

As she sat eating cornbread and smoked sausage, and drinking bitter but bracing chicory coffee, she asked those nearby, "Have any of you seen a boy here this evening? He's thin, with hazel eyes, and has a black and white dog with him."

"A mop-haired kid? Too smart-mouthed for his own good?" asked a private who was shucking corn.

Kathryn, having to admit that might suggest Natty, nodded agreement. This was received with a startling bellow from a brawny, hirsute sergeant, who was apparently the supervisor and official taster, because he sampled everything that came out of the ovens. "Forsooth, fair lady, that young knave made off with the best of the bread! Two loaves and half a Virginia ham he took to feed his youthful gluttony. *'O brave new world that has such people in't!'* "

Kathryn smiled in surprise. "I doubt the 'young knave'

prefers being in *The Tempest*, Sergeant, any more than the rest of us do."

"Egad, that it should come to such a pass—when women as I have met of recent possess more learning than do the men! Please allow me to introduce myself. I am Claudius Berringer, lately thespian, and delighted to make your acquaintance."

"I am Kathryn Llyr, currently nurse, and also delighted, sir."

His shaggy eyebrows shot upward, followed by a booming "No! Can this be true? Yet another beauteous daughter of Wales has graced my path? Why did the first not say: '*A ministering angel shall my sister be*'?"

"Sister? Is it possible, Sergeant, that you have met Bronwen?"

" '*She that looketh forth as the morning, fair as the moon, clear as the sun, and terrible as an army with banners*'?"

"It seems you have met her."

Still smiling, Kathryn got to her feet, feeling somewhat guilty for enjoying herself when she should be back at surgery. She didn't offer Sergeant Berringer the information that Bronwen was here; given her sister's perilous occupation, she couldn't know under what circumstance they might have met. She did ask again if anyone had seen Natty.

"Not since he stole the bread and ham," the private answered.

"Ah, well, may I ask when that was?"

"This afternoon. You some relation to that little bandit?"

Shaking her head, Kathryn edged to the door, slipping out into the wet night with Sergeant Berringer's "Come tarry again, oh rare and radiant maiden!" thundering behind her.

Where could Natty be? Into mischief no doubt.

Rain had made the stone walk slippery, and when Kathryn glanced up at the approach of another light, she misstepped and went skidding forward to be caught by a soldier holding the other lantern.

"Is that you, Miss Llyr?" came a vaguely familiar voice.

She looked up into the earnest young face of Private Randy Hall. He had been an invaluable ally at the Seven Pines field hospital when male nurses had ignored her pleas for assistance.

"Private Hall, how good to see you again. What a coincidence to run, literally, into you."

"Not such a coincidence. After Seven Pines I requested a transfer to hospital detail. I think Dr. Travis pulled a few strings so it would be approved, and he's put my name in for promotion, too."

It did not surprise her. Gregg would make every effort to advance someone he saw as capable. "That's admirable, Private Hall. Especially since I might have thought, given the terrible conditions at Seven Pines, that you'd stay as far as possible from field hospitals."

He mumbled sheepishly, "Thought maybe I could do more good there, 'cause I'm not much use on a battlefield."

"Hospital detail can be just as dangerous, and Union soldiers are lucky to have you."

She received a boyish duck of his head, but he looked pleased. "I volunteered to come up here with some newly arrived wounded, Miss Llyr, 'cause somebody wanted to know if you were working in the big house."

"Who . . . *who* wanted to know?"

His responding grin made her grasp at hope, even before he said, "Member of a New York regiment camped down near Herring Creek—name of Lieutenant Llyr."

She clasped his hand in gratitude. "Is my brother in good health?"

"He said to tell you he's okay, he got a promotion, and

he'll come see you himself when he can. They're still thinking Rebs could attack, so officers can't leave their regiments."

"It's enough for now to know he's safe."

"He wants word of your sister, too, if you have any."

"Ah . . . yes, please tell him she's here." There was no
point in worrying Seth over Bronwen now, when he could
do nothing for her. And how extraordinary, she suddenly
realized, that the winds of war had tossed three children
of the same western New York family here, together, at
Harrison's Landing in Virginia. But not so extraordinary
considering the entire Army of the Potomac was gathering
here.

Voices made them both turn to see several dozen
stretchermen trudging toward them.

"We've got sick coming in with the wounded," Private
Hall told her as he motioned for the men with the litters
to wait. "Should we take them to the house, too?"

"No, only the ones who might need surgery and don't
have regimental surgeons. The sick are to go temporarily
into one of those," she said, indicating the two large white
hospital tents.

"I'll be back," he said before trotting to tell the stretchermen.

They split off in two directions, all except one pair, who
stood there shifting their feet. Kathryn, raising the lantern
and seeing their indecisive expressions, went to where they
were waiting.

"I'm a nurse at the big house," she told them, steeling
herself for skepticism. "Is there some question about where
you should take that soldier?"

"Yeah," one replied with no hesitation, or else he was
too tired to question whether she was really a nurse. "Some
navy ensign down at the river said this one just all of a
sudden upped and passed out cold. He ain't s'posed to be

sick—all he's got is a bruise on his head. Not that we looked too close for anythin' else," he admitted wearily.

"I'll see what he needs," Kathryn said, "if you take him to that second tent."

She chose it because the other looked full, and this one proved to still have vacant space along the far canvas wall.

"Put him in the empty back row of cots for now," she told the stretchermen, "in case he needs surgery." Gregg was convinced that diseases spread like wildfire among men housed in close quarters, and in the Washington hospital he had even separated soldiers with different illnesses from one another.

The male army nurse in attendance sent her an annoyed glance that Kathryn did her best to ignore. She should be used to it by now. After the stretchermen had deposited the soldier on a cot and left, she put her lantern on the ground and looked down at what must be a fresh recruit. His face carried not even a hint of beard, and when she removed his forage cap, the stiff hair was longer than that of most veteran campaigners. Its color was an odd dark brown, and Kathryn had the fleeting thought that it might have been dyed to make him look older. She pushed back his hair to see the contusion at one side of his forehead. The skin was red, but not broken, and it was not readily apparent how it had happened. Had it been made before he passed out, and was thus possibly the cause, or had he struck something when falling?

Kathryn took his slender wrist and found the pulse to be steady. "Soldier, I'm a nurse. If you can hear me, let me know by squeezing my hand."

The response was a soft groan. If he was concussed, it would simply require bed rest, but he might have additional injuries. His forehead did not feel feverish, and from the look of him, she instinctively doubted he had any of the diseases that took such terrible tolls. Deciding to check for further injuries before leaving him here, she began unbuttoning his shirt. She stopped suddenly, yanking her hand back as if burned, and stared down in stunned disbelief.

She looked away, and then looked down again, trying to convince herself that what her eyes told her must be fact. When a furtive glance at the other nurse gave assurance that he was busy, Kathryn seated herself on the edge of the cot, hurriedly rebuttoning the shirt while shielding the soldier from view.

The soldier who was not a man.

What were the army's penalties for impostors? No matter what they were, she couldn't leave a female here among sick men. It then occurred to her that this woman might, like Bronwen, be an intelligence agent—otherwise why on earth would she be masquerading as a soldier? And how long had she been passing for male?

While Kathryn tried to think what to do before Private Hall returned, the woman groaned again and her eyes blinked open. She looked around in obvious confusion, but meeting Kathryn's troubled gaze, she attempted to pull herself upright. When she winced, her hand flew immediately to the shirt buttons, then to her hairline, and she winced again.

"You've been injured," Kathryn said softly as she pressed down on the woman's shoulders to restrain her. She now appeared somewhat older, and was made unusually attractive by large and luminous deep brown eyes.

"Please lie back and calm yourself," Kathryn told her, glancing again toward the male nurse. He still had his back to her.

"Where am I?" The woman had stopped struggling, and spoke in a throaty timbre, which could have been taken for that of a young man.

"You're in a field hospital. And I suggest you keep your voice down."

"Why am I here?"

"You may have suffered a concussion. Did you fall?"

"Fall? Yes, I must have done. But I am quite all right now, so there's no reason for me to be here."

"I think there is." Kathryn, who saw growing desperation in the strained face, added in a whisper, "How long did you expect to remain undetected?"

The remarkable eyes instantly reflected fear, and her hand went again to her shirt buttons. "You know?"

Kathryn nodded, and from the corner of her eye spotted Randy Hall entering the tent.

"Please, *please* don't give me away," the woman said in agitation. "I must find my son. He's only a child and—"

She broke off as Randy Hall approached, and with a frenzied lunge she wrenched from Kathryn's grasp. When her boots hit the ground, she staggered forward a few steps before clapping a hand to her head. Kathryn caught her as she fell, and seized a thin cotton blanket from the cot to place under her head. Was the woman unconscious again . . . or was she feigning it for the private's benefit, gambling that Kathryn would not betray her?

She was looking for a son? If she thought he could be here at Harrison's Landing, it might be a compelling reason to disguise herself as a soldier.

With mixed emotions Kathryn looked aside to see Randy Hall standing there.

"Is this a surgical patient?" he asked, lifting his lantern. "Need to be taken to the house?"

"I'm not sure yet," she said evasively, moving to stand between the light and the woman.

"I saw him struggling with you just now. Is he delirious?"

Kathryn, remembering how resourceful and kind-hearted he had been at Seven Pines, and having no solution to this dilemma herself, whispered, "Private Hall, we have a problem here."

Checking to be certain no one could overhear, she told him of her discovery.

After his initial gaping look of shock had receded, he said reasonably, "She might be insane. Why else would anybody want to fake being a soldier?"

"I don't fully know why. And while I suppose she could be insane, she could also simply be . . . misguided."

"She could be in big trouble, too."

"I imagine so. But I'd like to learn more before I report her deception. Is there some out-of-the-way place we can take her until I decide what to do? I don't like putting you in a compromising position, Private Hall, but I have no one else to turn to for help."

He nodded readily enough. "There's a pantry off the back porch of the mansion. It's empty right now—I know, 'cause I just went in there searching for candles. But I don't s'pect it'll be a good hiding place for long."

"Thank you, and I promise no one will learn you had any part in this. Now, can you find us a litter to carry her there?"

AFTER Kathryn thanked Private Hall again, she prodded him to the door of the small pantry.

"I think you should put this out of your mind," she said as he lingered in the doorway. "Just go on with your work, but please remember to tell my brother I send him love."

He looked doubtful about leaving her there, so she gave him a gentle push to send him on his way before someone discovered him missing.

When she bent over the litter they had lowered to the pantry floor, the woman's eyes were shut. Kathryn was unsure how much time might have elapsed since she'd left the mansion, but it could have been as much as thirty or forty minutes, and she was needed back there. After checking that the blanket was wrapped securely around the woman, and that the bread and the water pitcher Private Hall had brought were within reach, she straightened and started toward the door.

"Please wait," said a voice behind her.

She turned to see the woman pushing herself to a seated position. "Have you been conscious all along?"

"Yes, but I was afraid the soldier might give me away if he saw I was unhurt."

"How does your head feel?"

"I just have a slight headache. It's nothing, really."

"My name is Kathryn Llyr. And yours?"

"It's Hobart. Frances Hobart. I'm a widow."

Kathryn noticed that an enigmatic expression she could not quite pin down had replaced the woman's former desperate one. It must be that of resolve, because surely only strong resolve could have led her to take such risk.

"Mrs. Hobart, why would you think your son is here?"

"Because I received a letter from him saying the regiment he'd joined would be withdrawing to here. But Paul's just a child, Miss Llyr, only thirteen years old."

"I know boys that young attempt to enlist," Kathryn said, "but if their age is discovered, they're turned away. What regiment is it that took your son?"

"An Ohio one, but Paul looks mature for his age."

"Number of the regiment?"

"The Second," she said quickly with a trace of impatience, and rushed on, "Please, Miss Llyr, please try to understand. I must find Paul! He's my only child, and my husband—Paul's father—was killed at Williamsburg. The boy's all I have left now."

"I'm very sorry about your loss, Mrs. Hobart. And I

understand your desire to find your son, if not necessarily the way you've gone about it."

"There *was* no other way. I wrote to the War Department trying to locate him and received no reply."

"But surely under the circumstances your son will return to Ohio and—"

"He doesn't know about his father," Frances Hobart interrupted, her voice trembling. "He left home before I received notification of my husband's death. And I'm afraid when Paul finds out he'll insist on taking his father's place. If I can just find him, I think he could be convinced to come home. That I need him . . ."

Her voice broke, and she buried her face in her hands.

"Mrs. Hobart," Kathryn said, touching the woman's shoulder, "I am truly sorry. You should try to rest now. I have to leave, but I'll come back in the morning. In the meantime, I'll make some inquiries—"

"No, please don't! It could go hard for Paul if it's discovered he lied at his enlistment. But thank you, Miss Llyr, for your kindness."

"Again, try to rest, and tomorrow we can think about how to find your son."

When Bronwen heard of this, she would probably know what should be done, Kathryn thought as she made for the mansion's rear door. She had just passed the guards posted there when something began to tug at the back of her mind. Whatever it meant, she was too tired to bring it forward and figure it out. Tomorrow would be soon enough.

When she opened the study door, she found Gregg Travis in a chair, slumped over the cluttered desktop with his head resting on his arms. From the sound of his steady breathing, he must have been asleep for some time. Bronwen also appeared to be sleeping, but Kathryn saw that the uniform jacket was now lying folded on the empty cot;

instead, an army blanket had been tucked around her sister. And the bandaging on her arm was fresh.

Kathryn crouched beside the sofa and placed the back of her hand across Bronwen's forehead. Her skin no longer felt clammy, but warm to the touch.

"Bronwen?" she whispered. "Can you hear me?"

"No."

Kathryn smiled with relief. "How do you feel?"

"It's hot in here."

"You were in shock, so the windows were closed to keep you warm, but I'll raise one now. Will you tell me, honestly, how your arm is?"

"It hurts."

Kathryn almost fell forward in surprise, thinking the arm must be terribly painful for Bronwen to admit it. Once, when she had been a child and thrown from her first horse, she had limped around for days, black and blue from head to toe, insisting she'd never felt better. She had also climbed right back on the horse.

Kathryn glanced at the black medical case on the desk. It was closed, and she didn't want to open it without asking Gregg, but she also did not want to wake him.

"I'll go up the hall to the surgery," she told her sister, "and fetch an opium pill for your pain. It should take me only a minute or two."

As she went to slip out the door she looked with longing at the cot.

WHEN she left the dining room with a cache of pills, she was forced to step around the waiting soldiers and the exhausted attendants who were seated with them on the floor. Voices told her stretchermen were coming in, so she flattened herself against the archway as they went by.

She heard a steward mumble to them sleepily, "Are all those men wounded?"

"One of 'em's sick," came the reply. "Real sick."

"Take him out of here!" Micah Rosen ordered.

Kathryn was afraid the stretchermen might not obey a civilian, but they headed back through the arch. As they were passing her again on the way to the entry hall, she looked down at the motionless soldier they carried. And her heart leapt into her throat.

"Oh, no! Stop, please stop!" she begged the litter bearers. "I know this man."

17

I wonder how the North will take this. "On to Richmond" and the Fourth [of July] to be celebrated there in the Rebel Capitol is harder than they had thought.

— Catherine Ann Devereux Edmondston,
North Carolina, July 1862

Seneca Falls, New York

"Here's the one from Britain you've been expecting, Miss Tryon," said her assistant. "It's Dickens's *Great Expectations*."

Glynis stood at the tall windows of her library, watching the bustling traffic on the canal below and frequently turning, as she did now, to see the stack of books on the cart beside her desk growing higher. She and Jonathan Quant had been adding to it all morning as they uncrated arrivals from New York and London publishers. Some, like the Dickens, had been ordered as much as a year ago.

Jonathan's face reflected an inner glow Glynis recognized all too well. It meant that a few of those crates held the romantic novels to which her assistant was joyfully addicted. Ordinarily his infectious cheeriness, and the arrival of a new Dickens, would have lifted her spirits, but of late her spirits did not rise readily. She knew why this was so, and she also knew she was not alone in it.

On the surface, this Seneca Falls summer seemed very nearly the same as those of years past. The winter wheat harvest had been a bountiful one, and the new corn was already knee-high. Boys continued to disregard their elders, stealing away to a favorite swimming hole and smoking tobacco behind the barn, while girls worked beside their mothers in hot kitchens, preserving and pickling for the winter ahead. Come tomorrow, the Fourth of July bandstand would host endless speeches on patriotism from politicians who had themselves dodged Lincoln's call for more troops; beer and gossip would flow freely, and someone's prize hog and piglets would break loose to create havoc on Fall Street, just as they did every Fourth. But this year, under the comforting sameness, ran an ever-present, spine-prickling current of foreboding. Since almost everyone in a small town knew almost everyone else, they were all joined in waiting. Waiting for the newspaper that listed the war's latest casualties, and for the telegram that would change some family's life forever. And which, by the myriad intertwining lines of blood, marriage, camaraderie, and even enmity, would in turn change all other families' lives.

Glynis also recognized another source of her melancholy, because Cullen Stuart had once before left Seneca Falls. Then it had been to work briefly for Pinkerton's Detective Agency. Now it was war that had made him leave.

"Here's another one you've been wanting," Jonathan sang out, while peering at her through his thick-glassed spectacles.

Glynis realized he was trying to cheer her, and responded dutifully, "Which is it?"

"*Les Misérables.* It's an immense volume."

"That's because it's Hugo," she said, bringing a smile from him, although to her the title was darkly apt.

She should try to resist this frame of mind. On balance,

the Union's massive Virginia campaign could be as successful as hoped. And perhaps, as some Republicans predicted and most Northerners prayed, Richmond would fall, and with it the seceding states' Confederacy. If so, the war could be over by summer's end, and the men would come home. She took a deep breath and resolved to turn her attention elsewhere.

As if on cue, the library door swung open to admit a welcome sight. Her niece Emma swept across the floor, looking beautifully elegant despite carrying her new infant daughter and being trailed by a housekeeper whose arms overflowed with articles of clothing. Among the garments, Glynis spied a skirt of the same fabric as the dress Emma was wearing, one of the printed plaids made a fashion rage on both sides of the Atlantic by Queen Victoria's love of all things Scottish. Trust Emma to be fashionable no matter motherhood or war. The creations from her dress shop had given many a woman fleeting respite from both.

Glynis rose and had rounded her desk by the time Emma reached it and held out the baby, who was swathed in a lacey white blanket woven through with rose-colored grosgrain ribbon.

"Would you please take Miranda for a minute, Aunt Glyn? I feel as if I've grown some new limb that's useless for anything except tending." As if rethinking this, she smiled and added quickly, "I suppose it's like planting a garden and then having to wait for something interesting to show itself."

Seeming to recognize this as no noticeable improvement, she turned to her housekeeper. "The mailing crate is in my aunt's back office, Mrs. Reeves." She paused and looked to Glynis for confirmation, and upon receiving a nod, continued, "Just lay those things on the table in there."

As they followed the housekeeper into the small office,

Emma said, "I think those skirts and blouses should take Kathryn and Bronwen through the summer. Adam says that surely this wretched rebellion will be over by then!"

Her husband was known to be an inveterate optimist, and if the war could be decided by one man's confidence alone, Union soldiers would be home before mid-summer.

"I hope Adam's right," Glynis murmured, looking down at her grandniece and godchild, whose middle name was the same as her own. Although the infant's eyes were still the misty indeterminate color of most newborns, sunlight coming through the windows revealed distinct flecks of green.

"Why is Miranda always so angelic with you, Aunt Glyn, when she's such a little tyrant at home?"

" 'How can tyrants safely govern home, unless abroad they purchase great alliance?' " Glynis quoted, smiling as always when Shakespeare once again proved ageless. But it was the curse of a librarian's exhaustive reading to also know that Sic semper tyrannis—Thus always to tyrants—was the motto of the state of Virginia.

Emma knelt on the floor beside a crate holding the items to be sent south, the bright blue-and-tan-plaid skirt fanning behind her like a Federal peacock's tail. The last letter from Kathryn had said things could be sent to her and Bronwen by way of Washington. So far the crate contained a few books, chemises and drawers and two petticoats, and other skirts and blouses that Emma had made for her cousins during her confinement.

"Aunt Glyn, your gray cotton-lawn dress is finished, too, and it's lovely—like a column of silver smoke. You can wear it to the holiday festivities tomorrow. Just substitute a deep Federal-blue sash for the gray one."

She took the other garments that her housekeeper was handing her, carefully folding each before placing it in the crate for her cousins. When given two skirts, a blue plaid

with a flounce at the hem, a green plaid without, she said
with a mischievous smile, "I don't need to put name tags
on these, do I?"

Glynis smiled, too, at the rhetorical question, and was
shaking her head when Jonathan's voice came from the
doorway.

"Miss Tryon?"

She turned to see an uncommonly sober expression on
his face. "Yes, Jonathan, what is it?"

"Ah, well . . ." He paused and stepped into the room,
sending Emma a look shot through with anxiety.

Glynis, responding to this with a feeling of undefined
dread, barely heard Emma ask, "What *is* it, Mr. Quant?"

"It's Mr. Grimes," Jonathan said to Glynis. "He's come
with a telegram for you."

The only sound following this was Emma's quick intake
of breath. Glynis somehow forced enough composure to
hand Miranda to her young mother and follow Jonathan
into the library room.

"Good morning, Miss Tryon," said Mr. Grimes, his features arranged in what an amateur acting coach might have
labeled: The Expression Of Sympathy.

A folded piece of yellow paper he held just beyond her
reach swam before Glynis's eyes.

"I'll have that," she said, stepping forward and seizing
the telegram. "Thank you and good day, Mr. Grimes."

"But, Miss Tryon, I need a signature—"

"Mr. Quant will sign for it. *Good day,* Mr. Grimes!"

She turned and went back into the office, walking directly to its window and unfolding the paper quickly before she could imagine anything worse than what she
already had.

"It's from Virginia," she managed to tell the white-faced
Emma. "Somewhere called Harrison's Landing."

As Emma silently inched closer to her, Glynis held the paper in a death grip to read:

CULLEN STUART GRAVELY ILL HERE. IF YOU CAN COME DO SO WITH HASTE. RHYS BEVAN IN WASHINGTON PREPARED TO ASSIST YOU. LOVE, KATHRYN

18

Full of wiles, full of guile, at all times, in all ways, are the children of Men.

—Aristophanes, 414 B.C.

Berkeley Plantation at Harrison's Landing

At mid-morning, and just before the enemy struck again, Dr. Travis diagnosed Cullen Stuart's raging fever as caused by malaria.

"I was afraid it must be that," Kathryn said. "Shortly after being brought here last night he was wracked with shaking chills, and the fever began about two hours later."

"He's in such critical condition I doubt this is the first cycle of paroxysms," Gregg replied. "If, as you said, he's been only semi-conscious since his arrival, we have no way of knowing when they started. But given the severity of his symptoms—"

He broke off at a rumble of cannon. "Where the devil is *that* coming from? I thought we were done with shelling after that shower of rockets last night."

"Private Hall said enemy cavalry was occupying a ridge northeast of here."

"Those heights hadn't been secured? Our entire army is

on that plain down there, and with only the one road out! What in hell has McClellan been doing if not fortifying the area? It's bad enough that—"

He stopped himself. Kathryn, taken aback by his outburst, remained silent until she realized that he was replacing his stethoscope in the medical case as if about to leave the hospital tent. Cullen Stuart's fever finally seemed to be subsiding, and with it, she prayed, the risk of brain damage, but now would come the profuse sweating stage of malarial paroxysms. Within forty-eight hours the whole cycle would begin again. In the meantime Cullen lay in a near stupor.

"Shouldn't I start him on quinine?" she asked Gregg.

"You *should*, but it's been reported we have none left. And won't have more until the next medical supply ship arrives."

"When will that be?"

"It ought to be sometime today, unless the Rebels are planning to attack full force. In which case, our gunboats will be deployed offshore and other ships won't be allowed within range."

"There isn't *any* quinine? Not even in one of the regiments?"

He closed the case and looked down at Cullen Stuart. "This man's a family friend you said. A close friend?"

"Yes, especially of my aunt. For years Constable Stuart and Aunt Glynis have been . . . that is . . . yes, they're close friends."

While she'd been inanely stammering, Gregg had stared at her with raised eyebrows, but now he began to smile, a sardonic smile she had seen before, and she braced herself.

"My, my, my! Are you suggesting, Miss Llyr, that there's a libertine in your family?"

"Certainly not! That's not at all what I meant. I just

didn't know how to describe . . . I don't think I care to discuss it further."

Kathryn knew she was flushing and glanced around to see who might be overhearing this. Fortunately, there were still several rows of empty cots between Cullen and the other sick men. She made an effort to move around Gregg, but he stepped into her path.

"Please let me by," she said, determined not to look at him.

"Kathryn—"

"I'd like to ask Private Hall," she interrupted, "to see if there's quinine in the medical supplies of one of the regiments. May I assume that has your consent?"

"I intended to make that inquiry myself. And since there's no evidence to prove malaria's contagious, I'll see to it that Stuart's moved into the newly prepared hospital unit. It's in the second brick outbuilding near the mansion."

Surprised, Kathryn murmured, "Thank you."

Another rumble of artillery, followed by the muffled crackling of musketry made him wheel around and start for the tent entrance. Over his shoulder he said, "Eat something substantial, Miss Llyr, and be back at the surgery by noon . . . please."

KATHRYN was just leaving the tent, having changed the perspiration-soaked blanket on Cullen Stuart's cot and given him the first dose of quinine, when she heard shells exploding.

"It's not over," came Private Hall's voice from behind her. "The fighting, I mean."

"Will it ever be? I would have thought there'd been enough bloodletting on Malvern Hill to make the James River run red. It does sound some distance away, though."

"I better go find the stretchermen."

"You'll keep an eye out for the boy?" she asked. Natty had not been accounted for since yesterday afternoon.

"Yes, and I'll ask around."

"Thank you again, Private Hall. And for bringing the quinine, too," she called after him as he sloshed off in the rain. He didn't seem as enthusiastic about his job as he had the night before.

Which reminded her that she hadn't yet seen Frances Hobart today and had best do it now before checking again on her sister. Bronwen had been sleeping soundly when Kathryn left her early this morning.

When she reached the mansion porch, she glanced cautiously around before rapping on the pantry door. Receiving no answer, she opened it and stepped inside. The woman wasn't there. Although Kathryn hadn't found a chance to discreetly inquire of anyone how Mrs. Hobart's son might be located, why had the woman left without waiting to hear if Kathryn *had* learned something? But she noticed that the lantern and blanket were still there, so perhaps the woman had left simply to use one of the mansion's water closets.

As Kathryn started across the porch to the mansion's rear entrance, several shells arced through the gray sky, exploding on the plain above the river. Soldiers who had been standing ankle-deep in mud around campfires grabbed the harnesses of terrified horses and mules and began wading into columns, while officers shouted orders. Kathryn stood there in stunned disbelief that the Confederates, who had lost more troops at Malvern Hill than the Union had, could be attacking again so soon. Advancing from those heights, they could overpower McClellan's scattered, exhausted army and sweep all the way to the river. And other Union soldiers were still straggling in from battlefields farther north.

"Dr. Rosen," she said to Micah as he emerged from the mansion, "do you know what's happening?"

"Only that McClellan himself is actually leading a force to defend the heights. Granted it wasn't until after he learned there's only Rebel cavalry up there with a single piece of horse artillery."

"But could more of their army be coming behind?"

"That's the fear. And Jeb Stuart, who I'm told is one of their best officers, is reported to be commanding that cavalry, so conventional military wisdom says he would never attack if he didn't have infantry right behind him. I myself can't imagine Rebel troops regrouping this fast after the brutal beating they took at Malvern Hill."

"That's what I had thought," Kathryn agreed.

"But you and I are civilians, and since we're here to *save* lives, we presumably lack the killer instinct that makes officers. Right now, though, I'm on my way to the kitchen to feed my self-preservation instinct. And you'd better take shelter inside, Kathryn, until we know more."

"Yes, but I'm uneasy about Natty. He hasn't been spotted since yesterday, so would you please ask if anyone in the kitchen has seen him?"

"I'll ask, but the odds are good that he's off somewhere fleecing soldiers at cards and merrily pocketing their money."

For once, Kathryn hoped that gambling actually might be the reason behind his disappearance.

WHEN she reached the study, she found Bronwen slumped in the desk chair and staring absently out the windows. Kathryn stood in the doorway, debating whether to reveal that earlier she had located the telegraph tent and wired Aunt Glynis, and Rhys Bevan too, but that would mean also telling her sister of Cullen Stuart's perilous condition. Bronwen had always liked him; during the summer weeks she had spent with Aunt Glynis in Seneca Falls, Cullen had been the one who taught her to shoot. But that he could survive the malaria was questionable, and it probably would be wise to avoid shocking Bronwen again, so soon after the loss of Marsh, until she was stronger herself.

Thinking she would be leaving for the kitchen shortly, Kathryn left the door ajar as she stepped into the room.

"Bronwen, how are you feeling?"

"All right."

On the desk sat a tray that held a plate of beefsteak and onions, cornbread, a small bowl of cherries, and a glass of milk. Two-thirds of the glass was empty, but the food looked virtually untouched.

"Aren't you hungry?" Kathryn asked.

"Not very. And not enough to help eat one of the cattle herded here from White House Landing. But have some of it yourself."

"Where did the tray come from?"

"Travis had it sent in."

"Gregg did?" Kathryn said in astonishment, forking a piece of steak.

Bronwen nodded. "He checked the arm again, too, so please don't bother looking at it. He said it's healing fast now—not that it matters much."

Kathryn sank onto the sofa and reached for another piece of steak while regarding her sister with concern. "I wish you'd eat. You sound in very low spirits."

"I expect so."

What unsettled Kathryn most was Bronwen's expressionless face and the lethargic way she slumped in the chair. It was totally unlike her, but Kathryn recalled she had thought that before now. It could be, in addition to the shock of Marsh's death and the wounds Bronwen had received, that her lethargy was caused by forced inactivity.

"I expect you heard the artillery fire?" Kathryn said, attempting to prompt a more typical response. "It's from some heights north of here."

Bronwen merely nodded again.

"I've heard only a little," Kathryn persisted, "but apparently some Rebel cavalry found the encampment and is occupying those heights."

When Bronwen slowly turned toward her, Kathryn hoped the flicker of interest in the green eyes was real and not just wishful thinking on her own part.

"Rebel cavalry?" repeated Bronwen. "Did you hear who's leading it?" She picked up the wedge of cornbread and began to nibble at it.

"Dr. Rosen said it was Jeb Stuart. Isn't he the one who embarrassed General McClellan some weeks ago by riding a circle around the Union army? Even the Northern newspapers admired his daring."

Bronwen's shoulders somewhat straightened, and an inscrutable expression crossed her face. "What's being done about it?"

"The Rebel cavalry?"

"No, I imagine it's being driven off. After Malvern Hill, even McClellan must be forced to accept he has far more troops than Lee ever had. I meant what's being done with the fact that Jeb Stuart found this encampment."

"I have no idea. Would the camp be that hard to find?"

"No, especially if someone pointed the way," Bronwen answered, staring out the window again with the same odd expression. "Kathryn, where is O'Hara?"

The question was so unexpected that Kathryn was momentarily thrown off balance. "Where's . . . O'Hara? I really don't know."

"When did you last see him?"

"Let me think. I believe it was right after we evacuated Malvern House."

Bronwen's face went frighteningly blank, and as if she had no recollection of that night. Kathryn couldn't decide whether to try prodding her sister's memory, or to keep silent and hope she would recover it on her own.

At last Bronwen said, "Was that right before we came here?"

"Yes, do you remember it?"

"I think so, but it's blurry. Didn't we make some long trek across flooded wheat fields to reach here?"

"Yes. And do you recall what happened before that?"

But Bronwen's expression had changed to a stricken one, and she looked away, saying quietly, "I remember a shell exploding . . . and O'Hara telling me . . ."

She left the rest unsaid, pressing the heel of her clenched hands against her eyes. "I can't talk about it."

"I understand that, but what about your arm?" Kathryn asked. "Another exploding shell sent fragments into it. And then O'Hara brought you back to Malvern House. Natty and the dog were there, too. Can you remember any of it?"

"Now I do, but it feels distant, as if I were watching it happen to someone else. Kathryn, you said O'Hara left Malvern House when we did?"

"I think he was still with us when we reached River Road."

"And then?"

"I don't recall seeing him since. I assumed we were separated because of the evacuation chaos. Now that you mention it, it does seem strange that he hasn't come to see how you are. Although he would know you're receiving good care."

"There might be another reason he hasn't surfaced."

"Bronwen, he seemed genuinely concerned about your injuries. And when I wanted to stay at Malvern House with the wounded, he spoke up, saying you could be in danger of capture if the Confederates came back."

"There could be a reason for that."

"What reason?"

"Because he wanted us both out of his way."

"To do what?" asked Kathryn, the Malvern House episode of O'Hara's drawn gun and Bronwen's reaction to it
having jumped to mind. "What *is* it you distrust about
O'Hara?"

Bronwen just shook her head and slumped back in the
chair.

Afraid her sister was sinking back into lassitude, Kathryn had risen to her feet and had gotten as far as the desk
when movement in the hallway beyond the ajar door
caught her eye.

She hurried to the doorway, and called, "Wait! Please
wait!" to the trousered figure going down the hall.

The figure paused in what seemed to be indecision, and
then half-turned toward Kathryn.

"Oh, it's you, Miss Llyr," came Frances Hobart's throaty
timbre.

"Yes, and could you come in here, please?"

Again what looked like indecision, or possibly apprehension, crossed the woman's face. It cleared before she
came back and stepped into the room. Kathryn closed the
door firmly behind her, saying, "Mrs. Hobart, this is my
sister."

Bronwen was looking at the woman with a perplexed
expression, and Kathryn added, "I haven't told her what
brings you here to the encampment, Mrs. Hobart, but I
think you should explain it to her. She may be able to
help."

"Miss Llyr, I really don't—that is, I'm afraid to involve
anyone else in this. I wouldn't want to cause trouble for
you and your sister."

"It's no trouble, Mrs. Hobart, and my sister might be
able to assist you, because she's—"

Kathryn had stopped herself even before Bronwen rose, shaking her head, and went on to say, smoothly she hoped, "She's very clever at solving problems."

She saw that Bronwen was now scrutinizing Mrs. Hobart with a peculiar intensity that even Kathryn found disconcerting, so it would be no wonder if the woman did.

"I believe the 'problem' may already be solved, Miss Llyr."

"So soon?"

"Yes, some regiments are just now arriving here that were involved in last week's battles. They may hold the solution."

"Ohio regiments?"

She gave a quick nod. "That's why I left the place you so kindly found for me. I shan't trouble you anymore, and again, thank you for your kindness."

She had started to back into the hall when out of the blue Bronwen asked, "Mrs. Hobart, were you in Washington recently?"

"Why, no."

When Bronwen's eyes narrowed in even more thorough scrutiny, the woman sent her a faint smile. "That is to say, I did visit Washington briefly, but it was some months ago. Now, if you will both excuse me, I must locate those regiments."

She was through the doorway and down the hall toward the rear mansion entrance before Kathryn could react. To her surprise, Bronwen went to the door and looked after the disappearing figure, but then shrugged and returned to the chair.

"Why did you stare at her so?" Kathryn asked.

"Because I think I've seen her before."

"Where?"

"I don't remember. Maybe in Washington," she said, her forehead furrowed in concentration. "Or maybe not. What's her story?"

"Story?"

"Yes, this 'problem' that she said brought her here?"

"She's looking for her thirteen-year-old son, who en-listed without, of course, giving his true age. Mrs. Hobart's sure, from a letter she received from him, that he was with the troops retreating here from White House Landing."

"This son had enlisted in an Ohio regiment that was retreating to Harrison's Landing," Bronwen said flatly, without giving it the inflection of a question.

"Yes, he . . ." Kathryn broke off, something nùdging at her mind as it had the night before.

It must have showed, because Bronwen said, "Is your memory ringing a warning bell?"

"There's something, but I can't seem to place it."

"How many wounded have you treated from Ohio reg-iments?"

Kathryn stared at her sister as the bell began to toll clearly. "Last night in the surgery," she answered, "I thought to myself that I'd seen men from every single Northern state—all save one."

Bronwen nodded and reached for a handful of cherries. "There may be a regiment or two coming in today, as that woman just said, but if so, they'll be the first ones here on the Peninsula from Ohio."

19

———

*What, to the American slave, is your Fourth of
July? I answer . . . to him your celebration is a
sham.*

—Frederick Douglass, July 4, 1852

Berkeley Plantation at Harrison's Landing

What finally awakened Kathryn was not the bright alien
sunlight streaming through the window, but a resounding
crash. Her heart thudded with dread until a trumpet fan-
fare and drumroll, followed by a second crash of cymbals,
gave her reason to hope that Berkeley Plantation had not
overnight become a combat zone.

But why on earth would a band be playing now? Unless
. . . yes, today would be the Fourth of July.

It must have been well after midnight when she fell
asleep here in the chair next to Cullen Stuart's cot, having
come straight from the surgery to give him another dose
of quinine. Yesterday Gregg Travis had made good his
intention to move Cullen to this room in the outbuilding
housing the new hospital unit.

Pushing aside a light cotton blanket that covered her,
she rose and went to look at Cullen. He was shivering, his
chest moving rapidly up and down as he labored to

breathe. Another cycle of the malarial paroxysms had begun sooner than expected. Cullen's skin, browned from the sun, looked as dry as parchment, as did his sand-colored hair and mustache, but even in the grip of dire illness he remained a handsome man.

She wrapped a blanket around him before slipping an arm under the back of his neck, then lifting his head enough to drink the water in a glass she held to his lips. He swallowed only a few times before choking.

"You have to drink more," she told him, raising his head higher.

Dehydration was one of the worst perils for malaria victims. While medicine had named the condition only a decade before, the danger of the disease's sweating stage had been known for much longer; it drained a sufferer of vital fluids faster than they could be restored.

"Please take a few more swallows," Kathryn begged, but the water ran out the corners of his mouth, and there was no sign he could even hear her. She put down the glass and felt his forehead. It was clammy to the touch, and his shivering had increased. She added another blanket, at the same time fearing the start of the next fever onslaught promised by the chills.

Strains of martial music took her to the window, where she looked out on a landscape transformed. The summer sun, climbing in a cleared sky, had already dried much of the mud on the plain, while on the higher ground, row upon row of white tents was being raised. Here and there vibrant green patches of grass had somehow survived.

Several regimental bands were assembled in front of the mansion. At present one of them was playing "The Star-Spangled Banner," its tune that of an old British drinking song.

"Good morning, Miss Llyr," said the cheerful voice of

Private Hall from the doorway. "I've brought you some coffee. Figured the band would rouse you."

"It did that," Kathryn agreed, thanking him as he handed her a mug of still-steaming coffee. "Do you know the time?"

"It's around nine."

"That late?"

"Dr. Travis said to let you sleep. And that when you woke up you were to get something to eat next door in the kitchen house."

Gregg must have come in while she was asleep, because she hadn't seen him since leaving the surgery. And the blanket that covered her had not been there when she arrived. His attention was serving to confuse her, and although she wished the terrible scene at White House Landing could be erased, the memory of it intruded every time she saw him.

"Private Hall, do you know if there's still a threat from that Confederate cavalry on the heights?"

His smile gave her hope. "Word is they've withdrawn after the fight we gave them this morning. We're occupying those heights now, and everybody's saying the Rebs will think twice before risking the range of our navy gunboats. Later today General McClellan will give a speech, but in the meantime, he's ordered the regimental bands to lift everybody's spirits."

"I expect spirits could use some lifting," she murmured, "but the sun may help more than anything."

"I heard one soldier say, after what the troops went through in the swamps north of here, that once the mud dries this place'll be the Eden of Virginia."

Kathryn, glancing at the dangerously sick Cullen Stuart, was not quite so optimistic. What came to mind again was the biblical land east of Eden.

She then glanced toward the window, astonished by

what she was now hearing. "Private Hall, surely that band can't be playing 'Dixie'!"

He smiled and nodded. "First time they played it, there was a lot of whooping and hollering from across the river. Some Rebs are camped on the opposite side, so I s'pect our band's telling them we know they're there."

And now the faint sound of cheering reached Kathryn. This seemed as poignant, and bizarre, to her as when the pickets of either side called a momentary cease-fire to exchange newspapers. As if the common soldiers, unlike their commanders, were undergoing what they imagined was only a temporary estrangement. But the terrible mounting casualty figures said otherwise, and made the lively strains of "Dixie" even more heartrending.

She shut the window while asking Private Hall, "Have you managed to learn anything yet about Natty?"

"Uh, not exactly."

"What does 'not exactly' mean?"

"It means that another ham was stolen . . . taken from the kitchen, along with four loaves of bread. Some lemons and potatoes, too."

"And someone thinks Natty took them?"

"The soldiers on kitchen detail said they spotted a real short fellow, or a midget, hightailing it away. They didn't get a good look at him, but they did see a black-and-white dog."

"There might be some mistake," Kathryn said without much conviction. "Why would Natty take all that food? He couldn't possibly eat it himself."

"That big Sergeant Berringer, the one who talks so weird, said he wagered—now, let me get this right—that 'the rascal is either a merchant bandit or a Robin Hood.' Do you know what he meant?"

"I'm afraid so."

She should be relieved that Natty was apparently all

right, but shuddered to think what would happen if he were caught selling the army's food supplies.

"Kathryn?" came another voice from the doorway.

"Bronwen, how did you find me?" she said, moving to stand between the door and the cot. "You must be feeling better."

"I'm okay."

"Your arm?"

"Can't feel anything. Travis told me you were here— said you were caring for a sick family friend. Who is that?" Bronwen asked, gesturing toward the cot.

"Let me know if you need anything, Miss Llyr," said Private Hall, as he tactfully backed out of the room.

Kathryn sighed, saying, "I wanted to spare you, Bronwen, so I avoided telling you." As she stepped aside, she added, "You'd better prepare yourself."

Bronwen's puzzled expression, as she moved toward the cot, changed to one of stunned distress when she recognized Cullen Stuart.

"Oh, God, no!" She whirled to Kathryn. "How long has he been here?"

"He was brought in the first night."

"Night before last? But why didn't you tell me?"

"Because I was so worried about you. And not just about your arm, but your frame of mind, too."

To Kathryn's grateful surprise, Bronwen's accusatory look instantly withdrew, and as she stood over Cullen, tears began to well in her eyes. Even as a child, Bronwen had rarely, if ever, cried.

When she asked, "What's Cullen sick with?" her voice was fearful.

"It's malaria."

"Malaria! Are you sure?"

"I'm afraid so, yes."

Bronwen's shoulders drooped as she lowered herself to the floor beside the cot. "Is he unconscious?"

"Not fully, but I doubt he hears us."

When Bronwen looked up at her, tears were spilling down her cheeks. What was even more unusual, she didn't make any effort to hide them. "He looks so cold, almost as if . . . but he won't . . . he'll be all right, won't he?" she finally got out.

"He's very sick, Bronwen."

"Aunt Glynis! She should be told."

"I wired her yesterday morning. And last night, on the way here, I stopped at the telegraph tent to see if she'd sent a reply. There wasn't one."

"That pea-wit telegraph operator in Seneca Falls might not have delivered it yet," Bronwen said, sounding only slightly more like herself.

"Mr. Grimes isn't stupid enough to risk arrest, is he?"

Bronwen shrugged and rose on her knees to look at Cullen. "Did you explain how sick he is? Or maybe she can't come—I just remembered that Cousin Emma's expecting a baby."

"But we know how determined Aunt Glyn can be when she puts her mind to something. I went ahead and wired Rhys Bevan as well, thinking that if she made it by train as far as Washington, he could help her get the rest of the way here."

"That was smart, Kathryn." Bronwen laid her hand against Cullen's cheek. "His skin's like dried corn husks. And he looks so defenseless. I used to think he was the strongest man in the world. And the most handsome, too—except for Jacques Sundown."

She darted a sideways glance at Cullen. "I hope he didn't hear that."

Jacques Sundown, half-French and half–Seneca Iroquois,

had been Cullen Stuart's friend and deputy, until something happened to make Sundown abruptly leave Seneca Falls. Even now, five years later, on the periodic occasions when he returned to western New York, Cullen and he kept clear of each other. The break between them, so Bronwen and Kathryn speculated, had come when Cullen realized that both he and Sundown loved the same woman. The exact nature of their aunt's continuing relationship with these two men was a source of even more speculation.

"I'm not sure I agree with you about Sundown," Kathryn said softly. "He has a dangerous look about him."

"Strange you should say that, Kathryn, because Sundown doesn't look much more dangerous than Travis does."

Startled, Kathryn couldn't think of a response before Bronwen said, "I think I'll check the telegraph to see if Aunt Glyn has answered your wire by now—although today's a holiday, so the telegraph office in Seneca Falls might be closed. But even assuming she got your message yesterday, if she didn't leave there immediately, it will be tomorrow or the next day before she can catch a train."

After getting to her feet she looked at Cullen again, and whispered, "Will tomorrow be . . . soon enough?"

"I don't know, Bronwen. Only God does."

It was the honest answer, but inwardly Kathryn doubted whether Cullen Stuart could survive another soaring fever to see the sun set on this day.

Her sister, as she went toward the door, stopped and turned back to gaze at Cullen. "I hate this," she said in an intense voice, and with her eyes once again filling. "I hate this war!"

·   ·   ·   ·

KATHRYN cringed in alarm, as did everyone else leaving the kitchen, when the air was suddenly split by a thundering roar of cannon. It was followed by another roar, and then another. As the ground trembled underfoot, people began scrambling for cover before someone yelled, "It ain't Rebs!"

"It's Little Mac!" someone else hollered. "He ordered a national salute for Independence Day."

"The citizens of Richmond," said Sergeant Berringer in a wry tone, "must be mystified as to why we're using cannonballs for Young Napoleon instead of on their city."

He gestured to where a black horse with McClellan astride was cantering up the slope from Harrison's Landing. A gust of cheering swept before and after the general, and the band, which had been playing "Yankee Doodle," hastily switched to "Hail! Columbia." When McClellan reined in before the bandstand, cheers rose in swelling waves from the mud-covered soldiers standing in columns that stretched all the way to the James. While navy gunboats continued to fire deafening salvos, Kathryn stood there in baffled amazement. From the celebratory mood, one would almost think McClellan had just led his army through the gates of Richmond, but all she could think of were the thousands of casualties at Seven Pines and Malvern Hill; those who had died and those who would never be whole again. And for what? What had been accomplished in the past weeks of indescribable slaughter? It made her realize anew how little she understood of men and war.

As the soldiers crowded toward the bandstand for a closer glimpse of their commander, she and Sergeant Berringer were left standing alone near the kitchen, and Kathryn now saw her sister coming from the direction of the telegraph tent. Bronwen gave a quick shake of the head in response to Kathryn's raised brows. There had apparently been no reply from Seneca Falls.

"Do my eyes deceive me?" bellowed Sergeant Berringer. "Forsooth, they do not. Welcome to Camp Hog Pen, oh, fair daughter of Llyr!"

Bronwen received this with a spontaneous smile, the first Kathryn had seen from her in a very long time.

"We meet again, Sergeant Bear," she said to him, grasping his large extended hand.

"My cup runneth over with delight. But brace yourselves, dear ladies," he said to them, with a flamboyant flourish toward the bandstand.

Someone had given McClellan a megaphone, but the cheers quieted with only a commanding wave of his hand.

After a greeting, followed by more cheers, he solemnly addressed his army. "Your achievements of the last ten days have illustrated the valor and endurance of the American soldier."

After again waving the responding hurrahs to quiet, McClellan went on, "Attacked by vastly superior forces, and without hope of reinforcements, you have succeeded in changing your base of operations by a flank movement, always regarded as the most hazardous of all military expedients. You have saved all your matériel, all your trains, and all your guns—"

"But not all your wounded," Kathryn could not stop herself from murmuring.

Bronwen looked at her with surprise, but nodded.

And Sergeant Berringer muttered, "What must also have slipped his mind were all those guns and all those wagons left on the road from Malvern Hill. Or all the tonnage of supplies and equipment set aflame at White House Landing. But then again, he could not be expected to see that from his vantage point on yon river."

While Kathryn and Bronwen waited, both sure something pithy was coming in conclusion, Berringer instead smiled and whispered dramatically, "The great bard ne'er penned truer words: *'What a piece of work is a man.'*"

McClellan went on at length, congratulating himself by way of praising his troops, and blaming his government and his enemy for his failures. Most of the soldiers gave their general's speech rapt attention. Some officers appeared more skeptical. They avoided looking at McClellan and stared studiously at the sky, where rain clouds had so often thwarted the Richmond campaign; or at the river, where navy gunboats had saved the army from another round of Confederate attacks.

Kathryn glanced over the thronged soldiers in hopes of spotting Natty, and noticed a handful of Negroes gathered by some cabin-like structures at the edge of a trampled field. They must be plantation slaves. Did they recognize that, with the Federal army's arrival at Berkeley, they were no longer bound to remain? And that they were perhaps the few Americans here today who had real reason to celebrate this Fourth of July?

McClellan, if not by design, had accomplished something after all.

AS the soldiers returned to tent raising and mud shoveling, Bronwen asked, "Are you going to the surgery?"

"Yes, the nurse in charge of Cullen Stuart's ward said he would let me know if there's any change."

"Just the same, I'll go and sit with Cullen. What should I watch for—some kind of seizures?"

Kathryn was explaining when Bronwen interrupted her by pointing toward the Landing, where a few minutes earlier a small, dark blue steamship had docked. The first to disembark had been three people, unidentifiable at this distance but seemingly non-uniformed, and they were now coming up the gravel path leading to Berkeley House. As the three drew nearer, Kathryn could make out a lissome woman of medium height, flanked by two tall men whose longer strides, even when checked, kept them a step or two ahead of her. One of the men was slim, the other more muscular, but both carried themselves with marked self-assurance.

The nearby soldiers, to a man, stopped what they were doing to watch the woman's graceful passage up the slope. A light wind tossed the trailing ends of a sheer chiffon scarf tied under her chin, holding in place a large-brimmed hat; what hair was visible beneath it glinted in the sun, its color like that of ripened chestnuts. From the woman's sure, measured step, and even before she was close enough to be seen distinctly, Kathryn knew the smoke-gray of the long flowing dress would match exactly the eyes of its wearer.

Aunt Glynis had come. So had Rhys Bevan and Jacques Sundown.

20

*A steamer has got in from Liverpool & brings
as a present from the Liverpool merchants to
the Confederate States thirteen batteries of
Light Artillery.*
— Cathérine Ann Devereux Edmondston, July 1862

Berkeley Plantation at Harrison's Landing

Bronwen watched her aunt and Kathryn hurry toward
the outbuilding's hospital unit, and then turned reluctantly to Rhys Bevan, who was saying to her, "We need
somewhere private to talk."

"That might be hard to find. There are eighty to ninety
thousand soldiers camped hereabouts."

She threw a sideways glance at Jacques Sundown, who
looked absolutely nothing like a soldier, or, for that matter,
like a government agent either. And neither the military
nor the Treasury had succeeded in recruiting him, although both McClellan and Rhys Bevan had tried.

"What are those cabins over there?" Rhys asked.

"Slave quarters," Jacques said. He did not explain how
he knew this. He rarely explained anything. There was the
inscrutable quality of a mystic about Sundown, which
served to make him even more compelling than his looks
alone did, but it took some getting used to.

Rhys scanned the surroundings with impatience. "We need something more secure than slave quarters."

Bronwen's first impulse was to avoid seclusion, delaying as long as possible the moment when she had to tell Rhys about Marsh. And that she intended to leave Treasury's intelligence force. But stalling was spineless, and she might as well have done with it quickly.

"Dr. Travis has taken a room in the mansion for his office," she suggested. "I think he's in surgery now, but if you're willing to risk being interrupted by him, the room's probably as private as you'll find around here."

"All right, we'll go there," Rhys agreed. As they started toward the mansion, he said, "Can I assume that Travis's disposition hasn't improved any?"

"He's just very abrupt, and doesn't suffer fools gladly, if at all," Bronwen answered.

In fact, Travis had acted unfailingly considerate of her, even if it had only been to please Kathryn. Since he was not a man who went out of his way to please anyone, he must truly be taken with her sister. Kathryn, strangely enough, given her kind, responsive nature, seemed to be one of the few persons who would challenge the forceful Travis, as when she had left White House Landing despite his demand that she stay. Then again, Bronwen had always suspected her sister of being stronger than shyness allowed her to appear. Perhaps with Travis, who could be ferociously arrogant, Kathryn felt freer to exercise that strength. And while society might frown on strong-willed women, Bronwen saw this new side to her sister as an attractive one.

"Jacques, the last time we saw each other," she said now, "you were about to head west. Did your plans change?"

"No."

"You've been west? Then why are you here?"

He looked down at her with his usual flat brown stare,

as if the answer must be obvious. But regarding Jacques, hardly anything was obvious.

"Where's this office located?" Rhys said. "Do we need to go through the main house?"

"Not unless you want to wade through suffering men who've been waiting hours for surgery."

"I can forgo that." Then, as casually as if he were inquiring about the weather, he added, "And how's your arm?"

Was she unknowingly favoring it? With only an exaggerated shrug as reply, she pointed to the back porch and led the two men past the pantry, where Kathryn said she had taken the mysterious Frances Hobart, and they entered the hallway.

As she had anticipated, Travis's office was unoccupied.

"Close the windows," Rhys said—unnecessarily, since Jacques was already pulling them down—and scanned the room as if expecting to see Confederate spies in every corner. He had obviously meant it when he said "private."

Bronwen spread a blanket over the jumble of papers and journals on the desk, thinking the doctor also deserved some privacy.

"Sit down," Rhys said to her, indicating the sofa as he seated himself in the desk chair. Jacques went to stand with his back against the door.

"Now, Agent Llyr, how is that *arm*?" Rhys asked again, regarding her with his I-want-the-truth gaze.

"It's all right, but how did you know?"

"Is it usable?"

Bronwen bent her left elbow and flexed the arm several times, managing to wince only slightly.

"Make a fist," Rhys directed with a swift glance at Jacques.

"Why don't you just ask Travis about it?" but she dutifully balled her hand into a fist. And then whirled in the direction of the door, ducking as something came flying at her.

Whatever Jacques had tossed cleared the top of her head and skipped when it hit the thick carpet. She looked down at a roll of bandaging.

"As you see, my reflexes weren't damaged," she said evenly. She had a strong suspicion as to how he knew about her injury, but wouldn't ask him again. There was something else much more important.

"Rhys, before we go any further," she said quietly, "I have to tell you that Marsh . . . Marsh is dead."

There was not even the faintest flicker of shock in his cool blue eyes. He already knew. And there was only one person who could have reported it.

"Yes, I know about Marshall's death, for which I am very sorry," he said. "I also know the circumstances."

"Then I assume O'Hara told you it shouldn't have happened. But when did he—"

"No," Rhys interrupted, "O'Hara did not tell me that. He said that under the combat conditions, it was a random strike. A case of Marshall being in the wrong place at the wrong time."

"Marsh should never have been on that battlefield. And it's my fault that he was."

His frown was a puzzled one. "That's not what I heard."

"I should have made certain he went to the field hospital and stayed there. Instead, I just went off and . . . and I forgot about him. But any fool could have predicted he would follow. He should have been left at Chimborazo."

Swallowing, she swiped at her eyes, helpless to overcome the wrenching guilt, and dismayed to have broken the pledge she'd made to herself not to talk about Marsh's death. It was her burden, caused by her own failings, and no one else could lift it.

Rhys was regarding her with what appeared to be concern, which was the last thing she wanted. Only Marsh deserved sympathy. She choked back the tears as she straightened on the sofa and glanced at Jacques. He had not shifted an inch from the door, but an odd light moved in his eyes as he regarded her.

"If you need to place blame somewhere," Rhys said, "blame the war. Your instinct to move Marshall from Chimborazo was sound, but as I've told you more than once, even the best-laid plan can go awry. Not every contingency can be covered, and never is that more true than in time of war."

When she didn't respond, he went on, "I assume you made the decision to go after the boy with the same noble intention that sent you to free your brother. Just as Marsh made the one to follow you. You are not responsible for the consequences of his decision."

"Marsh was in no shape to be making any kind of life-or-death decisions."

"And you were?" he said sharply. "You are an agent of Treasury, not of God."

Where is Abel thy brother? echoed Malvern Hill's bloodied field.

"I'm not fit to be anyone's agent," she responded. "I want to leave Treasury's intelligence force."

"That option is not available," he said in brusque dismissal. "And you were so informed when you joined the unit. Voluntarily joined."

"You'd make me remain against my will?"

"It was your *will* that took you into an agreement with Treasury, and you are obligated to carry out its terms. And since that's all I intend to say about it, we need to move on."

He did not sound like the same man in whose house she had stayed in Washington, but he always had been able to switch his roles rapidly. Bronwen glanced again at the expressionless Sundown, wanting but not expecting any help there. Jacques was the one who had said—often said—that he did not take oaths.

"Right now you have an assignment to complete," Rhys continued crisply, and as if he couldn't see her distress. "It's taken on even greater urgency, because we've just received a report that once again a blockade-runner has slipped past Norfolk. Its cargo was British rifles and ammunition."

His words barely registered. How could she remain with Treasury, never knowing if she was making a decision that would exact too high a price to bear. She kept seeing over and over again that shell striking Marsh.

Hoping to reduce the pain caused by the memory, she got to her feet and rounded the sofa to look out the window. If she refused to comply, would Rhys have her placed under arrest? Put on trial for . . . what? Failure to fulfill a contract? Dereliction of duty? Disloyalty?

It didn't matter what. If he would not allow her to resign from the Treasury unit, then she'd have to find another way to leave.

He startled her by saying, "When did you last see James Quiller?"

"What?" She swung from the window to stare at him blankly. "When did I *what*?"

"Last see the president's friend, James Quiller?"

"At Chimborazo Hospital."

"That was the *last* time you saw him?"

"Yes, why?"

"Tell me the circumstances."

"If you've talked to O'Hara, who was there, then you know them."

"At the moment, I'm talking to you."

"It was when we were in Quiller's room and sent him out through the window. Natty, who'd spotted us shortly after we docked the sloop, was making a diversionary ruckus up the hall—as only he can do. O'Hara followed Quiller through the window. I was to find Kathryn, and then Marsh, and we were all to meet at the wharves. But O'Hara must have told you that."

"Go on."

"That's the last time I saw Quiller. But why—"

"O'Hara said immediately after he arrived at the wharves with Quiller," Rhys interrupted, "an unexpected situation arose because Confederate naval officers had just docked there with a hospital supply ship. Or, in retrospect," he added dryly, "I suppose it might even have been a blockade-runner."

Such a possibility had never entered her mind. But what better place to surreptitiously unload smuggled weapons than hospital wharves on the James, only a short distance from the Confederate capital? If a ship were stopped on its way upriver, it was unlikely the U.S. Navy would thoroughly search one whose manifest listed medical supplies, or prohibit them from being delivered either. In which case, a smart blockade-running captain would foresee the need to have those supplies aboard to act as camouflage. And if deliveries were being made at Chimborazo, a worker there would probably be involved.

But let someone else figure it out. She was done with this war.

Since for some reason Rhys wanted her to confirm O'Hara's account, and was now waiting for her to do it, she said, "We—O'Hara and I—had agreed beforehand that if trouble arose, he would leave with Quiller, and then pick us up later downstream."

"Did you see Confederate officers at the wharves?"

"Yes. Natty did, too."

Rhys nodded once or twice, as if satisfied, but about what, she couldn't tell.

"Why these questions?" she asked, growing uneasy about his refusal to elaborate. "Isn't Mr. Quiller now in Washington?"

He gave her a lengthy speculative look, as if he were weighing alternatives, and then motioned to the sofa.

When she didn't move to seat herself, he said, "This morning, the War Department's telegraph operator notified Treasury that he had received a communiqué from Fort Monroe. A body washed ashore there had been positively identified as that of James Quiller."

Reeling, Bronwen sank to the sofa and clutched the seat cushion. She managed to ask, "Does Mr. Lincoln know?"

"I would think he does by now, since before leaving Washington I contacted Secretary Chase about it. I came here with your aunt, because, among other things, I needed a report from you. And I wanted it in person."

"But what happened to Quiller?"

"You tell me."

"How could *I* know?" she said and then saw the more obvious question. "Didn't O'Hara tell you that he put Quiller aboard one of our ships? Before he returned in a sloop for the rest of us?"

"He told me."

"What does *he* think happened?"

"As yet O'Hara presumably doesn't know about Quiller's death. I wanted to hear your recollection first."

Did Rhys finally have some doubts about O'Hara? Her previous distrust of him came rushing back to her, but she didn't dare voice it again, not now. It might look as if she were trying to pass off responsibility for poor Quiller's death on O'Hara, when it might have been at least partly her own. Should she have insisted on taking the man downriver to safety herself?

Her face must have reflected her agitation, because Rhys said, "Agent Llyr, it is one thing to grieve. It's quite another to sink into a morass of self-blame over events beyond your control."

"But Marsh and Quiller both . . . both of them *gone?*"

"I'll repeat what I said earlier: You are not an agent of God. And I sincerely hope you do not harbor some delusionary idea that you are!"

He could have a sound argument. She did not have power over the outcome of things beyond her control—which, when it came down to it, meant almost everything. A slight movement at the door made her glance toward Jacques, and expecting to receive his flat stare, she was startled by what might have been approval crossing his usually impassive face.

"In addition," Rhys said to her, "and lest you fear that anyone in Treasury might think you even remotely blameworthy in Quiller's death, there is another aspect of it that absolves you altogether."

"What?"

"That message from Fort Monroe included the information that James Quiller had likely not died from drowning, but, rather, from a bullet."

A bullet? As the room started to spin, Rhys continued, "It was apparently from a revolver, whether an army-issued one or not we will probably never know. But while it's common knowledge that Treasury agents are armed, you have steadfastly refused to carry a revolver."

Bronwen guessed she could for once be grateful for stubbornness until a forgotten incident came back to her. It was that of O'Hara removing a dead young signal officer's revolver. And handing it to her, saying, "Here, take it, Red."

She did not have it now, only her derringer and her stiletto, and O'Hara might have taken it from her on the battlefield. What had followed Marsh being hit by the shell was mostly a blur she had not wanted to remember.

But the revolver detail now served to jog her memory about something else.

"Rhys, when did O'Hara arrive back in Washington?"

"Why?"

"Because this is the Fourth, so it must have been within the past two days. The Malvern Hill battle was on the first day of July, and Kathryn said we evacuated the field hospital there late that same night or in the early morning hours. She also said that was the last time she saw O'Hara."

"What are you getting at?"

"Did you know this encampment was fired on by enemy cavalry?"

"No, I didn't. When was that?"

"The night after we arrived, and yesterday morning, too. I remember thinking how lucky it was for the Rebels, that they'd discovered the camp so quickly, and at a time when the heights north of here hadn't yet been secured. Our troops were exhausted, too disorganized and dispirited to deploy rapidly. While Rebel cavalry might have followed the path of Union retreat, what if instead they had been informed exactly where our army would be?"

Rhys's expression hardened, and he answered her initial question. "O'Hara returned to Washington in response to a telegram I sent on the first of July. I knew advance units and supply trains had already arrived here at Harrison's Landing, and that the military telegraph was operational. My wire was recalling both of you."

"Both of us? Why?"

"Because by then we'd received the report about the blockade-runner, along with some crucial information giving us a lead on it. O'Hara, when he came back alone, explained what had happened at Malvern Hill."

"But *when* did he arrive in Washington?" Bronwen asked again.

"I assume shortly before I saw him at Treasury yesterday

morning. Said he'd caught a supply ship returning from Harrison's Landing."

"Which could have given him time to alert Confederate cavalry following our evacuation in the early hours of the second. And before he received your wire here."

She looked at Jacques, hoping against hope that he would indicate even mild interest in her speculation, since she doubted Rhys would. Still standing at the door, Jacques had obviously heard it, but typically gave no sign of his opinion one way or the other.

"Agent Llyr," said Rhys, "can you give me one good reason for this accusation of yours? Which, I must add, is only your latest in a long string of accusations against O'Hara. None of which have borne fruit."

She felt a surge of anger, thinking that none had borne fruit because Rhys refused to consider them credible, not because they weren't legitimate. But she refrained from saying so. It wouldn't help. Also, the anger had surprised her. It was the first time since Malvern Hill she had felt any emotion other than grief or guilt.

"I'm waiting for a reason," Rhys said, but he didn't sound as annoyed as she'd expected. He looked almost worried. Maybe by now he'd remembered the same thing she had, and was dreading confirmation of it.

The only path open meant risking his disapproval once again, and it shouldn't matter to her, but it did. James Quiller's death made it matter. And Mr. Lincoln would trust her to learn as much as she could about his friend. Had the death of Quiller, like that of Marsh, been another random strike of war? Or had it been murder?

"All right," she said, "here's the reason. When O'Hara and I were in northern Virginia several months ago, on our first assignment for Treasury, we accidentally ran into a Confederate cavalry officer. At the time I was concerned—no, I was frightened to death—because that officer exhibited such familiarity with my fellow agent. He even mentioned gambling with O'Hara on some Mississippi riverboat. Do you remember me telling you that?"

"I remember," he answered tersely. "Go on."

"You discounted my concern on the grounds that O'Hara had gone to the U.S. Military Academy. And so he naturally knew not only that particular Rebel officer but also a number of others now in Confederate command. It was, you said, one of the items that made him valuable as a Federal agent. And while O'Hara was a native of Virginia, he was from *western* Virginia, the area now seeking Union statehood."

"There is no need to remind me of that."

"But I think maybe there is, Rhys. O'Hara introduced me to the cavalry officer we encountered that day very reluctantly, and only when pressed."

Rhys stood up and put his hands in his trouser pockets as he gazed out the window. "I assume you will now tell me, Agent Llyr, that the cavalry unit firing on this camp was led by General Jeb Stuart?"

"Please, at least consider it might be more than sheer coincidence." She said this knowing that Rhys Bevan disliked conclusions based on coincidence as much as anyone else in intelligence work. Blaming chance could mean taking a fatal misstep.

He continued to stare beyond the window, and then turned and said briskly, "At the moment, O'Hara is in Washington. He was instructed to wait there until I assessed whether you had recovered enough to pursue the blockade-running lead we've been given. I believe you have. We need to discuss how to stop those weapon shipments from flowing into Richmond. Discuss it now."

He leveled a direct look at Jacques Sundown, the meaning of which Bronwen could only guess.

21

Do ye hear the children weeping, O my brothers,
Ere the sorrow comes with years?
—Elizabeth Barrett Browning

Berkeley Plantation

"I'm afraid he's worse than when I left him," Kathryn said with concern to Glynis, who stood helplessly beside Cullen's cot. He did look perilously ill, his skin flushed a deep scarlet and his breath coming in short, rapid gasps.

"His fever is climbing, and I should find Dr. Travis," said Kathryn over her shoulder as she started for the door.

"Is the water in that bucket clean?"

"Not clean enough to drink," answered her niece, picking up the bucket. "I'll stop at the mansion's well on my way back, but in the meantime, try to help him take what's left in that dipper. With a soaring fever he needs water desperately."

"I don't suppose there's any ice to be found here?" asked Glynis with scant hope.

"None that I've been able to locate. But the plantation might have an ice house, so I'll ask again," Kathryn said as she hurried out, disappearing into the second-story hall-way.

Glynis pulled the room's one chair closer to the cot, sat down, and grasped one of Cullen's hands.

"Can you hear me, Cullen? If you can, please open your eyes."

There was no response, and his hand lay lifeless in hers. Thus far she had managed to fend off despair, but now it was all she could do to keep from weeping. Stroking his cheek, she wished she could stop reliving the past; that if she had married him when he first asked, he might not be here. But the past was just that, and mourning what might have been was wasted effort. It rarely changed the present. Decisions made for what at the time seemed a good reason could haunt one's life for years after that reason had paled into insignificance. Her own decision not to marry, but to instead pursue education and the independence it could offer, was made before she had even met Cullen, and had been forced by the limited choices open to a woman. During the few times when she had regretted her choice, she tried to remember that on the whole it had been the right one. But now, once again, her belief in it was being severely strained.

"It's Glynis, Cullen," she tried again. "Please, let me know if you can hear my voice."

The room held only the sound of his labored breathing.

"Cullen, how did we come to this? I cannot imagine my life without you in it."

Why did it take so long for each generation to learn what had already been painfully learned by those who went before? And why did it so often take tragedy, whether in love or in war, to bring that wisdom home?

She released Cullen's hand and went to the window that overlooked the vast encampment of the Union army. It was spread over several square miles of rolling fields and marshy lowlands threaded with creeks that ran to the James. Its river frontage included Harrison's Landing and the wharves of a neighboring plantation. She could see, plying the broad river, navy gunboats and ironclads, civilian canal boats and transports, barges and supply steamships, and even sailing vessels. The scene resembled the face of a busy seaport city. And it was a city, one that held more than twenty times the population of Seneca Falls.

East and west of the river stood open acreage of what had been the two plantations' wheat and corn, much of it now lying ruined. On the way here, Rhys Bevan had told her this land had seen its first white colonists in the early sixteen hundreds, come from England and calling themselves the Berkeley Company. From Indian corn these colonists had brewed an unsurpassed bourbon whiskey, and they had exported thousands of hogsheads packed with fine tobacco. The land was eventually acquired by the Harrison family, one of their descendants a signer of the Declaration of Independence, a member of the Continental Congress, and three times the governor of Virginia. His son, born on this plantation, had become a United States president.

She wondered what this family would have thought, knowing the country it had helped to build and unite was now being torn apart. And that the United States Constitution's provision for slavery, which Virginians had demanded be included, stood at the core of the conflict.

If she narrowed her eyes she could also see, on one of the far, level fields, perhaps two dozen soldiers, half of them gathered together in a group, the other half scattered and standing at some distance from one another. Those in the group suddenly started leaping up and down as one of them broke away to dash around the field as if chased by hellhounds. Glynis's puzzled gaze followed the runner, whose route took him past three of the scattered men. All became clear when she realized four of them formed a configuration that was diamond-shaped.

She usually enjoyed watching hometown baseball games, but now men's seemingly boundless urge to compete took her back to the chair. Because the trivial was so often more comforting than the momentous, she grasped Cullen's hand again and, choking back tears, said to him, "You must get well. If you don't, what will become of the Seneca Falls baseball team?"

She began fumbling in a skirt pocket for her handkerchief, but abruptly stopped and leaned toward him. Was it only wishful thinking, or had she really felt a slight pressure from the fingers held in her hand?

"Did you hear me, Cullen? Please move your hand or squeeze mine, so I'll know."

His hand didn't move. But his lips did, and she bent her head close to them, hearing with a heart-lifting surge of hope the two whispered words, "Glynis . . . water."

"I doubt there's an ice house here," Gregg Travis said to Kathryn. "It may never get cold long enough for ice to form, much less to be chopped into blocks for storage."

They had begun to climb the stairs to the second floor, so Kathryn raised the filthy hem of her skirt to keep from tripping. She refused to look down at it, covered with mud and who-knew-what-else, and thought of the crate her aunt said had arrived with her. Whoever would have thought such commonplace items as clean clothes could seem more precious than gold.

At the top of the stairs, Gregg kept her from starting down the corridor by grasping her arm. "Kathryn, there's been no opportunity to talk without an audience since you came here. Now isn't the time, but we have to do it."

"At White House Landing I think you said all I can bear to hear."

His hand on her arm tightened. "There were reasons I said what I did then. I want to explain myself, which I realize I should have done better at the time. And I want to——" he paused and then went on "——I want to apologize."

She could only believe from his obvious difficulty in saying it that he might never have made an apology.

"Not for everything I said," he amended quickly, "but for the way I said it. It may have sounded as if——"

"As if you found me intolerable," she finished.

"Never!"

"But you said . . . Gregg, this is not the time."

"No, but I need to know you'll listen when there is time."

Kathryn thought she heard someone's voice at the foot of the stairs, and her emotions were too tangled to straighten out now. Since Gregg clearly did not intend to release her until she answered, she said, "Yes, I'll listen."

She heard what could have been a sigh when he removed his hand from her arm and touched her cheek.

When they reached the doorway of Cullen's room, she stepped inside, and stopped short. Her aunt was kneeling beside the cot, holding the dipper, and when she looked up Kathryn saw tears welling in the smoke-gray eyes.

"Aunt Glynis! Is Cullen . . . has——"

"He recognizes me," her aunt said. "I'm sure he does."

Kathryn rushed to the cot and saw that for the first time since Cullen Stuart had arrived, his eyes were open.

"Did he drink any water?" she asked her aunt.

"All that was left."

Kathryn turned to look back at Gregg, who was still standing in the doorway, holding the water bucket, and staring at her aunt. He was so obviously stunned that Kathryn nearly smiled. It was hard to recall exactly what she'd said to him about Aunt Glynis, but probably no more than that she was a small-town, unmarried librarian. From the look on his face, he must have heard this as describing an aged spinster, and not the striking woman who was now rising to her feet with such timeless grace.

"You must be Dr. Travis," she said, coming around the cot to extend her hand.

"Miss Tryon?" Gregg responded.

As her aunt nodded, Cullen made an inarticulate sound, and Kathryn seized the dipper. "I think his fever's breaking and he needs more water."

Gregg placed his stethoscope against Cullen's chest, and after listening for a time, he stepped back and said, "There's a fair amount of fluid in his lungs. Is he ordinarily a physically active man, Miss Tryon?"

"Yes, very active."

"Some of us are coming to think that forcing inactivity for long periods can be harmful." He turned to Kathryn, saying, "See if there are any pillows in one of the other rooms—or something else we can use to prop him into a more upright position."

As Kathryn left the room she heard Gregg say, "Let's try to get more water into him."

She returned minutes later with an armful of blankets, pillows being a non-existent luxury here.

As they rolled them to place behind Cullen, Gregg asked her aunt, "Do you know if he's ever had malaria before?"

"Not since I've known him. But, perhaps . . ." She gazed toward the window as if searching her memory, and then said, "Years ago Cullen had something that looked similar to this."

"Tell me the progression of the symptoms. And when they started."

"He'd been tracking some train robbers and had to camp

several days in marshland. When he returned, violent shivering was the first sign he was sick, and that was followed by high fever. I thought at the time it was ague or swamp fever, or what we in western New York call Genesee fever, because it was associated with wetlands bordering the Genesee River. His symptoms were very much the same."

"It was likely malaria," Gregg said. "As far as we can tell, it's a disease found worldwide, responsible for more deaths than any other. As you might guess, it's known by different names in different places, but the common factor appears, as you pointed out, to be marshes and low-lying swampland. How was Stuart treated earlier?"

"Our village doctor gave him quinine."

"It's still the only thing we know that works. Some people can't tolerate it, but if Stuart responded to it before, I think there's reason to be optimistic."

"And he really looks better," Kathryn added, "although I expect it's due as much to Aunt Glynis as the quinine."

Gregg was smiling at her aunt, an engaging smile that appeared very seldom. "Many a sick man would be better for having two beautiful women hovering over him."

He said it so effortlessly, Kathryn thought, and with such genuine warmth, that it didn't sound as banal or condescending as it might from another man. Why didn't this side of him emerge more often?

"Continue with the quinine," he told her, "and I'll check him again after—"

A sharp rap on the open door interrupted him.

Kathryn turned to see Private Randy Hall standing in the doorway, his salute reminding her that Gregg was an army officer.

"Excuse me, Major Travis, but I, ah, have a message for Miss Llyr."

"Well, give it to her," he was told. It was the first Kathryn knew that Gregg had received a promotion.

She couldn't miss the anxious glances Private Hall was sending her, and she now noticed he was also unusually pale. "Are you ill?" she asked him.

"Not exactly," he answered evasively as he stepped backward into the corridor.

"Excuse me," Kathryn murmured and followed him out. He moved up the hallway some distance before stopping.

"What is it?" Kathryn asked.

"Maybe I was wrong, Miss Llyr, but I didn't think your aunt should hear this."

"Has something happened to my sister? Or my brother?"

"No, no, it's not them. It's about that Mrs. Hobart."

"Mrs. Hobart? Why, is she unwell again?"

"She's not unwell, Miss Llyr. She's dead."

22

Three may keep a secret, if two of them are dead.

—Benjamin Franklin

Harrison's Landing

Standing beside her sister, Bronwen watched as Private Hall and another soldier approached with a stretcher. It bore Mrs. Hobart's body, covered by a blanket, and they carried it past the army telegraph tent situated near the wharves.

"Go to the tent's far side," Bronwen had quietly directed Private Hall. "It's secluded, and not readily visible from anywhere except the river."

And from Thaddeus Lowe's gas balloon *Intrepid*. Anchored by wires it towered a thousand feet overhead, while Professor Lowe kept watch for signs of a Confederate advance.

Scorching heat had driven most soldiers to the nearby creeks. The men had also taken to spreading pine boughs over their tents for shade, imitating the troops lucky enough to be camped under trees at the fringe of a wood.

Most of the tent rows were on the broad plain which had quickly been denuded of trees.

Kathryn seemed to believe the woman's death was something that she could and should have prevented. "I can't help but think that if I'd paid more attention to her head injury, this wouldn't have happened," she had said repeatedly as they followed Private Hall down the slope from the hospital unit.

Bronwen, recalling Rhys Bevan's words about assuming omnipotence, had told her, "There was nothing more you could have done for her. It's not as if you had no one else needing care."

When Kathryn appeared unconvinced, Bronwen had gone further and cautioned, "Because you didn't make the woman's deception known, you could face trouble. I think you need to take that seriously and keep silent. So should Private Hall," she added, calculating that while her sister's honest nature might lead her to disclosure, she would hesitate before involving the young soldier.

"I have no choice," Kathryn had surprised her by saying, but looked uncomfortable about it. "I gave my word to Private Hall that he'd not be blamed, and there would be no avoiding it if I were to speak out."

"I think that's a wise decision, Kathryn."

"But an underhanded one. As Sergeant Berringer would undoubtedly quote: '*Oh, what a tangled web we weave when first we practice to deceive.*' "

"Let's not forget Mrs. Hobart's deception. I would guess she recognized your kind nature and then played on your sympathy. Otherwise, why was she so secretive?"

"Because of her son's age."

"To deal with that, she didn't need to go through a risky masquerade. All she had to do was contact his Ohio regiment. Except that, just to remind us both, Ohio did not have troops fighting on the Peninsula."

"Private Hall said several Ohio regiments arrived today by ship."

"Meaning they weren't here before."

They had stopped trying to analyze it before reaching the foot of the slope. Kathryn in her skirt had already drawn enough attention just by being there, but Bronwen hadn't been too concerned. Her sister's nursing headdress was self-explanatory, and she herself still wore trousers. More reassuring than either was Jacques Sundown's presence directly behind them.

The telegraph operators paid little attention to what was simply one more passing stretcher.

"Tell me where you found the body?" Bronwen now asked Private Hall, having waited until the other stretcher-bearer had left.

"It was first spotted under a pier by some soldiers patrolling the waterfront. When I saw who it was, I offered to help retrieve it," he said to Kathryn. "I thought you'd want to know before the body was shipped north for burial."

"Was the body in the water?" asked Bronwen.

"No, looked like it had either washed ashore, or she had died at the water's edge. But I don't know why she'd even be down here at the wharves."

"Waiting for a ship that she might have thought was bringing her son?" offered Kathryn.

After Bronwen warily peeled back the blanket, exposing the corpse's shoulders and head, she asked Private Hall, "Did the other attendant know this was a woman's body?"

"I don't think so. He wasn't paying much attention, and the uniform and forage cap gave him no reason to think it wasn't a soldier."

Bronwen saw that although the cap was askew, its visor

covered the woman's forehead. "Private Hall, the eyes are closed. Were they when you first found her?"

"No, the other attendant closed them. It's customary."

Even so, Bronwen again had the sense of having seen this face before. But where could it have been?

"Kathryn, if, as you assume, the Hobart woman had a concussion, and it was a severe enough injury to cause death, wouldn't it have been painful?"

"Probably, but not necessarily. Why?"

"Because if she were in pain, wouldn't her first impulse be to rip the cap off and knead her forehead?"

"Disguise was for a reason," said Jacques, whom Bronwen had filled in as to Mrs. Hobart's purpose. Her alleged purpose.

"But for so crucial a reason that it would be uppermost in her mind during acute pain?" Bronwen asked. "I can't quite believe that, not if the story she gave Kathryn was even half true."

When she bent down to lift off the cap, it wouldn't budge. She gently rolled the head to one side, noting that there was no rigor mortis yet, and saw that the cap had been pinned in place. While pulling out the pins, she was struck by the hair's texture. It was so stiff that not a hair had ruffled. Then she saw something else, and straightened as she took a step back.

"Kathryn, show me the bruise on her forehead."

"The contusion is there to the side," her sister said, indicating a faint, bluish mark on the forehead.

"The skin's not even broken."

"That doesn't mean there was no concussion. The severity of impact is what causes one."

"She may have sustained a concussion, but it alone didn't kill her. A bullet did."

Bronwen pointed to a small hole at the hairline behind the left ear. The others gaped in shocked silence, except for Jacques, who never seemed surprised and instead moved in for a closer look.

"It must have been accidental," said Kathryn in a stunned voice. "Caused by a soldier's stray bullet. Or perhaps a misfire while a gun was being cleaned, because why would anyone want to kill that woman?"

"She wasn't dressed like a woman," Jacques said laconically. And if that hadn't scuttled Kathryn's conjecture, his next remark did. "She was shot at close range."

"How can you tell?" asked Kathryn doubtfully.

After pressing two fingers to the corpse's neck, he held them up to show a trace of black powder. "Not dead long."

"That's what I concluded," Bronwen agreed. "No rigor's set in yet."

When she pushed back the dark hair she heard her sister's sharp intake of breath when what resembled horsehair webbing had been revealed.

"It's a wig!" Kathryn whispered. "You know, something like that crossed my mind the night I first saw her, but I didn't seriously consider it."

"It's a wig, all right," Bronwen said. She tugged off the hairpiece woven into a tight-fitting webbed net, revealing the frizzed, brassy blond hair underneath. It held an orangish hue that the harsh nitric and muriatic acids used to lighten hair often produced.

Her sense of having seen this woman before was now even stronger, but since she couldn't recollect the time or place, maybe it was based on only a passing glance, as a face glimpsed in a crowd. She had traveled through so many places in the past four months, it could have been just about anywhere. But solely men in uniform had populated most of those places. So could it have been on a busy street in Washington? In Richmond? Maybe in a restaurant or hotel or dry goods store in those cities? And there was something else, an association or connection that was nagging at her, but she couldn't pinpoint it either.

She turned to her sister. "Kathryn, had you ever seen this woman before you did here?"

"No, but you thought you had."

"I'm almost sure of it, but I can't remember where. It's frustrating."

"It may come when you're not trying so hard," Kathryn suggested. "In the meantime, what shall we do?" She gestured toward the body.

"Better be done fast," Jacques said.

Since they were all perspiring in the heat, Bronwen took his meaning. "I agree, but I doubt in a military camp we have authority to do anything with a suspected murder victim. Rhys Bevan would know who does."

"Mrs. Hobart's son," her sister said. "What about him?"

"Kathryn, I'd be willing to wager there's no son and that nothing else she told you was true either."

"Then why was she here? And if her death wasn't accidental, who could have killed her?"

Bronwen shook her head. They might never know who or why, but there was clearly more to this than simply a stray bullet. Her near certainty that she had seen the woman before made the murder all the more troubling.

"EXECUTION style, quick and tidy," muttered Rhys Bevan when she told him of the woman's alleged background and of her death.

"Execution?"

"A bullet to the head fired at close range."

He looked uncharacteristically disturbed by this, which was curious, since presumably he didn't even know the victim.

"Which side of the head?" he asked.

"The bullet hole? Behind the ear on the left side."

Frowning, he seemed to be searching his mind, and finally said, "I don't trust coincidence."

"What coincidence?"

"The telegram from Fort Monroe concerning James Quiller's death. It included the information that he'd been shot behind the left ear."

Startled, Bronwen wondered why he hadn't told her that before. Was he seriously considering some link between the two apparent murders? Between James Quiller and Frances Hobart? How could there be? And then it crossed her mind that in March two Treasury agents had been killed in Baltimore by the same method. She started to remind Rhys of it, but pushed the memory aside, as surely those killings had been too long ago to have any bearing on these two.

"A connection seems highly improbable, if not altogether impossible," he was saying as if thinking aloud. "Which means we are forced, unhappily, to at least bear in mind the factor of chance."

"I expect we are," Bronwen agreed, although she noticed that he sounded worried by it.

"I think you should leave today," he announced abruptly.

"Today? I thought we were waiting for a signal from Navy Secretary Fox."

Seeming to ignore this, he said, "There's been another element of urgency injected. I told you earlier that the president has been contemplating a review of Union troops. Earlier Fox wired that Lincoln's just made up his mind to assess the situation here himself. And that he intends to do it shortly."

"The president is coming here? In the near future?"

"Very near. He's finding increasingly painful the comments of politicians and newspapers describing the Army of the Potomac as 'McClellan's bodyguard.' "

Bronwen did not even try to stifle her groan.

"It seems the general has portrayed the army," Rhys went on, "as threatened on every side, the troops too weary and too sick and their numbers too depleted, for him to continue the advance on Richmond. Therefore, before he can even contemplate such a movement, he says he must demand and receive . . . the usual."

"More troops."

"In excess of one hundred thousand more."

Swallowing her incredulous response, she waited for Rhys to explain why this meant she should leave Berkeley today.

They were now standing in front of the mansion, and the Army of the Potomac camped below did not look anywhere near as debilitated or even as scanty in number as McClellan's imagination led him to believe. In fact, the soldiers who had survived the swamps and rains and battles of the past week appeared to be recovering rapidly, although they were no doubt grateful for a respite. But idle men far from home could grow impatient with just lounging in the sun. She'd had ample opportunity on the Peninsula to observe that soldiers preferred to be on the move. It had been the long siege of inactivity at Yorktown that had made Jacques Sundown, at the time one of McClellan's scouts, quit his post and head west. That, and the general's refusal to accept any report of enemy strength that refuted his cherished delusion that he was outnumbered two to one.

"Rhys, how did Sundown come to be in Washington when Aunt Glynis arrived there? Another coincidence?"

"Not this time. He and I had kept in touch, and you're aware that I've wanted him on the Treasury force."

"Where was he?"

"Serving as scout for General Grant, who's about to be promoted in the western war theater. Heard of him?"

"I have, yes. Mr. Lincoln seems to think well of him."

"Grant usually does what he sets out to do, which these days is a welcome novelty. But I wired Sundown with an offer on another matter, one you might find interesting. On the same day as the Malvern Hill battle, the president signed a bill approving construction of a transcontinental railroad."

"One's actually going to be built?"

"It was only a matter of time. Lincoln has been its strongest political supporter, and he's been pressing Congress to act. Treasury wants to stay informed of where its money is spent, and the railroad companies will need scouts."

"Sundown?"

"If he accepts. But as to the business at hand, I want you to proceed now with the blockade-running assignment. It's crucial we have answers about how a foreign ship can slip into the James before the president leaves Washington. Likely to be within the next week."

"So soon?" When he nodded, she said, "It's nearly time to move forward on that information from the anonymous source, anyway. But why did you emphasize the president's visit?" she added uneasily. "Are you worried about his safety?"

He deflected the question by saying, "I've become more concerned about the circumstances of James Quiller's death. And there's been another development that might be remotely connected. Repeat: *might be.*"

He paused, giving her a probing look before he continued, "After I first talked to you, I sent a wire to Washington. I've just received a response from the War Department telegraph operator, notifying me that the intended recipient of my wire could not be located. And that he is presumed to have left the city."

Bronwen felt a nasty sensation in the pit of her stomach.

Hoping she wasn't right, she asked, "O'Hara?"

His answer came with obvious reluctance. "Yes, O'Hara."

"You said he met with you yesterday morning. Did you see him again in Washington?"

"No."

Which meant O'Hara could have left anytime after that.

"Rhys, have there been threats against the president?"

"You, of all people, know there have been threats."

She knew he was referring to the pre-inaugural Baltimore assassination plot. Although the attempt on Lincoln's life had been thwarted, the conspirators had not been caught, and only their fanatical secessionist leader had been identified: Cypriano Ferrandini had managed to vanish. Which meant he might again be planning to strike at the president.

"Recent threats?" she persisted, while trying to ignore a sudden staccato drumming in her head, much as if her memory were sending an encoded message. Whatever it was, she could not read it.

"Why do you ask that?" he sidestepped.

"Because you said there might be a 'remote connection' between O'Hara's apparent disappearance, Quiller's death, and the arrival of the president here next week."

"Again: *might be!* I fervently hope there is no connection, but we had damn well better find out if there is before the president sets foot outside Washington."

23

The destiny of the colored American, however this mighty war shall terminate, is the destiny of America.

—Frederick Douglass, 1862

Berkeley Plantation at Harrison's Landing

Bronwen, climbing the steps to the second story of the hospital unit, heard her sister's voice come floating down the stairwell. It carried such a lilt of optimism that it stopped her in mid-flight. She concluded that Cullen's condition must have improved.

Then she heard Gregg Travis say, "I agree it's remarkable news."

"And so honorable of General Lee," came Kathryn's astonishing reply.

What on earth could that mean? wondered Bronwen, waiting on the stairs, since it sounded as if they were descending. When the pair appeared above her, she sensed that the current, which before being interrupted had run between them like a live telegraph wire, was again thrumming.

"How is Cullen?" she asked.

"Stable," Travis told her. "Certainly no worse, and possibly improving."

"He's sleeping without any visible discomfort," Kathryn said, the lilt in her voice even more distinct. "And we've added good news. Dr. Swinburne, the surgeon who remained at Malvern House, sent a letter to General Lee's headquarters about the suffering of our wounded who are now prisoners of war."

"He contacted Confederate *command*?"

Travis nodded. "And Lee has replied to the effect that he would have Federal wounded of the past week's combat collected and brought to Savage's Station. Also that he'd be willing to parole those who agree not to bear arms."

Bronwen gripped the railing in disbelief. "Do you mean to say that Lee is prepared to just release them? After those ferocious battles, some of which, like Malvern Hill, the Confederates lost?"

Their expressions were answer enough. Before she could gather her wits, Kathryn said to her, "Were you going to Cullen's room, or looking for me?"

She couldn't sink her sister's buoyed spirits by announcing she would shortly be leaving Berkeley. In any event, Rhys had sent another wire to Washington, asking for more information about O'Hara's possible whereabouts, and she had to remain here until a reply came. Meanwhile she also wanted to question the boy.

"Looking for you, if Cullen's not in danger. Have you located Natty?"

"We now have some idea where he is," Travis replied. He turned to Kathryn, saying, "We need to get back to the surgery. But I know you won't be satisfied until you've seen the boy safe yourself."

"I'll not be too long," Kathryn told him.

As he went down the stairs two at a time, he called over

his shoulder, "Be firm with him, Kathryn! If you can't bring yourself to do it, then I'll deal with him."

He sounded like an exasperated father, Bronwen thought; rather like her own had sounded on rare occasions, almost always ones involving her. But unlike Travis, her father was a patient man, so she must have pushed him beyond bearable limits. Had she meant to be so trying? No, and probably neither did Natty. *Thoughtless* might be a better word. There were other words, too, but dwelling on her faults right now could not help her or her president. It would have to wait until she finished her current assignment and took leave of Treasury. She was determined to have done with this war, even if it meant imprisonment. Whatever she might once have envisioned as worthy, when risking one's life for someone else's cause, had died with Marsh.

"What does Travis want you to be firm about?" she asked her sister as they followed him down the stairs.

"Natty is rumored to be taking sizable quantities of food from the kitchen," Kathryn said with a sigh. "But it's *only* a rumor."

"Why?"

"Why is he taking food?"

"No, why would you think it's only a rumor? You know that little scamp—he's probably selling it."

"Oh, Lord, I hope not."

"I doubt it will bankrupt the Union. So where is he? I need to ask him a question or two."

"He's been seen down near the slave cabins."

"THEY'RE playing baseball!" Bronwen said when they neared the cabins at the far edge of a field.

"Aunt Glynis said she saw it from the window."

"I thought baseball was a Northern game, and most

particularly a New York one. But if our troops are importing it to Virginia, the Confederacy ought to be grateful we're here. Better flying balls than flying bullets."

"Bronwen, isn't that Natty over there, slouching against the oak tree? With the dog tied to it?"

"It's Natty, but why is he scowling?"

At Kathryn's call he looked up, and when they approached, his eyes darted around as if looking for somewhere to hide. The dog, at least, swung his tail in greeting.

"Where have you been?" asked Kathryn. "I've worried about you."

"What fer?" Scuffing the toe of his boot in the dirt, Natty added, "Ya got 'nuff ta do without worryin' 'bout me."

Bronwen wondered if he was suggesting that Kathryn should be relieved to have him out of the way. Which seemed so out-of-character it bordered on the implausible. What deviltry had he been into other than raiding the Union larder?

"Just the same, my sister was worried about you," she told him. "You should have let her know where you were. And why are you looking so put out?"

"It's them guys," he said, jerking a thumb over his shoulder at a loosely formed line of soldiers, who appeared to be waiting their turn at bat.

"The ones playing baseball?" Kathryn asked.

"They're *all* playin'," Natty said with disgust. "Even them Reb prison-ers."

Bronwen thought about asking if he was sulking because they wouldn't let him join the game, but decided it might embarrass him. And only a moment later one of the soldiers shouted at the boy, "Hey, li'l slugger! C'mon, you're next at bat."

Natty scowled again, looking conspicuously reluctant. When Kathryn started to say that he didn't have to do it,

Bronwen seized her sister's sleeve. "Let him handle it," she whispered. "This is men's business, and he'll be humiliated if you coddle him."

To her surprise, Natty sent her a curt nod. She had forgotten he owned the ears of a cat. To her further surprise, he then straightened and walked—or, more accurately, he swaggered—up to a flattened burlap bag staked to the ground. It was apparently serving as home plate. With a show of nonchalance that must be forced, he picked up one of several wooden clubs, which looked exactly like the bats Bronwen had seen used by Rochester's intercity baseball teams. Clearly the Army of the Potomac had come prepared for more than war.

As she and Kathryn inched closer, her sister whispered, "He can't possibly hit a ball with that club, can he? It looks too heavy to swing."

"Those soldiers look as if they expect him to hit. Unless they're just patronizing him."

But if he were shamed in front of all these men, it could be devastating for him. Would it help if she and Kathryn were to leave? Or would he then think they had so little faith in him that they were fleeing to avoid association with failure? She should have thought this through sooner, because Natty was already standing at the plate. He had positioned his thin wiry legs in the typical batter's stance and held the bat just above his shoulder, as though mimicking what he had seen the soldiers do. Unfortunately, he continued to stand there, unmoving, as three pitches of a yarn-wrapped rubber ball sailed past him.

A few of the nearby soldiers were hollering what Bronwen dearly hoped were words of encouragement, and she could sense the same sympathetic concern radiating from Kathryn. Were these soldiers allowing Natty to bat so they could make fun of him? Had they forgotten what it felt like to be a boy trying to be a man?

This did not seem to be the case when one of them yelled good-naturedly, "Atta boy, slugger! Wait for a good one!"

Kathryn was saying, "He's too young to be competing with grown men," when they heard a resounding *whump*.

Flinging the bat, Natty took off running as if he'd been shot from a cannon. Bronwen rushed forward, trying to see between exuberantly cheering soldiers. By craning her neck, she finally got a glimpse of Natty. He had rounded second base and was sliding on his stomach, arms outstretched, into third. His fingers touched the burlap only seconds ahead of the ball.

When Bronwen realized she was jumping up and down like everyone else, she restrained herself, shouting over the noise to a grinning soldier beside her, "Has he ever done that before?"

" 'Most every time. Kid's a slugger!"

"I wouldn't have thought he could swing the bat that hard," said Kathryn coming up behind her and looking as weak with relief as Bronwen felt.

"We found out he's a whole lot stronger than he looks," laughed the soldier. "But it's not just how hard he swings. He's got a good eye, and he waits so's he can hit a ball just right. Kid's gonna be a champ!"

The noise quieted abruptly when the next batter stepped up to the plate. On the first pitch he sent the ball bouncing toward third base. Even before it was scooped up by the infielder, Natty was tearing toward home plate. The catcher took a few steps toward third, and after he fielded the thrown ball, the boy jumped, feet first, knocking the ball out of the catcher's hands. And scrabbled the few remaining inches to the plate.

Amidst the riotous yelling and cheering, Bronwen turned to smile at her sister, both of them simply shaking their heads. But a lively controversy was erupting over whether Natty's tactic had been unsporting and even impermissible. When he came off the field, his ragged hair was dripping with perspiration. For some reason he still looked peeved.

"That was pretty spectacular," Bronwen said to him, since her sister seemed speechless.

He shrugged. Reminding her of the times she had won shooting matches. And shrugged. *Nothing to it.* As if anyone would believe that.

"Why the frowning face . . . slugger?"

" 'Cause they're makin' me be on this team."

The soldier who had spoken to Bronwen earlier grinned at Natty and said, "Too bad, champ, 'cause we're stuck with it."

"I don't wanna play with no Rebs."

"Who does?" said the soldier.

Bronwen turned to him saying, "Are you a Confederate prisoner?"

"No, but me and Slugger here are 'bout the only ones on this team who ain't. Gotta spread us winners round," he told Natty, "or we ain't got enough men to play."

Bronwen had to smile at the soldier's unerring instinct; the word "men" instantly cleared Natty's frown and even straightened his shoulders.

Since the argument was continuing apace, she said to him, "I need to ask you something. I can wait, though, until they decide whether your run should be scored."

"Aw, they jest likes to yell an' pro-test everythin'. 'Course it was a run."

"I think so, too. Where did you learn that kick maneuver?"

"Dint learn it. Just knowed to do it. Ya gotta score, else there's no use hittin' the ball."

That about summed it up. A winning philosophy.

A gust of nearby cheers announced the end of the protest. The soldiers began to disperse, some of them stopping

to thump Natty between the shoulder blades or to tousle
his hair, and Bronwen now understood what had fueled
the argument. Natty's had been the game-winning run.

He started to walk in the direction of the slave cabins,
and from Kathryn's expression she was just as surprised by
it as Bronwen. Coming out from behind the tree to meet
him was a sweet-faced young girl whom Bronwen had not
spotted before, now leading the dog by its rope. When she
fell into step beside Natty, Bronwen thought she recognized her.

"Isn't that Absinthe?" she said to Kathryn while they
followed the pair. "The slave girl from White House
Landing? Or former slave, since her mother had been
manumitted."

"I think it is. Didn't you tell me Natty brought her here
on his way into Richmond?"

"Yes, of course! Absinthe had wanted to find her brother
who'd been . . . been sold as a slave to Berkeley."

She had stumbled over the words, because slavery had
become the last compelling reason for her to stay with this
war for the current assignment. Her earlier argument with
Rhys, when she had wanted to resign from Treasury effective immediately, had ended because of it. He had finally
told her why the most recent threat against Lincoln was
feared to be credible.

"It's not as yet known by many of the president's cabi-
net," he had said, "that Lincoln has all but decided to draft
a preliminary emancipation proclamation. It would strike
at slaveholders in the seceding states by disrupting their
labor force, weakening their ability to wage war. The president believes that if emancipation is seen as a military
necessity, it will eventually be accepted by most Northerners."

"But for whatever reason, those slaves will be free?"

When he had nodded, the enormity of it began to sink

in. A few strokes of Lincoln's pen would change the face of this war so profoundly that she could imagine the Virginia soil already starting to heave underfoot. And if slaves in seceding states were declared free, freedom for all slaves could follow if the Union were successful.

"The president will also state," Rhys had gone on, "that the Federal government won't repress slaves who are trying to gain their own freedom. In other words, it would end the controversy over whether the droves of them fleeing to Union lines should be returned to the South."

Bronwen had recalled the comment made by Secretary Fox before she left Washington: that Europe was watching for signs the South could win this war. Echoing Lincoln's oft-expressed concern that Britain and France might decide to aid the Confederacy. But Britain was vigorously opposed to slavery, so had McClellan's failure to capture Richmond forced the president's hand? If so, it would be a colossal irony, since McClellan himself passionately argued against abolition.

"Clearly, this is an extraordinarily sensitive issue," Rhys had warned. "While every effort is being made to keep it quiet until the president formally announces it, there may already have been leaks. If there have, it gives us more reason to fear that an assassin could be prodded into acting."

"When will Lincoln announce it?"

"Possibly in a few weeks. In the meantime, it was thought that you, among a few others in the Treasury unit, should be informed."

Bronwen, after giving this last remark some reflection, had regarded him warily. "Am I being told this because of my regrettable acquaintance with Britain's Colonel de Warde?"

"What do you think?"

Now, as she and Kathryn were nearing the cabins, she saw a handful of Negroes eating at a long wooden table.

Were they the slaves Berkeley's owner had left in charge of his plantation? Although Natty had for some reason disappeared into the nearest cabin, Absinthe turned toward Bronwen and Kathryn.

"Come set a spell if y'all like," she said with a shy smile, pointing at the table where a large black kettle held pride of place. "Y'all can have some soup, 'cause there's lots of it."

When Bronwen approached the table, the pungent smell of the soup triggered a sudden suspicion, and she shot a sideways glance at Kathryn. Her sister was smiling and nodding to the four others there—three men who had quickly risen to their feet and an ancient woman who had not—and was asking them to please sit back down. Maybe she hadn't yet noticed the incriminating aroma.

Natty, emerging from the cabin with a basketful of what looked very much like the bread made in the army's kitchen, reached over to plunk it down on the table. He then wriggled himself in between two of the men seated on a wooden bench, all as if this was something he did routinely. When the men laughed and called him "Slugger," it occurred to Bronwen that he probably did.

Another glance at her sister told her that Kathryn had also just realized where Natty had been keeping himself.

"That's my brother Shandy," Absinthe said to Bronwen, and indicated a strapping young man with guarded dark eyes set in a square face. "He's freed now, like me and Mama. 'Member I told you 'bout him?"

"I remember," Bronwen answered as she returned the man's reserved nod. "You didn't wait for me to come back for you that night, Absinthe."

"That weren't Ab-sent's doin'," Natty mumbled around a mouthful of bread he had stuffed in after a gulp of the ham-bone soup. "I made her run 'way."

"Why? Didn't you trust me?"

"Nope. Dint trust nobody who was a spy."

Bronwen saw the sideways glances cast her way, and cut off Kathryn's murmur of reproof with, "That seems reasonable enough." The less made of it the better. "And what about now?" she asked him.

Natty's head came up from the soup bowl, his hazel eyes boring straight into her own. "If'n I dint trust ya, think ya'd be sittin' here?"

Bronwen's responding laugh lifted the veiled expressions around the table, and two of the men laughed with her. Shandy did not, but he looked like a man who'd had little experience with laughter.

Then a sudden, intruding blast from a ship's steam whistle made her unhappily recall why she *was* sitting there. Since she had already been labeled a spy, it probably didn't matter if she questioned Natty without taking him aside. Dragging him away from the table would not only be rude to his friends, but would make him more uncooperative.

"Natty, my man, I need some information."

"Yeah, I s'pect so," he said in untypical lowered voice.

"You do?"

"Ya wanna hear why I was takin' ham and stuff from the kitchen—"

"As a matter of fact, I don't," she interrupted. "That seems fairly obvious."

"It was 'cause they dint have no food here. Sol-jurs went an' trampled everythin'—you *don't* wanna hear thet?"

"No, I don't." She noticed that Kathryn was staring at the sky as if utterly unaware of this dialogue.

"Okay," he said nonchalantly, but darted a glance at her sister. " 'Sides, thet there big hairy sol-jur knows 'bout it— the one thet talks like he's crazier'n a bedbug."

"You mean Sergeant Berringer?" asked Kathryn, and

then looked as if she wished she hadn't, since she supposedly wasn't hearing this confessional.

"Yeah, him. He even gives me stuff so I kin bring it here." This said as he was slipping chunks of bread soaked in soup to the waiting dog.

"Partners in crime," said Bronwen.

"Huh?"

"To take a different path, I need to know something about that Confederate hospital where you stayed with Lady."

"Ya mean thet there Chimp's bor-acho?"

"Chimborazo, yes."

"What 'bout it?"

"I know you make it your business to keep your eyes open for opportunity. So, did you ever see steamers dock at the wharves there that didn't look like the usual hospital supply ships?"

"Ya mean like a kind thet stowed guns 'long with medsin?"

Pay dirt! "Yes, indeed, my man, that's exactly what I mean."

"Yeah, I seen one."

"When?"

Natty shrugged, "Dunno. Mebbe a coupl'a days after we got there."

"You never told me that," Kathryn said.

"Ya dint ask me."

"Okay," Bronwen said, shaking her head at her sister, who, like the others there, was hanging on every word. "Now, this is important, Natty. Were the guns stowed under the medical supplies?"

"Yep, they was. Couldn't figger why the Chimps wanted guns, less'n they was gonna shoot all them sick sol-jurs. Seemed kinda stupid, 'cause they was dyin' anyhow."

"Can you tell me if you recognized anyone?" Bronwen

persisted, sending her sister a warning look, determined not to be sidetracked by a lesson about compassion. "Was anyone you knew present at the wharves when those guns arrived? For example, someone who might have worked at the hospital?"

"Shure. There was thet ole bat—Missus Lynne."

Her sister's gasp brought another shake of Bronwen's head. "Please, Kathryn, no reprimands while I'm trying to get answers."

"But I know who he means," her sister protested.

"You do?"

"Yes, Mrs. Lynne—she's a matron at Chimborazo."

"Yeah, an' she's one a' them there loos pained wimmin, too," Natty agreed.

Bronwen, fearing she was losing her grip on this, tried translating. "Do you by any chance mean 'loose painted women'? And if so, *what* are you talking about?"

"The pay-as-y'all-go ladies," offered one of the men, not trying to hide a grin.

"Thank you for clearing that up," said Bronwen, assuming a modest expression as if she couldn't have known. But she was still groping in the dark as to the woman.

Kathryn, looking upset, said firmly, "I think perhaps Natty is under a mistaken impression. Mrs. Lynne is a *nurse.*"

"Lady," he protested, "I ain't mis-impressed. Ya dint see what thet ole bat an' thet there Reb navy off-cer was a'ways doin'!"

"*What* Reb navy officer?" Bronwen asked, half-rising from the bench.

"The one she was meetin' in thet kitchen all's the time. An' I kin tell ya, the stuff they did was 'nuff to make ya—"

"Natty!" Kathryn interrupted. "We do not need details."

"Yes, we do!" Bronwen had nearly snapped it, and quickly sent her sister an apologetic look.

Flushing, Kathryn rose from the bench and picked up her empty soup bowl and Natty's. "May I help wash these, Absinthe?"

Shandy was instantly on his feet. "No need," he said to her brusquely.

"Please, I'd like to," Kathryn replied.

"She jest wants to git outta here," Natty commented with his sometimes-remarkable perception. He then ruined the effect by saying, "Lady, when we goes back to Washing-town, kin we take Ab-sent?"

Kathryn first looked dumbfounded, swiftly followed by flustered. "Well, ah, Natty, I expect Absinthe wants to stay here with her family."

"Nope. Shandy's gonna go north an' be a Union soljur."

Bronwen, nearly beside herself with impatience, glanced at Shandy. He nodded.

"An' nobody else here is Ab-sent's relay-shuns," Natty pressed. "Why cain't we all of us take her?"

" '*All* of us?' " Kathryn repeated with a confused expression.

"Yeah, me an' you an' Dog, an' the doc. Yer gonna marry him, ain't ya?"

Bronwen, shifting restlessly on the bench, was making every effort to curb her frustration. Instead, she should be enjoying this unfolding domestic drama. Natty, who had never known a family, was plainly orchestrating one for himself. Thus in a matter of mere weeks, her sister stood poised to acquire two children, a husband, and a dog.

Kathryn had flushed to a deep shade of pink. She sent Bronwen a pleading look as she backed away from the table, striving for dignity by acting as if she hadn't seen the nudges and amused expressions following her.

"Natty," said Bronwen firmly, "let Lady decide what she wants to do. And then ask her again. Now, tell me about the ship with guns. And about the Reb navy officer, and the 'loos pained' *nurse* at Chimborazo."

FROM the corridor outside the hospital room she had heard the murmur of voices, but after entering she whispered to her aunt, "Is Cullen asleep?"

"No," came a hoarse response from the cot.

"You're better!" Bronwen said, although she could tell that from her aunt's face alone. When she took Cullen's hand, his grip was weak, but his smile had been restored to full strength.

"Why are you here in Virginia?" he asked, although the effort made him cough.

"Came to see you."

This brought the trace of a smile from her aunt, who put down the immense book she had apparently been reading aloud to him. Bronwen, glancing at it, thought *Les Misérables* was a curious choice of title for bedside reading, but it might have been the only book her aunt brought with her. From its size, it could easily last her through Christmas.

"Aunt Glyn, can we talk a minute?"

She relied on her aunt's astuteness, and rightly so, since she wasn't even asked "why."

Rising from the chair, her aunt said to Cullen, "I'll be back soon."

Once out of the room, they walked to the end of the hall, where beyond the window a waxing moon was climbing. That moon could be an unforeseen obstacle. Blockade-runners pursued their stealthy trade on only the darkest nights, but days ago Elizabeth Van Lew's unknown source had said that a steamer from Nassau could be anticipated tomorrow night or the next one. Priceless information, if it were accurate.

"Aunt Glyn, I have to leave Berkeley in less than an hour. Please don't ask why or where."

"May I know if you intend to come back here?"

"Yes, of course, I do. But that brings me to something I need to request. I can't ask Kathryn—in fact, I don't even want her to know I'm leaving. Or Seth either, if you should see him."

"He was here earlier, looking for you. I assume your reason is one of consideration for them, Bronwen, since I would never believe it's a lack of courage."

"Truthfully, it's probably some of both. Kathryn will know soon enough tomorrow. If it eases your mind any, I'm not going alone. Jacques Sundown agreed to come."

Proving to her that Rhys Bevan was seriously worried about O'Hara's unexplained absence. The situation had been presented to Jacques in Rhys's usual persuasive manner; even so, Bronwen thought he had been surprised when Jacques, with a nod at her, had said, "If she goes, I go. A lot riding on it."

Her aunt, who had been gazing out at the moon with an oddly poignant expression, now turned and said, "I spoke with Rhys Bevan earlier, before he left for Washington. He had offered Jacques another Treasury position, and asked if I knew whether the offer would be accepted. I told him I had no idea. Does this departure of yours signal that Jacques has agreed to it?"

"No, this concerns something else. And there will be at least one other Treasury agent involved, too."

Bronwen didn't know yet who it would be, only that it would not be O'Hara. Rhys, by the time he left Berkeley, had not received a reply from his wire to Secretary Fox, inquiring about his missing agent. But Rhys had heard from Treasury, and the reason they were now moving ahead

so rapidly was because the date for the president's trip to
Berkeley had been set. It would take place only three days
from now.

Rhys disagreed with the haste. But too much advance
notice, it was felt by those in the War Department, would
be more dangerous to Lincoln's safety than too little.
Added to this was the desire of the president to see his
commanding general and his army as soon as possible.
Treasury had been given no alternative but to act.

"Aunt Glyn, if, for some reason I don't—no, let me put
it another way. I promised myself I would go to see Marsh's
mother, because it might give her some comfort if she
knew why he died. Not how, but why. Could you . . .
would you be able . . ." Her voice broke as the tears that
were threatening could no longer be checked. For years she
had not allowed herself to cry, and yet in the past days it
seemed the dam had broken.

Her aunt stepped forward, gathering her in a warm,
lavender-scented embrace. "Where does his mother live?"
was all she asked.

"In a little Pennsylvania crossroads town. Place named
Gettysburg."

"Please be safe, Bronwen," her aunt whispered. "So you
can tell her yourself."

24

Already the floodgates of treasonable intelligence flowing North seem to be thrown open wide.

—John B. Jones, Richmond, July 1862

Hampton Roads, Virginia

The dilapidated Black Gull Tavern, looming alone against the night sky, perched on a remote finger of land pointing toward Chesapeake Bay. Its very isolation made Bronwen imagine the two-story structure might once have served as a pirate hideout. From its north attic window approaching merchant vessels could have been sighted, and then lured into shallows by the swinging lanterns that promised safe harbor. When the hapless ships ran aground, their cargo would have been ripe for plunder.

The Black Gull, sagging on its foundation, looked easily a century old. And the dark deeds it might witness today were not piracy but the reverse; illicit cargoes running into Virginia rather than running out.

At present, a feeble glow of its lanterns, barely visible through grime-streaked windows, did not begin to reach the nearby wharves jutting darkly into Hampton Roads. Although *roads* was maritime jargon for safe anchorage,

Bronwen thought as she cautiously circled the tavern that *bridge* would be a better term for this body of water. It connected the Chesapeake and the Atlantic with three rivers, the Elizabeth, the Nansemond, and the James. The surrounding flat terrain made it one of America's finest natural harbors; ironically, given her current assignment, it had been the first port targeted by the Federal blockade. Across Hampton Roads and due north of where she was skulking stood Fortress Monroe. For all the protection the Federal fort afforded her now, the few miles of tidewater that separated it from the Black Gull might as well have been an ocean.

When her circuit again brought her to the tavern's front door, hanging cockeyed from only two of its three rusty hinges, she heard loud voices coming through it. Quickly retracing her steps until she reached a safe distance from it, she dropped to a crouch. While she waited, she rubbed her left arm. It didn't hurt anymore, but the scar tissue itched.

The waxing moon gave unreliable light as it sailed in and out of clouds, so she could no more than intermittently see the trio of dark-clothed men staggering from the tavern.

"Bloody friggin' ships! All of 'em oughta be sunk!" The owner of these comments was evidently three sheets to the wind, because he stumbled over his own feet and went sprawling into the path of the others.

Boisterous guffawing followed as his companions hauled him upright, while Bronwen verified that these were U.S. Navy seamen. Presumably they were on shore leave, because if they were on active duty, it was a wonder blockade-runners weren't flooding into the James.

As the men lurched toward the wharves, Bronwen maintained her distance from the tavern. She was expecting that whichever Treasury agent Rhys Bevan had told her to meet here would come outside and make himself known. Otherwise she would have to enter blindly, even though she was not fully satisfied that no one had followed her from Norfolk.

Jacques Sundown had remained there to track down Colonel de Warde, while she had come north to meet the agent. She could only hope he would be recognizable. Most of the special intelligence operatives had not seen one another since the unit's formation. The exceptions were Marsh and O'Hara and herself, as well as a traitorous double agent whom O'Hara had shot in a Richmond tavern.

"O'Hara!" she had shouted at the time, "stop shooting! You've probably killed him!"

"That was the intention. Why are you so riled up, Red? I fired because he was trying to kill you."

"We needed information from him," she had said accusingly, after finding that the turncoat agent was indeed dead. "About his connections with Confederate intelligence."

"Bevan told me to use any means necessary to stop this bastard."

"I'm certain Bevan *meant* stop, not permanently silence him."

As she later discovered, the double agent had been carrying a "Proceed at Once" order to destroy the *Monitor*. The one to whom the order had been directed was ultimately thwarted, but thanks in part to O'Hara's fatal shots, the one or ones who had ordered the sabotage remained unknown. The episode had only deepened her distrust of Kerry O'Hara.

She thought now that if she'd known beforehand what a godforsaken spot this would be, she wouldn't have made the hike to the Black Gull alone. Or she would have waited until daybreak. But time was too valuable to waste second-guessing herself.

She wore the blue cloth jacket and trousers of a seaman, since Norfolk and its surroundings were in the U.S. Navy's hands. Not too many hands were needed, because the whole area was sparsely populated. Two months ago President Lincoln himself directed the bloodless recapture of the Navy Yard, and shortly after she had landed here from Fort Monroe with Union troops. Her assignment at that time, coordinated with Secretary Fox's navy men, had been to intercept the *Monitor*'s saboteur. And here she was again, playing yet another hazardous role directed by Fox and Rhys Bevan.

Only a few more seamen had left the tavern in the past minutes, none of them an agent she recognized. He must be waiting inside. She took another scan around before creeping to stand beside the door. Her black cloth navy cap had no visor, and her upper face felt naked. Before leaving Berkeley she had found an army barber, and her hair now curled just above her collar, so she pulled her neckerchief up to her chin. Since this couldn't be put off any longer, she would soon find out if she passed for a sailor.

Once through the noisily groaning door, smoke and the smell of stale beer and whiskey hit her, and something once again began tugging urgently at the back of her mind. This sensation kept happening, and she couldn't find the source of it. If some memory was important enough to keep calling her, why didn't it show itself? Or could it have been formed so long ago that it signified nothing in the present?

She had taken two steps into the barroom, trying to see through the smoke, when a hand clamped her shoulder. Her own hand curled around the derringer nestled in her jacket pocket.

"Got a match on ye, boy?" growled a raw voice, belonging to a bewhiskered, unkempt man of indeterminate age. The butt of a cigar, just being pulled from his dirty overalls, brought Bronwen's recall to heel.

She should have expected him. Who else among the Treasury agents would lodge at this place other than the eccentric, or maybe half-mad, Mr. White. His first name was unknown by anyone other than Rhys Bevan, who had hired the convicted counterfeiter. White's services had undoubtedly come cheap.

"Where's the Injun?" he grunted.

Bronwen pulled out of his grasp and lied, "*Mr.* Sundown is waiting just outside. I assume from your question that you've been in contact with the chief?"

"Thee's correct. Infernal telegraph machine's down the road apiece."

She glanced around to see who might be interested in this conversation and spotted only a few shabbily dressed civilians slumped over the bar, all of them holding cigarettes, whose smoke added to what had surely lingered there for years. Beyond them, another three men in seamen's blue were raucously shooting darts in between their swigs of beer. Bronwen guessed, on the basis of the carefree navy men she had seen at this tavern tonight, that she might be in the wrong branch of her country's service.

"Ya want somethin', boy?" called the plump, pink-faced man behind the bar, who was probably the tavern owner. He was peering at her through the haze with what seemed intense scrutiny, but given the tavern's desolate location, strangers were unlikely to wander in here often. A new face might be a noteworthy event.

"No, Lester, but thank ye kindly," White answered the man. "This boy has taken the pledge, and what ye see here is a reformed drunk." His description did have the effect of dampening any further interest in her by Lester and his customers.

White clamped her shoulder again and propelled her down a dingy narrow corridor. Once beyond sight of those in the barroom, Bronwen dug in her heels and brought them to a halt.

"Where are you taking me?"

"Room," he muttered.

"I'd rather not."

"Ye scared? Thought the Injun was just outside."

From the way it was said, he knew she was alone. And, she reminded herself, half-mad did not mean half-witted, or Rhys wouldn't have hired White, cheap or not.

"Ye have nothin' to fear," White said in a patronizing tone. "When the Lord plucked me outta the gutter, He shook me like a rat 'til I swore to give up me sinful ways. No more gamblin', no drinkin', and no fornicatin'!"

She had already noted that he smelled of coffee, not whiskey, but had no like evidence regarding the other two sins.

"I take it smoking is exempt," she mumbled under her breath, reluctantly trailing him down a dank narrow hall while the floorboards squealed underfoot. Feeling her way along, her hand kept encountering holes in the wall that had probably been made by bullets. The idea of being ambushed in the Black Gull made her grip the derringer in her pocket.

When he shoved open a creaking door with his boot, she pulled back. Given Mr. White's casual approach to personal cleanliness, she did not look forward to seeing his room.

"Thee looks like a trapped hare," he said. "Can't abide shrinkin' women!"

She was about to remind him that he'd sworn off women, but when he fixed her with a gimlet eye, she guessed this would not be well received.

After waiting until he lit a lantern, she stepped into a room as dingy and musty smelling as the rest of the Black Gull, and size of a closet. Wine stains and more bullet and possibly knife holes graced the wall. On the floor lay a thin mattress carrying other stains that might have been made in Blackbeard's day.

There was one telling exception to the tawdry gloom. A table had been crammed into the center of the floor, and its ancient gouged top looked recently cleaned and polished. Placed in a tidy row on it were tools of Mr. White's trade; an inkwell sat beside a set of sharpened quill pens in various sizes, along with a jeweler's glass, a chunk of sealing wax, and what looked like official U.S. government stamps. Hanging over the table, and pinned to a line running between a wall hook and the one window frame, were pieces of paper with writing on them. Two were large, and Bronwen assumed they were some variety of forged documents. The others were the size of banknotes.

While the Lord had been shaking Mr. White like a rat, a mention of larceny must have slipped His mind.

White unpinned the two large pieces of paper and spread them on the tabletop. After wedging the jeweler's glass in place over one eye, he adjusted the lantern and sat down in a rickety chair. And proceeded to examine each paper with far more attention than Bronwen had seen surgeons give a fractured bone.

She waited quietly, but the examination proved to be a lengthy procedure. Finally, as a preliminary to what she most wanted to know, she asked, "How long have you been here?"

"Long enough," he muttered.

"Have you spotted agent O'Hara anywhere in Norfolk?"

Receiving an unintelligible grunt, she tried again. "Do you know what O'Hara looks like?"

"Like he's cock o' the walk."

"That's him."

"Ain't seen him."

"What about an Englishman named Colonel de Warde?

Slim, well-dressed, features sharp like a bird of prey, always carries a black walking stick?"

"Ain't seen him neither. Ain't been lookin' for cocks nor Brits."

"Mr. White, in addition to, ah, printing, what might you have been doing here?"

"Hangin' round barrooms. Good place to pick up things. Bevan said to learn what I could 'bout a dead man named Quiller."

"And what did you learn?" she asked eagerly.

"That he's dead."

In frustration she wondered if she wasn't asking the right questions. "Ah, did you find out anything other than the fact that Quiller's dead?"

"One sailor allowed as how he helped pull Quiller's body outta Hampton Roads."

"Anything more?"

"Had a bullet hole in his head. Here's your papers," White added, giving her the two documents.

"What are these?"

"Boarding passes. Works of art. Should get ye on any ship, Yank or Reb. Bevan approved the one with Fox's signature, and t'other one's Reb navy secretary Mallory's."

He got to his feet and unpinned two smaller pieces of paper. These he gave only a cursory glance before handing them to her.

"And these are what?" she asked.

"Credentials. Says thee's a special agent for Navy Secretary Fox, or for Mallory, dependin' on the occasion. Have ye made peace with the Lord?"

Startled, she just nodded at the ominous question, afraid anything else might bring forth a revivalist rant. Had he already made plans to attend her funeral?

"Mr. White, why would I need these documents?"

"Are ye deaf? So's ye can board a ship!"

"Yes, but why would I want to do that?"

"Mebbe ye do and mebbe ye don't."

Bronwen stepped to the door and backed against it to assume a defensive position, wondering if Rhys might have overestimated White's sanity. Maybe those bygone days of sin had addled his brain.

"Ah, Mr. White, I don't wish to be rude, but would you please *be more specific*?"

"No need to get testy, woman. Why didn't ye just say so?"

"I apologize. Let's start again. You must believe I might want to board a boat—"

"Ship!"

"Why do you believe that?"

"On account of what that Miz Van Lew said."

"Elizabeth Van Lew? Have you seen her?"

"Nope. Got a message from one of her farmers, tho."

Elizabeth Van Lew owned parcels of land along the James, renting them out to loyalist farmers who had become part of her spy network. They passed information in relay fashion to Fort Monroe.

"A message about what?" she asked, trying to curb her impatience.

" 'Nother shipment's due in on a blockade-runner, tomorrow night or the next."

Since they already knew that, Bronwen simply nodded in disappointment. It then occurred to her to wonder how anyone, including the anonymous source, would know *when* a shipment was due.

"Did this come from the person who's been giving information to Miss Van Lew?" she asked.

"So she said in the message. She weren't sure it got through afore."

"Mr. White, do you have Miss Van Lew's message here?"

" 'Course not. An agent's s'posed to destroy sensitive correspondence."

"You destroyed it?"

"Are ye deaf? I said so. Why can't ye listen, so's I don't have to keep repeatin' myself? Lord, give me strength!"

He got up abruptly and yanked open a duffel bag to withdraw a tall brown bottle. Its label, which Bronwen had to crane her neck to see, read: DR. ABERNATHY'S AMAZING RESTORATIVE TONIC. White yanked out the cork and swilled down a goodly amount, grimaced, and set the bottle on the floor with a thump.

He looked at Bronwen with a smile of satisfaction, saying, "Can't offer ye none of that, 'cause ye ain't old enough to need it."

Was it possible he didn't know these so-called restorative tonics were usually ninety proof? No, it was not possible.

"Ah, Mr. White—"

"Now woman, ye just got to keep quiet whilst I tell this. I ain't got all night."

Bronwen agreed, pressing her back against the door.

"Good," he said in a heartier voice. "Now, Miz Van Lew, she just learned 'bout that Quiller feller's death. So's she sends this message by way of her farmers, who I was talkin' to yesterday. Are ye with me?"

"I am."

"Seems Miz Van Lew had told this feller Quiller—'fore he died, a' course—that she got information from that anonymous source 'bout the date and place to look for a blockade-runner comin' through. Quiller told her he would make a map of where the ship was due to pass, so she could send it on to Fort Monroe. Did ye know that poor dead feller, Quiller, was a mapmaker?"

"Yes," she answered absently, because jumping to her mind was Kathryn's recollection that Van Lew had visited

Quiller at Chimborazo. And had brought some papers with her. Had it been the information from the anonymous source that was too valuable to trust to memory?

She nodded at White, but held her breath with anxiety, fearing the effect of Dr. Abernathy's tonic in loosening the man's tongue would wear off too soon.

"According to her message, Miz Van Lew never saw Quiller agin, nor got that map neither. She thinks Quiller took it to his death, so's she wrote down all he told her. Ye listenin'?"

"To every word."

White looked skeptical, which was apparently reason enough to restore himself again. After he had plunked the bottle down on the floor a second time, Bronwen began to fear he might pass out before giving her Elizabeth Van Lew's entire message, and she said firmly, "Please go on, Mr. White."

Showing no ill effects whatever, he turned nimbly to unpin the last piece of paper from the line and handed it to her with an overly friendly smile. "How old are ye, woman?"

"Not old enough!" She moved to the far side of the table and flattened the paper under the lantern.

It held White's detailed map. She had copied maps herself and recognized that this was excellent work. From what she could recall of the ones she'd seen of the Virginia peninsula, this map even looked to scale. She would need to apologize to Rhys for having doubted his judgment about recruiting White. O'Hara was another matter. As she peered down at the Chesapeake, Hampton Roads, and the James River, she noticed a tiny strip of land with an X on it.

"Mr. White, does this X mark the Black Gull? Here?"

"It does."

"Why?"

"Do ye think I'm in this infernal hovel by choice? That's where Miz Van Lew's message said the signal's comin' from?"

"What signal?"

"The signal tellin' the blockade-runner the coast is clear."

Feeling weak at the knees, Bronwen leaned her weight on the table. "How does the one signaling from here know the runner has arrived out there?"

" 'Nother signal."

"One sent from the ship when it arrives in Hampton Roads?"

"Ye are smart enough for a woman's who's deaf. Ye ain't too bad to look at, neither."

"Signal?" she repeated, thinking furiously. "What kind of signal? To be seen after dark, it must be from a lantern."

"Flashin' light."

"Who gives it? Did Miss Van Lew's source happen to mention the blockade-runner's name? Was it Lockwood?"

White, looking put out by these excessive demands, reached for Dr. Abernathy, saying, "If I knew all that, I would have told ye."

SHE had wanted to depart by way of the window, but when she tried to open it, years' worth of paint, none of it recent, had sealed it shut. By this point Mr. White was so restored he couldn't move, so she gave up on the window and crept down the hallway. Waiting until she made sure Lester and his customers were not watching, she dashed past the barroom. Only in the nick of time did she remember the groaning entrance door.

Someone in that barroom might be the one who sent signals to the blockade-runner. It took a toll on her nerves, and what little remaining strength she had in her left arm, to carefully lift the ancient door on its remaining hinges.

"Hey, you damn crook!" came a nearby shout. "Put that dart back and quit cheatin'."

She forced herself to wait until a gust of laughter from the barroom covered any noise she might make slipping through the crack she had opened. Rounding a corner of the tavern, she pressed against its wall, attempting to scan the surroundings. It was too dark to see any distance, but she had to leave, since the hike to Norfolk could take until dawn. After checking once again, she raced from the tavern, and gave it wide berth as she struck out wearily for the narrow dirt road ahead.

Suddenly a shadowy figure moved into her path. She sucked in her breath, but managed to yank out the derringer.

"Too slow," said a voice.

"You're right," she agreed. "I'm out of practice." But no one other than Jacques Sundown could have materialized without even a whisper of sound. "What are you doing here?"

"Brought a horse."

"My hero! I was doubtful I could make it back to Norfolk."

"Horse is faster."

As they went toward the horse, and the moon slid from behind feathered clouds, Bronwen looked sideways at Jacques. The man never seemed to change. Not since she had been a girl and he had taught her to throw a knife. Day after day she had practiced it, over and over until her arm and shoulder ached unbearably, desperate to do it perfectly so he would give her more than a passing glance. As Kathryn had said, there was a dangerous look about him, almost as if he had taken on the spirit of a wolf; the wolf of his Seneca mother's clan.

As she expected, the horse he had ridden here was a

handsome black-and-white paint. Jacques rarely rode any other, and how he found these paints everywhere he went was just as inexplicable as the man himself. Bronwen had once fantasized that they were all the same horse, conjured by Jacques whenever he needed it.

After she climbed up behind him, and they started at a slow canter for Norfolk, she said, "I assume you found de Warde." Jacques wouldn't be here otherwise.

"Found him. Sure you want to see him?"

"I don't *want* to see him, but I have to."

"Man's got the look of a twisted snake."

"What's a twisted snake?"

"More dangerous than most snakes. Makes like he's sleeping, so you can't know he's ready to strike."

"That sounds like de Warde. Did you tell him I need to see him?"

"You don't tell a twisted snake anything. Not until you have a knife ready, gun aimed, and getaway route in sight."

"I've dealt with de Warde before, keeping all those things pretty much in mind."

Jacques half-turned in the saddle. "If you lived to tell it, that twisted snake got himself outsmarted. Could have told him you want to see him."

25

I agree . . . we ought ourselves to recognize the
Southern States as an independent State.
—Lord John Russell, letter to British prime minister
Lord Henry Palmerston, England, 1862

Norfolk, Virginia

"Miss Llyr, what a delightful surprise! How kind of
you to come."

Despite Colonel Dorian de Warde's quick recovery and
effusive greeting, he had at first looked suitably startled
by Bronwen's arrival at his waterfront office. The sign on
its door read: OFFICE OF CROWN IMPORTS AND EXPORTS.
She suspected it should also read: OFFICE OF BLOCKADE-
RUNNING, LTD.

"I believe we have several items to discuss, Colonel de
Warde."

"Do we indeed?" he said, as if she habitually paid him
social calls solely for the dubious pleasure of his company.
He also seemed amused at her use of his rank, since in the
past she had confined her address to simply "de Warde."

"Please do sit down, my dear," he told her, having risen
from his chair when she entered, and now pulled out the
room's only other chair opposite an undersized desk. She

wondered if he actually did any work here. The minuscule office might be only a convenient place to receive messages and an occasional visitor, as for instance, a disguised agent of Confederate Intelligence.

Before seating herself, she gathered up the skirt of her cotton dress, purchased this morning at a Norfolk dry goods store. She could hardly meet with de Warde wearing a Union navy seaman's garb, and would have felt at a disadvantage in shabby farmer's overalls. In the past year and a half that she'd been forced into contact with the Englishman, he had always been dressed in elegant fashion, as though at any minute he might be summoned for an audience with his queen.

As she sat down, a single, sepia-toned photograph on his desk caught her attention. It was that of a lovely dark-haired woman wearing an Indian sari. De Warde, who must have seen her observing it, asked, "Would you have heard of the Sepoy Mutiny, Miss Llyr?"

"I recall learning something about it. Wasn't it a revolt against the British by some of the Bengal army?"

"Yes, in 'fifty-seven. I had left my post in Delhi a year before that, intending to return shortly, but events in England kept me there longer than expected. By the time I could return to India, the woman in that photograph had been killed in the Sepoy uprising. Killed because she had married an Englishman. Bakula was my wife."

For a shocked moment, Bronwen could only stare at him dumbly, before recovering enough to murmur the banal, "I'm sorry, I didn't know."

Of course she couldn't have known, and wished she didn't now. It had never occurred to her that de Warde might have a wife, or a family, or any life at all beyond his devious dealings in the United States. Not that learning he did made him any less dangerous. She reminded herself that he had caused one death and been indirectly responsible for who knew how many others, and the story behind the photograph only put a more human face on de Warde. But enemies should not have faces.

He was scrutinizing her while he lightly fingered the blade of a letter-opener, almost as if he regretted divulging something about himself and now felt subtle intimidation was necessary to balance the scales.

"I do not flatter myself," he said, "that you have come merely to wish me *bon voyage*."

"Why, are you planning a cruise? Perhaps to somewhere such as the smuggler's port of Nassau?"

Ignoring the barb, he answered, "My dear, you didn't know? I have been recalled to London."

It was not hard to keep from visibly reacting to this piece of news, because Bronwen didn't know whether to rejoice, or to worry that his successor might be even more treacherous. That seemed unlikely.

"Surely you aren't abandoning your business investments in America," she said, pretending disbelief. "For instance, your railroad interests and your tobacco that remains in Richmond."

"Alas, my queen needs me, my dear, and one does not ignore Her Royal Highness. Thus I have divested myself of the Southern railroad interests, although at a lamentable loss. As for the tobacco, after you so cleverly salvaged the bulk of it for the queen, some of my own modest portion also found its way to England."

"How did you accomplish that?"

When he didn't respond, she made an educated guess, saying, "One of your English ships ran the blockade with it. And I'll wager its captain's name was Lockwood."

He smiled, and while not denying it, he asked, "Why would you think that?"

"Do you believe we don't know that Lockwood has been steaming in and out of Richmond with relative ease?"

"And are plans afoot to stop him?"

She matched his smile, not ready to use her one bargaining chip for information she might already own. There was something more urgent, although related, that she wanted from de Warde. The trick would be to catch him off guard, which, while not easily done, she had managed to do once before. A few preliminary feints might pave the way.

"Colonel de Warde, did you know that the president's friend James Quiller has been murdered?"

"Indeed I did not!"

His expression of shock was persuasive, but she couldn't rely on her sense that it was sincere. "Who do you suppose might have done it?" she asked him with practiced innocence.

"I cannot imagine. My dear, you surely cannot harbor even a hint of suspicion that I would countenance such a perfidious act."

Forgoing the obvious skeptical reply, she said only, "Then perhaps one of your Confederate friends, for example an agent of Major Norris's intelligence network?"

Without a trace of hesitation he replied, "I think not! Major Norris has given me every assurance that civilians would not be targeted. And I judge that he has seen the error of any such previous excesses."

It was such a revealing, and damning, denial that she half-believed him. In the meantime, the sudden nature of his forthcoming departure had fully registered and was troubling her. Given Secretary Fox's grim prediction, and Rhys Bevan's disclosure, she should press the matter.

"Why are you *really* leaving?" she asked abruptly.

"As I said, my queen has need of me."

"Forgive me, de Warde, but you and I have fenced too often for me to miss an evasion when I hear one."

To her surprise, he put down the letter-opener and said,

"You are quite right. I have in the past underestimated you, and will not do it again."

"So?"

"I am returning to England to join the debate—which will soon become a formal one—regarding recognition of the Southern Confederacy."

"Why at this time?" Although she could predict his answer, she asked because Rhys would demand a word-by-word account.

Again de Warde surprised her by answering bluntly, "The Federal campaign to capture Richmond was an ignominious failure. It has led a number of those influential in British politics to believe that the Confederate states will succeed in winning their independence."

"How large a number believe it?"

"Perhaps sufficiently large."

"Then you had best advise your countrymen, Colonel de Warde, that Lincoln will not allow the South to gain its independence. No one in Britain should doubt that, not for a minute."

De Warde sat back in his chair, silently regarding her, while she waited. At last he said, "I tend to believe your president's resolve. The question is not *his* will, but the willingness of the North to stay the course with him. As casualty figures mount, due to ineptly led campaigns such as the latest one, Northerners may simply refuse the sacrifice."

"Lincoln will keep the North with him."

"Perhaps. He must recognize that a split between North and South would produce the same endless petty wars over territorial boundaries, trade, and religion that have plagued the European countries for centuries."

Bronwen, seizing the opportunity, sat forward to say, "And here there would always be the inflammatory issue of slavery. Lincoln is determined to win this war, and he intends to address slavery as the root of it."

De Warde straightened in the chair. "Is that an opinion, Miss Llyr, or do you have evidence to support it? Before you answer, I am confident you will give my query careful thought."

"It doesn't require thought," she said, thereby telling him that she was merely acting as messenger. "The president is now drafting a preliminary emancipation proclamation. He will announce it within the next few months."

"Indeed," was all de Warde said. "Indeed."

It was all she had expected him to say.

When she rose from the chair as if intending to leave, he also got to his feet, rounding the desk to position himself by the door. The first thing she had done when entering was check to see that his lethal walking stick was in the umbrella stand, so it was more habit than apprehension that made her thrust her hand into her skirt pocket and curl it around her derringer. It was only a precaution in case he felt an urge to kill the messenger.

"Before we part, Miss Llyr, I must tell you that I greatly admire much about your young country. No, do not look skeptical, it is quite true. And in many ways you are yourself a mirror of it. Bold, inventive, courageous—altogether a most worthy adversary."

"You neglected to mention one thing, Colonel de Warde," she said lightly, with a rare smile she hoped would lower his guard still more.

"Beauty is randomly bestowed and not earned, as are your other assets."

"Reminding me that you are a businessman, and are obliged to maintain a balance sheet."

"Ah, yes—as in credits and debits, perhaps?"

"Surely you didn't expect me to forget a certain debt?"

"If so, it seems I was woefully in error. Tell me, my

dear, how I can repay it, and I shall make every effort to do so."

De Warde being de Warde, he would anticipate only what he would consider payment. Since she needed him flustered, she answered immediately with her eyes riveted on his, "How credible is the rumor of an attempt on the president's life?"

And she caught it, just a fleeting flicker in the black eyes. "Who's behind it?" she demanded.

"My dear, I don't know——"

"You *do* know! You owe me, de Warde, and I'm calling for repayment now."

"And here I believed that when saving my life you did it for the most noble of motives." When she didn't reply, he sighed, saying, "Very well. I heard the rumor, but have learned nothing more and have no names for you. That is the truth, Miss Llyr."

"Will you swear to it on the head of your queen?"

"My dear girl!"

"On the memory of that woman on your desk who was killed because of you?"

He blanched and took a step backward. "Miss Llyr, I regret that you have become quite ruthless."

"And where do you suppose I learned it? When you double-crossed me in Richmond, de Warde, you had no inkling I expected you to do exactly that. As a result, by the time you reneged on our agreement, your role in it was already unnecessary. My brother was free of Libby Prison."

"He had escaped? How extremely fortunate," he added, but not soon enough to cover his surprise at learning he had been outmaneuvered.

She was gaining ground, but had to keep him off balance.

"For all you knew or cared, de Warde, my brother would have hanged. And then there was Pinkerton agent Timothy Webster, who *did* hang, with your pounds sterling helping to pay his betrayer. Of course there was also the *Monitor* saboteur, the one you killed before he could——"

"I do *not* have the name of a possible assassin," he interrupted, an uncharacteristic sheen of perspiration appearing on his forehead. Perhaps he had just now seen that she had insinuated herself between him and the umbrella stand.

"I think you do," she contradicted. "You understand, I assume, that one word from me will prevent you leaving Norfolk?"

"That threat's unworthy of you, my dear. If you were to have me arrested, it could only be on some trumped-up charge that could never be proved."

"It doesn't have to be provable. Just imaginative enough for Treasury to keep you in a dirty prison cell for a good long time. The *habeas corpus* privilege has been suspended here, or hadn't you heard? So don't tempt me!"

His moist face told her that he recognized she might be able to have him detained. It was also possible that he didn't know the name of the would-be assassin. But she was sure he knew something.

"I want a name," she said again, "or you won't see England and your queen until long after they've forgotten you exist."

"If I had the name, Miss Llyr, I would give it to you. If only because I believe assassination is a foolish and dangerous idea. The South and Britain could find themselves dealing with someone far less intelligent or restrained than Lincoln."

"I'll be sure to make mention of that while you're being held for questioning," she said, strengthening her bluff by reaching for the doorknob. "Although I doubt it will do you much good. U.S. courts won't like the notion that Britain is involved in a plot to kill our president."

"*Britain* involved? That is completely untrue!"

"Pity, because if anyone suspects it is true you'll be languishing in prison for nothing."

He whipped a snow-white handkerchief from a breast pocket and wiped his forehead.

"Who's behind it? Is it Major Norris and Confederate intelligence? The lunatic secessionists of that Baltimore cabal?" she persisted as he applied the handkerchief again. "The Confederate military, or agents of British intelligence—in other words, de Warde, one of yours?"

"No! It's one of *yours*."

26

—⁊⁊⁊—

With Cain go wander through the shade of night,
And never show thy head by day or light.
                                                    —Shakespeare

Hampton Roads

$\mathcal{B}$ronwen crouched in the stern of the navy cutter *Ramrod*, frequently raising her field glasses to scan the southern shore. She did it more from nervousness than because she expected to see anything. Some time ago a cloudbank had swept over the moon, plunging the shores and tidal waters of Hampton Roads into darkness. While the clouds obscured vision, they might be a stroke of good luck if they encouraged a wary blockade-running captain to make a dash for the James.

She drew in a deep breath of salt-tanged air to ease her tension. All she could do at this point was wait. Wait and worry that too much rested on information given Elizabeth Van Lew by an unknown source. But what else did they have? The greatest fear now was that if a blockade-runner could slip undetected through the Roads, so too could an assassin's ship whose cargo was not contraband weapons but something even more deadly.

Too dispiriting to dwell on was the distinct possibility that the source's information had been accurate, but Captain Lockwood had somehow been alerted and was now far from here on another course.

She raised the glasses again, this time whacking the bridge of her nose as the anchored, light-draft cutter bobbed in the wake of a larger ship.

"You sure we're in the right place?" the *Ramrod*'s helmsman asked her for the second time.

"As sure as I can be," she answered in a whisper, the nervousness making her throat so dry she couldn't speak much louder.

"Okay, we'll stand by." He sounded even more dubious than he had the first time they'd been through this. "Just remember we need to stoke the engine to get under way."

She simply nodded, avoiding comment on the obvious need for patience, a quality which had never been her own strong suit.

Where was Lockwood? Could he be riding at anchor, too, lurking somewhere farther downstream? Still en route to the Chesapeake? Or maybe she and the others aboard the *Ramrod* had missed the cue, and the blockade-runner was already in the James.

Anxiously raising the glasses again, she swung them over the surrounding water. Only a handful of ship lights could be seen winking through the blackness. Apparently Treasury had been successful in persuading the Navy to order some of its patrolling Federal ships to temporarily change course. Not enough of them to cause suspicion, she had emphasized in the telegram sent to Rhys Bevan following her session with de Warde; only enough to make a sparsely traveled open Roads irres: tible to a captain seeking safe passage. Rhys obviously would have preferred to bait this trap himself, but there had not been enough time for him to reach Norfolk. Not if Lockwood was intending to make the run tonight.

Secretary Fox had left Washington for the trans-Mississippi theater of war two days ago, or so Rhys's return telegram had stated. Which explained why Fox had not responded to the wires sent him from Harrison's Landing. And they still had no lead at all to the possible whereabouts of O'Hara.

When de Warde's emphatic "It's one of *yours!*" had finally confirmed Bronwen's worst fears, the sharp pang of regret she had felt surprised her. Despite all her suspicions, she must have been harboring some hope that O'Hara was not a double agent, using Treasury to keep abreast of the North's intelligence-gathering activity. Her telegram to Rhys had contained an adamant demand for secrecy regarding this mission, the details of which she didn't dare spell out in a wire. O'Hara was better than anyone when it came to tapping telegraph lines. Rhys's response had been ready agreement. Which told her that he at last recognized O'Hara's duplicity.

A sudden movement at her elbow made her jump, but it was just Lieutenant Minor, the *Ramrod*'s young commanding officer. "Want some coffee, Miss Llyr?"

"Thank you, yes," she answered, taking the tin mug he handed her. The coffee was cool, but strong.

"Still too dark to spot much," he said to her. Unlike his helmsman, the lieutenant had enthusiasm for the mission that was transparent, although he had learned the particulars of it only after casting off from Norfolk. She was taking no chances. O'Hara could have collaborators anywhere.

"What do you think now?" he asked.

"I think we pray hard that our informant is reliable. And we wait until he proves otherwise. Or until dawn."

The night was hot and the humid air oppressive. When,

after steaming into the Roads, she had removed her cap and outer jacket, the lieutenant's stunned expression said it had never crossed his mind that Agent Llyr might be female.

"It must be exciting, what you do," he said now, his voice bearing some envy. "Don't mean to offend you, but I've got three sisters, and I can't see any of them . . . that is, I can't picture a woman in this kind of work."

"That's exactly the point, Lieutenant. The other side can't picture it either."

With a shake of his head, he moved off. Having a woman on his hands plainly troubled him. But Bronwen was just as troubled by having an inexperienced officer in charge if and when the trap was sprung.

There were so many spies in Washington that she had feared word could leak out if a more ambitious operation were mounted. The *Ramrod*'s twelve-man crew was fewer than she had wanted, but again, time was the determining factor. Without Fox available to cut through red tape, it could have taken hours, even days, to commandeer a larger ship and crew. Mr. White's forgeries had done their job, if only because the eager Lieutenant Minor had barely examined them. Stationed for weeks off Norfolk, he had seemed overjoyed at the prospect of taking part in some action.

"I don't like it, Pilot," said Lockwood, watching from the *Portia*'s deck as the moon slowly emerged from behind the cloudbank.

"Won't last," replied Artemis, who was also studying the sky.

"Even so, the tide's ebbing, and the wind's shifting. One hurdle to jump is bad enough, but together with that moon they make me think the fates are against us this night. A prudent man would turn around."

"Didn't know you was superstitious, Capt'n. Do know you ain't got repute for prudence!"

It drew a faint smile from Lockwood, but he sobered when a wave splashed against the *Portia*'s hull. "Steady!" he called softly, and ordered steam to be reduced still more. They were at a near standstill.

With the wind lightly ruffling his red beard, Artemis raised his telescope and scanned westward toward the distant mouth of the James River. Lockwood did the same, but swung his glass to follow the south shore of Hampton Roads. Then suddenly it was as black as the inside of a witch's cauldron, the moon once more covered by clouds.

Before leaving Nassau, Lockwood had weighed whether the danger of running up the James again was worth what even he acknowledged to be an exorbitant fee. His price to take the weapons directly to Richmond was significantly more than if they were forced to go there by rail from the port of Wilmington. No one, including the Englishman de Warde, had protested it too bitterly as yet, but the passage through Hampton Roads was becoming increasingly hazardous. The money would do him no damn good in a prison cell.

"Wind's down," Artemis announced a short while later, staring at his motionless beard, and not even glancing at the ship's vane. "Down to stay."

Lockwood figured that for what he paid his pilot, he should be entitled to a less primitive weather indicator. Not that Artemis had ever been wrong.

"So's we got only the moon and tide to plague us," the pilot said, "and traffic in the Roads tonight is thin. Huggin' the shore should keep us out of harm's way."

Lockwood nodded, but had already decided to wait and see what the next minutes brought in the way of moonlight. He had little flexibility, since tomorrow's moon would be fuller, and there might be no cloud cover. Also, Artemis was right; the Roads seemed to hold fewer ships tonight than of late. When a vague sense of uneasiness rose, he dismissed it. The reason for fewer ships might be due to an advance of Confederate forces on the Federal encampment at Harrison's Landing. In which case the U.S. Navy would have its attention focused on the land, not the river. The *Portia* could slide like a shadow along the James, where on its south bank Confederate shore batteries would have been alerted. If a Union ship stopped her then, the medical supplies in the hold could account for her trip upriver.

When the moon had been fully obscured for some time, Lockwood made his decision. "Send the signal!"

One if by land, two if by sea.

Telescope to his eye, Lockwood watched the south shore. When a period of time elapsed with no answering flashes, he began to say, "Repeat signal," but stopped himself because the vague uneasiness had returned. He again considered ordering the *Portia* back to the Chesapeake without further tempting fate.

"There it be, Capt'n!" Artemis was pointing toward the south shore, where a blue light blinked: *Two by sea.* Repeated twice.

"All set to run," the pilot said, tugging his beard in a rare display of enthusiasm. "Can hear them pretty Richmond ladies callin' loud and clear!"

Lockwood glanced at the dark sky again, shaking off the formless misgivings. "Fire the boiler," he called down the engine room tube.

As the *Portia* moved forward, gathering steam, Lockwood glanced over the side, turning his head to listen as water slid past the hull. Frowning, he told his pilot, "I want a sounding. That last reading you gave me indicated more depth than what I'm sensing."

Artemis mumbled, "Ebb tide," but did as he was ordered.

The moon was creeping from behind the clouds when, minutes later and the *Portia* well under way, Lockwood again thought he sensed shallows. "Pilot," he called, "what's the depth?"

Artemis was bending over the tidal current charts and didn't immediately answer.

"Capt'n!" came the lookout's voice. "Ship approaching to starboard. No lights on it 'til just now."

"Steady as she goes," Lockwood ordered, raising his telescope and swinging it to his right. His jaw clenched when the other ship began flashing a signal for the *Portia* to stop.

The moon was half-hidden, but the bobbing lights of the approaching vessel indicated a light-draft ship. With some relief Lockwood concluded it was too small for a Federal gunboat.

"Capt'n," said Artemis at his shoulder, "they're comin' on fast! What d'you reckon they want?"

"I'm not stopping to find out. How much depth have I got?"

"Much as you want for now."

Before Lockwood could respond, an order for the *Portia* to halt came booming across the water by means of a megaphone.

"How in hell did it come on us so fast?" Lockwood muttered, peering across the brightening moonlit water. But the answer to his question was obvious. That ship, a cutter from what he could see, had been laying in wait. And its draft would be lighter than his fully loaded sidewheeler. Despite his pilot's reassurance, Lockwood knew there were shallows ahead, and if he tried to escape by speed alone, the *Portia* might run aground before the other ship did. Now, with the cutter approaching at an angle, the *Portia* was caught between its trajectory and the shore.

"It's Federal, Capt'n," said Artemis, the telescope screwed to his eye. "Which means it's armed."

"And if it's been waiting for us, it knows we aren't."

Another order to cut his engine boomed from the Federal ship, approaching at a faster speed than the *Portia* was steaming forward. Lockwood knew its next maneuver would be a warning shot across his bow. An attempt to turn his ship into midstream for a run back to the Chesapeake would put the ships on a collision course. The other captain knew that, which was why his approach was angled. The only chance to evade the cutter would be to slow the *Portia*, and wait until the other ship closed the distance and reduced its speed. Its captain would assume Lockwood was complying. Like hell he would!

Ordering the engine room to decrease steam, he told Artemis, "We're going to run. How far ahead are those shallows now?"

When Lockwood's ship slowed, the cutter also did, drawing nearer to the *Portia*'s starboard bow. Meanwhile Artemis pored over his charts in the stark moonlight.

"Stand by for boarding!" came the cutter's order.

"Depth *now*, Pilot!" snapped Lockwood.

Artemis looked up and nodded. "If you want depth, Capt'n, you still got plenty of it."

"Stand by while I alert the engine room. Once that cutter slows enough to come alongside, we'll slip past and head out into the Roads. It'll take that captain too long to fire his own engine and turn to hit us broadside. He must be either a fool or a new hand at this!"

He waited, his impatience reined by self-control, waited and watched the cutter's approach until the ship was within hailing distance. Then he shouted down the tube "Full steam!"

With a quiver, the *Portia* gathered herself and leaped forward.

Lockwood heard a shot hitting the water off his stern. Moments later the impact of another shot hurled him to the deck. Wrenching shudders were shaking his ship, and together with a series of grinding, thudding groans, they made his blood run cold.

"SHE'S aground!" Bronwen yelled in astonishment to Lieutenant Minor. "Bring *Ramrod* about! Fast!"

"That side-wheeler's not goin' anywhere," a nearby crewmember told her as he unholstered his revolver.

"That's what you told me earlier," she responded, "and her captain almost outfoxed us. How do you know he and his ship won't sprout wings?"

"Wouldn't be more peculiar than getting himself aground," he agreed. "Can't figger it."

She peered through the moonlight at the slate-gray blockade-runner, which appeared to be maybe two hundred feet long, and saw a flurry of activity taking place amidships. It looked as if a lifeboat was about to be lowered. Since Lieutenant Minor seemed to have his hands full bringing the cutter about, she grabbed the megaphone and with little confidence yelled into it, "Surrender peaceably now, or we'll commence firing! And move away from that lifeboat!"

A sudden lurch of the *Ramrod* nearly threw her off her feet, but she regained her balance and repeated the threat. To her surprise, she saw hands being raised on the other ship. They were giving up, just like that?

Glancing aside, she saw the *Ramrod*'s crew lining up along the bow with their rifles and revolvers drawn, aimed at the high and dry targets.

As they steamed closer to the stern of the powerless vessel, her name *Portia* now visible, Lieutenant Minor remarked, "Bet they're all Brits."

"Why do you say that?"

"British crewman are legally non-combatants, so they know they won't be held as prisoners of war."

Bronwen's gaze was locked on the lifeboat, afraid she would see it magically float away with the man she wanted aboard. "It's only the captain I need, and if it's Lockwood, he's South Carolinian," she said, withdrawing the revolver she had obtained this morning after she and Jacques Sundown had gone over their plan. A plan inspired by the pirate treacheries she had imagined while waiting outside the Black Gull Tavern.

"We can't lose that captain, Lieutenant."

"He's all yours," said Minor, pointing toward a lone figure standing at the other ship's bridge.

Bronwen scanned the shoreline, trying to spot an outline of the Black Gull. Jacques had presumably been concealed in its attic, ready to capture the one sending an "all clear" signal to Lockwood. Bronwen wagered it would be the tavern owner, Lester. From her crouch aboard the anchored *Ramrod*, it had been far easier to spot the flashed signal than she had feared.

The navy men had by now jumped aboard the *Portia*, and were beginning to herd its non-resisting crew members together to be manacled. Bronwen, once aboard the side-wheeler's stern, immediately started forward. She had already asked one of the captured crew if his captain was named Lockwood, and had received a sullen nod.

She crept along the *Portia*'s starboard gunwale and stopped, rearing backward when a large shape in front of her suddenly wavered.

"Hands up!" she ordered, her revolver raised.

"They're up," the man answered, lifting his arms. "But it ain't me you're lookin' for."

"Move out into the light," she directed, "and while you're doing it, tell me who *you* are."

As he stepped slowly into the moonlight, she could see a long luxuriant beard, but not much of his features.

"Name's Artemis," he said. "I'm pilot of this here ship."

"In that case, there might be some who think you deserve to be keel-hauled for running her aground. I'd imagine your captain's one of them, although I thank you kindly for it."

Peering down at her, he asked, "You a woman agent?"

Bronwen took a step backward. "Who says I'm an agent?"

"Miz Van Lew. Leastways she told me she's in touch with gov'ment agents."

"*What?*"

"You think I beached this ship by accident? Me, best pilot this side of the Atlantic?"

"Why did you?" she asked, cautious despite the telling reference to Elizabeth Van Lew.

" 'Cause I'm a loyal Unionist, that's why!"

"So it wasn't because you'd made as much money on these trips as you needed? Feared Lockwood was taking too many risks, and decided it might be time for you to retire? And thought you'd ensure your own freedom by putting us onto the captain?"

"You're a suspicious one, ain't you?" But he was smiling, so she probably wasn't far off the mark.

"Why not identify yourself to Miss Van Lew?"

" 'Cause I didn't know where what I was tellin' her was goin'!" he said emphatically. "Damn Rebs got spies all over! How'd I know it weren't goin' to one of them?"

How indeed, she thought bleakly, reminded of de

Warde's chilling revelation. "All right, Artemis, I'll check your story with Miss Van Lew."

When he nodded without hesitation, saying, "She'll tell you it's gospel truth," her skepticism lessened.

"My superior at Treasury will also want to talk with you, so report yourself to Lieutenant Minor back there. And where's Lockwood?"

"He's waitin' on the bridge, bidin' his time 'til he can do some bargainin'. Won't be the first time. An' you watch yourself, miss, 'cause he's a mighty persuasive man. Got himself out of many a tight spot before."

"Apparently he's in this one because he's also a trusting man," she couldn't resist saying. They owed this pilot a vast debt, but even so, disloyalty was never attractive.

Some disloyalties, though, went far beyond being merely unattractive. Some, like O'Hara's, made their owners worthy candidates for firing squads. And despite herself, she felt another stab of regret.

To relieve it, she concentrated on the assassination threat against the president. The first attempt on his life hadn't succeeded owing to timely information and a preemptive defense. But an unforeseen assassin, cunningly concealed and with unknown means of striking, would be nearly impossible to stop.

After watching Artemis lumber toward the bow, Bronwen started for the bridge, but paused, imagining she heard a single, fairly distant boom. From a ship's gun?

She must have been mistaken. What in the waters of Hampton Roads this night could require artillery fire?

When she approached the bridge, the figure she saw leaning against the rail did not remotely resemble the grizzled, leather-skinned seaman she had expected. He looked more like the figure of a dashing Mississippi riverboat gambler in a sketch she'd once seen. Despite this man's seemingly casual stance, arms crossed over his chest, she could sense his tension. By the time she was near enough to take in the handsome profile, and the short, neatly trimmed black hair and beard, he had turned to face her.

"Captain Lockwood," she said, her hand at her side but the revolver in it deliberately visible.

"If I'd known it was a beautiful woman chasing me," he answered in a mocking baritone, "I would have stopped. Running aground makes for a bad first impression."

"Your pilot was responsible for that. I don't think for a minute that you would have stopped."

"And you are?" he asked, his keen eyes measuring her.

"Treasury agent."

"Treasury? I'm no counterfeiter, Miss . . . it is *Miss*?" Without waiting for a response he probably guessed wouldn't be given, he went on, "Your gun isn't necessary, and neither is tying up my crew. Obviously we're not armed."

"And it's a damn good thing you aren't, Captain!"

His black brows lifted and the dark eyes beneath them narrowed as he regarded her more closely. "We're on a humanitarian trip, Miss——may I have your name?"

"Llyr."

"You're right, I wouldn't have stopped," he said, smiling faintly. "You Welsh are a bloodthirsty lot."

"I'm a United States American, Captain. As apparently you were, until South Carolina began this war. But you were saying?"

Only a rueful smile indicated surprise that she knew his background. "My cargo is nothing more martial than medical supplies."

"In that case, you won't mind showing me those supplies. They're bound, I assume, for Chimborazo Hospital."

His smile didn't change, but his eyes widened. He began to reply, but broke off and whirled, as Bronwen did, toward the roar of a ship's gun. By the time water sprayed over the deck, they had both dropped to a crouch.

"What the hell was that?" he said accusingly. "My crew's surrendered!"

Shaking her head, Bronwen climbed to her knees, keeping him in her line of sight while attempting to glance sideways over the rail. Another blast, making the *Portia* rock, sent her scrambling for cover behind the smokestack.

Lockwood yelled, "That's one of your ships!"

"Why would the U.S. Navy fire on its own cutter?" Unless, she thought, it were too dark to identify.

Now on his feet, Lockwood grabbed at her shoulder, shouting, "Get away from that stack—it's too good a target!"

His warning surprised her, but it was likely meant to make him seem more friend and less foe. Evoking for her the pilot's cautionary "He's a mighty persuasive man."

Frenzied shouts were now erupting from the *Ramrod*. Training her gaze and her revolver on Lockwood, she edged sideways to take a quick look around the huge paddlewheel's casing. He moved to stand along the rail, looking down as she did at white signal flags waving from the cutter, along with flashing lights sending what must be identifying messages. And now visible on the moonlit waters of Hampton Roads was the sleek silhouette of a Federal gunboat. It had stopped firing and was steaming toward them, its oil-burning search light slicing through the night with a long yellow beam.

When she saw Lockwood glance toward shore, she followed his look. The ebb tide was pulling water away from the hulls of both his ship and the *Ramrod*, and unless it turned soon, reaching dry land would mean only a short wade.

He was a strongly built man. She didn't doubt that, given the opportunity, he would try to escape and make for shore. It would be reckless to chance being overpowered by him while the *Ramrod*'s crew and Lieutenant Minor were preoccupied with not only the blockade-runner's men, but also the approaching gunboat.

Maintaining a safe distance from Lockwood, her revolver trained on him, she curbed her impatience to wait until the gunboat dispatched a boarding party.

"You might be interested in knowing," she said to him, "that your friends ashore—the ones who signaled when the coast was clear—are being tracked and rounded up even as we speak. How long did you expect to keep running the James without being discovered?"

"As long as wounded troops needed medical supplies." He added in an offhand manner, "How much do Treasury agents get paid?"

"Not as much as blockade-runners. But enough," she said, looking him in the eye. "I'm not greedy, Captain, so don't waste your breath."

"Greed takes different shapes. Almost everyone has a price."

"Which immediately brings to mind a mutual acquaintance. What's Colonel de Warde's price, Lockwood? A share of the sizable profits?"

"You don't expect me to answer that."

It was answer enough. But she was surprised that he had given up so easily an effort to bribe her. Or was he considering something more strenuous than bribery?

She heard with relief the splashing of oars that announced a longboat's arrival with some of the gunboat's crew. A short time later, a staccato bark of commands signaled that navy men were preparing to board. They would hear an account of the blockade-runner's capture from Lieutenant Minor, and probably from Artemis, too, and come looking for her in the hold.

She picked up a lantern with her free hand and gestured

toward the hatchway with her revolver. "Now, about those supplies, Captain Lockwood."

When he stepped aside, the gentleman waiting for the lady to precede him down the companionway steps, she had to smile at this test of her naïveté masked by apparent courtesy.

"Thank you, but no, Captain. You first."

He gave a small shrug and went down the few narrow steps.

The hold was dark and close, with little headroom, owing to the ship's shallow draft, and Lockwood's head barely cleared the planking of the deck above. Bronwen placed the lantern on a nearby cask to free her left hand in case she needed it.

"Move over to that far bulkhead," she directed, pointing toward what was essentially a partition wall separating sections of the hold.

Sudden thumping noises, along with a chorus of male voices on the deck above, indicated crew of the gunboat were boarding. Bronwen could distinguish only the voice of Lieutenant Minor protesting, "But I *did* have orders, sir!"

She glanced uneasily at Lockwood, standing motionless and obviously listening to whoever was questioning Minor's actions. Exactly what was being said was spoken too quietly for her to hear.

She had just decided to announce her presence and that of her prisoner when Minor's voice came again, now more clearly and presumably closer to the hatchway.

"No, sir, I didn't examine any of those papers too closely. It just didn't occur to me, sir, that they might not be authentic. I was told that a blockade-runner was due and—"

His protestation had apparently been cut off, and now Bronwen heard more thumping of boots. While she waited for someone to appear, she tried to think what difference the forged papers could make, assuming it was her papers that were being challenged. She abruptly realized that the thumping sounds were diminishing. With alarm that those above were leaving, she stepped backward toward the companionway.

From the corner of her eye, she saw Lockwood shift in the dim light, and again sensed a coiled-spring tension in him. She raised the revolver and strained to shout as loudly as she could, "Lockwood, I'm a good shot!"

When he stopped, eyes again narrowed and watching her, she yelled, "Lieutenant Minor? I have Captain Lockwood here in the hold!"

A resounding silence followed. And then a series of dull, far-away thuds told her that the navy men must be moving aft or leaving the ship. Meaning she was alone here with Lockwood?

He obviously recognized it, too, sending her a sardonic smile as she inched along the bulkhead behind her, placing herself to the left of the companionway steps so she could follow him back to the deck. For the moment, inspecting his cargo of medical supplies, and the weapons she was positive were stowed beneath them, would have to wait.

She was motioning Lockwood toward the companionway when boots came pounding down the steps. A strapping, dark-coated figure leaped into the hold. Lockwood dropped to the planking a split-second before a revolver shot ripped into the bulkhead behind him.

In the confined area the explosion was deafening. Her ears ringing, Bronwen saw Lockwood dive behind a cask, and could barely hear herself scream, "Don't shoot! He's unarmed!"

The broad-shouldered man in navy uniform swung toward her, his revolver leveled at her chest. When she recognized him, her jolt of shock was seemingly reflected in his voice when he said, "Braveheart! What in God's name are *you* doing here?"

The lieutenant commander's ice-blue eyes were darting glances in the direction of the cask as she sagged back against the bulkhead. "Farrar, I can't think of anyone I'd rather see. But you didn't have to shoot. He's not armed."

"Thought he was holding a hostage down here. You do manage to get yourself into some devilish spots, Braveheart, but why don't you go back on deck while I dispose of this scurrilous bastard."

"Dispose . . . you mean to kill him?"

"How many do you think were killed by guns he ran to Richmond through our blockade?"

"But he's unarmed. And Treasury needs information from him."

"Afraid Treasury will have to do without. I'll not chance him bribing his way past a prison sentence," Farrar replied, and pulled the revolver's trigger.

Wood chips flew from the cask, and amid the ringing in her ears Bronwen heard a shouted curse. She thought it had come from Lockwood, but then saw beside her on the steps a blur of movement.

"Drop the gun, Farrar!" came a familiar voice, its owner dressed in navy seaman's shirt and trousers.

Bronwen, stunned by disbelief and sudden fear, managed to raise her revolver and aim it at Kerry O'Hara.

27

—⁓—

The curse is mutual 'twixt thy sire and thee.
But for thy sons and brothers?

—Byron, *Cain*

Hampton Roads

"Drop the gun *now*!" O'Hara ordered Farrar again, "or I swear I'll kill you without a twitch of conscience."

Farrar had stopped midway to the cask, his revolver lowering as he turned sideways to see O'Hara. "And just who the hell are you?"

Bronwen's throat was so dry she had to swallow several times before she could say, "O'Hara calls himself a U.S. Treasury agent, but he's available to the highest bidder."

Farrar's eyes moved to her. "You mean he's a Rebel spy? A double agent?"

She saw O'Hara's jaw clench. His gaze was fixed on Farrar, but he said out of the corner of his mouth, "Red, what're you talking about?"

With her gun trained on O'Hara, standing between herself and Farrar, a nightmarish memory rose in Bronwen's mind of the similar standoff, two short months ago in a

Richmond tavern, involving the first traitor cloaked in the guise of a Treasury agent.

"O'Hara, I know about you."

"Know what?"

"De Warde *told* me!"

With a crash, the cask toppled and rolled across the floor, drawing Farrar's fire. Lockwood came leaping sideways toward Bronwen and barely avoided the next bullet roaring from Farrar's gun.

With the memory of that earlier, missed opportunity for information, Bronwen sprang in front of Lockwood to cover him. "Farrar, hold your fire! And O'Hara, don't move."

O'Hara, his revolver still aimed at Farrar, said, "Red, what *is* this? And since when did you believe anything that rotten Brit told you? On second thought, don't bother answering. Just go ahead and shoot Farrar!"

"Braveheart, you and I have obviously been laboring under a misunderstanding," Farrar said with his compelling smile. "I had no idea you were so determined to save this blockade-runner's miserable life. But since you are, I will harness what admittedly was my urge to take the law into my own hands. Now, I suggest we disarm your double agent here and put an end to this. We have a bigger war to fight."

While she considered agreeing, O'Hara suddenly laughed. What startled her even more was Lockwood's laugh.

"Such a prince of a fellow you are!" chuckled O'Hara, his revolver trained on Farrar wavering not an inch.

Bronwen tried to concentrate on the indistinct shadows that were gathering in her head, stirred by Lockwood's response. They might serve to clear her confusion if she could find the key to free them.

When she did not move to disarm O'Hara, the three of them continued to stand there. She was aware that Lockwood behind her might at any moment lunge forward and hold her as a shield while attempting an escape, and it could have worried her more than it did if she thought he was a man who would hide behind a woman. But O'Hara might not hesitate to kill her if his masquerade were endangered. Rhys might suspect him, but that suspicion could not save her now.

As if reading her mind, O'Hara said, "I don't know what you're blaming me for, Red, but whatever it is, I'm the wrong target. Where do you think I've been for the past two days?"

When she didn't reply, he said, "Okay, since you're so eager to know, I'll tell you. Secretary Fox sent me on a mission."

"O'Hara, I know Fox has left Washington."

"But not before he gave me permission to investigate Quiller's untimely demise. I felt kind of responsible, since I was the last of us good folks to see him alive."

"Go on," she said, praying it wasn't some perverse affection for him that made her agree to listen.

"One place I've been," he said, "was stowed aboard Farrar's ship. I followed him here."

Now it was Farrar who laughed, but at the same time Bronwen saw his hand move infinitesimally. "Take your finger off the trigger, Farrar."

"Braveheart, this is absurd—"

"Let him finish! Keep going, O'Hara."

"I was interested in Farrar's gunboat because that's where I dropped Quiller after leaving Chimborazo."

O'Hara had never said *which* gunboat it had been. And she had never asked.

"That is nonsense!" Farrar said to her. "He's only toying

with you. I've never seen this buffoon before, and I certainly never saw anyone named Quiller."

"Before I went cruising with our friend here, though," O'Hara said to Bronwen, ignoring Farrar's denial but not his revolver, "I went looking for an answer to that question you asked me a couple of times. Remember? Who, you wanted to know, was the navy commander who shot a blockade-running captain on the Chesapeake? Shot him with the excuse that the prisoner was trying to escape. It was the day the Union recaptured Norfolk."

Bronwen felt air stir in the close hold as Lockwood behind her shifted. Perspiration was threatening to drip into her eyes from her hair as she took a small step forward.

"Imagine my surprise," O'Hara said, "when I learned it was Lieutenant Commander Farrar here who did that shooting. And if you recall, Red, it happened to be Colonel de Warde's cotton aboard that blockade-runner. The slippery Brit's name was on the ship's manifest, and his place of residence was listed, if you can believe it, as Maryland."

For no apparent reason, an item jumped forward from her memory, although it seemed to have no bearing on this. Or . . . maybe it did. Major William Norris, head of Confederate intelligence, was from a town just outside of Baltimore, Maryland.

Baltimore. Where the first, pre-inaugural plot to assassinate Lincoln had originated. And there was something else about Baltimore . . .

"I don't deny the incident," Farrar was saying with annoyance. "That blockade-running captain *was* trying to escape."

"Why were you even in the Chesapeake that day?" O'Hara asked, as if he knew the answer. "Your specific orders were to patrol the York River. Don't trouble yourself with another denial, because the Navy Department already checked it for me."

"And that was on the day Norfolk was retaken?" Bronwen said, wanting to be certain she had heard him correctly.

"It was," said O'Hara. "While you were busily dispatching some ensign."

"De Warde did the dispatching," she said, for the opportunity to study Farrar's face. It told her nothing, but something else had begun to work its way out of her memory, if she could grasp it before it slipped back.

Ensign. Baltimore.

"While I was stowed away on this commander's gunboat, I did some poking around," O'Hara continued. "I think Farrar killed Quiller, although I haven't figured out why."

While Farrar scoffed at this seemingly bizarre accusation, Bronwen suddenly recalled what Mr. White had told her at Black Gull Tavern after the restorative tonic had loosened his tongue: Quiller intended to make a map from the information given to Van Lew by the anonymous source. The source Bronwen now knew had been Lockwood's pilot Artemis. But according to White, Van Lew had never seen Quiller again, and had never received the map either.

White had said: *She thinks maybe Quiller took it to his death.*

When Quiller had been on the James River—in either a gunboat *or* a sloop—wouldn't it have been natural for him to ask someone about his map's accuracy? Someone who presumably knew the river and Hampton Roads, because that someone was either a navy officer *or* a self-professed river scout? She had only O'Hara's word for it that he had left Quiller on Farrar's gunboat. When, instead, *he* might have permanently silenced Quiller and destroyed his map.

Which one of these two men was lying?

". . . and remember, Red," O'Hara was saying, "when our sloop was fired on? Near Haxall's Landing?"

She could hardly forget it.

"I trust you're not accusing me of that, too," Farrar said with a tone of bored irritation, as if this had until now been somewhat amusing but was fast becoming a nuisance.

"Oh, but I am accusing you," O'Hara contradicted. "Three of your artillery crew told me you gave the order to fire on a sloop that day, because it was a Rebel one carrying explosives."

A sloop carrying explosives.

She remembered thinking, on the night she and O'Hara had sailed up the James to Chimborazo, that even ships bearing explosives would be as inconspicuous on the broad river as their small sloop had been.

Keeping her voice as matter-of-fact as possible, Bronwen asked Farrar, "How did you and your ship happen to arrive here so quickly tonight?"

His brows lifted, but he answered readily enough, "Nothing mysterious about it. I'd been assigned patrolling duty in the Roads, as I am on a regular basis. My ensign saw signal lights flashing, so he thought there might be some trouble."

Bronwen barely heard more than the word "ensign."

Ensign. Explosives. Map. Baltimore.

"You're welcome to check my duty schedule yourself, Braveheart. If you're not satisfied, then telegraph Navy's Secretary Fox from Fort Monroe if you like—we'll be taking our prisoners there." Instead of reassuring Bronwen, it sounded almost like a threat. "But in the meantime," Farrar added, "I hope you're not too distressed by this drivel from your double agent. It sounds to me like the hallucinations of someone who spends too much time drinking in smoke-filled taverns."

Smoke-filled taverns. Navy—telegraph. Ensign. Baltimore.
And de Warde's *"It's one of yours!"*

The shadows in her head cleared as scattered pieces of the puzzle merged to reveal a picture. But she needed one last piece of it, so she said quickly, hoping to catch her target off guard, "When in Baltimore did you first meet Frances Hobart?"

As his revolver whipped toward her, Bronwen fired.

The bullet hit his right forearm as she intended, but he grabbed his revolver with the other hand. O'Hara's first shot sent the revolver spinning. The second hit Farrar's right knee, dropping him to the planking.

"Don't fire again, O'Hara!"

"I didn't intend to. But who the hell is Frances Hobart?"

Lockwood was lunging toward the gun. A split-second ahead of him, Bronwen snatched it up.

When she motioned him back against the bulkhead, he glanced down to where O'Hara was lashing rope around Farrar's ankles and wrists, and said to her, "You sure you've got the right man?"

"I'm sure. How does this sound, Lockwood? Farrar's duty schedule, in his own words, regularly brought him into the Roads, and you could time your arrivals from Nassau to coincide with that schedule. Remember, we can confirm this with your pilot. Farrar's secessionist cohorts in Norfolk signaled when it was safe for you to pass into the James under the protection of a U.S. Navy gunboat commander. Farrar, I assume, shared your profit? Yours and de Warde's?"

He said as he had earlier, "You don't expect me to answer that."

"Farrar was ready to kill to keep you quiet. And, if you recall, I kept him from succeeding. So yes, I do expect answers. Was Farrar accumulating explosives?"

"You are, in other words, requesting information from me?" Lockwood asked, eyeing her with the sardonic smile.

Before answering, she glanced back at O'Hara, who was making sure Farrar was securely hobbled even though he looked unconscious. "I want information, Lockwood."

"My price could be high."

"How high?" As if she didn't know.

She had already made one decision tonight, after vowing never to make another that might cause death. Could her conscience bear another one, possibly allowing Lockwood to escape and continue running weapons to the enemy? If it might mean, as she suspected, preventing Lincoln's assassination?

O'Hara was on his feet, wiping his forehead on his sleeve. "It sure took you long enough to see the light, Red. I damn near thought you didn't believe me."

"I didn't, not at first."

"Oh, hell, Bronwen! You must think I should've prevented Marshall's death. I couldn't! He was dead before—"

"I know," she interrupted. "I know that, O'Hara. I needed a reason for Marsh's death, something I could understand. But war is too irrational to understand."

"You finally got that right. So why'd you decide to believe me?"

"Farrar's arrogance. Elaborating for effect on items that instead came together to damn him."

"Like what?"

"I'll tell you above deck. It's hotter than Hades down here, and we need to put Farrar—" she deliberately paused and looked at the blockade-runner "—and Lockwood under armed guard. If you'll go up and find a navy officer with some rank, I'll stay here and guard these two."

To her relief, O'Hara promptly agreed.

When she heard his footsteps receding, she made her

decision. An escaped blockade-runner could be recaptured. Lincoln could not be replaced.

"All right, Lockwood, here's my offer. I can't assist an escape attempt. But I might not see an attempt. Take it or leave it."

"Am I supposed to trust your word?"

"I don't give my word to enemies. But I'll stand by my offer, and it's as good as you'll get."

"What do you want in return?" he said.

"Answers."

"Fair enough."

"How did you meet Farrar?"

"Knew him before the war, when I was running U.S. mail ships."

That jibed with the information Fox had about Lockwood. "Go on," she told him.

"I had an import business on the side. Did some trading with Farrar's family—a wealthy, secessionist family until his father gambled away an inherited fortune."

So Farrar's motive had been money after all. One of the main reasons for dismissing him from suspicion in the *Monitor* plot had been Secretary Fox's mention of the Farrar family's wealth.

She asked Lockwood, "Was I right about Farrar's role in allowing you to slip through the blockade?"

"Let's just say it was an inspired guess."

"I'd also wager you had help at Chimborazo Hospital. I think a nurse serving there notified her lover, a Confederate navy officer in league with Federal navy officer Farrar, when a shipment of medical supplies had arrived. The Confederate officer then saw to it that the weapons hidden under those supplies were unloaded and transported into Richmond. By ambulance wagons?"

"You just might win that wager," was all Lockwood said, but it was plenty.

"Now, about explosives—"

"I'm not involved with those," Lockwood interrupted. "I'm a businessman, not a saboteur."

"Not good enough."

His eyes narrowed, and then he shrugged, before answering in roundabout fashion, "This trip, I had just a two-night opening to run the James—the only reason I chanced it with that moon. I was told the coast wouldn't be clear again until after the ninth of the month. Is that what you're looking for?"

Bronwen, chilled by his indifference, said, "The president is making a trip up the James on the eighth. Given what you were told, did you think there might be a connection?"

"I knew nothing about any trip."

"Now that you do know, what might be the link, Lockwood?"

He gave her a peculiar look, as if he rightly thought she could be testing him. And when he didn't reply, she said, "No answer? Then I withdraw my offer."

After a pause, he said, "If you're asking me did I hear of a threat against Lincoln, of course I did. There are plenty of them. Some are more credible than others."

"And this most recent one?"

"Farrar was the one dealing the cards here. De Warde and I were just players. So when I was told to stay out of the Roads for a period of time, only Farrar would know why."

With her ear cocked for approaching footsteps, Bronwen said, "Did you know de Warde is returning to Britain?"

He looked so surprised she tended to believe his "No."

Meaning that de Warde's "recall" had been a sudden decision. Because he didn't want to be on American soil when its president was murdered?

"Lockwood, I want to know if Farrar could conceal surplus explosives on his gunboat."

"Easily."

"Tell me why he might do that?"

"He could manage one hell of an explosion if he used his ship as a battering ram, or ran it into a wharf at a busy landing."

Bronwen heard the sound of approaching footsteps, and since Lockwood must have heard them too, she gave him a look indicating she expected more.

"Have your Treasury chum talk to Farrar's artillerists," he responded. "They'll know if extra gunpowder's being taken aboard."

When she nodded to herself, he added without prompting, "You could be right. Wouldn't be the first time that Baltimore family hatched a cuckoo's egg."

"*What* family?" Bronwen said, her mind racing down the side streets of Baltimore.

"Name Ferrandini sound familiar?"

Boots thumped down the steps, and O'Hara, followed by a naval officer and a seaman, stepped into the hold.

WHEN they arrived back on deck, the moon was slipping in and out of clouds and ribbons of mist wrapped the ship. The ebbing tide had left only pooled water between it and the natural shoreline.

O'Hara and the seaman were carrying the partially conscious Farrar, Lockwood followed them, and Bronwen and her revolver brought up the rear. At the naval officer's shouted orders, crewmembers came forward to collect the prisoner. But O'Hara dropped Farrar's tied feet, and then he tripped over them to go stumbling into the path of the approaching crew. In the ensuing commotion, Bronwen stepped forward to see what had happened. She was given a powerful shove, and after grabbing a cleat to steady herself, she looked up in time to see a figure vaulting over the rail. Regaining her balance, she went to the rail to see the mist swallow a running man.

"SO what did Lockwood tell you?" O'Hara said, drawing on a cigarette when he and Bronwen at last stood on the deck of the gunboat. They should arrive at Fort Monroe within the hour.

She decided it was in her own best interests not to question his clumsiness on the *Portia*, but she had never known the nimble O'Hara to make a misstep. Lockwood, by the time she alerted the crew to his disappearance, had vanished. He might have stopped at the Black Gull for a pint of beer as she had recommended earlier, but she doubted it. If he had, he would have walked straight into Jacques Sundown's grasp.

"What Lockwood told me," she answered, "should keep telegraph wires humming all night between Fort Monroe and Washington."

It had been Farrar's bluff, suggesting that she wire the absent Assistant Navy Secretary Fox, that made her recall the cut telegraph lines at Union headquarters the day of General Lee's surprise assault. After discovering them, Sergeant Berringer had mentioned the naval officers arrived there earlier by train from White House Landing. And it had been at White House later the same day that she had found Farrar. He would have had more than enough time to make the short return train trip after cutting the lines. Such an act of sabotage, which isolated Union headquarters at a crucial time, could only have aided the attack by Lee's Confederate troops.

She now realized that this was one of the final pieces of the puzzle that had first presented itself over three months ago.

O'Hara listened without interruption while she told him why she believed Farrar had murdered poor mapmaker Quiller, and then related what she had learned from Lockwood. "You need to question those artillerists about explosives," she finished. "The ones who told you that Farrar ordered them to fire on the sloop."

"Don't have to," he said. "They already told me the crew had been disturbed by his order, because they'd seen the boy and the dog and figured the sloop only carried civilians. And they said Farrar had been stockpiling ammunition at Norfolk. Their guess was that he planned to sell it at an inflated price. He had enough, in their words, to blow half the harbor sky high."

"My Lord, O'Hara, I've just remembered something! When I met Farrar at White House Landing, he was paying very close attention to the barrels being loaded onto his ship. I joked at the time about his supervision, because the barrels were labeled flour, but now I'll stake money they held gunpowder. What kind of mind would invent such a scheme? Stealing United States gunpowder to use in assassinating its president."

O'Hara tossed his cigarette over the ship's rail, and asked, "What about Baltimore?"

"Treasury can find out if any members of the Ferrandini family changed their name to Farrar. It's a common practice among immigrants."

"Especially if one of them had been rolling around their new homeland like a loose cannon, trying to murder presidents."

"Cypriano Ferrandini was never caught. Rhys Bevan believes he fled the country."

"So maybe Farrar decided to carry on the family tradition and finish the job a relative started. But that's not what I meant when I asked about Baltimore. It triggered your fateful question about Frances Hobart. Again, who is she?"

"A woman killed down by the wharves at Harrison's Landing. Farrar's gunboat traveled between Norfolk and the Landing, and I think he killed her."

"Why?"

"She must have told him I had seen her there at Berkeley Plantation."

"You've lost me. What was she doing at the Union encampment?"

"She was most likely associated with Confederate intelligence, like Farrar surely is, and she had probably been sent to gather information about McClellan's future intentions."

"Well, that was a wasted effort! What do the Rebs think Mac is planning—an advance on Richmond? He'll do that when hell freezes over."

"She could also have been trying to learn the details of Lincoln's trip to Harrison's Landing. Farrar knew if I had recognized her, I could link her to him. He may have intended to dispose of her body, but was interrupted. Or he might have thrown her overboard and her body drifted into shore like Quiller's did."

"Why could you link her to Farrar?"

"When I saw her at Berkeley, she was wearing a wig. But even so, I had the strong sense that I'd seen her before, although I had the devil's own time trying to remember where. It finally came to me when Farrar said 'smoke-filled taverns'—last March three men chased me into one of those in Baltimore. I'd fled there, because I knew Treasury had a deep-cover agent planted at the tavern. Except that I had no idea who it was."

"This goes back to March?"

She nodded. "After I'd been cowering inside the bar-room for a few minutes, frantically flashing a Treasury coin in hopes the contact would see it, an orangish-haired woman directed me to the tavern's back hallway. A woman whose name I now know was Frances Hobart. At the end of that hallway, Farrar was standing by a door, but those thugs were right behind me, so I shoved past him, yanked open the door and plunged into the room. Where I found a group of navy men playing cards—one of them, inci-dentally, his traitorous ensign. I'll bet the Hobart woman alerted Farrar when I first entered the tavern."

"But Farrar couldn't very well dispose of you in front of witnesses."

"No, he played the role of gallant rescuer, and I didn't suspect he was otherwise. Later, after I'd returned to Wash-ington, Rhys told me the tavern keeper's wife was the Treasury contact. Frances Hobart could have assumed her identity that day. Either that, or Hobart *was* the tavern keeper's wife, but a double agent."

"Unlike me, Red. In case you've forgotten."

Bronwen winced, but continued, "Before I was nearly done in by those thugs, two Treasury agents in Baltimore had been murdered. Later Rhys and I concluded that Far-rar's ensign had killed them. Maybe he did, but Farrar probably ordered it. And those thugs, put in the brig aboard Farrar's ship, managed to 'escape' on their way to Washington. Which is why, before I homed in on the ensign, I had suspected Farrar of being allied with Con-federate intelligence and of plotting to sabotage the *Mon-itor*. In retrospect, it's ironic that I had been on the right track about him, but then got sidetracked by the ensign."

"You told me de Warde killed him."

"He did. And there was no question that the ensign intended to light a fuse leading to *Monitor*'s gunpowder magazine. But ever since then I've questioned whether he acted alone."

"Why did de Warde kill him?"

"Because he knew Farrar was involved in the conspiracy. He couldn't afford to have Treasury question that ensign, who, to save his own skin, might have exposed Farrar's treachery. And, far worse from the Englishman's viewpoint, the ensign could also implicate de Warde in the lucrative blockade-running business."

Colonel Dorian de Warde was indeed Jacques Sundown's twisted snake, using the same cunning forked tongue as his infamous ancestor in Eden's garden.

The lights of Fort Monroe were just becoming visible when O'Hara remarked, "One other thing, Red. What in hell did de Warde say that made you think I was a double agent?"

"I had threatened him with arrest unless he told me who was plotting Lincoln's assassination. It was a desperate tactic on my part, and he might have guessed that, but it was still enough to make him nervous. So after I demanded to know if the plotters included Confederate military or intelligence, he said, 'No. It's one of *yours*!' "

"And?"

"And I assumed he meant 'one of yours' as in Treasury's intelligence force."

"That's what you assumed."

"Yes, O'Hara, I did. But as evidence tonight began to point to Farrar, I realized I had misinterpreted de Warde's words. That when he said 'one of yours,' he had meant one of the Union *military*."

"And?"

"And I apologize for misjudging you."

"Which you have done consistently and without just cause. Done erroneously and with malice aforethought. Et cetera, et cetera, and et cetera!"

Bronwen sighed, but decided she probably deserved this. "I was wrong, O'Hara. I am truly sorry, and I hope you will forgive me."

To her surprise, instead of the flip retort she expected him to make, he said, "Not too long ago you would still have been arguing that your suspicions of me were justified. And from your viewpoint maybe some of them were. Apology accepted."

"Thank you."

"It's more than you deserve, but give me a minute and I'll think of a suitable penance."

Smiling at his perennial impish look, Bronwen turned her gaze back to the disappearing lights of Norfolk. By now Jacques Sundown and the navy force should be well on their way to rounding up Farrar's accomplices. Making her wonder if Lockwood had made good his escape. Despite herself, she almost hoped he had, until she remembered the weapons he had delivered. At least he would not try the James again for some time to come.

When she turned back, the huge fortress was looming ahead, guarding the Roads and the Chesapeake, and looking in the moonlight like a drawing of an old walled city. She remembered her aunt saying that ancient Man built the walls to protect against unknown strangers who might threaten his gates. Perhaps he didn't yet know that the threat could come from within as well as without, and that a brother might be no less dangerous than a stranger.

But lacking that knowledge, no wall could ever be high enough or wide enough or long enough, because Man was the child of Cain.

28

*I am all the daughters of my father's house,
And all the brothers too.*

—Shakespeare

JULY 8, 1862
Harrison's Landing

After watching the president's ship steam from the wharf into mid-river, the handful of civilians began making their way back up the long slope to Berkeley Mansion.

"Will the president replace McClellan?" Bronwen asked Rhys Bevan, as she watched Seth head back across the creek to the camp of his New York regiment.

"Not just yet. The common soldier in McClellan's army still reveres his commanding general. But more important, Lincoln at the moment has no one he thinks is any better."

O'Hara made a rude sound that said even Natty's dog would be an improvement. Then, his expression uncharacteristically somber, he caught her arm. "It's time to say so long for now, Red. I'm off to ply the lower Mississippi."

"Why there?"

"Because Chief Bevan here has decided Treasury needs

an experienced river scout like me at the delta. And as you can imagine, the New Orleans ladies are breathlessly awaiting my arrival."

He seized her shoulders and gave her a brief but seemingly heartfelt kiss. "See you again, Yankee gal!" he said lightly, despite a misted cast to his eyes. He turned from her quickly and loped back to the wharves, jumping aboard a sloop just casting off.

Bronwen found herself swiping at her own eyes, and returning his wave with an unexpected rush of regret.

Their speculations of two nights ago on the gunboat deck had proved to be accurate. A search of the Norfolk naval base had been ordered, which unearthed Farrar's frightening hoard of explosives. Also found were what Treasury believed to be solid evidence of Farrar's ties to Confederate intelligence. And he had not denied murdering Frances Hobart. Not after Rhys had wired a Treasury agent working in Baltimore, who reported back that the tavern keeper's wife there had run off, so the man said, with "some damn navy officer" who frequented the establishment's gambling rooms. And that he "sure as hell could" identify the officer.

When a military tribunal was finished with Farrar, he probably would have preferred to die in the hold of Lockwood's *Portia*.

Lockwood himself had completely disappeared from Norfolk. At least for the time being.

Last night O'Hara had admitted that before leaving for Washington, he had deliberately visited Jeb Stuart and his cavalry on the heights above Berkeley. And had convinced Stuart, who had only the single piece of artillery, that General Longstreet's Confederate infantry was coming right behind him with reinforcements.

"So, hearing that, ole gambler Jeb starts firing down on the Union encampment," O'Hara had chuckled. "Which was one *big* mistake, because he brought attention to the fact that those heights hadn't been secured. Allowing McClellan, after putting away his champagne glass and oyster fork, time to safely correct his oversight. We know Young Napoleon needs that guarantee of safety before he'll move an inch."

As Bronwen now waved to O'Hara again, she looked around for Kathryn. She must have rushed back to the surgery. Gregg Travis, ever the devoted doctor, had not been free to watch Lincoln's review of Union troops. Earlier Bronwen had asked her sister, "Have you made any future plans?"

Kathryn, with her customary aplomb, had answered calmly, "Gregg has asked me to marry him."

"He did? Somehow you don't sound as elated as I think you're supposed to, Kathryn. How did you answer him?"

"That I needed time to consider it. Meanwhile, I'll continue as a field nurse with his surgical unit."

"You'll keep Natty with you?"

"Yes, and Gregg said if we marry, he's prepared to legally adopt Natty."

"My Lord, Kathryn, his proposal must really be a serious one!"

Smiling, her sister had said, "I'll keep Absinthe with me, too. She has no family other than Shandy, and if Union troops leave Berkeley, there's a real danger she'll be forced back into slavery."

Bronwen, after throwing another backward glance at O'Hara's departing sloop, now continued walking up the path between Rhys Bevan and Jacques Sundown. This position was a calculated maneuver on her part, Rhys having earlier said that before he left for Washington, they needed to discuss something. Since then she'd been trying to avoid him, not eager to hear what new peril he was dreaming up for her. But surely he wouldn't bring up a future assignment with Jacques here. As far as Rhys knew, the question of whether she would willingly stay with Treasury was still an open one. She thought for the moment she was safe.

She thought wrong.

Rhys, acting as if her leaving Treasury had never been mentioned, said, "Agent Llyr, although I know it may break your heart, I must order you to depart Virginia. Not to return in the foreseeable future."

She stopped walking to give him a stunned look. Jacques too had stopped, and stood staring up the slope, while Rhys gazed down at her with a cryptic expression.

"Are you making some joke?" she asked. "Or can I hope you're sincere?"

"You've become altogether too notorious here to be of further use to Treasury."

"I couldn't agree more!"

"Thus, after a suitable period of rest—by which I mean a brief one—you will be heading west."

"West? As in *the* West?"

"Sundown here has accepted the offer I made regarding Treasury's interest in the transcontinental railroad. Because of your Pinkerton training, you'll be going along to employ your unique methods of intelligence gathering. And, as Sundown so quaintly put it, to 'ride shotgun' for him."

Now that could be interesting, she thought, but did not say so. If she seemed overly eager, Rhys might change his mind, and assign her to deskwork in Washington.

Stealing a glance at Jacques, she saw that his gaze was focused on two people seated ahead on a bench under a spreading elm. The bench was still some distance up the path, but she could tell the two were her aunt and Cullen Stuart.

Cullen had been severely weakened by the malaria, making Gregg Travis predict it could be some time before he regained his strength, even after a long recovery period. Travis had then signed a medical discharge.

Bronwen was forced to wonder, with another glance at the silent man beside her, how much Cullen's condition had colored Jacques's decision to accept the Treasury offer.

She also had made a decision. Marsh's senseless death still affected her, and she would not forget him. But the president's stand on emancipation, whether or not it swayed European thought, had ended her own uncertainty. For however long Lincoln needed soldiers to fight this war, on whatever front necessary, she would stay the course.

GLYNIS watched Jacques Sundown veer away from the others on the path to go striding across the slope in the opposite direction. She had told him earlier of her intention.

Now, turning to Cullen, she said, "Several ships are leaving here today for Washington. From there Rhys Bevan said he would make transport available for you to the rail station, where trains run to the North."

Cullen, who had also been watching Jacques, responded with a preoccupied nod, and then shifted suddenly on the bench, his eyes searching her face, "Glynis," he asked, drawing her closer to him, "what are you planning to do now?"

She caught his hand, holding it fast when she answered, "I'm taking you home, Cullen."

AFTERWORD

—⚉—

> Nothing occurred during the whole war so
> much to give new life, spirit, energy, and cour-
> age to the Confederate Army and people as this
> untoward retreat of McClellan from the Pen-
> insula.
>
> —John Minor Boggs, Richmond politician and
> Union loyalist, 1862

For six weeks following Malvern Hill, the Army of the
Potomac sat at Harrison's Landing, broiling under a hot
Virginia sun. Union soldiers fought biting flies, rampant
diseases, and boredom, while McClellan continued to insist
that he would march forth and capture Richmond if only
he were given more troops. Without reinforcements, he
claimed, even he could not hope to overcome two hundred
thousand Rebels. While his estimate of enemy strength
remained consistent, it also remained delusionary; although Lee was fielding the largest force he ever had, and
ever would have, he did not command more than ninety
thousand troops on the Peninsula.

Finally, Lincoln, his patience exhausted, replaced Mc-
Clellan. Ships bearing the last Union troops left Harrison's
Landing on August 16, 1862, making a quiet finish of the
much-ballyhooed Federal campaign to capture Richmond
and end the war of secession. For the Union it had been a

costly failure. But Lee's brilliant strategy for keeping Northern invaders from the gates of his capital had also been costly. From the first fighting at Yorktown to the last at Malvern Hill, almost one in every four of the quarter million Federal and Confederate men on the Peninsula were lost: counted as missing, wounded, or dead by reason of battle or disease. The Civil War raged on for another three years, and hundreds of thousands more men were lost.

Lincoln issued his preliminary emancipation document in September of 1862. And on January 1, 1863, his Emancipation Proclamation declared that all slaves in rebelling states should be free. This effectively ended the European debate over recognition of the Confederacy. In 1865 the Thirteenth Amendment to the United States Constitution legally abolished slavery in America. Seven months before its passage, Abraham Lincoln had been assassinated.

HISTORICAL NOTES

—✐—

Items that previously appeared in the Historical Notes sections of *Sisters of Cain* and *Brothers of Cain* have not been repeated here.

Intelligence

Mid-nineteenth-century intelligence gathering was far simpler in scope and operation than it is today, and as ever, it is a mistake to view historical events solely through the lens of the present. "Codes and ciphers were either primitive or non-existent," writes Edwin C. Fishel in his groundbreaking *The Secret War for the Union* (Houghton Mifflin, 1996). The Civil War equivalent of today's observation satellites was Thaddeus Lowe's balloons, which were severely limited by the weather conditions, the means of transporting them (horse-drawn launching platforms and occasionally river barges), the available gas supply, and the bravery of an unprotected balloonist under threat of hostile fire. Visual sighting, which required close proximity to the enemy, was almost always the method of detecting troop movements. Messages relayed by signal flags had the obvious disadvantage of being seen by friend and foe alike, and required high ground or rooftops to be seen at all. The telegraph was vulnerable to sabotage and telegraph messages to enemy interception.

The Federal government did not have an organized intelligence presence until, following the failed Peninsula Campaign, General Joseph Hooker originated the Bureau of Military Information. To head the bureau, Hooker called on George Sharpe, a lawyer-colonel from upstate New York. Sharpe, in large part through his own initiative and ability, built an efficient, successful organization. Not surprisingly, the Civil War general who most valued, and effectively used, intelligence information was Ulysses S. Grant.

Lockwood, Thomas

Lockwood's name appears in nearly all reference material on Civil War blockade-running, and he is described variously as dashing and daring, and so successful that he became known as the "Father of the Trade." (Although Lockwood captained a number of different ships, such as the *Kate*, the *Carolina*, and the *Theodora*, the fictional *Portia* was not among them.) Thomas Haines Dudley, the United States consul at Liverpool, in his Dispatch No. 38 of 1864, described Lockwood as "The notorious Tom Lockwood . . . [who] used to boast that his success lay in his 'making arrangements' with our naval officers to let him pass."

Swinburne, John

When General McClellan ordered the army's retreat to Harrison's Landing following the Battle of Malvern Hill, acting surgeon Dr. John Swinburne, USA, heroically remained with the Union wounded. On July 3 Swinburne wrote to General Lee requesting assistance on humanitarian grounds. Swinburne proposed, among other things, that arrangements be made for the wounded by "condensing them at Savage's Station . . .

or, what would be more agreeable to the demands of humanity, the unconditional parole of these sufferers." Lee's answer of July 4 included the statement "I will do all that lies within my power to alleviate their suffering. I am willing to release the sick and wounded on their parole not to bear arms."

For readers who would like to know more about the Peninsula Campaign, I found the following non-fiction resources to be among the most useful and widely available. *The Richmond Campaign of 1862: The Peninsula and the Seven Days,* edited by Gary W. Gallagher, is a collection of essays by Civil War historians who address wide-ranging facets of the campaign. *To The Gates of Richmond: The Peninsula Campaign,* by Stephen W. Sears, gives a comprehensive and highly readable account with military emphasis. *With Courage and Delicacy: Civil War on the Peninsula,* by Nancy Scripture Garrison, is a narrative treatment of women and the Sanitary Commission in the 1862 campaign. *Lifeline of the Confederacy: Blockade Running during the Civil War,* by Stephen R. Wise, provides an overview of the crucial role blockade-runners played in supplying the Confederate armies and civilian populations. And *The Secret War for the Union: The Untold Story of Military Intelligence in the Civil War,* by Edwin C. Fishel, remains the single most comprehensive source to date on this aspect of the war.

Children of Cain was completed in the near aftermath of September 11, 2001. On that day another generation of Americans learned all too graphically what the lack of coordinated intelligence information could bring. Readers of the Cain trilogy will know this lack was not without precedent.
M.G.M.
December 2001